The Sundering: Immortal

Michael J. Wyant, Jr.

No part of this publication may be reproduced, distributed, or transmitted in any form or by any means, including photocopying, recording, or other electronic or mechanical methods, without the prior written permission of the publisher, except in the case of brief quotations embodied in critical reviews and certain other noncommercial uses permitted by copyright law.

The Sundering: Immortal

Copyright © 2013 by Michael J. Wyant Jr.
Original Cover Art Copyright © 2013 Michael J. Wyant Jr.
Original Cover Design by Ethan Kocak of Black Mud Puppy

All rights reserved.

ISBN-13: 978-0615764986
ISBN-10: 0615764983
BISAC: Fiction / Science Fiction / General

First Edition: April 2013

Acknowledgements

This book has been a labor of love. From a strange fragment of an idea to NaNoWriMo and back again, this group of characters has consistently guided my life in every day of the past three years. I have rewritten entire sections of this book based off of value judgments I've made in life that were, in turn, based off decisions Dervy or Weynie would have made in my stead. To see it coming to fruition is a lot like what I imagine giving birth to feel like... a joyous occasion filled with overwhelming pain and paranoia. Regardless, I now give this book to the world, the first of three. I hope that it brings the joy, the sadness, and, ultimately, the enlightenment it has brought me.

Now, this could go under the dedication, but I was pretty explicit in my wording, so I'm holding true to that. I am, if nothing else, a stickler for detail.

First: Kickstarter. Thank you. Only in a world like today could you crowd-source the publication costs of a book, somehow overshoot that goal by one hundred percent, and have everyone be okay with that. You've created something magical and wonderful; it's given me a little bit more hope in the human race.

Everyone who pledged any money to the Kickstarter, big or small, deserves as much thanks as I can heap into these pages. I toyed with the idea of writing haikus or something similar about everyone and realized that I wouldn't be able to afford the printing cost of the book anymore if I did that. It wouldn't be much of a Kickstarter to publish a book if I then had to run another one, would it?

To all of my backers: you have my sincerest thanks.

Now, in order of pledge date, my Kickstarter backers: Alec Suits, Ryan Baldwin, Andrea Reynolds, Mike Mirizio, Chris Shaughnessy, Anthony Cianciosi, Kevin Lindsay (who will have a minor character modeled and named after him in the next book), Keith Coit and Tammy Abend (and their son Austin Coit), Andrew Gemmell, Ethan Kocak (he designed the cover art), Joan Hart, Dawn Wyant (my mom), Shaun Burdick, Sherry Nepton (my favorite mother-in-law), Jenn Davis, Melissann Ashton-Patton and Kevin Ashton, Katelyn-Lily Holubek Greer, Casey Re, Scott Sanders, Adam Wickert, Simon Stearns, Mike Taffet, Jeanie Robinson-Pownall, Caleb Coy, Matt Molanare, Patrick Ellis, Kristopher Volter, Miles Nielsen, Cathy Boudreau (for Shelby Mehmet), and Beau G. Bolle (who will have a secondary, non-storyline character based on him).

Again thank you all. Without you, this would not have happened for a good long while.

This is dedicated to my wife Amy.

She urged and guided, supported and pushed

until I thought she might brain me with something.

Luckily, it didn't come to that.

I love you Amy. Thank you for reminding me of my dream.

Prologue
San Francisco, CA
3:19 AM March 1, 2010

    Alex Mamsin dropped the last foot to the deck of the Golden Gate Bridge and staggered to the ground. Something fell from his pocket as his knee slammed into the concrete, one hand carefully protecting the bottle of whiskey he'd somehow managed to avoid dropping. A brown leather wallet sat a few feet away from him in a puddle, iridescent water rippling away from its edges. Grimacing, Alex took another long pull on the nearly empty bottle and moved away from the fence and toward the center of the bridge. He left it behind. It wasn't like he needed anything in there anymore.

    The fog rolled heavily across the road and sidewalk ahead of him carrying the deep salty bite of the ocean. The mist dragged like a lethargic stream through the night, eddying around the steel supports of the Golden Gate Bridge. Those ruddy beams rose skyward, fading to gray as they disappeared a scant few feet above him. They reappeared briefly beyond--long and purple in the deep night--where a lamp hung here or there, small blobs of light in an intangible ocean of gray.

Alex moved steadily, though in a slight zigzag, stopping only to pull long and hard on the bottle in his fist. The walk was endless; just he and the mist. He didn't hurry. He'd taken his time getting here; there was no reason to rush this.

He breathed deeply, filling his lungs with the crisp, cold of the early spring night. The tingle of the salt air filled his nostrils and the surreal sensation of condensing moisture on his bare arms made him shiver. The half-tucked polo shirt that belonged to Nawat Industries did little to warm him. A grin crept across his face as he took another sip.

They'd have a fit over the ruined shirt.

Quietly, Alex trailed his hand over the guiding rail of the bridge, calming his staggering pattern and allowing his eyes to follow the roiling mass of gray below. Everything disappeared, faded, as he looked down and away to the pylons below.

Everything was silent. Still. Even the cars had stopped their inexorable march from San Francisco to San Rafael for this. Crying seemed like the appropriate response, but instead he felt only relief. Finally, he had the courage to follow through with his decision. Alex couldn't remember when it had become so clear--so obvious a solution--but here he was. Now that he accepted it was happening, he was quite calm. Those roiling clouds below cast out their arms in an embrace, waiting for him to join them so they could take him to Mary.

There was comfort in the finality of death.

Alex took another drink, but found only stale droplets on his tongue. He looked at the bottle for a long time, and felt the first inkling of uncertainty creeping back into his mind.

"No," Alex said out loud, shaking his head violently. "This is the way it needs to be."

He nodded, though his assertion didn't keep the tears from building or the vice-like grip from compressing his chest. The world swirled around Alex as he fought down the sudden feelings of panic and despair. Familiar demons whirled in his mind.

Alex had come too far to give up like this. Just like when his parents died, he would prevail; he'd survive.

As he wiped away tears, an image of a young woman entered his mind. Her shoulder-length brown hair danced around a face only slightly touched by makeup as she moved, pulling away from his embrace with a tinkling laugh.

She winked at him and then there was a hole beneath her left eye. Blood poured, covering the side of her face...

Alex stood, screaming at the world with everything he had left. He collapsed to the ground, sobbing. With a cry, he lashed out at the bridge with the bottle. It exploded, spraying shards of glass across the deck like dead little diamonds.

"Hey there," a voice said, quiet and soothing.

Immediately, Alex was on his feet again, the neck of the bottle held limply in hand. He turned toward the voice, which belonged to an older woman dressed in some sort of uniform. She was further down the walkway than he'd expected, just behind the next large post.

"Just go away," Alex said quickly, backing up against the railing. The broken bottle knocked against the barricade.

The woman stepped forward slowly, hands out to the sides.

"Why don't we go over this way?" She asked, nodding toward the barrier between the walkway and the road.

Alex shook his head violently. "No, I'm here for a reason."

"Okay, okay," she said soothingly, though she continued to move toward him. Slowly. "What reason is that?"

Alex grimaced. "I'm guessing you already know. Just go away."

She shifted uncomfortably.

"Please?" Alex pleaded.

She shook her head and took another step forward. She was only about ten feet away. "My name is Sarah. I work for the transportation department. I'm just here on the overnight shift. What's your name?"

Alex held up the hand with the bottle in a warding motion and Sarah finally stopped moving. "Listen, this is happening and all you're doing is speeding it up."

Sarah nodded, taking a step backward. "Okay, okay. Why don't you tell me what's going on? Maybe I can help?"

Alex's face fell as he looked at yet another person willing to put their life on hold to help him. What good would it do, though? Nothing ever changed... Mary was still dead, his parents were dead and the only people alive that knew his name would rather avoid him.

Moisture slid down his cheeks--or was that mist--as he glanced behind him, into the deep, eternally swirling fog.

It seemed welcoming... so peaceful and graceful.

Like the pillow of God.

"I'm sorry, Sarah. I appreciate the offer, but you can't help me any more than I already have been helped," Alex said weakly.

Lights flashed suddenly to his right as a car sped by. Sarah glanced away. It was just a flash, a quick distraction, but it was enough.

In that moment, Alex picked himself up over the edge of the railing and jumped toward the fog and the bay below.

The wind rose to a fevered pitch as he shot into the night, darkness swirling around him. Alex smiled, letting his body relax as he dropped, the broken bottle in his hand slipping easily from his fingers. It hovered for a just a moment beside him before the clouds cleared and he slammed into the black water.

1
San Francisco, CA
6:25 AM August 20, 2010

Alex needed a drink.

He removed his cell phone from the center console of his car, checking to see if he had any messages. There weren't any, but he already knew that. The phone had been next to him during his entire nerve-wracking commute, but it was a routine he'd developed over the last six years as a Systems Administrator of Nawat Industries.

A beer would be really nice...

Thoughts like that seemed to be happening more and more lately. It was enough to make Alex wonder if he should go to those Alcoholics Anonymous meetings. A court order was nothing to sniff at, especially the latest strongly worded reminder, but Alex just wasn't an alcoholic... past events notwithstanding.

With a stretch and a groan, Alex opened the car door and stepped out into the echoing emptiness of the parking garage. He glanced around, noticing the usual Audis and BMWs in their parking spots. Executives who showed up just early enough to make an excuse to leave earlier than everyone else owned those cars. There wasn't much else.

Then again, it would have been strange to see anyone since no one else was ever there when he arrived. Alex had been working at Nawat Industries since 2004 and during six years of early arrivals he'd only seen one other person at 6:30 AM. That man had been drunk after getting fired the day before. Apparently, he'd passed out in his car.

An Audi, Alex recalled with a sigh.

Lazily, Alex reached into the back seat of his Toyota and pulled his work backpack free from a mess of fast food wrappers.

"Aww hell," he groaned, peeling one from the front of the bag and tossing it into the rest of the filth behind him.

His eyes passed over the mishmash of wrappers he'd tossed into his backseat for the past three months. All the major chains were represented as well as a plethora of unmarked wax paper with the telltale signs of Mexican food.

El Matate. Not fast food, but far too delicious to pass up.

Alex grinned and shut the car door.

There weren't any booze bottles in his car anymore, so that was a good sign. Not that he'd ever drink and drive, of course. He just didn't like cabs and sometimes you needed to sleep it off.

Alex bit his lip in consideration. Combine that fun fact with a suicide attempt, also while inebriated, mind you, and any judge would scream "AA or Jail."

He shook his head and thought more about lunch.

Idly, Alex tongued the tooth he had filled yesterday afternoon and was surprised to find it wasn't tender in the least, though there was some crud left over from the filling.

A lot of crud.

Confused, Alex maneuvered the bit of amalgam to his tongue and pulled it out. It was a few millimeters across and a brilliant white. Cursing, he checked the tooth on the lower left-hand side of his mouth with his finger, expecting to find a large gap where the filling should be and found nothing.

That's weird.

Alex had spent most of the night rolling around, loaded up on pain relievers, trying to ignore the throbbing ache from the filling. All night it felt like he hadn't taken anything, so he wasn't going to argue now that it felt fine.

Despite the confusion, Alex's mouth was already watering at the thought of a couple carne-asada super-burritos as he made his way over to the elevator. Suppressing a yawn, he slapped the up button.

As the unsteady drone of the elevator chugged along, Alex began mentally organizing his task list.

He'd spent the entire previous day on one particular issue. Unfortunately for him, there were still people complaining...and of course they were in Marketing.

Behind him, Alex heard hurried footsteps just as the elevator dinged its arrival. He stepped in and glanced back toward the person approaching.

The man was coming down the parking garage ramp on foot. He was tall and balding with a large, crooked nose. With a wave, he gestured for Alex to hold the elevator and picked up his pace.

It may have been the way the other man moved, his smile, or some instinct that came from living in cities for nearly a decade, but a tingle of doubt and warning fell between Alex's shoulder blades. He found himself hitting his floor number and the door-closed button simultaneously, while smiling and pretending that he was doing quite the opposite.

As the doors shut Alex shrugged in false defeat and mouthed the word "Sorry" to the other man who waved it off with an easy-going smile.

"I'll get the next one," the man said as the heavy aluminum doors snapped shut and the elevator lifted toward the seventeenth floor.

The further away from the garage Alex got, the less intense the annoying itch at the back of his neck was, until it faded entirely and he forgot the incident completely. By the time Alex was swiping his security badge to the server room, he was thinking about block sizes and packet routing rather than the man with the pockmarked face and crooked nose.

Michael J. Wyant Jr.

Well, block sizes, packet routing and burritos, anyway.

* * *

The night I was born most of my village was destroyed.
My father saved me, as far as I can tell.
Though I've been told I shouldn't be able to, I recall the sound of wood shattering as he ran into the room where my mother had just died giving birth to me.
I have a vague, blurry memory of my father from that moment. A small man, only slightly taller than I am now, bent down and picked me up gently. He was almost entirely bald and what was left was gray.
He only lived a few years beyond that event. I don't remember his name, but I remember his eyes.
They were a beautiful violet color that I've only seen twice since then...one was a child in Byzantium.
The other I see everyday on the other side of a mirror.

* * *

"Dervy!"
The shout broke her concentration and Dervy found herself staring at the dim laptop screen, little vertical cursor flashing slowly at the end of the word 'mirror'. She closed her eyes and sighed, rubbing a hand through her shoulder-length dyed brown hair.
Dervy closed the lid with a sharp snap.
She went over to the mirror above the hotel's short dresser and put in her contacts even though her eyes were perfect.
Better than perfect, actually.
Superhuman would be the more accurate term. For years people had told her how lucky she was to have vision that good. She shrugged. It wasn't as important nowadays, what with LASEK and binoculars.
Dervy blinked away tears as the second contact went in. The contacts only changed her eye color from violet to a very dark brown. It wreaked havoc with her low light vision, but walking around unrecognized was more than a fair tradeoff. If she had to go outside at night, she'd just take them out anyway.
"Dervy! What are you even doing in there?"

"Relax Simon! I'm coming!" Dervy yelled as she moved back to the desk and stuffed the laptop into her brown bag, letting her fingers trail over the worn, well-kept leather. It had been a surprise that the old messenger bag could house these portable computers so well, now that she'd finally been assigned one. Dervy hadn't been thrilled about it, but Jalal had been insistent.

She smiled as she shifted the bag on her shoulder. A little stitching to reinforce the corners, the old thread had long ago eroded and torn, some patching to cover the bullet holes and some polish to cover the bloodstains. It was good as new.

"We were supposed to be gone an hour ago," Simon whispered from the other room.

She smiled. Despite the annoyance in Simon's voice, Dervy didn't move any faster. She knew exactly how much time she had. There was no rush. Being as old as she was made you understand how time flowed better than most.

Simon Vanderwell on the other hand was rather new to the Life. So new, in fact, that he still hadn't gotten used to being around other people with enhanced hearing. He'd managed to run under the radar for nearly eighty years. Simon's face and sparse pate indicated that he'd been Taken in his mid-thirties, a fact that made him very unhappy. Simon constantly whined about joints popping and random aches and pains that Dervy had never experienced as she had been Taken in her late teens. She would never feel those aches and pains, not until she entered the Return anyway... then it would all come in a rush.

And she'd be dead within a week.

Finally.

Dervy lowered her arms and stared into the mirror for a moment, taking in her youthful features. With one hand she traced the skin around her left eye wishing and hoping for something, anything, to disturb the smooth contours. As Dervy's fingers slid, a deep ache grew in the pit of her stomach as her skin traced smooth and nearly flawless. There were only two imperfections: the small freckle right below her left eye and the single smile line she'd developed before being Taken.

Tears welled up as the ache broadened, but Dervy forced it back down and straightened up, taking a deep, steadying breath.

Dervy had looked the same for nearly four thousand years.

In that moment, she just wanted it to be over.

With a few quick wipes, she made sure her eyes were dry and her hair straight before picking up the satchel and heading out into the well-lit common room of the suite.

The room was gorgeous. Furnished with designer brands, it had huge picture windows overlooking foggy San Francisco. The penthouse was a testament to excessiveness and waste that the rich and powerful of every age seemed to find attractive. It wasn't that Dervy found it distasteful or unsatisfying, she enjoyed Jacuzzis and heated floors as much as the next person, but it all seemed so... unnecessary.

"You're impatient," Dervy said to Simon as she moved toward the kitchen.

She ignored the pulsing tingle of the freshly Taken's chi at the back of her neck. It was so clear that, by comparison, the chi of the humans might as well not exist. Like a homing beacon, it directed her to the southwest.

Simon sat on one of the beige couches, a thick silver platter on his lap. Most of its contents were gone. He looked up with a grin at her comment.

"Oh, that's because I'm only trying to get in your pants," Simon said. "Once we seal the deal I'll be out of here."

Dervy faked a toothy smile at Simon as he finished buttering a piece of toast, grinning at his own comment. He scratched absentmindedly at the thick strap of black fabric that ran tight around his neck.

Simon hadn't taken well to wearing the collar, the Taenova, though in his defense few did. The band indicated you were a newcomer and garnered leniency from others of the Life. Other strigoi. As far as she knew, Simon hadn't met any strigoi outside the Arktois besides a couple newly Taken.

Dervy considered him, wondering again at how he had managed to avoid detection for nearly a century. For all his crudeness, Simon was remarkably intelligent, which explained his longevity outside of the safety of the Arktois. He maintained that he'd been a banker during that time, though Dervy didn't believe it for a minute.

Maybe he'd been a con artist or a thief, but not a banker. She could easily see him in the early twentieth century selling mercury to expectant mothers as a diuretic.

Handling other people's money though? She couldn't picture that without picturing him wearing a clown nose.

The thought brought a real smile to Dervy's face as she filled a glass with water. She sniffed at the container to confirm its cleanliness, an old habit, and took a drink, sparing only a casual glance for the pre-bottled water next to the faucet with a $4.99 price tag attached to it. The idea of bottling clean water still baffled her. Maybe if it had some ale or wine in it, but just water? It was enough to make your head spin.

"I know this guy is that way someplace," Simon gestured to the southwest as he set the platter down. "But how do we actually find him?

"I mean, I can't just go asking everyone in San Francisco if they've noticed that they've been having trouble dying recently," Simon chuckled.

Dervy grimaced. Simon was supposed to be running lead this time around. He should already know how to track someone.

"Weren't you trained before they decided to send you out?" Dervy asked, taking a sip of water.

Simon shrugged. "Not really. They told me I'd learn it from you."

Learn from her? The leaders of the Arktois, the Ankousti, had sent her out to find out where all of the missing Taken were and they expected her to train someone while she did it? Dervy was going to have a talk with Primator Searle when she got back to Heathshome.

"You know there are thirteen Taken a year, right?" Dervy asked, setting her cup down on the counter roughly.

Simon looked ready to give a snarky response, but held his tongue. He nodded.

Thirteen a year and the Gatherers hadn't found a single one. Not one. That was the only reason the Ankousti had asked Dervy to help. Or rather, that was the only reason Esok Johnson had asked. The Ankousti seemed...preoccupied lately.

At least she'd found that Taken in Beijing. Simon had been of little help then, though now she realized why he hadn't had any idea what he was doing. He was a very gifted faker, this one.

"Good," Dervy said with a scowl. "And how long does their chi shine?"

"A year," Simon mumbled. "They shine for a year, which means we have a year to find them."

Dervy took a deep breath. There was no need to take it out on him. It wasn't Simon's fault he was an idiot. She was just angry with everyone else.

"Okay then," she continued, "So whoever picks us--god, gods, spirits, whatever--gave us a year where our chi shines so bright that we're easily found by others of our kind."

Dervy paused and sipped her water.

"Others like us."

Simon looked like he was going to stay something, but held his tongue.

"What?" Dervy asked.

"I know all of this Dervy. If I didn't, I wouldn't have been able to keep up in Beijing. I just need to know the tracking piece."

Fine.

"You can feel him over that way right now, correct?" Dervy gestured off to the southwest and Simon nodded.

"How did I do it in Beijing?" Dervy asked.

Li Li had been abnormal. She was a Chinese woman, but that wasn't what made her odd. When Li Li's chi led Dervy to the small apartment building in Beijing, she had expected the usual; a teenager or early twenties youth with an attitude. Instead an old, grandmotherly woman answered the door. Dervy had been shocked, to say the least. Others had been Taken while they were older in the past, thirties and forties, but this was the first time that Dervy knew of where a sixty-year-old woman had been Taken.

And Li Li only spoke Mandarin. It couldn't have been French, Latin, Spanish, or anything else Dervy actually could speak. It had to be Mandarin.

For some reason she just couldn't wrap her head around those Far East languages.

Simon hadn't known Mandarin either.

She grinned, which made him frown. "You said that you focused on it until it became a sharp pain. I guess that let's you narrow down on a single person?"

Dervy nodded. "Basically, yes."

Of course, it was much more complicated than that. The ability to narrow down a single being using nothing more than a buzzing at the nape of your neck took decades to really learn and a few centuries to master. It was kind of like grabbing a buzzing mosquito from the air; if you tried too hard, you killed the mosquito, but if you were too delicate, it escaped.

Once you mastered the skill the rules changed. At that point everyone buzzes a little bit, an ever-present hum just like that annoying mosquito. That single frustrating drone becomes a swarm, merging together into a dissonant symphony. Picking out the higher pitched squeal of a newly Taken is almost easier in that environment because they stand out like the brassy screech of an out-of-tune trombone amidst the rest of the cacophony.

Cities were the worst because of the sheer number of humans populating the area. It was especially bad in places as large as San Francisco. That was why Dervy always stayed in high-rise hotels when she had to travel to one. She always got the worst headaches in cities. At least the height gave her a little buffer from everyone's incessant whine.

Beijing had been a nightmare.

If anyone else could track like she could, it would be considered amongst the Six Gifts. Then again, no one else had the same proficiency as Dervy. They hadn't even been able to learn it.

She smiled to herself. It was easier this way; if they added another power, the Ankousti would spend a fortune reprinting training materials.

Dervy almost laughed as she looked over at the couch. Simon's face was bright red, beads of sweat rolling down his face, his hands balled into fists at his sides.

"Don't push yourself too hard or we'll have to keep running back to the room so you can shit," Dervy said with a smirk as she refilled her glass, sniffed, and sipped.

Simon glared at her and grunted. The blood drained out of his face as he started breathing again.

"Is there another way to do this?" Simon asked, slapping his knees in frustration. "It seems kind of, well, hard."

"Life is hard Simon, even when you don't die," Dervy said, tipping her glass toward him in emphasis.

"Yeah, whatever, but there has to be a better way to do this," Simon countered, rubbing his neck. "I can feel this prick, but it's really faint and pushing like that just makes it feel like someone is pushing harder. It isn't helping me narrow him down."

"That's normal," Dervy said, "and it's what you're looking for. The more you do it, the more you can focus on it, though, so it feels less like a thumb pushing on your spine and more like a red-hot needle sticking in a nerve-ending," Dervy grinned at Simon's grimace. "Just like anything, it takes practice. When we get close enough, you'll just know who he is."

Simon gave her a look, "All right. I'll keep doing it."

Dervy leaned back up against the fridge. It was a brushed steel monstrosity with an ice machine. Who on earth needed an ice machine? What was wrong with waiting for it to freeze in a freezer? Or better yet chipping your own on a warm winter day; feeling its icy bite snap at your teeth? That was the best.

It had to be a nice day, though. Only then. She hated the cold.

Lost in her own thoughts, Dervy waited in silence, watching Simon practice. After a few minutes she leaned forward.

"Since you're supposed to be taking the lead on this one, how do you want to do the pickup?" Dervy asked.

"I'm taking the lead?"

"Yes."

"Okay then," Simon sighed. "Let's try something a little subtler than what you did in Beijing."

"It worked, though, didn't it?" Dervy asked, pointing back at him as she put her empty glass in the sink. "You have to be flexible if you're going to do this. Taken need to know there is a community and a support structure or they'll go crazy or do something stupid. It's even more important than their personal safety."

Simon stared at her, mouth open, "I know that better than most, but Dervy... you broke her legs."

"She got back up afterwards, didn't she?" Dervy said bluntly. "Flexibility applies to all different scenarios."

Her headache had been immense in Beijing. All those people...

Dervy shuddered despite herself, but forced a grin for Simon's benefit. "And it's not my fault you don't speak Mandarin."

"I didn't know I was supposed to, all right. I didn't even know we were going to China," Simon said reflexively, averting his eyes.

Li Li was supposed to have been his first Gathering job. Dervy had thought Simon knew Mandarin, but that turned out to be... incorrect. She had just met him on the plane and assumed that the reason he'd been sent along with her was because he was, well, useful.

When neither of them could explain to Li Li why there were two Americans standing on her doorstep, she ran. Simon tried to talk her down as they ran through the tight, packed streets, but that failed. Again, it had been because of a lack of a common language.

Then Dervy took over. She caught up to Li Li, broke her legs, gagged her, and stuffed her into the trunk of their rental car until they could get ahold of an Arktois interpreter. It was certainly a lot easier to convince the panicking woman that she was no longer human when her legs knit back together in minutes.

After a few weeks in Heathshome, Li Li was finally adjusting nicely.

She still couldn't look at Dervy.

"Now," Dervy asked again, "What's your plan?"

Simon leaned forward on the couch. "I'm thinking of running a con--"

"Of course you are."

"--I'll make him think I went to college with him or something and convince him to let me in the house."

"And then break his legs?" Dervy grinned.

"No, not break his legs," Simon said irritably. "Maybe get him to chat about the weird stuff that's probably been happening over the past couple months instead."

"Where's the break?" she asked.

"I'm not breaking his damn legs, Dervy!" Simon yelled, throwing his hands in the air.

Dervy shook her head. "No, I mean where do you convince him he's a strigoi and offer to take him to Heathshome?"

"Oh," Simon said, leaning back into the couch with a knowing process. "There are other ways to convince people of crazy stuff like living forever, just look at Billy Graham."

"Yeah, well there is a rush on him," Dervy said, pointing at him again. "Afterwards we still have eleven more Taken to pick up before the new batch starts Shining in January."

Simon nodded, leaning forward with a big smile, "Don't worry, I'll be 'flexible' if I need to."

"Glad to hear it, because it's August and that only leaves us four months," Dervy said, barely feeling that little pinprick of pain indicating that the Taken was heading downtown on his way to work.

After a pause, Simon asked, "Do they all start Shining in January at the same time or is it staggered?"

"It's usually staggered," Dervy said. "They get Taken at different parts of the year, but it always starts with the first one sometime in January. A couple centuries ago they all started Shining on the same day, at the same time. We only found that out after we Gathered them and compared notes."

"No phones or telegraph, I'm guessing?" Simon asked.

"Nope. Nothing but written correspondence and hope," Dervy said, remembering.

Dervy cocked her head to the side in annoyance. "Didn't anyone teach you this yet? This is basic introductory stuff."

Simon shrugged.

Dervy was going to have a long talk with the Ankousti when she returned. This was basic knowledge that every strigoi, certainly every Sirgil, should know. It was their common history, the thing that tied them all together.

Dervy shook her head. There wasn't much she could do about it now. She had to focus on the Gathering.

Luckily, there wasn't a whole lot of legwork left to finding this newest Taken, so she wasn't worried.

When they arrived the night before, Dervy had tracked down their target and gotten a name so they would be able to plan their attack. She had found him in a hole-in-the-wall apartment down in the Hayes Valley district. A little Internet research had turned up a lot more about this Taken living down on Fell Street. His name, his job, and even a couple police blotters from Rochester were available within minutes of their arrival.

She hadn't told Simon this since he was supposed to track this one on his own, but with all the missed Taken, Dervy didn't want to leave anything to chance.

The day a person learns they're a strigoi is always bad. That's why the Arktois established the Gatherers. A Gatherer's job is to make the transition to the Life, and hopefully, the Arktois, as easy and seamless as possible.

Given the rush on this job, however, Dervy had a feeling that Alex Mamsin was about to have a really bad day.

2
San Francisco, CA
8:05 PM August 20, 2010

    Alex leaned back in his office chair and threw his third box of rice into the overflowing trashcan across the room. It bounced off an empty container that had recently held Orange Chicken and hit the floor, sprawling bits of rice across the server room. He hadn't been able to leave yet, but order-in Chinese was always a delicious alternative to nothing at all.

    "Swish," Alex said to himself with a frown.

    "Go home Alex," came a loud, authoritative voice from the other side of the rack, barely audible over the roar of server fans and a noisy HVAC. "You're just making a mess and getting me all self-conscious."

    "Well you've been doing a shitty job, Bruce," Alex yelled back, spinning his chair around with a grin. "You should be self-conscious."

    "Go to hell, dude," came the expected response. "I'm busting my ass over here and you're eating Chinese food for the third time tonight."

"Oh, stop getting all angry, you're writing down serial numbers for an audit," Alex stood up, stretching and yawning. "I had to rebuild that damn SAN again today. That's real work."

Bruce kneeled down so he could see through one of the gaps between servers in the main rack. His glasses were slipping down his large nose and sweat dotted his red cheeks.

"You spent two hours reconfiguring some block sizes and have been sitting on your ass all day waiting for the RAID to rebuild, so piss off."

Alex laughed and said sarcastically, "I migrated the image cache server to the cloud, too."

Alex leaned over his desk and began tapping on the keyboard of his laptop. With a few strokes he typed out a one-line command that he would send to all three of the servers to shut them all down at the same time.

"In fact, the only reason I'm still here is so I can do this," Alex hit 'Return' on the keyboard and watched the machines flash for about fifteen seconds and then power off simultaneously.

Bruce laughed from behind the rack.

"Somebody is feeling confident today," Bruce called out. "Don't you usually let stuff like that run over the weekend before shutting down?"

Alex smiled as he tested the main website one more time to be certain that all was working.

It was.

"Usually, but I guess I'm looking for trouble this weekend."

After glancing around to make sure Bruce couldn't see him, Alex double-checked to make sure no traffic was still going to the old servers. It still wasn't.

He let out a small sigh of relief.

"That and the CDN is already updated. Traffic has been dead on those machines for an hour," Alex said casually, wiping a bead of sweat from his forehead as he closed his laptop.

"Well why don't you go have a weekend for once. Maybe you should try going out or something," Bruce said. "God knows getting laid wouldn't hurt your personality any," he added just loud enough to be heard over the roar of the equipment.

Alex laughed half-heartedly at the comment as he tossed his laptop and other gear into his backpack. "We're at work, Bruce, you have to watch that chauvinist streak of yours or you won't have a job at Nawat Industries very long."

Bruce came from around the last rack and tossed a clipboard down on the desk next to Alex. He was a tall man, maybe six foot four, and really thin with a slight scoliosis-inspired bend in his back that gave him periodic trouble.

Alex on the other hand was quite average by his own estimation. He was five foot seven, one hundred and eighty pounds with brown hair that hadn't shown any indication of receding yet, despite baldness running on his father's side.

His only outstanding feature was his eyes. They were a deep purple, almost black, that optometrists always wanted to examine in detail. Luckily, perfect eyesight seemed to come right along with the purple color so those visits were infrequent and usually quite quick.

Bruce pushed on the small of his back, stretching out after spending the last hour and a half digging around behind the racks.

"I'm not going to be around here much longer anyway," Bruce confided quietly.

Alex glanced over at him as he shouldered his bag, shaking his head. "You've been saying that for the past four years Bruce. What makes today different?"

Bruce looked at him and Alex could see the nervous tension building in his face. Bruce had this twitch in his lower lip that usually started ticking when he was getting called out during a staff meeting. Right now it was going crazy.

Alex set his bag down and cocked his head slightly. "Did you get another job?"

Bruce smiled awkwardly, his lip still jumping away, "Yeah. Senior Systems Administrator at a non-profit in Oakland. More money, less hours, and I won't have to drive the Bay Bridge anymore."

Alex put on his best fake smile and walked over, slapping Bruce in the shoulder. The other man almost fell over from the force of the blow, just barely catching himself on the table.

"Oh, sorry about that," Alex said, brushing it off. "Congratulations," he said, working hard to keep himself from going numb. "When is your last day?"

"Two weeks from today, actually," Bruce said, rubbing his arm and eyeing Alex warily.

"Well, hey, tell Janet congrats on getting her husband back," Alex winked, feeling depression well up into his chest. "I'm assuming we'll still be on for poker on Saturdays?"

Bruce smiled finally. "Absolutely, though not this weekend, with the wedding and all."

Alex nodded, though he couldn't remember what the hell Bruce was talking about... not with the roaring in his ears. "Yeah, definitely."

Bruce paused, a concerned look etching lines in his face. "So you're okay with this, right? You'll be fine?"

Alex smiled again, forcing it to stay. "Definitely, definitely. I'm good."

The taller man exhaled deeply and rubbed his chest. "Good, good. Janet was worried about you, you know?"

She was right to be worried...

"Worried?" Alex asked innocently. "About what?"

Worried he'd crack like after Mary died? Worried he'd drink himself into a stupor and jump off a goddamn bridge again because he was alone in a dead-end job? Worried that he felt like he dragged everyone down? Worried that everyone he ever loved was dead?

Bruce's smile faded and his lip started to twitch again.

Alex feigned surprise. "Oh, that. No worries, I'm good." He tapped his bag, giving off a little rattle. "Still taking my pills so, like I said, no worries."

"Good, good," Brian said quietly.

They stood there for a moment, two men awkwardly facing off, nodding their assent at the lie that sat between them. They both knew Alex had stopped taking the cocktail of medications in his backpack. Alex could almost see the six pill bottles spread out next to each other like a little rainbow of coma-inducing happiness.

Three months ago he took a mix of them, maybe forty or fifty all together. Nothing happened. Alex stopped taking them and hadn't told anyone, though Bruce knew.

Bruce always knew those things.

Alex broke the silence and shouldered his bag again, the slight rattle of useless pills punctuating the action.

"Well, I've got to get going, but congratulations again and give Janet my best," Alex said and he left the secure room in a rush.

A small group of people who looked significantly different from the average Nawat Industries employee archetype was blocking the elevator. Instead of mid-grade suits and loose ties, they wore pretty much anything they wanted.

One man was wearing a Mountain Dew faded tee and a pair of torn jeans that he probably paid a hundred dollars for. Next to him stood a woman wearing a flowing sundress. She was pretty enough, but she didn't shave and he just couldn't get over it. It might be sexist, even intolerant, but Alex liked his women with no armpit hair.

Leg hair in the winter was okay, but not hairy armpits.

Ugh.

This was the extreme neo-hippy element in the media group. Everyone else in the throng was presentable, even if they didn't conform to the usual dress code. For the most part they were good people, but they had inflated egos that weren't commensurate with the quality of work they produced. The least egotistical of the media group was Janice and she still had the haughtiness of a first year VP.

Appropriately, Rhonda Vasquez, VP of Media and Marketing, was the most narcissistic. Given her position in upper management she was forced to wear a pantsuit, but once the workday was over, out came the Birkenstocks--though Alex noticed she wasn't wearing them now.

Which meant the workday wasn't over yet.

Alex cringed inwardly.

Rhonda had a remarkable way of making people feel like they were stupid, whether they were or not. She would just talk at you as if the quantity of nonsense coming out of her mouth could overcome her complete and utter idiocy.

Alex had been dealing with her for two weeks because of his latest project. Each time he'd discussed it with her, she had given some piece of harsh criticism or added another feature that "we just need."

As he approached her and she saw him, Alex cringed visibly. He could see yet another one of these meetings about to take place. Bracing himself, he walked forward, pointedly ignoring her, and pushed the down arrow on the elevator.

"Alex, how are *things?*" Rhonda asked, brandishing her fake smile.

Alex glanced around at the people who now surrounded him and felt like an injured antelope alone in the Savannah. They all looked at him like lions, each smiling toothily. He could smell their combined coffee breath.

Rob Hollisnit apparently had a peppermint mocha earlier.

After a fourteen-hour day, Alex just wasn't in the mood to cater to their desires. "It went well," was all he said.

Come on, elevator.

"Well it doesn't seem to be working, Alex," Rhonda said, crossing her arms. "How long is this going to take? My people need to work and every minute they aren't is losing the company thousands."

If she had actually listened to the project plan or read her email... Alex bit his tongue and let loose the political speak instead.

"As we discussed during the project meeting, there is going to be some downtime since the RAID needs to rebuild..." Alex said quietly, as the elevator door popped open and he stepped in.

Rhonda followed him into the elevator, Rob Hollisnit trailing behind. "And as *I* said during the meeting, any downtime that infringes on the weekend rush is detrimental to the business and is unacceptable."

Disgust flooded Alex at the thought of spending any more time with her, let alone in a confined space.

Didn't she have something else to do? Why couldn't she just go argue with her boss or something?

To Alex's complete surprise, Rhonda stopped in mid-step, turned around--almost knocking over a very confused Rob--and marched back out into the hallway.

"I'm going to take this up with James!" Rhonda shouted as she stomped away with purpose, leaving her peons staring slack-jawed in her wake.

Rob glanced over at Alex. "What the hell was that?" Rob asked.

Alex shrugged, smiling to himself. "I dunno."

But it was nice.

Maybe he should go out. Alex let the smile linger as the back of his neck started to tingle.

The elevator slowed to a stop at the thirteenth floor, the doors sliding open. A tall man with a crooked nose and pockmarked face entered. He wore a gray pinstriped suit with a red silk tie. Politely, he stepped between Alex and Rob and turned around as the doors shut so he could watch the floors countdown.

"Thanks for holding the door this time," the other man said with a grin and Alex suddenly recognized him as the man from this morning.

"Heh, no problem," Alex said, cringing.

What department did he work in? Alex wracked his memory to see if he could identify this guy, but nothing rung a bell. There were a lot of employees at Nawat Industries and he rarely even left the seventeenth floor unless he was going home for the night.

Was he wearing a suit that morning?

Why hadn't he held the door that morning? Alex couldn't remember clearly.

"I work in HR," the other man said, as if reading his mind. "I just came on as the Recruiting Manager today," he continued easily, extending a hand to Alex and ignoring Rob. "Zeke, Zeke Dunfee."

Alex smiled.

"Alex Mamsin, Senior Systems Administrator," Alex shook Zeke's hand. "Nice to meet you."

Zeke nodded and turned back, ignoring Rob. They sat in silence, Rob visibly stewing.

"I heard that the traffic is pretty horrible today," Zeke said as they hit the garage and the doors opened. "You live in the East Bay?"

Zeke motioned for Alex to step out and he did so, followed by Rob.

Zeke was frowning as the three of them walked toward Alex's Toyota. Rob's bike was locked down to the bike rack near the elevators, so he made his way there.

"No, I live down in Hayes Valley, but I hate bikes and public transit. Call me what you'd like, I have a parking spot at my apartment and at work, so it makes sense to have a car," Alex said as he unlocked the car and tossed his bag in.

"At least I have a hybrid," Alex added at the sign of disapproval that flashed over Zeke's face.

As quickly as it came, the look passed and Zeke was smiling. "Of course. Have to help the environment in little ways here and there."

"Yep," Alex said.

Zeke glanced over to where Rob was unlocking his bike. "I used to live down in Hayes Valley before I moved to the Richmond. Where do you live?"

"Down on Fell, near Laguna," Alex said, turning back and extending his hand. "And sadly, I need to be going."

Zeke looked at the hand, glanced over at Rob, and then smiled and gripped it tightly.

"Nice meeting you, Alex," Zeke said, smiling. "I hope we run into one another soon."

Alex smiled back, "I'm sure we will."

With a grunt Alex got into his car and started it.

"It was nice meeting you!" Alex said as he pulled away, the electric hum of the engine winding up with the accelerator.

As he left, he saw Rhonda exit the elevator, face furious. Alex shook his head and pretended not to see her.

What a nice guy, Alex found himself thinking as he pulled out onto Fourth Street and made his way toward 101 South. Maybe there was still time for a pit stop at El Matate.

Absentmindedly he scratched at the back of his neck as the tingle faded away. He smiled.

Burritos sounded great.

*   *   *

Rhonda Vasquez threw her bike helmet onto the cement floor, but immediately rebuked herself for the outburst when she noticed the man in the nice suit was watching her. She turned back to Rob, who was leaning away from her in that way he did. He was the only person she'd ever met that could seem to pull off a fetal position while standing and it frustrated her to no end.

Rob was incredibly intelligent, she could see that in his attention to detail and daily reports, but he was spineless to the point of uselessness. However, Rhonda kept working with Rob because he reminded her a little of herself when she first entered the corporate world from non-profit land. He was coy and uncomfortable, but driven. Rhonda intended to give him what he needed to succeed, but it was getting harder and harder to maintain her resolve.

And then there was Alex Mamsin.

Mamsin she did not like, not at all.

He was always so pretentious and self-important, throwing down timelines without any research and almost always underestimating the downtime. If Rhonda Vasquez did that, she would have been out the door years ago, but this, this... punk kid could talk down to her and get away with it time and time again.

It just made her so angry!

Quietly, Rhonda took a deep breath and exhaled through her nose before turning back to a panicked Rob.

"Rob," Rhonda began, calm and composed despite him. "Head back upstairs and tell the rest of the team to plan on not having access for the weekend," she paused, and then added. "Actually, have them take a couple days off. Paid."

If Mamsin wanted to stall production then let him be responsible for the payroll.

Rob nodded, confusion clear on his face and made his way quickly toward the elevators, nodding at the gentleman in the suit as he did so.

Someone dressed like that had to be important, but who was he? Was he a new director? Rhonda mentally prepared herself for the introduction she was about make. She did a couple practice runs as she retrieved her helmet.

Putting on her best smile, Rhonda walked over to where the man was still standing, staring at the exit with a thoughtful look on his face.

The suit was of good quality, though not a brand she recognized. Classic, with good lines, gray pin stripes and a high waist that made her think more of a Twenties businessman than a Twenty-First century executive. Likewise, his shoes were well worn, but well kept. They were old leather, oiled and buffed repeatedly. They reminded her vaguely of vintage sketches she'd looked at in college.

The more she stared, the more something seemed slightly off. Everything was a little too well put together, matched with disjointed period clothing to a pseudo-modern look. Even the gold pocket watch that he glanced at seemed purposeful.

Maybe he was gay? She dismissed the thought.

It wasn't important if he was or not. Rhonda just needed to mend the bridge she damaged with her outburst. It was hard enough being a ranking female executive and maintaining respect amongst male staff without ruining it with something like a temper tantrum. There were enough imagined slights without her adding to the mix.

It had just been a bad day.

Sales were down and Harrison Nawat and Karen Jenkins, the CEO and CFO respectively, were breathing down her neck. They kept pointing at Marketing as the source of the failure. She'd argued that there wasn't a market for self-sustaining solar plant holders, but they didn't want to hear it. Harrison was huge into the green movement. Karen was a prick and a follower. There wasn't much to be done there.

Rhonda had spent years trying to get access to the military division--now there were products she could market--but, as Harrison was always quick to remind her, those contracts were military only. Regenerative tissue, personal defense systems; there were limitless possibilities. She wasn't even supposed to know about those things, but word traveled quickly at Nawat Industries.

If only she could get a chance to pitch some of those products to the shareholders! She could picture the billboards already.

Rhonda sighed. She was a realist and that meant she was stuck marketing solar powered plant holders. It also meant she could use all the help she could get.

"I'm sorry," Rhonda started as she approached the man with a hand extended in greeting, "I don't think we were introduced. I'm Rhonda Vas—"

"I don't care what your name is," the man said, eyes moving slightly to the left as if he was tracking something in the distance.

"Excuse me?" Rhonda asked, shocked.

"I said I don't care what your name is," he said again, still looking off into the distance, "I don't care about your failing product line, your angst at upper management, your questions about my sexuality, your self-perceived benevolence, or the disgust with which most of your coworkers view you.

"I care about you enough to know that I despise you precisely for these thoughts and feelings and the fact that this type of anger and hate-mongering is seen as being 'competitive' rather than what it actually is," he turned and met her eyes, face full of annoyance and disgust.

"Stupidity. Complete and utter stupidity," He glanced toward her for a moment and shook his head sadly. "With my kind as advisors you could have been so much more."

He turned a pitying look on her before turning away to stare into the distance again. "But I guess that's just not going to happen, is it?"

Rhonda stood there, aghast. Anger roiled within her. She was tempted to tell him off right there, regardless of his position or clout. Stupid? She was stupid? Then how did she end up becoming a Vice President of one of the largest military contractors in the world!

Then again, Rhonda conceded to herself worriedly, glancing around and realizing that she was alone with him in the basement, he might rape and kill her. No one would ever get there in time to help.

"Go with that one," he said suddenly, waving her off to the side, "I'd rape and kill you for sure."

A sudden haze seemed to descend across her vision. The world became soft, pliable as Rhonda glanced around, trying desperately to hold onto... something. Hold onto what?

"You would rape and kill me for sure," she said numbly, watching in fascination as the garage turned fuzzy, as if she was staring through cheesecloth. "I should go home."

"I'm a homeless guy who harassed you outside the parking garage," he said in that smooth, even voice--it seemed even slightly melodic with his mid-western accent. "And you're pretty sure I was a vet from the Iraq War. I was wearing a bronze star underneath a ragged camouflage jacket. I called you a dirty whore when you ignored me."

"I should go home before you catch up to me," Rhonda said quietly, moving to her bike and mounting it.

"Don't forget to pull up your pant leg," he reminded her quietly, like a parent to a child. "You weren't assaulted until you left the garage, so you need that up."

She looked down and saw that she forgot to roll up the leg of her pantsuit.

"Thank you," she said, smiling. "That's very nice of you."

"Stop talking to yourself," he said as he walked away toward the stairs that led to the lower level of the garage. "People will start thinking you're crazy."

Rhonda nodded as she finished rolling her pants, put on her helmet, and took off, whistling.

What a nice guy, Rhonda thought as she pedaled up the exit ramp.

The streetlights blazed around her suddenly as she exited onto Stockton Street, the glaze that had been present a moment earlier burned away in the incandescent light. Rhonda stopped, looking around in sudden confusion, trying to remember where she was or what she was doing.

"Spare some change ma'am?"

The voice came from her right and suddenly all of the memories slammed into her; the vicious attack, the attempted rape.

Rhonda screamed and kicked the homeless man to the side of the exit in the face. He fell to the ground, clutching his bloodied nose as she pedaled frantically into the street.

Some lights flashed to her right--a horn sounding, high and loud--and a moment later she was flying through the air, one leg twisted the wrong direction, the ground rushing up to meet her.

Unbidden, an image of a man in a vintage Twenties suit and a sad smile flashed through her mind.

What a nice guy, Rhonda thought through the pain just before everything went black.

* * *

It was nearing midnight when Alex dropped his beer. It poured out onto the stained wall-to-wall carpet. Not that there was much of it; the two bedroom apartment was tiny.

Leaning limply to the side, Alex watched the beer surge out as gunfire erupted around him and his companions screamed for help.

A shot echoed around Alex in full surround sound and the character on the large television in front of him suddenly fell backwards as the round ended. With a curse he grabbed the empty can and tossed it onto a large pile in his kitchen. He was already well into his second case when he reached down and grabbed another.

He groaned as his eyes lit on the clock across the room.

"Hey, I'm out for now," Alex said into his microphone, since it was getting close to midnight. "See ya."

A chorus of "see ya's" came over the headset as he turned off his system and made his way to the toilet. Alex tossed the controller and headset back onto the couch with a grunt.

It was a short walk given that the apartment was all of three or four hundred square feet. Cramped and claustrophobic were the two words that had popped into his mind when he decided to rent the place after Mary died, but it had been cheap and the right size.

Alex certainly didn't need a three-bedroom house anymore that was for sure.

He was still a bit fuzzy on what happened on his way out of work, but he was pretty sure that come Monday he'd be referred to as the "Former Senior Systems Administrator" at Nawat Industries.

Alex frowned as he urinated.

If Rhonda was on the warpath and she actually went to his boss then, well, it wouldn't be good.

Couple that with Brian's announcement and Alex had found himself at the checkout line with two thirty packs of Natural Ice and a bag of beef jerky. The rest of the night had been a haze of virtual gunfire and flowing booze.

Idly, Alex pulled the last bit of the meat from the bag that was in his pocket for some god-awful reason and popped it in his mouth. There would have been a time when doing that would have disgusted him, but that care disappeared with the house and Mary.

Alex had come a long way. With a shake, he moved to the sink. He looked at the man in the toothpaste-spattered mirror and shook his head. There were deep bags under his purple eyes and some light stubble of in what counted for his version of five-o-clock shadow. At least his bloodline helped keep that from getting out of hand.

Mary would have kicked his ass to see him like that.

"At least I'm still going to the dentist," Alex said defiantly at the mirror as he gnawed on the jerky, doing his best to imitate a western cowboy.

Chewing the bit of jerky reminded him of the piece of filling from earlier, so he shook his hands off and pulled back his cheek.

What the hell?

Alex took a step back, shook his head and leaned into the sink. He got as close to the mirror as he could, but nothing changed. On the bicuspid that had been drilled and worked on the day before there was nothing but pure, white enamel. He tongued at the tooth, looking for seams and found none.

He was certain the filling had been a rough texture afterwards. It had also been a pristine white rather than the slight ivory of his actual tooth.

It had hurt like hell all night. Alex tongued at the tooth for sensitivity, but felt nothing.

"Huh," he said to no one in particular.

"Guess that dentist is better than I thought," Alex murmured, rubbing at the back of his neck as it began to tingle.

He shrugged, dried his hands and went back into the tiny living room that was dominated by his 56" LED television and entertainment system. Grabbing another beer--and taking care not to scatter the pile of thirty plus cans in the kitchen--he plopped down on the couch just in time to hear a knock at the door.

"Goddamn it..."

He grunted as he stood back up and made his way to the door, rubbing at the annoying itch.

"Stupid old lady," Alex mumbled to himself as he kicked some shoes away from the door and got situated at the peephole.

His next-door neighbor--an ancient Jewish woman named Frieda--had been part of the building when he moved in. As long as Alex didn't make any loud noises, snore, flush the toilet, or scuff his feet on the laminate in the kitchen, Frieda was great. If he happened to do any of the above--or cough--then there was always hell to pay.

Instead of an elderly woman in a wig, Alex was shocked to see a man standing there, glancing around casually. Squinting at the darkened fisheye image--the light outside Alex's door had blown a few days prior--he tried to identify the stranger and failed.

Alex could tell the man was of average height and build, but beside the fact that he didn't appear to be a bum there wasn't any way to find out who he was without opening the door.

And Alex didn't open the door for anyone, let alone strangers. Unless it was a screaming neighbor, he maintained his distance and ignored all solicitors.

Despite himself, Alex stood there staring for a long moment, the buzz in the back of his neck growing stronger and spreading out into three distinct points. He reached up and scratched at it, wondering if he was developing a rash.

Who would come this late unless he knew them? Alex found himself wondering as he met the eyes of the man--black pools with tiny white specs--through the looking glass.

The longer he sat there, the more Alex found features that reminded him of a kid he used to party with in college... someone that followed him and Mark Sacco around when they got in trouble with the cops.

Alex could almost picture this man with a full head of hair, sitting next to him on the sidewalk, laughing hysterically despite the handcuffs as Mark Sacco--complete with gigantic Styrofoam head worn as a helmet--shouted down at the police: "When I am wearing this, I am above the law!"

And he was wearing a sport coat.

Alex laughed. He opened the door.

Simon grinned as the light hit him.

3
San Francisco, CA
2:38 AM August 21, 2010

The car was a tiny oasis of darkness and silence on the otherwise well-lit San Francisco street.

Inside of its hushed interior Dervy sat, eyes closed, focusing on three distinct vibrations amongst the throbbing presence that blanketed the rest of the city. Two were together indicating that Simon had managed to get inside the apartment. It had taken her a millennium to perfect the ability, but all that practice seemed worth the effort at times like this.

One of the three--the newly Taken, Alex--was like the Sun on a bright day, so intense that all the stars were wiped away. Or rather, it was like that to every other strigoi.

Dervy saw things differently.

The sun still shone, but she could see everything else as if it was nighttime. And right now, against the backdrop of her mind, two other people stood out. One was Simon.

Who was the other?

As she had mastered the skill, Dervy began to notice unique patterns in the way each person's chi vibrated. Taken were the strongest and nearly impossible to tell apart, but that wasn't as significant since the effect only lasted a year. After that, their signals faded to until they were nearly indistinguishable from other strigoi. Strigoi themselves gave off something a lot less detectable, but still more intense than the average human. Each one seemed unique; a distinct note on a larger scale. This made them the easiest to identify on a person-by-person basis. Dervy had taken care to identify as many strigoi she could.

That's what made her so nervous.

Another strigoi was watching Alex's apartment and she couldn't identify who they were. The briefing stated that there were no Sirgili in the area and no known strigoi inhabiting San Francisco beyond her contact. Even he had been passing through on business; he didn't live here.

That either meant the strigoi she detected was in hiding--quite likely given the rebellion a little over a century ago--or had arrived when news of a Taken in San Francisco got to Heathshome.

Honestly, either situation was bad since that person was sitting in an alleyway across from Alex Mamsin's apartment waiting for... something. Dervy grimaced and focused down on the vibration, searching it for pieces of familiarity that might help her identify someone who had been exiled.

Most of them had been exiled during either the Dunfee Rebellion of 1878 or the Vendée Rebellion of 1794. Pardons had been issued, but overall there had been several hundred Sirgili stripped of their ranks and cast out from the Arktois.

Dervy wasn't excited about meeting any of them.

Both uprisings had been well organized and led by dozens of powerful and intelligent strigoi. Dervy had fought for the Arktois against both rebellions, which wouldn't put her high on the sympathy list for anyone involved with either. On the other hand, it was only one strigoi.

But who was it...?

This might be her chance to find out what was happening to the other Taken. If this strigoi was involved, Dervy should be able to get some information out of them if they really were alone.

Dervy was interrupted by another vibration, this time coming from the cell phone in her front pocket.

She pulled it out and took a quick look at the Caller ID.

"Bonne nuit, William," Dervy answered with a grin.

A deep laugh came back over the line.

"Bonne nuit Derval. How is it going over there?" William responded with a voice accented by the slightest of Liverpool accents.

Well, a Liverpool accent, as Dervy would identify it. These days there were few people who'd be able to narrow down the town where a young William Searle was born based on the intonations of his voice. Well, unless they had been alive in the sixteenth century. The first time she'd ever graced the streets of the city had been to find this man and introduce him to the Arktois.

Dervy had found more than she anticipated. Subsequent centuries had been… complicated by his presence. William was more than just handsome; he was beautiful in a way that made her teenage physiology tingle with excitement every time he was around.

Beyond that William was amazingly intelligent. After two decades living in poverty in a then-rural England, William had devoured every piece of literature available to him in the Arktois Library. The man could argue the nuances of Cicero while translating Ovid's *Metamorphoses* into English.

That made it worse every time William betrayed her trust. Dervy wished she could say that it had only happened once or twice over the centuries since she found him lifting crates on a dock, but that would be a lie. She hated herself for it, but he hadn't broken the one promise that mattered; the one he made to her under a dark canopy of stars in the years leading up to the Vendée Rebellion.

William had never told anyone her age. For that she could forgive all of his other indiscretions, as irrational as it seemed.

Not that he was hers to forgive. Not anymore.

Dervy shook her head, clearing her head. "Things are going smoothly so far," she replied, "though I do have a strigoi watching the house."

There was a pause on the other end of the line. "Just one?"

"Yeah," Dervy said, focusing on the minute vibration.

Something about it was just so…familiar.

Dervy thought she heard a sigh on the other end.

"One will not be a problem, I hope," William said.

"So far there hasn't been anything," Dervy said, "but, regardless, there should be no problem on my end."

"Glad to hear," William said, voice growing quiet. "We need a rushed removal."

Dervy paused for a moment, considering the change in tone. "I have Vanderwell inside with him now," she said, referring to Simon. "How quick does this need to be? We're already working on an accelerated extraction here."

"Quick enough that it will make Simon uncomfortable," William answered honestly.

"I'll call him now," Dervy said, glancing toward the apartment a couple houses down from where she was parked. "But why am I rushing his first pull?"

"We have received confirmation of a Taken being kidnapped in Elmira," William said quietly. "A computer consultant named Craig Seamon. Apparently his wife Julie saw him airlifted after a car accident."

"Elmira, New York?" Dervy asked.

"Right."

"That's only a few hours away from Heathshome," Dervy said, tapping her fingers on the steering wheel thoughtfully. "How do we know he was a Taken. And who kidnapped him?"

She didn't ask how they had managed something like this so close to Heathshome.

Since the end of World War II, the Arktois center of government had been situated in a rural area of New York State between Albany and New York City. It was about the size of a small village. Mostly it was a gathering area for the Ankousti, but it also provided a living area for a few thousand people and a couple larger events each year. Despite that, it was the heart of the Arktois. The area was kept under tight surveillance and had the highest population of strigoi in the world. Dervy just couldn't fathom how a Taken was kidnapped a couple hundred miles away from there.

"A woman who worked in the building across the street called the police when she saw a man dragging himself down the sidewalk after a car accident," William said. "He was all broken up-- legs shattered, face cut to hell--and then he apparently started using his legs, 'all of a sudden.'"

"When did this happen?" Dervy asked.

"Back in January," William said dismissively. "But we missed it until Porter in AIC found the two incidents and realized they were related."

"Damn," she cursed quietly, though she knew that there was nothing she could have done about it.

Dervy had been in Switzerland in late December through the end of January. She had left suddenly to say farewell to Tobias Ender, an old friend who had Returned. It had taken a while to wrap up his finances and a few other personal matters before she got back to Heathshome just before February.

"Do we know who kidnapped him?" Dervy asked finally.

"We got three sketches from Julie Seamon before she disappeared late last week," William said hesitantly.

"Disappeared?" Dervy asked, incredulous.

A pause.

"Yes," William responded.

"Just 'yes?'" Dervy asked. "Did she have a guard?"

"Yes," William repeated, refusing further details.

You didn't just disappear when the Arktois was watching you. She felt the first tendrils of anxiety and concern.

"Okay," Dervy conceded finally, rubbing her face with her free hand. "How good are the sketches? Did we get a hit off any them?"

There was another pause on William's side, "All three actually," he said, pausing as though considering every word. "The Ankousti is performing additional verification on the third one due to its severity."

"Who is it, William?" Dervy asked, annoyance crawling into her voice.

"As I said, the Ankousti are--" William began, but Dervy cut him off.

"We both know..." Dervy stopped speaking, but she finished the statement in her head. *We both know there wouldn't be an Ankousti if it weren't for me.*

She took a deep breath before continuing. "So just tell me who you think it is so I can be prepared in case you *are* right."

There was a long silence before William's voice crackled over the cell phone. It seemed quieter than before.

"It looks like Kevin, Derval."

"I..." Dervy stuttered into the phone.

Caoimhín? Dervy pictured the short Irishman with the blazing red beard. He'd always been so dedicated to strigoi well being. Why would he kidnap a Taken? It just didn't make any sense...

"I see why you're verifying," Dervy said finally. "Is there any possibility that the drawing is accurate?"

"After Julie Seamon disappeared he left Heathshome and has not been in contact with anyone," William said and Dervy could hear the concern in his voice. "That was three days ago."

That would be a 'yes'. She drummed her fingers nervously on the steering wheel.

Maybe that was who was waiting in the alley? A quick focus on the vibration told her no. Dervy knew what Caoimhín's tone felt like and it wasn't his.

"If he's involved that only gives him a week to do whatever he is planning," Dervy said, mind spinning as she began to work through various scenarios that would push a man like Caoimhín to kidnap another strigoi. "He started the Return before I left New York, which means he has six days at the most."

Maybe it had something to do with the Return. It wouldn't be the first time that a respectable strigoi--or even a member of the Ankousti--had tried to cheat death.

They all failed.

"The council believes that he is seeking solitude before he dies, so I would rather you not concern yourself with that just yet," William said calmly, though there was still a trace of concern that he was trying hard to hide. "I will let you know if I can confirm it. We both know how Kevin is when he is on a mission, so rest assured that I am moving as quickly as I possibly can."

"I told him not to change his name," Dervy said quietly, realizing that if William was speaking this openly about the subject, regardless of pressure from her, that it was already confirmed. "He's been different since he stopped going by Caoimhín."

William sighed. "It is the same name, Dervy, just easier for the newer generations to say."

"Regardless," Dervy said, shaking her head, not wanting to get into it. "What about the other two?"

"One is Nathan Potts, who I'm sure you remember," William said.

"I remember him," Dervy said, gritting her teeth.

Nathan Potts had been a lead player in the Dunfee Rebellion and was currently in exile. He was also an ex-slave who had joined the Union during the American Civil War. No one knew exactly when he was Taken--no one even knew how old Nathan was--but the man was huge and impossibly strong, even for a strigoi.

Nathan had overpowered her during a desperate raid on the old Vendée stronghold right before the end of the uprising. Caoimhín had beaten Nathan back with a piece of wrought iron and given Dervy the time she needed to recover and overwhelm her assailant.

If Dervy had to fight Nathan again, he would be near the peak of his strength. Dervy had come to a plateau almost a millennium ago and she probably wouldn't be able to overpower him next time. Unless he was older than they all thought.

Dervy could still remember his cocky smile.

She'd knocked his teeth out for it.

"Sorry," Dervy said, realizing that William had continued speaking. "What was that?"

"I said," William started again, obviously annoyed at having to repeat himself, "the other person identified was a human doctor named Eustace Williamson. He was a pioneer of stem cell research and was developing a couple new cancer treatments when he disappeared three years ago."

"I guess he didn't die three years ago then," Dervy said. "But you said 'was?'"

"One of his legs and an arm washed up down near Haverstraw back in April," William said. "We just found out about it last month so, before you ask, there is no point in sending Weynie."

Dervy snorted. "Did she say that or did you?"

"She did after seeing the case photos," William said tersely. "You would almost think I knew how to do this job by now, huh?"

"Was that sarcasm?" Dervy said, smiling to herself, "From William Searle?"

"I know; I must be getting old," he responded sarcastically.

"I don't think this is Nathan," Dervy said abruptly.

"Who?" William asked.

"The strigoi across the street," Dervy said, reaching out one more time to confirm that the pattern didn't match her memory of Nathan Potts. "The tone seems familiar, though. I definitely know them."

"You know everyone whether they know you or not," William said, the playful tone fading from his voice quickly.

"That's my job."

"That was your job in the late teens," William said, referring to the prior half of the past millennium. "For now I just need you to get the Taken back to Heathshome."

"Will do," Dervy said. "But I thought you wanted me to find out what was happening to these missing Taken?"

"I do," he paused. "I don't suppose you can Scry him?" William asked hopefully.

Scrying, formally referred to as Animi Pellegi, was one of Six Gifts that sometimes developed in a strigoi as they aged. The definition varied to either include or exclude the ability to alter a target's memory, but both camps agreed that Scrying was--at its most basic--the ability to read someone's thoughts. If you were untrained and touched a mind, you would be blinded with a flurry of sounds and images that didn't make much sense. However, a skilled Scryer could read your thoughts as quickly and efficiently as you thought them. A few could almost control someone, though they were rare.

Simon was great at reading thoughts and could sometimes inject images into a person's mind, but it was a skill she'd never really developed.

She frowned. "You know I've never been able to Scry without touching someone, William."

"I know, but I had to ask," William said.

There was another long pause and they both sat in uncomfortable silence, waiting for the other to say something.

"Well, I—" Dervy began.

William cut her off. "Oh, there is one more thing," he said, finally speaking at a normal volume.

"What?" Dervy asked.

"Marie is pregnant," William said.

Even with numbers as few as theirs, it wasn't easy to be on a first name basis with someone, but Dervy knew whom he meant. She had seen the signs William gave off when he spoke to the Taken the Gatherers had found the previous year. She was a South African woman--girl, really--in her late teens. Marie. Dervy admitted that she was beautiful, but the girl was just so... young.

He always liked them young. That was a good part of why they weren't together.

"She'll abort soon, I went a full month one time," Dervy said dismissively, trying her best to cover up the disgust welling up inside her.

Maybe it wasn't his? Something climbed into her throat just as it always did when William talked about his women.

He cleared his throat. "She is twelve weeks in."

"That's impossible," Dervy said firmly, slapping the steering wheel.

Strigoi can't get pregnant. Dervy reeled, memories of miscarriage after miscarriage flooding her mind.

"Impossible or not, the baby is in there and has a heartbeat," William said, voice crackling over the cell phone.

Dervy didn't know where to begin; words failed her. "I..."

William cleared his throat again, "'Congratulations,' would be nice if you run into her."

"But, but that can't happen and you're passing it off like it's no big deal!" Dervy finally stammered out.

In four thousand years, not a single strigoi woman had given birth, not unless they were Taken in their last weeks of pregnancy, and even that was uncertain. In all of those cases, if it carried to term, the baby was always mortal. Not one strigoi had ever gotten pregnant after being Taken and gone longer than six weeks.

Ever.

"She is still a Taken. Maybe things are changing. We have all seen it the last few generations," William said softly. "They are different than us."

"Who's the father?" Dervy asked, suddenly needing to know.

Another pause. "I am, Derval."

"Wow," Dervy heard herself say.

"Yeah, I know," William said happily.

He continued. "Almost five hundred years old and going to be a father."

There was a long pause as Dervy tried to digest everything.

How could he do this to her again? Her heart raced.

"You are okay with this?" William asked tentatively.

"I just didn't know you were picking from the Taken now. Isn't she a little young?" Dervy said acidly.

The quiet tone... the happy announcement.

"I probably should not have said anything right now--" William started, obviously trying to calm her down.

Dervy cut him off as the pieces fell into place.

"Is she sitting there with you?" She asked incredulously.

"That's none of your business," William said firmly, but still hushed. "I just wanted you to hear from me instead of someone like Simon."

How the hell would Simon know? Dervy looked around her dark car in amazement.

She wanted to scream at him, call him a liar, a whore. Dervy wanted to light them both on fire and smile, holding a gas can as they turned to ash. Then she'd wait for the bodies to regenerate so she could start over. But behind those thoughts, Dervy just wanted to cry to him that she loved him and beg him to come back to her.

But she wouldn't. Those days were long over, no matter how much her heart yearned for them back. With no remorse, Dervy burned all of the thoughts away and scattered the ashes to the wind.

She had more important things to take care of at the moment.

"Thanks anyway," Dervy said quietly, feeling calm spread across her like a cool wave. "I'll take care of Alex and get him back to Heathshome."

"Alex is the newly Taken?" William ask, curiosity tingeing his voice.

"Yes, Alex Mamsin," Dervy said.

"Huh. Interesting." William said, interest fading.

"Why?" Dervy asked.

"It is not important," William said quickly, "but getting him back here safe is, so I will leave you to it."

"Mm-hmm," Dervy said. "Give Marie my best."

"Thanks," William said uncertainly.

Dervy disconnected the call and, with a steadying breath, she dialed out a number on her cell phone.

"What's up, woman," came Simon's carefree voice on the other end. "I thought I told you not to call me tonight unless it's important."

"We need to make this a rush job," Dervy said, ignoring Simon's act and getting out of the car. "I'll be there in three minutes."

"Wait a second baby," Simon said urgently. "We can work this out without—"

Dervy slammed the car door and the window spider-webbed on impact, pieces of glass falling inside across the driver's seat. A moment later she heard the echo across the cell phone and Simon's alarmed screech.

"Two minutes and fifty seconds, Simon."

Disconnecting the call, Dervy walked toward the apartment, fully aware that the strigoi across the street was moving as well, albeit slowly.

She smiled to herself.

As Dervy passed millennia in constant solitude, the world had slowly faded, becoming a dull, ugly thing. Each decade caused a little more color to fade, until she was left with a gray, drab existence. Even sex, while still desired by her body, had lost any lasting satisfaction. Once the act was over, Dervy felt the emptiness fill her again.

Love had been a brief reprieve, but now that only brought anger.

Anger, however, led to a revelation. Since then there was one thing that always spoke to her, wrapping her in purpose in an otherwise empty world. And when there is only one thing that brings you back to yourself and makes the world vibrant again, you have to fulfill that desire; that need.

As the unknown strigoi started cautiously toward the apartment, she felt the craving fill her. Dervy grinned as the world slowed down. Her pulse was racing and sweat began dripping down her back as the adrenaline filled her veins. Her mouth watered as she took another step, the silence of the street screaming in her head.

At that moment, Derval desperately needed to kill something.

4
San Francisco, CA
2:47 AM August 21, 2010

Zeke Dunfee sat quietly in the dark alley. He was desperately trying to ignore the stench of stale urine and feces that permeated the tight space. There had been a few bums populating it when he'd arrived, but a few quick demonstrations had sent them scrambling away believing that they were in the presence of a demon or a flashback.

As it stood, Zeke wasn't exactly sure which one he preferred.

There were definitely times when charm was a better tool than fear, but for some reason the latter seemed to be the rule of order for this night. Zeke sniffed as a salty breeze wafted an odor of rot from the other end of the alley, bringing with it the memories of the evening and an accidental death.

Yes, fear had definitely become the norm for him.

Until a few days ago that hadn't been the case for the past one hundred and thirty years. When Kevin had called him desperately asking his help to locate a Taken in San Francisco, it had been hard to listen. Just speaking with the man who had almost single-handedly devastated his entire army during the revolution was difficult.

Instead, they had met in a neutral location on the edge of Wyoming and Kevin had offered him the one thing Zeke hadn't known he even wanted.

Dervy.

Zeke would have been much happier getting to spend a few years with Kevin, working over the successes and failures of the revolution in minute detail with a hot iron.

Nothing could have been better than to take the time to write the names of the dead into Kevin's skin, but he had to admit, Dervy was the next best thing. Getting the chance to inflict her with any of the pain he'd experienced over the last century would almost make up for the fact that he would be working for Kevin.

Zeke grunted to himself. He took a sip of his quad-shot mocha, taking care to breath in the rich, chocolaty aroma instead of the fetid stink around him.

Work for Kevin.

The man was obviously insane at this point. He was well into the Return and had acquired that strange fervor that sometimes infects those suddenly facing death. Kevin was certain he could beat it; that he could stop the Return. He was mad for sure, but the steps he'd taken over the past twenty years gave Zeke pause and made him consider that maybe, just maybe, there was something to what Kevin said.

Maybe Kevin could stop the Return...

Zeke grunted again and finished the last of his drink, luxuriating in the strong mix of chocolate and espresso at the bottom. Carefully, he set the cup next to him in a place where he wouldn't it.

He smiled. San Francisco had managed to change him, though Zeke would never admit that to anyone. It was hard not to care about the environment here. You actually had to stand against everyone if you were insistent on littering. Of course, Zeke had seen the world transformed from a green, easy-to-breathe landscape to a smog filled, nearly toxic wasteland. Or close enough to it, anyway. The air had finally begun clearing up over the past few decades after a century and a half of filth.

Zeke shook his head trying to refocus. The older he got, the more Zeke found his mind wandering through other times in his life. For hours he'd explore memories and old philosophies. Remember old friends... old dead friends who were supposed to have been immortal.

The memories were a lot more pleasant than the reality.

Across the street was Alex Mamsin's house, if you could call that thing a house. It was sandwiched between two brick buildings and appeared to be little more than a converted alleyway, much like the one Zeke currently sat in. Wood had been slapped on both ends and the rest framed up around that. The building was a faded green, though it appeared to be a drab gray in the night. There were a few windows up front, but all were dark at this hour.

He glanced at his watch. 2:47 AM.

No wonder his legs were starting to ache. Zeke had been sitting in this alley for near to six hours waiting for this young strigoi to finally fall asleep.

Zeke frowned. He could still feel the faint prickle on the back of his neck that Alex Mamsin was giving off, like a little itch he couldn't scratch. Alex was still moving around quite a bit.

There had been only one visitor to the building since Zeke had arrived, a man wearing a silly looking sport coat. After that, he'd seen nary a soul. That in and of itself was out of character for this part of town. Typically there were plenty of twenty-somethings meeting up before heading out for the night. Zeke hadn't seen anything tonight.

It almost reminded him of home.

Zeke shifted his weight as his right foot went numb. He wished he knew what was keeping Kevin's 'associate'. Whoever was supposed to meet so they could plan Alex's removal was hours late. In the meantime, Zeke had just decided to wait until the Taken had fallen asleep before heading inside.

If he had his choice, Zeke would have taken Alex back in the parking garage, but Kevin had told him to wait. Apparently there was a chance that Dervy would show tonight and Kevin didn't want to miss the chance to get the newly Taken as well as Dervy. Kevin seemed to think the safety of the new strigoi would distract her enough that Zeke and his mystery guest could capture her.

It was crazy. One didn't just capture Dervy. You had to maim her before she stopped getting up. Even then the only way you could keep her from tearing you apart a few minutes later was to box her so she couldn't regenerate her limbs.

Or at least, he hoped that would stop her. It had stopped everyone else in the past, anyway.

Zeke felt his heart sink. He really hoped Dervy wasn't going to show this night. He hoped that Kevin was wrong about her coming, while at the same time begging to God that Kevin was correct about her distraction.

Doubt weaseled into his mind. They hadn't taken the proper precautions for someone like her. Hell, if she showed up, he might not get away. Zeke might die. God knows Dervy hated him enough.

That said, he'd thought Kevin hated him like that, too. Maybe time had changed their temperament? Maybe he should stop his heart, just in case Dervy was there? At least then he might have a chance to get away if she tried to cripple him.

Zeke shuddered at the thought. It always felt so...unnatural when he did that. Sure, it made you harder to hurt and you didn't tire at all, but your blood didn't flow either. No blood meant no hormones, no adrenaline. You might as well be dead at that point.

That and going against Dervy like that would be a horrible idea. She was a master berserker and would just keep tearing limbs off until you couldn't move anymore.

Down the street a window shattered, causing him to jump to his feet. Zeke leaned out of the alley, glancing to the right. In all likelihood, someone's car was getting burgled. While he would usually step up and stop something like that, tonight he couldn't.

That didn't mean he couldn't look, though. Maybe he could report them later...

Zeke cursed. A short, slim figure was walking toward him from the opposite side of the road. The shadowy form moved purposefully, taking a moment to glance both ways before jogging across the street, quickly closing the gap between he and it.

He ducked back into the alley and squatted in the darkness, doing his best to act like one of the bums he'd kicked out earlier. Wrinkling his nose in disgust, Zeke grabbed some soiled cardboard and pulled it over him like a filthy blanket. Hopefully, the thief would pass him by, thinking him a small threat. At the most, he'd probably get stabbed, which wasn't that big of a deal when you healed like a strigoi. A shadow fell over him as the figure rounded the corner.

"Hey asshole."

The voice sounded small, feminine, and disturbingly familiar. It felt like someone had poured a glass of ice water down his back.

Zeke turned toward the woman taking care to keep his face covered and began mumbling incoherently.

A tremor of real fear entered his voice. "I didna see nuttin'," he sputtered, pulling himself in a half sliding motion.

It sounded like Dervy... but it couldn't be, right? Kevin's other guy hadn't gotten there yet.

"Bullshit," the woman said as she reached down and hauled him to his feet with unnatural strength.

"Aw shit," Zeke said as he finally locked eyes with Dervy, staring down into her menacing eyes... that were an odd brown color.

Dervy was a slight girl, slim at the waist, but muscular. He'd always thought she looked like a girl who grew up on a farm tossing hay bales with her brothers. That didn't make her any less beautiful, though. She had shoulder length brown hair pulled back into a loose ponytail at the moment, which struck him as odd.

Zeke remembered her hair being blonde and her eyes being a panic-inducing purple. Despite that, in another time and place Zeke would have fallen over himself trying to gain her attention.

Now he just wished he was anywhere other than in her sights.

Dervy glared at him, looking him over as if he really was a bum. "What are you doing here Zeke?"

"Umm..." Zeke mumbled, frantically scrambling for any other reason his presence than the truth. "Brown hair now? I thought you used to be a blonde."

Zeke cursed himself, but found he couldn't stop the words from coming out. "And are you wearing those new fangled contacts? Don't you have purple ey--?"

Starbursts erupted in his vision as his head was slammed up against the brick wall faster than he could react. Small fingers tore into the skin in the back of his head, ignoring the more easily accessible hair for the firm grip of his skull.

Dervy shifted her weight and Zeke felt his heart go into his throat as she drove him to his knees. The pressure on his skull increased; the world started to go fuzzy. He heard something cracking.

She put her lips up close to his ear and whispered. "You have fifteen seconds before I'm running behind schedule. What. Are. You. Doing. Here."

Zeke panicked.

Desperately, Zeke drew heat from the walls and ground and launched it at her in a bright flash, lighting the alley in bright blue flame. Dervy's fingers pulled away from his scalp and he tumbled away toward the opposite end of the alley, hands frantically digging through garbage and waste. Through his panic he considered pushing more power at her, but he dismissed it when he realized she wasn't screaming.

Zeke glanced back and cursed.

Dervy wasn't an average strigoi by any stretch of the imagination. She stood there, teeth clenched as the blue flames rippled up and down her body. It tore through clothes and flesh alike like a ravenous beast. The flames were already starting to die down, turning orange, but still vibrant.

Backpedaling, Zeke pushed on her with his mind using as much force as he could manage. Without being anchored to anything, he slid through the mess until colliding with a dumpster. At that point Dervy flew out into the street, tumbling head-over-feet like a doll tossed from a moving car.

Zeke grunted as he struggled to his feet, feeling his shoulder pop back into place and the skin on his head knit back together. Sometimes he hated telekinesis. He pulled broken glass from his hand and tossed it on the ground.

It was so...logical.

Zeke took a moment before he moved. He found himself staring, waiting, for something to happen... for Dervy to move.

A buzzing in his coat pocket interrupted his vigil. He reached into his pocket and pulled the cell phone free. Sitting bright on the screen was a text message from an anonymous number:

Get out she is coming.

Zeke laughed out loud, but stopped as he saw Dervy start to get to her feet.

"You don't have to tell me twice," Zeke said to no one in particular.

With an annoyed glance at his discarded coffee cup, Zeke turned and sprinted down the alleyway.

*   *   *

Alex sat on the couch, a beer hanging lazily in his hand. Simon leaned in across from him, spinning tales of his post-college adventures. Nodding with dull enthusiasm, Alex took another drink as Simon caught his eye during yet another fantastical flourish.

The conversation had long ago turned one-sided, though it had gotten ridiculous since Simon's girlfriend called. Since Alex had left out the parts of his life that included Mary, suicide attempts, and server configuration he'd found it pathetically easy to bring Simon up to speed on his life.

Alex now knew how many different ways could you say that you moved to San Francisco and became a System Administrator

Seven.

It had actually been a pretty depressing rundown of his life. He had graduated, moved to San Francisco, worked at a couple small businesses as a Systems Administrator and then moved on to Nawat Industries.

That was it.

Well, that was it if you left out Mary.

Alex nodded again with faked interest as he took a long pull from the can. He barely noticed the near panicked tone of Simon's voice as the minutes crawled by.

That girlfriend of his must be pretty horrible if Simon was that distracted by the prospect of her coming over. Regardless, Alex could hardly wait for this woman to show up and take the man home. Each minute was drowning him in his own uselessness and lack of accomplishment.

Simon had been talking about the places he'd traveled, the women he'd slept with--before meeting his girlfriend, of course--and the foods he had eaten. For someone at a startup, he had certainly been around the world enough times to put Donald Trump to shame. It seemed more than you could pack into a lifetime, for sure, but Simon assured him that it was all true.

If Simon tried to sell him on any more of that power of positive thinking crap though Alex was going to throw him out. The last thing he needed was someone trying to help him right now.

Abruptly, it dawned on him. Simon was one of those time-share people. Alex frowned, looking up at the frantic look on Simon's face as he described Istanbul in shockingly clear detail.

Simon framed imaginary walls with his hands. "And the buildings are things of extravagant beauty, though it changed a lot after the caliphate was abolished--"

Alex interrupted him mid-sentence. "What are you trying to sell me, Simon?"

Simon stopped, finally at a loss for words. Alex found himself similarly surprised by the sudden silence and nearly laughed.

Behind Simon the door exploded.

Or at least it seemed to. One moment it was there, locked and bolted and the next wood chips sprayed into the apartment, chunks flying as far as the kitchen.

Cursing, Alex dropped to the floor, instinctively covering his head with both arms. Alex looked around, shocked at the wood scattered around. Simon was on his feet screaming at someone coming down the hallway, obstructing his view. He was flailing in much the same way as he had been a moment earlier, but this time each movement was punctuated with a stabbing motion that Alex found entertaining for some odd reason.

Alex laughed. Simon was tossed to the side like a bag of rice, slamming into the television with a crash.

Alex stopped laughing.

Stunned, he turned away from his destroyed television and turned back toward what used to be his front door.

Standing in front of him was a short, bald woman who looked like she had just finished rolling around in a fire pit. Her clothes were charred, with huge holes burned through various places. He found himself staring at her left breast through one of those holes and then caught her eyes.

One was purple, the other brown.

And both were livid.

With a start, Alex jumped to his feet, dropping his beer in the process. "My god! Are you okay?"

Alex didn't know who he was talking to, it could have been Simon or the half naked crazy woman, but for some reason it didn't matter. He had just needed to say something.

"Jesus, Dervy," Simon mumbled as he got to his feet, pulling a piece of plastic from his forearm with a grimace. "Whatever happened to you, it's no reason to throw me around like that."

Dervy stood, eyes locked on Alex. He felt his knees growing weaker the longer it went on. He felt like he was some sort of microbe being weighed, measured, and otherwise examined under a microscope. Hesitantly, Alex sat back down, smiling awkwardly.

She looked back at Simon.

"We're leaving now," Dervy said icily.

Simon looked back and forth between them and then nodded. He turned and headed quickly for the door, taking care to avoid fragments of the television.

Alex stayed on the couch, not daring to move. Instinctively, he tried to make himself smaller. Never mind the fact that this *Dervy* had picked up a man twice her weight and thrown him across a room or the fact that it looked like she had recently been lit on fire. Alex could smell the stench of burnt flesh. It had a distinct bacon-y aroma to it.

He wasn't sure what bothered him more.

Bacon was going to be a little harder to eat after this.

Alex found himself praying to God that she would leave.

She pointed at him, beckoning him forward he cursed.

God hated him.

"I'm sure there must be some misunderstanding," Alex said as he stood.

He walked toward her, hoping to take a firm stance.

Alex tried very hard not to panic as she shifted her weight to the foot with a whole boot.

"I mean, if I have to buy something from your boyfriend so that we're all--"

She held up a hand and he stopped speaking, mid-sentence. Alex took a step back as his mouth snapped shut.

"You," Dervy said, pointing at him with a soot covered finger. "You are coming with us *now*."

"Yes, ma'am," Alex found himself saying, but he shook his head. "No, I won't. Why the hell would I?"

She stepped toward him and Alex's heart leapt into his throat, but for some reason he stood his ground. He couldn't explain why he did what happened next, but it happened.

With every ounce of courage he could muster Alex leaned forward, face contorting angrily and said: "Get out of my house."

She smiled.

And then the world was a blur. One moment she was standing there and the next her fist was coming at his head. Alex barely had time to recognize he was going to die before her delicate hand caught him in the temple and everything went black.

*   *   *

"Pick him up," Dervy said as she stepped past Simon, barely sparing him a glance.

Her heart pounded with adrenaline and rage as she left the apartment.

Simon cursed under his breath.

Dervy had hit Alex Mamsin.

Hard.

There had been quite a satisfying crunch when his skull caved in and his brains turned into a thick pudding. The slight pain his bones had caused when they lacerated her hand was already gone as were the cuts themselves.

She let the cool, salty air overtake her, though it did nothing to calm her mood. A shiver ran through her body. Dervy adjusted what was left of her shirt to cover some of the more sensitive portions as a stiff breeze streaked over her bare skin. Her heart slammed inside her chest.

Why couldn't she get it under control?

Was it because Zeke Dunfee had caught her by surprise and had escaped? No, that wasn't it. He'd always been crafty and incredibly quick with his powers, even as a Youngling. Dervy could accept defeat. It happened and you moved on.

The next time you didn't lose.

Then what was it?

Maybe it the weakness she'd shown herself in the mirror this morning when everything felt so heavy, so *long*?

Dervy shook her head at that. Those feelings had been with her for thousands of years and only rarely had they brought out the anger she felt right now.

She just wanted to scream into the night, to run wild through the streets.

To kill everyone she saw.

Howling at the street Dervy struck out at the wall behind her, pushing her fist easily through what she had thought was wood. Concrete shattered at the force of her blows, spraying around her. The bones in her hand disintegrated on impact.

She pulled back, holding herself steady against the pain with her left hand and forced her right to reform. The bones rejoined, knitting painfully as she hit the wall again, sending more shards flying onto the sidewalk. The corner of the apartment above buckled slightly, a harsh cracking sound erupting through the night though it held firm.

Again, Dervy willed her hand to reform, but this time she held back. One more time and the building would collapse.

Dervy knew what was making her angry, but it was the one thing she couldn't bring herself to admit. It was nothing to her.

He was nothing to her.

Inside the building, directly across from her a door opened and an old woman shuffled out.

"What is going on out here?" She yelled, looking around wildly.

Suddenly, Dervy felt drained, empty, as she stood there facing off against the old woman. The woman might have been eighty, but she looked ancient. A fake wig covering a bag of liver spotted skin. An old flower printed nightgown. Fuzzy slippers.

Dervy shook her head.

"You there!" The woman yelled, one hand on the loose wig. "Are you the one making all the noise out here?"

Weakly, Dervy nodded, wondering if the woman would notice her disheveled appearance or the smell of her burnt flesh.

"There are people trying to get some sleep around here!" She yelled, gesturing wildly with one crooked hand, a breeze catching the hem of her nightgown and lifting it disturbingly.

Humans were interesting. They tore through their short lives, screaming and demanding everything be their way, regardless of anyone else. Dervy remembered quite vividly when those self-servicing desires had dominated her life, though that had been a few thousand years earlier.

Now, though, she just didn't care. In some ways, she found herself relating more to this woman who stubbornly stood in the hallway yelling at her. It was certainly closer than she felt with other strigoi. What Dervy did, she did out of a disinterest in others--a slight, but very important philosophical difference in perspective.

Dervy didn't enjoy killing newly Taken, but the game of conniving and manipulation had grown old, stagnant. Why should she spend the time convincing someone that they were special if they were going to die before her? Age didn't make you special.

This applied to everything, not just humans; the land, the sea, the sky. Dervy had seen the land remade by wind and water; the oceans themselves expanded and shrunk like immense lungs. Stars had disappeared from the sky after centuries of twinkling reassurance.

These things she had found ways to accept.

Things changed.

Why couldn't she accept this?

Dervy was shocked back to the present by a skeletal finger pushing at her chest, touching at a point that was still tender from skin regrowth.

It had been nearly four hundred years since anyone had gotten close enough to touch Dervy without her permission, let alone lay a finger on her. How had that old doddering woman gotten so close? What had happened to her instincts?

"Are you even listening you little trollop?" The old woman spat at her.

Dervy looked at the old woman's milky eyes and found herself without words, mouth moving dumbly.

What just happened?

Simon appeared behind the woman, a body slung over his shoulder. He looked confused as he approached, but snapped on his token smile as he passed by the old crone.

"Evening, ma'am," Simon said politely, nodding as he walked past.

He began whistling.

"And to you, son," she said, nodding.

The lady froze as he passed by, mouth hanging open at the blood smeared mess that lay hung over his shoulder. Her face was a mix of horror, disgust, and curiosity that made Dervy laugh out loud.

Finally, Dervy's heart rate began to slow.

With a wave, she patted Alex's blood-soaked back. "No worries, we'll take good care of him."

"Simon," Dervy said lightly. "Sometimes you're just too much."

Simon grinned at her. "Yeah, I know."

"Let me get a quick look at him," Dervy said, stopping.

Simon stopped moving and remained still as she turned Alex's head back and forth. "He was drinking pretty heavily tonight, it might have slowed down his aura a bit."

Dervy twisted Alex's face, looking at both sides and struggling to find any indication she had just crushed his skull a couple minutes before.

"Hm." Dervy walked toward the car.

"What is it?" Simon asked, jogging to catch up with her.

"He's already healed," she said quietly, more to herself than Simon.

Simon whistled as they reached the car, pausing for a moment at the sight of the shattered glass. With a shake of his head he sat Alex down in the back seat. Dervy got into the driver's seat, taking a moment to wipe away some of the sharp debris left behind. Simon and the old woman had managed to snap her out of the furious rage she had felt at the doorway, but now she was just confused.

At the best of times, Dervy was dangerous, but when she lost herself in pain, regret, or anger, things tended to escalate much more quickly than they should.

Dunfee was a perfect example of that. Not only had she allowed him to escape during, but also there was little new knowledge for her to report from the interaction. Sure, she now knew Dunfee had been watching Alex, but she had no idea why.

The chances of him working with Caoimhín were slim at best. As it stood, she couldn't think of a single reason that Dunfee would even consider it, let alone putting him directly in her path. Zeke knew better than to do that. The fact that he ran after incapacitating her was telling.

Dervy shook her head in confusion. Was this part of her normal cycle? Did she do this every five hundred years? She just couldn't remember anymore. She'd gone through so many.

How was Dervy supposed to find all of these Taken if she couldn't even keep herself together?

With a sigh, she plopped into the front seat and started the car. Glancing in the rear view, she saw Simon still getting Alex set in the back.

"What are you doing back there? We have to go."

Simon backed out and slammed the door shut. Exhaling deeply, he sat down in the passenger seat and pulled his own door closed.

"Damn. You're right," he said, shaking his head in disbelief. "Completely regenerated."

Dervy put the car in drive and accelerated quickly to the next corner, where she took a right. "That's what I said. Do I usually exaggerate?"

Simon looked askance at her. "I don't know."

Dervy shrugged, looking for the signs to 101S. She saw one a street over and turned sharply.

"Shit!" Simon yelled, bracing himself against the dash and armrest as the car cornered tightly. "This is a one-way!"

Dervy shot him a questioning look as she pushed the accelerator to the floor. "Are you afraid of dying, Simon?"

"No," he said, putting his hands evenly to his sides. "I just don't want to hurt anyone else tonight."

The speedometer passed fifty-five. The car spat out into a strange intersection, where four or five roads all converged and she easily pointed it in the correct direction, following signs at this point.

Simon screeched and Dervy looked at him again. She raised an eyebrow in amusement.

"And it's a rental?" Simon asserted in a wavering voice.

Dervy finally slowed. They rode quietly in the night, eventually finding their way to 101S. They were heading to the San Francisco Airport where a private jet was waiting to take them back to Albany.

The highway spread ahead of them under the black sky and Dervy let her mind ease. The ebony strip stretched into the distance like a long sinuous creature of infinite length. Other highways merged with it, making it wider for short periods of time before it was once again shrunk down to its formidable six lanes.

Even at this late hour, other vehicles traveled the road, many joining from these disparate streams. They spun by; entirely oblivious to the three strigoi reclining inside the sedan, racing toward whatever they considered important that late at night.

Dervy stared ahead, watching the taillights of a small sports car fade into the distance. Twin rubies glittered as they shrunk and disappeared off a ramp heading to Pacifica.

It was easy to get lost in the road, especially at night. The night was peaceful and barring any accidents, driving tended to be uneventful. Dervy was happy for those who had created motor vehicles. Walking everywhere or caring for a beast of burden had just been a matter of living before the last century.

Cars and their ilk required maintenance, but nowhere near as much as a prize mare or a string of pack mules. She always laughed when overhearing someone complain of getting an oil change or replacing worn brakes. It would be hilarious to see one of them even attempt to shoe a horse.

"Dervy, you have to merge," Simon said, pointing to the left.

"I know," she said defensively, flicking on her turn signal and moving over a lane as the current one faded away.

Simon leaned his head against the window. "Sorry, it didn't look like it."

Dervy didn't answer, but instead turned on the radio with a free hand. She hoped it pretty clearly indicated that she didn't want to discuss it any further. She really hadn't been paying attention to the road. She'd been completely absorbed in her own wandering thoughts.

She forced herself to focus on the road for the rest of the drive, keeping the lanes clear in her view and the present firmly rooted in her mind. Simon quickly fell asleep to classical music tinkling out of the speakers as they progressed.

When they were a few miles out, Dervy reached out and tapped a sleeping Simon. He started.

"Hey, call ahead to Weynie and tell her to notify airport police that we'll be crossing the tarmac."

Yawning, Simon nodded and pulled out his cell phone. To her right she saw him pop it open, the dull green glow suffusing the cab, and tap out a series of numbers. Dervy signaled to the right and turned onto the exit for airport drop-offs.

"Weynie, we have the package, clear the runway," Simon said sleepily.

She followed the passenger drop-off signs, making sure to stay in the correct lane. There wouldn't be any more smart remarks about her driving.

"What?" Simon said in a confused voice. "Sorry, wrong number."

Dervy glanced at him. "What was that?"

"Dialed the wrong number," Simon mumbled. "Must have hit a three instead of a six or something."

"Well maybe you can try to actually call Weynie this time," Dervy spat as she began winding around the airport, avoiding the periodic human in a crosswalk. "We're coming up fast and I'd rather not have to deal with airport security."

Simon waved her off and tapped out another series of numbers. He put the phone up to his ear and a moment later he started talking.

"Hey Weynie, we have the package, clear the runway. Yep, he's fine, but a little smacked around. Yeah, already regenerated, believe it or not."

Dervy frowned at him, but Simon smiled back.

"We'll be there in a couple minutes so you best give them a call," he said, laughing at some unheard comment. "Yeah, see you soon. Bye."

Simon yawned again and put away his phone. "There shouldn't be any problems."

"Good."

A few minutes later, Dervy pulled up to a gate just outside the airport proper. There were a couple men in jackets chatting amicably to one side of the gate. One of them squinted as they pulled up and walked over to the driver-side window with a flashlight. Dervy rolled it down as he approached.

"This isn't a parking area," he said, flicking the flashlight into her eyes.

Dervy flinched as the light blinded her. She nearly tore the man's throat out, but managed to restrain herself just in time. A plane taking off in the distance drowned out her deep growl.

"We're not here to park, you should have gotten a call about letting Dervy and Simon drive through."

"One second," the guard said, taking a step back. "Hey, are we supposed to let a..." he turned back to her. "What were the names again?"

She sighed. "Dervy and Simon."

"Let a Dervy and a Simon in?" He yelled.

The other man nodded and went over to the gate, which he unlocked and opened.

"All right," the guard said, flashing the light at the ground. "You should be good to--"

He cut off as he looked in the back seat. He shone the flashlight on Alex's bloody face.

"Holy shit," he exclaimed, frozen in place.

Dervy sighed in annoyance. "Simon?"

Simon nodded and looked at the guard intently. Slowly, the other man's head turned, until their eyes met.

"He got into a fight and we're going home," Simon said slowly and purposefully, enunciating each syllable.

The guard nodded. "He got into a fight and you're going home."

He spoke dully and without emotion. Ahead of them the other guard was beginning to walk over, calling out to the man in the window.

Simon nodded. "Go back to your post and tell him that a guy in the car got into a fight, but was in good spirits."

The guard nodded. "He's in good spirits."

"Goodbye," Dervy said as the man pulled his head out of the window and she drove forward.

In the rearview she saw him walk over to his partner before they turned out onto the tarmac. "Thank you, Simon."

"No problem," he said quietly, settling back into the seat. "Do you think we'll have food on the way back?"

Dervy shrugged, "Maybe. It's a private jet, so probably."

Simon grinned. "I hope there are still some of those little bottles of liquor."

She drove out toward a small passenger jet set away from the larger commercial airlines. The tarmac spread out like a sheet of obsidian, dotted by perfectly spaced lines of lights. She drove across the black field, the plane in the distance growing ever larger.

It sat away from the airport proper, but close enough to be within the diffused orange glow of the lights. Standing next to the steps leading up to the cabin were three people, one shorter than the others. That figure wore a bright colored shawl over her otherwise dark outfit.

Weynie turned at their approach, orange shawl catching the sea breeze suddenly, and waved at them with a small smile Dervy could just make out.

Dervy smiled back as she pulled up, put the car in park, and killed the engine. As she undid her seatbelt, Weynie nodded to the two men with her and walked over to the driver side door.

Weynie was Indian and appeared to be in her late twenties, though in reality she had been walking the Earth since the early nineteenth century. Dervy smiled at the bright orange scarf sitting across her shoulders. It was unnecessary with the light jacket she also wore, but it was something that Weynie always wore, regardless of temperature.

Weynie was one of those who had maintained their religion after being Taken; she still wore the dot on her forehead. She said it was out of respect for her long deceased husband, but it was a concept Dervy didn't understand. He was dead and she was alive; why not move on and continue?

It was a topic they'd long since agreed not to discuss anymore.

One of the men was a strigoi--more specifically a Sirgil by the name of Esok Johnson. Esok was an Elder--though not a member of the Ankousti anymore, having retired the year before--born sometime in the mid-seventeenth century. He was tall, with a full head of black hair and a thick, matching beard that covered a weak chin and overbite. Traditionally, Esok wore clothing that appeared simple, but in the past few decades had taken to having every piece of his wardrobe custom-tailored to his exact specifications. The clothes remained... tasteful.

Esok was a dour man, always of foul spirit and mood and extremely religious. Dervy counted herself lucky if she could make it out of a conversation without being called out as a heathen or barbarian. How he maintained the Christian faith being what he was confused and astounded her.

It didn't confuse her as much as the other person's presence, however. He was a human, at least according to the faint buzzing Dervy picked up. His pressed suit and leather shoes gave him the appearance of a businessman, but, given the current setting, he looked more like a shady accountant for the mob.

Weynie opened the door and offered Dervy a hand. Dervy nodded in thanks and turned away from the men who appeared to be in a heated discussion. With a heavy slam, Weynie shut the door and leaned against the car. Behind her Simon closed his as well and was moving toward the backseat, pressing a fist to his back and groaning. He opened the door and leaned in, grumbling just loud enough so Dervy could hear him complain.

"What's the human doing here?" Dervy asked quietly, stretching, though it was unnecessary.

"He's from Nawat Industries," Weynie said with an edge to her voice.

Dervy raised an eyebrow. "The place where the Taken works?"

Weynie nodded.

"So why is he here?"

Weynie crossed her arms under her breasts and sighed. "They're laying claim to him."

"Humans are claiming a strigoi?" Dervy raised an eyebrow at that.

Official interaction between humans and strigoi, even the Arktois, was incredibly restricted. Only the highest levels of human governments even knew that the Arktois was anything other than a close-knit semi-religious group.

Weynie nodded, face impassive. "That would be it, yes."

Dervy glanced at Weynie's tapping foot before looking back over at the man. He quickly averted his eyes.

"And by what right do they presume to do this?" Dervy asked with little emotion, mind whirling.

How did they even know they could claim him? He certainly didn't appear to be a threat. The worse case scenario was that she could kill him and leave him for the scavengers someplace in Wisconsin. Dumping a body from a private plane was an easy way to eliminate evidence.

The thought gave her pause at the image of him dying, the brief light fading from his eyes and she found herself shaking in pleasure and disgust at herself.

There had to be another way.

Weynie sighed. "They claim that he signed paperwork that stated he was to donate his remains to the company in the event of his death."

Dervy looked over at Simon. "Is he dead?"

Simon shrugged, caught her glare, and then leaned inside the car.

He reappeared a few moments later. "Nope, quite alive, though bloodier than hell."

Dervy looked back at Weynie, who shook her head. "From what I understand he apparently died a few months back for a few minutes when he, uh, fell from a bridge."

Dervy snorted, but had nothing to say. She firmly trusted in Weynie's ability to digest and process legal documents, whereas she herself had no such skill. The problem with knowing hundreds of languages and dialects--many of which no longer existed--was that it became very difficult to master niche writings. At least things had standardized again after a few hundred years of confusion.

Latin, French, English; who cared? Just pick one for a few hundred years!

Simon knocked on the roof of the car. "Maybe I'm the only one who sees the elephant in the room--I have been drinking, mind you--but how the hell do they even know about us?"

Weynie frowned and started fingering her shawl, sheer orange fabric twining between her dark brown fingers. "Apparently someone in the Ankousti hired them to do something a couple decades ago and somehow they found out.

"After that, I'm guessing they wrote in the addendum that puts us in our current position, though that gaandu over there won't say anything."

Weynie spit when she finished as if she had a bad taste in her mouth. Dervy raised an eyebrow. Weynie rarely swore.

Frowning, Dervy looked at the man in the suit again. The fog was chill against her bare skin as she sat there. Was this something Caoimhín had done? What did they hire this Nawat Industries to do?

What business were they even in?

The man at the other end of her stare shifted uncomfortably, trying to ignore the gaze and failing. She saw his eyes flick back to her, nervousness beginning to show.

Unsteady shifting of the feet.

Fidgety hands.

Sweat.

"I'm going to talk to him," Dervy said abruptly.

She set off toward the man.

Weynie started. "What? No. Dervy. Esok is working it out."

But Dervy was already halfway to him, ignoring the way her shirt shifted to reveal her breast or the goose bumps that ran through her body at the chill as a breeze swept past. It was sharp from the bay salt and tinged with sweetness from spent jet fuel. Off to her right, a large airliner began pulling away from the airport, beginning its trek toward the runway. Dervy spared it only a quick glance as she closed in on Esok and the human.

The strigoi frowned as she approached. "Do you require assistance, Dervy?"

Esok gave her a quick glance, eyes passing quickly over her bare bosom with barely concealed disgust. "Like another shirt, possibly?"

"No," Dervy said dismissively, turning instead to the human who was finding it hard to take his eyes away from her partial nudity. "What is your name?"

"J-James Bruin, Vice-President of Technology at Nawat Industries," the man stuttered out, extending a hand and frowning at himself.

Dervy nodded and accepted the hand, taking care to squeeze it until his face clenched in pain. "Why are you here, Mr. Bruin?"

"Well," James Bruin said, extending a sheaf of papers with a hand that remained red from her grip. "I'm here to collect the body of Alex Mamsin."

Dervy cocked her head, ignoring the papers. "No, I asked why are *you* here?"

"I know," Mr. Bruin said with an uncomfortable laugh. "The VP of Technology is picking up a dead body. Who does that?"

Dervy looked at him silently, waiting for more.

With a cough, he looked away, apparently unwilling to continue with the topic.

Fine.

"What work did Nawat Industries do for the Arktois?" Dervy asked, placing her hands on her hips.

"I am not at liberty to say," James Bruin mumbled, looking askance at Esok.

Mr. Bruin received a shrug in return.

In this known lifetime, Esok was still her junior by nearly a century and, as such, would defer to her in nearly all things. Not that it stilled his tongue at times, but his silence told Dervy that he had grown tired of the human's games as well.

"Then I am not at liberty to deliver him to you," Dervy said simply.

That caused Mr. Bruin's backbone to snap back into place. He pushed the paper-clipped papers toward her again. "If you examine these papers, you'll find that Nawat Industries is well within its rights to assume possession of the body of our former employee Alex Mamsin."

Dervy shook her head. "You're well aware that he is not dead, right?"

Mr. Bruin shuffled his feet slightly, face flushed, though Dervy could not tell if it was in anger or embarrassment. "I have been informed that he has died and that you plan to exit the state with him, thus violating our contract and subjecting your Arktois to state and federal prosecution."

Dervy glanced at Esok who nodded reluctantly.

She felt more than heard his voice in her head, but the message was clear: there was nothing they could do. Legally.

She shook her head. "Since when do we give a damn about state and federal law, Esok?"

"Since the end of the last Great War, Dervy, you know that," Esok said evenly. "We agreed to abide by the laws of the United States for as long as--"

Dervy waved him off. "I know, I know."

There was something very wrong with the situation and the longer she stood there, hearing the hum of an airplane engine in the background, the more uncomfortable she was. If only there were some way to delay their claim so they could get out of there...

"Walk with me," Dervy said to the human and began walking away from Esok.

"Umm," he mumbled, looking again to the tall strigoi.

"He's no longer in charge, so stop asking him to help you," Dervy snarled. "Now come with me."

James Bruin wilted visibly, but followed, gripping his briefcase like a shield.

Together they walked toward the front of the plane, moving silently, the roar of a plane engine drowning the sounds of their footsteps as it took off, lifting into the air like an awkward bird. When they were beyond earshot of Esok and the others, Dervy turned on Mr. Bruin, causing him to take a step back in panic.

"What did the Arktois contract Nawat Industries to do?" Dervy asked again, face flat, emotionless.

He sighed. "I already told you that I'm not at lib--"

Faster than a striking snake, Dervy lashed out, smacking the man in the throat with the ridge of her hand. He dropped to his knees, grasping his throat and choking. The briefcase fell to the ground with a sharp thud.

Dervy raised a hand to the others. She looked up, making sure that they stayed where they were. Esok looked as if he was going to move forward for a moment, but then he nodded and turned away.

Slowly, Dervy crouched next to the gasping man. She looked him in the eyes and she saw the panic there.

Good.

"What did the Arktois contract Nawat Industries to do?" She asked again.

"I--," he choked out, then spat to his side.

"You...what?" Dervy asked quietly.

"Please, I don't know," he whispered, averting his eyes.

Dervy stood, sighing. "If you don't know and you can't give me a good reason for taking Alex, then we are at an impasse Mr. Bruin."

"W-what?" He asked, coughing and massaging his throat.

She walked around behind him, excitement rising in her chest as he turned slightly, his fear a palpable thing, like a thick, rich aroma that tickled her senses. Dervy could almost feel it, coating her skin as it passed, swirling around her.

Dervy swallowed down the exhilaration as she rested her hands on his shoulders. James shivered at the touch.

"I am not one to give away an asset without an exchange," Dervy said sweetly, leaning down to speak into his ear.

"If you have information, then I may consider relieving myself of the charge in that car over there, but lacking that, you will not get him."

Dervy leaned in close--he reeked of anxiety and terror--lips brushing his ear as she spoke. "Understood?"

James Bruin nodded slowly as her fingers tightened around his shoulder, digging in, pressing into his muscles like they were a paste. She felt blood vessels popping like tiny kernels of corn. A sharp gasp and a whimper escaped his lips as her thumb broke the skin through the suit and a small stream of blood soaked into the fabric.

Dervy held tight, feeling his heart rate pick up through her fingertips.

Or was it hers?

Once again, Dervy leaned in close, far closer than she had originally intended. His sweat beneath the smell of his cologne, the fresh blood seeping through the black fabric and wetting her fingernails... it called out to her quietly, urgently.

Begging.

Desperate.

Everything seemed to vibrate as she closed her eyes in pleasure...

"Please, don't."

Dervy blinked and found herself growling deep in her throat, ready to tear out the man's throat. She pulled back quickly, but not quite fast enough to let him think her guard was down.

Dervy's heart was fluttering as she looked at his brown hair.

With a final squeeze she let him go. James fell to the ground, just catching himself with his left hand as he reached up and gently touched the shoulder where the dark color of his coat was growing deeper by the second.

Dervy looked around, taking a quick, steadying breath.

What was happening tonight? How had she lost control so completely?

Dervy shook her head.

"You do not get Alex Mamsin tonight, but we will honor your contract upon his True Death, do you understand?" She asked quickly.

Too quickly.

James Bruin did not turn around when he spoke. "I understand."

Dervy nodded, turning away. "Good."

She walked, forcing herself to move slower than she wanted, pushing the growing self-loathing into a small ball in the pit of her stomach.

Dervy walked past Esok without acknowledging his presence and--ignoring the troubled look in his eyes--up the stairs into the plane. As she crested the last step, she turned and motioned them to follow.

Without waiting, Dervy moved toward the back of the plane, ignoring the clusters of brown leather seats and tables, and entered the small cabin at the rear.

She entered, taking a moment to pick up and throw Esok's small travel bag into the hallway before slamming the door and locking it.

Finally alone again, Dervy stood, staring at the door without seeing it, picturing a time long ago in a field covered with wild flowers and the glow of love encircling her in the form of a man's arms.

The image faded into white; the biting winds of a snowstorm tearing at her skin. Specks of blood dripping into that pure drift...

With a shudder, Dervy collapsed on the bed.

* * *

Alex wasn't sure what woke him up, but when he did his ears desperately needed to pop. His head was filled with the thrumming sound of a large engine that sounded like it was under water. A light leather scent mixed with another, less defined odor tickled his nostrils, causing him to reach up and rub at his nose.

He opened his eyes and shut them immediately as light flared into them, bringing a sharp pain at his temple. Gingerly, he tried again and a picture of rolling cumulous clouds began to take shape.

Behind him, Alex could hear people talking in hushed voices, just barely audible above the sound of the wind and engines. He looked around in confusion, seeing the groupings of brown leather seats--four to a unit, two facing another two--and carefully crafted woodwork that outlined most of the area. The cherry stained wood stood out against the dark plastic that covered the walls, a deep gray that looked nearly black. Small portals dotted the length, windows to the sky, but they were currently all closed except his.

Feeling a little sore, Alex turned to the side and closed his own window, shutting out the light that had caught him unawares a moment earlier.

That was a lot better.

He leaned back into the soft, padded leather. For some reason, Alex felt absolutely no reason to panic despite the tingle at the back of his neck. It was stronger than ever--like five distinct impressions--but it didn't make him wary.

When would he be able to enjoy such fantastic seating on a flight again? This was better than First Class.

It was best not to rock the boat.

Alex frowned, despite himself. He had a nagging memory of a short, attractive brunette punching him in the head and he could not shake it. For some reason, that bothered him, even though the possible kidnapping did not.

Maybe it was just his East Coast machismo coming out.

His head was a little tender, but since he'd never been in a fight sober, Alex had little experience with how well he could take a hit. Maybe she knocked him out and had Simon carry him to this extravagant hiding spot?

Alex laughed at that idea. The image of Simon trying to throw anything but a towel over his shoulder made him giggle for some reason. But... why was that funny?

He rubbed at his head, feeling confusion and just a tiny bit of panic beginning to develop. He had half-formed memories of Simon, diaphanous things of mist and confusion, but it was as if they were already beginning to fade.

One moment he could picture the balding man laughing with him in a bar, but the next, that man was someone else entirely--someone Alex actually remembered and could connect to other memories and history. What the hell was happening to him? He massaged his temples, ignoring the pain on the left side.

The throbbing was just starting to ease as a woman stepped around the chairs.

"It's nice to see you awake; you've been asleep for hours."

Alex raised an eyebrow at her. It was either that or run screaming through the plane. He figured the latter wouldn't help much given that they were in the air.

She wasn't the woman who had hit him, that much was certain, but she made him uncomfortable nonetheless. It probably had a lot to do with the characterization of Middle Eastern people in the media. She seemed like a conflicting duo of stereotypes--professional, self-assured woman mixed with a traditional...what?

He wracked his brain, trying to remember what culture wore the dot and did the shawl thing.

"Indian. Specifically Hindu," she said with a smile, sitting down in the chair diagonal from him and extended a dark hand. "I'm Weynie and it's nice to meet you."

Alex took it despite the overwhelmingly surreal experience of having someone answer a question he had only thought.

Her hand was warm.

"Alex," he said quietly, releasing and sitting back. "I'd like to say I'm happy to be here, but I'm a little confused as to the why and where of here."

"That's a little hard to explain," Weynie said as she lounged back into the leather chair, pulling her fluorescent orange shawl down across her chest. "It requires a suspension of belief that most aren't able to accept at this point in the process."

Alex gave her a look. "Try me."

She smiled at him, but said nothing. Instead she drummed her fingers on the armrest, skin nearly blending with the dark hide.

"Come on," Alex said, smiling what he knew to be his most charming smile.

Of course, that meant that it was nowhere near charming or endearing and, quite possibly, even disturbing. However, more times than he could count, it managed to bring about an attitude change in its target and get him what he was looking for.

Weynie shook her head, smiling at him. "Fine, but remember that I told you you're not ready yet."

First time for anything.

Alex grinned. "I'll keep it in mind."

She leaned forward, resting elbows on knees, the shawl falling easily between her legs. "Have you ever heard the word 'strigoi' before?"

He shook his head.

"How about 'Sirgili'? 'Ankousti'? 'Arktois'?" She asked as he shook his head at each.

"Well," Weynie said as she leaned back again. "These are terms you will become very familiar with as you have recently joined us in our culture."

Alex frowned. It all sounded a little fictional to him. "How exactly did I manage that?"

Weynie smiled at him. "You didn't do anything, it simply is."

"And this something that 'simply is' made you people come to my house and abduct me now for some reason?" Alex asked, raising an eyebrow.

Weynie shook her head from side to side as if weighing his words. "It could be put that way, yes."

He stared at her, aghast. Her face was entirely sincere, with just a hint of a look that he associated with his grandmother, even though she couldn't be older than Alex himself.

"Maybe you're right," Alex said, throwing his arms up in frustration. "Maybe I'm not going to get it."

Weynie sighed, leaning forward again. "Here it is in a nutshell, Alex. Every year, thirteen people the world over are changed. They cease being human, though there is rarely any immediate outward sign of the change. However, over time it will become apparent that they have stopped aging, instead seeming frozen--"

Alex cut her off with a wave. "Thirteen people?"

Weynie smiled. "Yes."

"Just thirteen?" He asked, raising an eyebrow.

"Yes."

Alex stared for what felt like eternity. He was either talking to a writer, a comedian, or a madwoman. She continued levying that smooth smile at him.

Well, he might as well hear the rest of the story.

"Okay," Alex said, eyeing her skeptically. "Go on."

"As I was saying," she began again, with a playful grin. "Thirteen people are changed--or some would say, chosen--each year. These people--who are no longer human--are called 'strigoi,' which we use as a blanket term to identify anyone who has been welcomed to The Life."

"'The Life'?" Alex asked.

"'The Life' is just what we call this existence we experience after we are Taken," Weynie said waving off his next question. "The word 'Taken' actually has two meanings here. First, it refers to the exact time that someone is changed. There is no common experience and many times you can't identify the point specifically, but you'll be able to track it down soon.

"The second meaning of the word refers to the newly Taken person themselves during the thirteen months following their change. During this period, a strigoi gives off something akin to a high-pitched frequency to other strigoi. It pricks the back of our necks, right here," she pointed to the very back of her neck, which was exactly where Alex was currently experiencing five distinct pinpricks.

"This allows us to track down new members of the community. Typically it is relatively easy once we are in close proximity to each other, though it has gotten more difficult of late, I hear," Weynie said with a shrug. "Regardless, after thirteen months, this broadcast, if you will, ceases and once again you are invisible to the rest of your brethren."

"Let's say I believe this," Alex interrupted, rubbing at the back of his neck. He stopped as soon as he realized what he was doing.

"Okay," Weynie said questioningly.

"Should I be able to feel these other Taken right now?" He asked, forcing himself to keep from scratching at his neck.

Weynie frowned. "It isn't common for a newly Taken to have this ability, but it isn't unprecedented either. You could simply have a gift for it."

Alex bit his cheek, considering his next words carefully. Quite a few events over the last four months were beginning to fall into place and it was sending his heart racing.

"Are there five Taken on the plane?" He asked, catching her eyes as disbelief flashed across her face.

"No," she said carefully. "No, there are not."

Alex examined her for a moment as she began rubbing the orange shawl with one hand, fabric sliding between her fingers smoothly.

"What?" He asked. "Did I say something wrong?"

Abruptly, Weynie stood, flashing a smile that was obviously forced. "No, no," she said quickly. "I simply need to return to my cohorts in the front and let them know you are awake and well."

Alex nodded and she took off back the way she came, leaving him alone and utterly confused.

What the hell was he supposed to think about all of this? Either she was a crazy woman holding him hostage or he was suddenly some inhuman abomination called a 'streegoy' or whatever that nonsense word was.

Alex knew which one he should believe, but for some reason he was beginning to lean toward the latter. It just explained so much about his life recently that he couldn't dismiss it out of hand.

You don't just swallow fifty anti-depressants and shrug it off with little more than some drowsiness the next morning.

You die.

He found himself thinking about that night on the Golden Gate when he'd driven to the Monterey side, dead drunk, and somehow managed to walk to the center. Alex could barely remember what happened, but the police report had said that a woman had seen him walking the bridge with a bottle of whiskey, sobbing to himself.

She'd called the police and reported a suicidal man. Before they got there, she'd asked him to step away from the edge, but instead he'd jumped.

He could still remember the wind whipping at his face, the deep fog of the bay permeating his clothes as he plummeted, screaming, into the chill, icy waters of the Golden Gate.

Sarah. Her name had been Sarah.

He'd been in the hospital for a couple days following that--a couple broken ribs--but then he'd gone home. The recovery was remarkable. According to the doctors he should have been dead.

It was only a short while later that he'd tried and failed with beer and pills. Nothing had seemed to change for him in the meantime--even the depression had remained constant.

Alex put his head back into the seat.

He just wasn't sure what to believe.

The droning sound of the engines was soothing, which Alex was suddenly very thankful for. With a finger, he reached over and cracked the window, letting his gaze wander over the crawling landscape.

It looked like they were somewhere in the Midwest, passing along huge stretches of undeveloped land that lay stark and yellowed as if blasted from the sky. Small groupings of homes--tiny flea eggs stacked in piles--dotted some of the sparse landscape, though infrequently.

Alex had never liked the Midwest. Too much nothing and not enough trees. Of course, he hated snow, as well, which was how he'd ended up in San Francisco in the first place.

No snow and a lot of trees.

Not that you could touch the trees, though. If it was green, some state government conservation agency was protecting it.

Suppressing a sigh, he leaned his head against the window, fogging it up with his breath. San Francisco had been hell since Mary died. Every tree, rock, or house brought back some vivid memory of her.

In a lot of ways, he was more than a little happy to be gone from the place, though he wished it involved a something a little more...sane.

Mary smiled at him from across a table... the small hole opening up, blood pumping in time with her failing heartbeat...

If they wanted him so badly, then he deserved some more answers. Why on earth should he wait for them to come bringing him information?

"What the hell am I doing?" Alex mumbled, unbuckling his belt and getting to his feet.

Alex stretched, looking toward the front of the plane. He could see Weynie leaning forward in her seat, facing him. She was speaking in a much more animated fashion than she had with him. He could tell that there was at least one other person sitting across from her--their arm was dropped from the seat lazily, swinging in the air like a pendulum.

Gritting his teeth, Alex stepped out into the walkway and moved toward them purposefully. Weynie saw him immediately and tapped the person sitting directly across from her. A man with black hair and sparse beard turned around in his seat, glancing at him as he did so, before returning to his place.

If he were a canine of any sort, Alex's hackles would have been bristling visibly, fangs bared. Alex came up to their seats, Weynie smiling carefully at him, and he found that the dangling arm belonged to none other than Simon, who turned with an easy smile of his own.

"Hey Alex," he said smoothly, motioning to the chair next to Weynie. "Take a seat and I'll get us some of those little bottles of liquor."

Alex narrowed his eyes at the balding man, but sat down nonetheless. "Please."

As Simon got to his feet, Weynie motioned to him to sit back down. "You drank all of those on the way out to California, Simon."

"Oh, I did?" Simon asked, looking nonplussed. "Sorry," he said as he sat back down.

Alex nodded, but didn't say anything. He was trying desperately to avoid looking at the man sitting next to Simon. It wasn't quite contempt that shown on his face, but it was close.

It was dismissal.

Alex could see the way the man looked at him and then, with barely a lift of his nose, all of his worth was tossed aside as if he was nothing--simply a child interrupting his parents during a party.

Alex lost his temper.

"What the hell is your problem, asshole?"

Weynie started. Simon grinned.

"You will watch your tongue around your elders," the man responded acidly, looking him up and down as if he was a foreign thing.

Dismissal was no longer part of the equation; that much was certain.

Alex snorted, but caught the look of astonishment and embarrassment that flashed across Weynie's face.

"Alex," she began, speaking quickly as if trying to move as quickly away from the confrontation as possible. "This is Esok Johnson, an Elder of the Arktois."

Alex looked the other man over just as dismissively as he had been a few moments earlier.

"Are you an Elder because you paid for it or because you're actually old, then?" He asked, feeling the warm glow of satisfaction fill him at Esok's expression.

"Because you are simply a Taken, I will forgive your indiscretions up to this point," Esok said, face growing dark. "However, if you insist on your continuing insubordination, then you will quickly find yourself locked away for a few decades in the Vault."

He waited for Alex to nod, which he did, albeit reluctantly. Alex had no idea what he was talking about.

"Good," Esok nodded. "To answer your question, a Sirgil may only achieve Elder status through age, much the same as other aspects of our culture."

Alex took a steadying breath. "How old are you, then?"

"I am three hundred and twenty-seven years old," Esok said with a dismissive wave of his hand.

Alex stared at him mouth slightly agape. "You were born in the, uh," he did some quick math in his head, "sixteen-hundreds?"

Esok nodded.

He kept staring at the other man for a moment, looking for signs of a lie or a joke--a twitch of the lip, a glance away, anything.

There was nothing.

"Where were you born, then?" Alex said quietly, trying hard to keep himself from believing the man.

Esok looked toward Simon. "Is this how Taken are initiated now? These questions used to be leveraged at the lead Gatherer of the expedition, yet now it seems anyone will do."

"You're doing a great job, Elder," Simon said with a wink. Esok glared at him.

"I was born in Jamestown," Esok said simply.

Alex looked at him for a moment, waiting for more information, but none was forthcoming. "Jamestown?" He asked.

Alex did a double take. "Wait? Jamestown? Like, Jamestown, first permanent U.S. settlement, Jamestown?"

Esok frowned. "First permanent European settlement on this continent, yes. That Jamestown. I was born during the third generation."

Alex rubbed at his temple and looked at Weynie. "And how old are you?"

Weynie smiled warmly, though she was still toying with her shawl. "Three hundred and two."

"I'm one-eleven," Simon spoke up with a grin.

"Jesus Christ," Alex mumbled.

They couldn't all be crazy? Could they?

If he were anywhere else besides a private jet heading across the United States Alex would think someone was playing an elaborate joke on him, but he didn't know anyone with that much spare cash. Not with San Francisco real estate costing what it did.

Esok sighed audibly.

With little more indication that something was going to happen beyond Esok turning in his seat, he grabbed Simon by the neck and twisted--the sound of tearing ligaments and scraping bone echoing in the small quarters--spinning the other man's head all the way around with barely any effort. Simon's shocked expression locked on his face, marred slightly by a grin.

Simon's body flopped over, landing at Alex's feet.

Alex screamed, scrambling back into the seat and pulling his legs up to his chest. Simon's dead eyes stared up at him, his neck torn from the force and lying at an impossible angle.

"What the fuck?" Alex screamed at Esok, standing on his chair. "Why did you do that?"

Esok put up a hand, motioning for him to sit back down, but Alex was having none of it. A man lay dead at his feet and he was stuck with his psychotic killer thousands of feet above the ground with nowhere to run or hide.

Weynie laid a hand on Alex's knee. "Alex--"

Alex swatted the hand away, refusing to be touched by someone who would just let something like that happen.

She glared at Esok. "You could have at least told Simon what you were going to do!"

Esok shrugged and gave a little smile. "I apologize. I'm not sure what came over me."

Weynie pointed at Alex, who was staring around like a trapped animal, his heart racing. "Well, look what you accomplished! Congratulations!"

Esok looked at Alex as if he was being childish. "Sit down, boy. He'll be fine in a moment!"

"You killed him you crazy fucker!" Alex screamed pointing at the body. "How the hell is he supposed to be 'fine in a moment'?"

At that moment, there was the now-distinct sound of bone scraping from below him, but he couldn't bring himself to look down again.

A moment later, Simon grunted and got to his knees, rubbing his neck. "Maybe a little warning next time, Elder?"

"Oh fuck."

Alex fainted.

5
Somewhere in the Midwest, USA
12:17 PM August 21, 2010

"He fainted?" Dervy asked, drumming her fingers along the armrest as she took a long drink from a water bottle.

It still felt strange to drink water from a bottle. It was even worse that it cost money, which Simon had been happy to remind her when he delivered it to her when she'd left the cabin a few moments earlier.

Weynie nodded in response and sat down next to her, adjusting her shawl as she did.

During her short reprieve, Dervy had changed into a set of jeans and a t-shirt she'd left in her luggage. The clothes were loose fitting so that she could move, but otherwise completely unadorned and unnoticeable. It stood in stark contrast to Esok's formal attire.

Dervy still wore the singed boots from her encounter with Zeke Dunfee--the scent of burnt flesh and melted plastic lingered about them--but getting lit on fire hadn't been something she'd anticipated when leaving from Heathshome. She grimaced down at the boot that had been damaged the most. Despite the fact that it still stayed on her foot, it would need to get thrown away. There was no salvaging it. The other one, maybe, but most likely it had seen the end of its days too.

She'd really liked those boots.

It had been incredibly painful getting them off since her flesh had actually merged with what had apparently been a plastic liner. Once they were off, everything healed back up and it was just a matter of imagining that the crackling noise she heard when putting them back on was something other than the sound of her own crisped skin still adhered to the leather.

Dervy glanced over to the set of seats next to her--taking another long pull from the bottle--where Simon had placed Alex before covering him with a thin blanket. She hadn't noticed before, but he was rather pleasant to look at. Alex's face was a little rounder than she was used to, but that seemed to be more from an Asian relative sometime back than from obesity. He seemed so peaceful lying there, cuddled up with a blanket, mouth twitching into a small grin. Alex's tongue darted out slightly to wet his lips as he dreamed.

"What are you smiling about?"

Weynie's voice shocked her.

Dervy sat up straight, looking over at Weynie, who was smiling knowingly.

"I'm smiling because we'll be landing soon," Dervy said quickly, stretching as if she was cramped, which, strangely, she was. "I hate flying."

"Uh-huh," Weynie said, smiling that annoying smile. "Are you sure that is all?"

Dervy glared at her and Weynie put up her hands defensively.

She hated this body, this mind. One moment she was herself: ancient and immortal, a force of nature. The next she devolved into a giggling, flushed girl. Dervy wished for the millionth time that she had been Taken later in life. Maybe then all of this youthful foolishness would have faded.

With a grunt, Dervy decided to change the subject.

"You spoke with him?" Dervy asked, glancing back over at Alex's sleeping form. There was still blood matted in his hair from where she had crushed his skull.

"I have," Weynie said, looking over at him as well. "He was able to detect all of us, even the pilot."

Dervy raised an eyebrow as her eyes traced the contours of his chest. "Oh?"

Not muscular, but certainly not soft. Dervy grimaced at herself.

"Oh?" Weynie exclaimed. "I say that he detected five strigoi in the plane when there are exactly five of us, and all you have to say is, 'oh?'"

"Wait," Dervy said, looking at Weynie. "He actually detected us, not just counted?"

Weynie nodded. "He said he felt five points in the back of his neck."

Interesting.

"These newer generations are different," Dervy said quietly, recalling her conversation with William.

"I'll say," Weynie said, looking back over at him. "He is such a child still..."

"Weren't we all at one point?" Dervy asked, pulling her gaze away from where Alex lay. She leaned back and closed her eyes.

Some more recently than others.

"Yes," Weynie said quietly. "But he just looks so...young. He has a baby face."

Dervy smiled to herself as she pictured rolling hills covered with ancient oaks and elms. "Some say I have a baby face."

Weynie laughed. "They would be right as well, Elder."

"Don't call me Elder, Weynie," Dervy said quietly, but firmly, opening her eyes and leveling a glare at the other woman. "We've talked about this."

Weynie shrugged uncomfortably and started rubbing her scarf again.

Dervy liked Weynie, which was something she had only been able to say about a handful of people over the past thousand years. She was funny, smart, witty and an amazing Bridge player. Dervy stopped herself just short of naming Weynie a friend, but only just.

Perhaps in a couple more decades.

"I mean you are almost five hundred years old, Dervy," Weynie said quietly. "It is respectful to call you by your actual title."

Dervy frowned.

Or a couple more centuries.

"How does my age gain me more respect than my actions?" Dervy asked, leaning forward. "The fact that I may or may not be five hundred years old means nothing of my experience. If I spent four hundred and eighty of those years in a basement in Orleans, would I have more knowledge and experience than a thirty year old who had traveled the world?"

Weynie shrugged. "But you didn't spend that time in a cellar someplace--you traveled the world," Weynie let go of the scarf and her back straightened perceptibly. "By your own example, you would seem to be qualified for the honorific I would like to bestow upon you."

Dervy smiled.

Okay. Maybe a couple more years.

Dervy changed the subject again. "Did you find out anything else from him?"

"Not directly, but I did Scry him while we spoke," Weynie said, eyes wandering over to Alex. "He has...issues that he needs to deal with."

Dervy shrugged. "I know of his wife and Simon says he is quite the drinker, what else is there?"

"He is suicidal for one," Weynie said with a look.

Dervy laughed. "Good luck on that one."

"It's not funny, Dervy," Weynie said with a frown. "I think he may have attempted a few days after being Taken if I read his memories correctly. Apparently he tried again about a short while after getting out of the hospital from the first attempt."

"What did he do?" Dervy asked, suddenly interested.

You could tell a lot about someone by how hard they tried to kill themselves.

"The first or second time?" Weynie asked.

"Both."

"The first time he jumped off a bridge," Weynie said, closing her eyes so she could focus on the observed memory. "I think it was the Golden Gate Bridge."

Dervy nodded. Alex had meant it then. That was good to know.

"The second time," Weynie continued, eyes still shut, "involved alcohol and a few bottles of prescription medication."

"Any idea how many pills?" Dervy asked.

Weynie shrugged. "The number he thinks is fifty, but I see bottle after bottle being taken. If they were even half full, that is probably more like a hundred pills."

Dervy nodded and looked back at Alex.

Why are you so intent on ending your life? She tapped her lips thoughtfully.

People tried to kill themselves all the time--they drank to excess, over ate, drove too fast--but actual taking the initiative to purposefully and irrevocably kill yourself was something that only a few of the most depressed, self-loathing individuals ever truly accomplished. And here, in the person of Alex Mamsin, she had just one of those people.

Jumping off the Golden Gate Bridge?

Taking a toxic cocktail of medication with alcohol while alone?

These were not half-hearted attempts to garner attention or desperate cries for help--these were true efforts to end one's life. Dervy found herself nodding in approval, a fact of which would make most other strigoi--let alone humans--queasy with discomfort. Yet the idea of self-annihilation was not anathema to her. She spent many hours of the day considering her own situation, five millennia beneath her belt, and wishing only for a final, permanent end.

This was one reason Dervy found herself on the opposite end of the table when it came to religious dialogue. For those with a limited lifespan--something that numbered in decades or centuries--immortality seemed a thing to desire, regardless of the existence.

It carried much more weight for her, however. Dervy imagined she felt much like God must, if a single God existed.

Separate and persistent.

Alone.

Why would she wish this existence upon anyone? She could barely maintain that single scrap of humanity that had been born into her.

"Are you okay Dervy?"

Weynie's voice snapped her back to the present. Her eyes were unfocused, staring off through the cabin walls, and into a history no living person had ever seen. For some reasons the echoes of screams stayed in her head, though she hadn't been thinking about battle.

"Je...j'étais pensais à choses," Dervy said quietly, feeling strangely disconnected. She fanned out her fingers in front of her eyes, and they spread, like so many feathers from an eagle's plume.

"Excuse me?" Weynie asked, a hint of worry creeping into her voice.

Sluggishly, Dervy looked up at Weynie and shook her head. The room was moving slowly, crawling past her vision, leaving streaks of light and sound in it's wake--a kaleidoscope of colors and music. An opera of sound and massacre.

"Was that French? Are you okay?" Weynie asked, leaning forward just as Dervy pitched forward into the aisle, bile and foam spitting from her mouth as her body began digesting itself. Through the sudden onslaught of pain and torment, Dervy laughed, spitting blood and chunks of something from deep in her throat.

Someone had poisoned her.

They'd used a good one, too; one she had never seen or experienced before, if her body's reaction was any indication.

Dervy smiled as spasms wracked her body and everything went black against the pathetic backdrop of Weynie screaming for help.

How... droll.

*   *   *

Weynie held Dervy's hand as the plane touched down in Elmira, shaking the cab enough to cause the convulsing woman to spew more blood.

They had tried calling ahead, both by radio and cell phone, but the radio wasn't functioning for some reason and no one's cell phones had a signal on the flight. It was infuriating and it reeked of sabotage, but the only thing Weynie concerned herself with for that moment was the terrible sickness Dervy was currently wracked with.

Esok had made the call to switch their destination. They had chosen to stop in Elmira instead of Albany for the simple reason that they had no radio. It would cause significantly more of an uproar if they landed in a populated city like Albany than in the tiny airport just outside of Elmira. Questions were inevitable in either scenario, but things were more likely to move faster here. They were used to smaller commercial craft, even if those craft typically had radios.

And if there was sabotage, then their flight plan said they were going to Albany. This would throw them off.

With one hand, Weynie wiped Dervy's forehead, smearing speckles of blood and streaming perspiration away. Under her breath Weynie kept reciting a short prayer, though she wasn't sure if it was for Dervy or herself.

Over the time she'd been a strigoi, Weynie had never seen one of her fellows laid low for this long, regardless of the injury. During a mission in Iraq in the early nineties, she had seen a man lose most of his lower torso from a landmine. Within five minutes, they had been moving forward again, though he was significantly more lethargic than before the incident. Dervy had been in this state for nearly three hours.

Weynie didn't want to consider it, but there were only a few people who could have poisoned Dervy. Suspicion was clearly written on each and every one of their faces--Esok eyed her, Simon watched Esok, and she couldn't help but look at Simon. It was like some childish board game gone awry.

Strangely, no one looked at Alex. Then again, he was still out cold.

Everything would be resolved when they arrived in Heathshome, of that she was certain...but there was still a long drive to their destination.

The plane rolled across the runway for a few minutes before finally stopping.

"We have a welcoming committee coming out, get her ready to move," the pilot's voice crackled through the cabin.

Esok stood to open the portal, but Simon waved him off. The cabin door cracked open as Simon turned the handle. It sighed as it opened out, letting in the mid-afternoon sun.

Simon looked stunned. "Kevin?"

A moment later Simon rocketed backwards, slamming into the side of the plane with such force that he left an impression on the wall, wood and plastic shattering on impact.

Weynie jumped to her feet, setting herself between the door and the prone forms of Dervy and Alex behind her. In front of her, Esok stood as well, though hesitantly. He glanced behind him; worry clearly written on his face.

Kevin cannot have them. It was more a feeling than words, but the meaning was clear to Weynie as she caught Esok's eyes. The urgency behind them brooked no argument. She nodded at him, turning her focus toward where a short man stepped up into the plane with a grunt.

Weynie cringed despite herself. While she hadn't forgotten that Kevin O'Ceallaigh had entered the Return, it was stunning to see the change. Where once he had stood straight and proud despite his short stature, Kevin was now stooped and old. His back was hunched over uncomfortably and he seemed to be favoring his right leg. Kevin's telltale flaming red beard was now a mess of silver, interspersed with streaks of orange and yellow as it tumbled away from his chin.

Kevin looked forward, taking in the stiff stances of Esok and Weynie, and shook his head. Frowning, he stepped forward and picked up the limp form of Simon. With little consideration, he tossed him back through the cabin door and out onto the tarmac.

Straining visibly, Kevin straightened. "I need you two to stand down," he commanded with a voice that belied his physical appearance.

It was the voice of Primator O'Ceallaigh, not of an old man. A shudder ran through Weynie's body at the sound.

Esok stepped aside as Kevin passed by with a nod. Weynie very nearly did as well, but caught herself. She knew that this man, once a legend and member of the Ankousti, had disappeared after entering the Return. She knew that the assault on Simon was excessive at the very least. The damage to the plane alone should have given Esok pause. Handing Alex and Dervy over to him didn't make any sense.

"I'm sorry, sir," Weynie said with more confidence than she felt, all the while eyeing Esok warily. "But I need to get these two to Heathshome as soon as possible. Those are my orders from the Ankousti."

Kevin walked forward, still favoring that right leg. "And do I not speak for the Ankousti, as all elected members do?"

Weynie shook her head slightly. "No longer, I'm afraid."

Kevin smiled toothily, a twinkle flashing in his eyes. Wrinkles spread across his once-youthful face, breaking it into a detailed tapestry of lines. "And who are you to make that choice?"

Weynie shuddered again. Something was definitely wrong. There was something wrong with his eyes, something she'd seen in the madmen of the '47 riots.

"Sir," Weynie said quietly, focusing and feeling the electric charge building inside, her hair rising on her arms and neck. "I need to ask you to leave."

"Oh?" Kevin said, looking surprised. "Why is that?"

"Because you are mortal, sir," Weynie said menacingly. "And I can kill you before you can reach me."

Kevin stopped, nodding. He looked around the cabin thoughtfully before turning around with a shrug. "Okay."

The charge fizzled, expelling harmlessly back into the air as Kevin exited the plane. Had Weynie just faced down one of the most powerful Sirgili of all time and won?

Weynie allowed herself a small smile as she sighed in relief.

Esok turned toward her, relief apparent on his face as well. "That was clo--"

The world erupted in flame.

*   *   *

Simon watched the plane burn with a smile, wishing he had some popcorn. Out in the debris, the big black guy--Nathan, was it--was searching through the charred bodies for Dervy. With all of the puddles of burning fuel and exploding patches of wreckage, it was proving difficult.

It had been easy enough to find the Taken. Within minutes of the explosion Alex had regenerated completely, sitting in molten rubble with little more than what God gave him. His regenerative power was maddeningly powerful.

It almost made Simon sick. Why should that pathetic, suicidal momma's boy get such power when Simon was sitting off to the side nursing a couple slow healing broken ribs?

Hopefully that would change soon, if Kevin were to be trusted. The old man just needed Dervy and one more Taken from this batch to make it happen.

Simon's smile widened as he thought about it again.

No Return.

Infinite power.

It made him all warm and fuzzy inside to think of the possibilities that lay in store for them when the secrets of their limited immortality were finally laid bare.

"I think this is her," Nathan called out from the rubble, stepping gingerly to avoid flaming potholes. In one hand, he held a reddish-black form that seemed to be shedding layers of flesh as he moved. Each step he took left more of the person behind in sickening, smoking heaps.

As Nathan stepped free, he tossed the body forward. It hit the ground with a sickening thud and rolled across the ground, where it peeled itself like an overcooked potato. Bare patches of milky white skin showed clearly beneath the greasy smears and charred flesh.

Simon looked over at Kevin who was grimacing. The old man--he finally looked the part--shook his head disapprovingly.

"Nathan, have more respect for your savior," Kevin said without humor. He reached inside a small, silver pickup truck and pulled free a cane, knocking over the now-spent RPG Nathan had used on the plane.

Nathan hopped free of the rubble, tsk-ing at the mess he had made of his clothes. "These suits are expensive..."

With a steady clicking noise, Kevin moved toward the body. He stood over it for a moment, then reached out with the cane and pushed free some of the cracked mess around what should be the head. It split and crumbled away, revealing half of a very youthful woman's face.

Kevin knelt down next to Dervy and leaned in close with much effort. How Kevin could deal with the smell was beyond Simon. Now that there were two charred shells lying out on the tarmac, the odor was beginning to get overwhelming.

Kevin stood, leaning heavily on his cane as he did so, and made his way back to the truck.

He waved to Nathan. "Grab her and get in the back of the ambulance."

Nathan grunted.

Kevin turned back to Simon and pointed at him with the cane as he reached the truck. "Simon, you're driving the ambulance."

Simon stood; feeling ribs that were not quite healed shift uncomfortably. "Um, should I really be driving them? What if they wake up?"

Kevin turned around and looked at him with a frown. "Hope that they don't."

With that simple statement, Kevin pulled himself up into the truck and drove off as the airport sirens finally blared.

Nathan grabbed Dervy with one hand and made his way toward the back of the fake ambulance, cursing as he did so. Simon just stared after the pickup truck as it left the field.

"Come on, boy!" Nathan's deep voice called out harshly as he tossed Dervy's body into the back seat. "The humans are coming!"

Shaking his head, Simon turned and hopped into the ambulance. With a flick of the ignition, he put it in drive. Nathan jumped back in shortly, dragging Alex's naked body up behind him. Nathan slammed the doors shut and gave the seat a tap. Simon turned on the sirens and tore out of the Elmira airport.

He couldn't shake an ill feeling that Kevin's stare had given him. There was something not quite right with him--something just a hair over crazy. For the first time since Simon had started working for Kevin nearly a century before, he had doubt.

Simon shook his head. Why would Kevin lead him astray now, after all these years? It didn't make any sense.

But there was a nagging voice in the back of his mind that kept repeating the answer he had known when he got a phone call in the middle of the night.

Kevin was dying.

That was enough to make anyone go a little crazy.

Turning out onto the side road, Simon made his way for a gate that led to the highway. Whoever it was that was watching the exit moved quickly, opening the gate just as Simon swept past, sirens blaring.

A few quick turns later and he was coming toward an onramp for route 17.

"East or West?" Simon called back to where Nathan was still securing the two naked captives.

"East," Nathan called back.

Simon grimaced. "Okay."

East took them closer to Heathshome and the rest of the Arktois. Kevin must be pretty confident in his base of operations if it was this close.

He came up to a red light, slowing as traffic stopped for him, and--engine revving--pulled out onto 17E. He put his foot to the floor, bringing the speed up to one hundred miles per hour before setting the cruise control and turning off the siren.

Simon left on the lights, though. Police wouldn't bother an ambulance with flashing lights. Or at least he didn't think they would.

"Thank God," Nathan muttered as he climbed into the passenger seat, smelling vaguely of a barbecue pit. "That noise was splitting my head."

Nathan pulled some napkins from the glove box and tried in futility to wipe off the greasy black dirt that coated his hands.

"Hopefully that's all that splits it today," Simon said, adjusting the rearview mirror so that he could see the two forms strapped to a stretcher--one on top of the other. "Are you sure that'll hold them?"

Nathan nodded, though he glanced back. "It's held everyone so far, don't see why this would be any different."

Simon snorted. "It's Dervy, that's why it might be different."

Nathan grimaced as he pulled a thick bristled brush from his pocket and quickly combed the ash out of his buzz cut. "I know it's Dervy, boy. I fought her before you were even born."

Simon doubted that, but kept it to himself.

"Besides," Nathan continued, tapping the small brush on the armrest before putting it back inside his coat pocket. "I used seventeen straps on the two of them."

"How many do you usually use?" Simon asked.

"Three," Nathan said with a smile as he fastened his seatbelt and leaned back.

Simon nodded. That along with the poison he had gotten from Kevin should be enough to keep her from busting out and wrecking the two of them.

The thought of the clear, viscous liquid Kevin had provided him on the breakfast cart at the hotel made him shiver. Simon had been made aware of the effects, but until he saw it, he just hadn't believed that it was possible to really poison a strigoi.

But there it was, something that affected strigoi and left them debilitated and weak. It even worked on someone like Dervy.

Simon reached out and turned down the air conditioning. The whole idea of it made him uncomfortable now that he had seen the results of one of Kevin's claims. If this was true, did that mean that the other things Kevin had said were also true?

Had he found a way to trigger the Return?

Simon glanced over at Nathan. The large man was already leaning backwards, feet up on the dash. He appeared to be taking a nap, though Simon felt confident Nathan was just as alert as he had been back at the airport.

Nathan shuddered out a snore that caused his entire chest to shake.

Pretty confident, anyway.

"Well," Simon said under his breath. "If I get lost, it isn't my ass on the platter."

"Won't be mine either," Nathan mumbled. "Just get off at exit 59, then we'll talk again."

Simon smiled to himself. "No problem."

"Better not be," Nathan grumbled as he crossed his thick arms across his chest.

A few minutes later, Nathan's deep snoring filled the cab, leaving Simon alone with his thoughts.

* * *

The frigid cold startled Weynie out of her regenerative coma. The world was a mixed mess of heat and cold, light and dark. As Weynie sat up, another fountain of liquid sprayed over her, knocking her to the ground. On hands and knees, Weynie crawled through the wreckage--a mass of twisted, blackened metal and slushy runoff.

She was filled with panic. What happened? Where was Dervy? Where was the Taken? Where was Esok?

Hands grabbed her suddenly around the shoulders, voice raised to a volume too high for her recently regrown eardrums to process. Weynie's instincts reacted before she could understand what was happening.

Moving faster than any human could hope to counter, Weynie grabbed the groping hands and twisted them out and up, dislocating both elbows of the figure grabbing her. Rage fueled her movements as Weynie pushed forward, a blur of movement, fists moving like pistons into its chest, throat, and stomach.

Weynie needed to find them. Bring them home.

Esok? Dervy? Alex? Simon?

She didn't know if she was yelling or if the words were echoing only in her head. The roar of flames and water drowned out everything else, even the sounds of her fists against this person in front of her.

With finality, Weynie brought a leg around in a wicked roundhouse, landing it solidly where the collarbone should be on the figure before her and it collapsed, dark green and iridescent fluorescents crumpling with him.

The world swam with choking smoke. A filthy red haze obscured her vision as she stepped out of the rubble, hot jets of air blowing across her bare, freshly grown flesh. Geysers of flame shot up around her; a turbine spun weakly to her right, engine roaring, flames shooting from both ends. A font of water slammed into flaming wreck, knocking it toward her. With a curse, Weynie leapt to the side, barely avoiding the steel tower as it collapsed to the ground, shooting bits of metal and debris everywhere.

Then, just as quickly as she had awoken, Weynie was free of the rubble and debris, sunlight spattering her with its benevolent rays through the billowing smoke above her.

With a short, shuddering breath, she turned around to see the carnage that lay behind. The entire plane had been reduced to a smoldering husk. Fire fighters were spraying down the wreckage from three separate engines, towering fountains swinging back and forth, coating the entire scene with water that barely contained the flames.

Heart fluttering with realization, she put a hand on her now smooth scalp. There were only a few ways to kill a strigoi and they all involved incineration or vaporization. If she had been closer to one of the engines or the fuel tank during the explosion, she could have died in the blaze.

Breath came in short gasps as she fell to her knees, grabbing at her chest. With an improbable amount of embarrassment, Weynie realized she was entirely naked save for a scrap of fabric stuck in a crease at her side. Apparently her skin had healed over it. With a pained grunt, she pulled it out. A small bunch of orange fabric, darkened and burned by heat came free. With a shake of her head, she tossed it back into the flames.

Weynie's eyes wandered over to the body of the man she had attacked just beyond the collapsed turbine and found herself looking at the crumpled form of a fireman, arms bent the wrong way and right shoulder caved in unnaturally.

Cursing, Weynie got to her feet, took a deep breath to fight down the panic attack that was encroaching on her psyche, and loped back into the wreckage, taking care to avoid the eyes of the other fire fighters. The smoke did more for that than any stealth she used. She squinted as the acrid fumes of burning plastic wafted into her eyes and burnt her nostrils. Blazing hot metal burnt her feet regularly and yet other pieces slashed open the tender skin as she picked her way across the debris. With a grunt, Weynie focused her regenerative power to her feet so that she could keep moving.

After what seemed like an eternity, Weynie bent and lifted the man effortlessly, taking care to take the weight of his oxygen tank off of his busted collarbone.

Stumbling away from the mess, Weynie set the man down and pressed her fingers to his neck. She sighed in relief as his pulse thundered through her fingertips. With great care, she examined his elbows, watching for any breakage from her attack and was surprised to find that there was none. Of course, that didn't mean there wasn't ligament damage or the like.

Biting her cheek, Weynie took a step back away from him. It was better if she left him as he was--she couldn't remember the correct procedures for helping him right then, anyway. It had been so long since she'd practiced first aid of any real sort that she was afraid that her only accomplishment would be in crippling the poor man for life, if she hadn't already.

Decision made, Weynie looked around for a way out. Luckily, no one beyond the unfortunate firefighter lying near her had noticed her miraculous reemergence from the flames. The roar of the fire hoses must have drowned out his cries and her screams of anger from earlier.

Weynie evaluated the situation. There were vehicles scattered near the fire trucks, probably owned by volunteers, and a clear route to a side road off in the distance. If she were lucky, she might be able to make it to the vehicles, get clothes of some sort, and maybe steal one of the trucks without being seen. The last thing she needed was someone screaming 'Terrorist' because a Middle Eastern person was near something like this, even if she was naked.

Moving quickly and quietly, Weynie crossed the distance to the nearest car--a four-door sedan with a spattering of different color panels--and let herself into the passenger side. The car was filthy, a mess of loose wrappers and cigarette butts spread around haphazardly. It smelled of stale smoke and french-fries, mixed together in a combination that caused her stomach to turn--no small feat considering she could still smell the wretchedness from outside. A radio was blaring in the small space, calling out for additional trucks at the airport, interspersed with various high-pitched squealing noises.

Cringing against the sound, Weynie looked in the back seat, throwing aside fast food wrappers and greasy tools before coming across a pair of oil-soaked overalls. Lying on the floor behind the seat was a flannel jacket and an old baseball cap.

Weynie grabbed the clothes and pulled them on, ignoring the stiffness and worn odor of the pants and jacket, and glanced around quickly for some footwear. She found a pair of men's work boots sitting neatly on the driver side floor, looking hastily discarded.

Quickly, she grabbed them and laced them up, despite the fact that they were huge on her small feet. It had a lot less to do with comfort and everything to do with appearances--you were looked at less if you wore footwear in the United States than otherwise. She had learned that pretty quickly on joining the Arktois Intelligence Center and moving to New York.

Weynie glanced out the window toward the billowing black smoke and felt guilt swirl around her like the tendrils of burnt ash and water around the firefighters' feet. She felt sure that Alex was gone, whatever that meant. Weynie couldn't feel his presence at all. Kevin must have been going after him. He had said as much.

The question was why?

Emotion rose in Weynie's throat as she scanned the wreckage one last time. Dervy, Esok, and Jerry had all been on board. What happened to them? Why had they not reappeared yet? She hated to consider it, but there was a slight chance--however slim--that one or all of them could have been immolated.

There was also the need to report back to the Ankousti with news of the kidnapping. They needed to know that Kevin had officially attacked them and gone rogue.

Steeling herself against the guilt that burned in her stomach, Weynie crawled over the shifter and started the car. She looked out the window one more time as the final flame was doused near where Esok had probably been. Wiping her eyes, she pulled away, still unnoticed.

Weynie had a failure to report.

*   *   *

Alex groaned. Or rather that was what he tried to do. His mouth was bone-dry and held open by some foul-tasting strap pulled tight across the corners of his mouth. There was a faint taste of copper mixed with the sickly sweet taste of something unidentifiable that made him want to gag.

Not that he could. His throat was too dry. Even a drop of water would be wonderful. At least it would get the taste out of his mouth.

There was something stacked on top of him, squeezing the breath out of him. Alex could just barely raise his chest enough to get a breath and he found himself gasping through the strap as panic began to build.

Desperately, Alex tried to open his eyes and found he couldn't. It was like his eyelids were stuck together, much like after waking from a sickness-induced sleep. He tried to wipe the goo from his eyes, but found that his arms were restrained as well. Alex's heart fluttered uncomfortably.

Great.

With strain, Alex forced his eyes to open, feeling something crack and break as he did so. He fluttered his eyelids, but the pieces fell in anyway, sharp and painful as they dug into his eyes.

Somehow Alex managed to make tears despite feeling as if he had no moisture left in his entire body. As they washed away the crud, he found himself staring at the back of a van. There were shelves to his left and right--some with latched cupboards--but they appeared empty for the most part.

Again, he tried to sit up, but something kept his head held tight, restricting his movement so much that he was a little surprised it hadn't crushed his skull. Desperate to move anything, Alex wiggled his fingers, feeling reassurance in their flexibility, if not in their overall mobility.

From somewhere he heard a radio turn on.

"...The fire took hours to put out, citing jet fuel as the primary factor. None of the six people aboard have been found and there is little hope any will be alive. The jet is privately owned and registered to a European corporation, Arktois United. Attempts to contact the company have failed--"

The radio switched off.

"What the hell are you doing, boy?" A deep male voice said threateningly.

"Listening to the goddamn radio is what I was doing."

Alex's heart jumped into his throat.

Simon.

"You've done this enough to know better than wake them up," the other voice continued, though much more quietly.

"Dervy's poisoned still, thanks to that shit Kevin gave me, and the Taken is a pansy," Simon said with a laugh as he turned the radio back on.

Alex flushed in anger. *That son of a bitch.*

Straining, he looked down, trying to get a better view of his restraints. Instead, he saw the scalp of someone, probably Dervy, if Simon's rant was to be believed. Simon laughed at something and Alex felt himself getting angry. He was going to kill him.

This was eminently different from the first kidnapping. Flying through the air in a private jet, having interesting, if disturbing, discussions with attractive women, and getting offers of tiny liquors from men who could stand back up after getting their necks broken was one thing.

Now Alex felt kidnapped. He was strapped to a surface, buttocks numb against a smooth bench of some sort, with another person tied on top of him. To top it off, he was inside a van that looked like it had been picked out of "Pedophilia Weekly," and was going god-only-knew-where. For all he knew, they'd arrive and Alex would be dressed up like a geisha and paraded around a small building to the sound of elderly Chinese men clapping.

The thought did little to calm his ire and Alex felt himself getting more and more frustrated. Gritting his teeth against the material in his mouth, he tested his right arm strap, pulling and twisting. It held fast, barely allowing him the freedom to perform this small test. Strangely, though, as he pulled, the strap on his left arm grew tighter.

They were connected beneath the table.

Alex tongued at the obstruction thoughtfully, trying to ignore the rancid flavors that accompanied the action. It felt like a seatbelt--all woven ridges along its length. Alex knew there was no chance in hell he could break a seatbelt, but at least he could try.

Balling his hands into fists, Alex pulled. The straps dug into his skin immediately, drawing deep gouges in his forearms, but he felt something happening. Pulling harder, he raised his arms, feeling the fabric stretching to accommodate the force he put on it. Getting to the breaking point.

At least he hoped.

Desperately, he tried to pull a little harder, to shatter the bonds that held him in place. Alex felt the belts go taut as if ready to snap. He knew that if he could just put a little more strength behind it... but after a moment he fell still, arms flapping lifelessly, blood streaming from deep fissures in his wrists. The table beneath him was now bowed up toward him, bent from the force of his efforts. At least that was something.

Barely able to get more air than a small breath anyway, Alex cursed at himself. He had been so close that he could almost taste freedom. Instead, he lay bloodied and bruised from the attempt with only an incessant itching along his forearms as reward for his efforts.

Abruptly, the pain faded away. With a sickening feeling, Alex realized that if he could look at his wrists, the wounds on his arms would be healed. There was still blood dripping down his skin, but no more was adding to the pool gathering around his buttocks.

Son of a bitch. They weren't lying.

Alex wasn't sure if he should be excited or excruciatingly depressed. If he couldn't die, he couldn't kill himself. How much longer would he be on this planet without Mary? The only thing that had kept him going since she died was periodic rage and the knowledge that it would all be over soon. Now what was going to happen? Was he doomed to live a life he loathed for all eternity, pining for a forever-lost love?

It was far too dramatic for a man like Alex and it certainly wasn't what it felt like, tied to the table with Dervy strapped to him. Right now he just felt like a fish waiting to be field dressed.

On the other hand, Weynie had certainly seemed convinced and Simon had gotten back up from a broken neck. Even if Alex could pass that off as a parlor trick, his arms had healed a moment after being torn into--not to mention the fact that he had somehow had the strength to dig seatbelt straps into his arms.

What was he to make of that? What was he even supposed to do?

Alex could feel the encroaching darkness, palpable and thick, as his depression welled up inside him for the first time since Simon arrived at his doorstep. Thoughts of failure, lost love, and hopelessness warred in his mind for dominance. How was he supposed to fight these things? He couldn't even keep himself from fainting. Fainting!

In his mind's eye, he could see Mary as she had been in the steely mortuary. Her face had been intact, though a pencil-width puncture wound had puckered the skin beneath her right eye. The doctor had said that was ultimately what had killed her--a tiny rod from the back of a semi-truck. The rest of the damage was from the accident that followed. Most of her upper torso was a bloody mess. He'd had been able to see it through the sheet, though just barely. They'd cleaned her up pretty well by the time he'd arrived.

December 9, 2009.

What a horrible day.

All of his memories of Mary held that same puncture wound, now. As hard as he tried he just couldn't get rid of it. Memories of Mary's laughing face during their first date, beautiful with red lipstick and blush were marred with a dark stab wound that dripped rivulets of blood from inside her eye shadow.

Alex blinked away tears. He was supposed to be dead. God knew he'd tried hard enough. How is someone still alive after a two hundred and forty-five foot drop? How was he supposed to know that jumping feet first would somehow keep him from dying?

And then they had put that goddamn net up under the bridge.

Alex closed his eyes. Maybe that isn't what saved him. Maybe he had already gotten to the point where he couldn't die.

Maybe the choice had already been gone by the time he jumped.

He just wanted to scream. Alex knew he needed to pull himself out, to move forward, but he couldn't. Everything would just be better without him there.

The straps on his arms itched. They scratched and tugged at his skin as the blood dried on his healed skin. Furious, he pulled again, this time putting everything into it. His face burned as the straps grew firm, arms flexing and bleeding-- bruising--under the force. Finally, lungs threatening to explode, vision fogged red, Alex screamed out his rage and frustration in one desperate bellow.

"What the hell?" Simon called out confusedly as the van lurched.

The strap snapped, slinging up and around the left side of table.

I did it, Alex realized as his arms moved freely.

"Get him Nathan! Shit, he broke the strap!" Simon yelled, panic streaking his words.

Alex heard the sound of a seatbelt disconnecting.

Cursing, Alex scrambled to pull himself free. Flailing, his hands found the tie down for the restraint around his mouth, and released it. With that free, Alex lifted his head up in time to see a huge man crawling into the back area. Dervy lay naked on top of him, spittle and blood tracing down her cheeks. Panic rose in his chest, but he didn't have time to check on her, so he ignored her.

There were more straps, seven or eight remaining, that he would need to release before the man got to him. There was no way he could do it, but Alex scrambled anyway.

He forced Dervy into a sitting position as he released each restraint, moving more quickly than he had ever thought possible, hands a blur of movement.

Come on, come on.

It wasn't fast enough.

Nathan stepped up to what Alex could now see was a gurney and looked him over. "Taken, my ass."

"Look, I don't know why you need us--" Alex started to say, but Nathan just shook his head and turned his dark brown eyes on him.

"Listen, boy, you're going to see the doctors whether I have to break your skull open every ten minutes until we get there or not," Nathan said, pointing at him with a thick finger.

Alex's heart sunk...all of it had been for nothing.

"I understand," Alex said despondently, laying back down, Dervy on top of him.

Nathan nodded and sat down next to him.

"Now, if you move, I'll break you open like an egg," he said quietly, making sure Alex saw that he meant it.

Alex nodded.

Simon sighed audibly as Nathan knelt with his back to the passenger seat, eyes locked on where Alex and Dervy lay. Nathan didn't even take the time to tie them back down.

The van rumbled along, continuing on toward these doctors Nathan mentioned.

As time passed, Alex felt the darkness consume him again as he sat helpless in the back of the van.

*   *   *

The night screamed at her, tore at her flesh; broke into her body and despoiled her. Each night it came again, violent, aroused; taking her by force as she lay shivering in the perpetual darkness of the barren cell. Bones were scattered about from other victims taken during the raid months before, but she still existed; full, wholesome.

Attractive.

The men came, round after round, like slavering beasts to take advantage of her beauty and willing behavior. She pretended to enjoy it, to satisfy their urges so they would give her food and water.

So that she would live.

But as time wore on, she began to dare, to consider an escape. They were everywhere. So many.

How were there so many? Had she not done enough for them? Had she not catered to their every whim?

Why would they not let her go home?

But she knew there was no home.

Not anymore.

Survival.

Survival and vengeance.

That was all there was now.

Outside, the voices came as the night began. Just like every night that followed a raid.

Feasting, revelry. The men yelled into the darkness, calling out in that tongue she had only just begun to understand.

Victory. Pillage.

Everything revolved around these two words. The other women who were thrown in with her were the latter as a result of the former. They cried, screamed, until one of the men grew impatient and would either silence them permanently or hit them until they quieted.

It didn't seem to matter which came first, only that there were pleasurable moaning or nothing at all.

The flap opened, casting just the faintest flicker of light into the cell. A man came in, wide and thickly muscled. He had a long beard that was usually combed, but not tonight. Tonight it was smeared with red, sticky with blood from another slaughter.

His eyes were clouded from drink as he stumbled toward her, growling lowly in his barbarous tongue. She understood the tone, understood his intentions.

Calmly, she lay back, spreading her legs as he pulled himself free and lay into her.

As usual it was painful, but most of all was the shame as she pretended to enjoy it for him.

For her safety.

But this time was different.

The shame grew too deep, she could feel his thrusting as harshly as a sword point--digging into her and twisting her pride; something she'd thought long gone. She bit her tongue in anger as he moved faster on top of her.

Something was happening. She felt strength in her limbs, a power filling her body. She didn't know what possessed her, but she reached up with both hands, put them around his head and looked into his drunken eyes. Surprise show there behind a hazy veil of lust.

"Die," she said flatly.

She snapped his neck.

It happened so suddenly. The frenzied palpitations of his body seemed oddly related as thrusting turned to spasms. After a few moments, movement stopped completely, save for the periodic twitch and she pushed him away and out of her.

She looked at his body, head turned to the side with strange dispassion, wondering at a strange urge bubbling up inside of her.

A voice, quiet and insistent, told her to kneel, so she did. She reached out with a trembling hand--which she found strange given that she barely felt anything at that moment--and touched the clammy skin of the man. The voice told her to get closer, urging her to put her mouth on his neck.

She did.

The urges told her to bite him--to tear his skin and swallow his flesh. She sat there, lips quivering against the salty tang of his unwashed body, his stink filling her nostrils. The sounds of the war party grew more frenzied outside her small cell. She knew that this was a moment that defined her--that changed who and what she was.

A yell came from outside.

Victory.

Dervy tore into him.

*   *   *

Dervy's eyes fluttered open, body and mouth numb and cold. She spit spasmodically, feeling the sharp tang of copper. She rasped incoherently, flailing, feeling the bonds holding her in place.

Rage filled her.

She was restrained.

"No," she gasped, pulling on the bonds. "Never again."

Dervy strained, pulling herself upright, tearing herself away from him.

Never again.

A voice told her to lie down, but she ignored it. She didn't listen to the voice any longer--not since then. She didn't need it. She was strong on her own.

Her vision swam, ribbons of rainbows mixing with kaleidoscopic lights.

"Never again."

A figure was in front of her, putting an arm out.

"NO!" She screamed and struck out, hand forced into a claw. Dervy felt as she connected, tearing through flesh and bone. She twisted and threw, sending a mass off to the side to slam into something radiant and shimmering.

The world lurched as the figure hit the barrier. Someone screamed. She vomited.

Suddenly, a sharp object pierced her neck. She swatted a hand away and pulled the needle into her line of sight. It had been emptied.

"Dervy?" The voice said.

She craned as the rainbows swirled, wrapping her in their comforting embrace once again.

There was a face, barely recognizable, on the verge of a memory. She felt she should know him.

The rounded face... the concern in his brown eyes.

"Alex?" She managed weakly just before everything disappeared in a shimmer of light.

6
Somewhere in the Urals
Night, Winter, ~2000 BCE

The screams entered her mind and she reveled in their blood. They ran, but they couldn't flee. No one escaped that night. Not the man with the missing nose or the one-handed man who liked to penetrate her from behind. Even the boy whom she had been presented to after the last raid fell to her.

He couldn't be past his twelfth year.

All died beneath her fists.

They struck her with clubs, but she used only her own limbs. Everything flowed so naturally when she moved--each action chaining into another with nary a thought.

They tried to unify against her, but they failed. She flowed around them like they stood still--weapons falling into empty air moments before they fell as well, too dumb to know they were dead. She was a force of nature, a spirit of vengeance set upon this war band by her ancestors. The sharp tang of copper still filled her mouth. The blood of the damned covered her chest and arms.

All who resisted died.

All who surrendered died.

All who ran died.

Michael J. Wyant Jr.

When the slaughter finished, her body covered in the blood of two-dozen men, the camp was still. Empty. No animal or sound dared interrupt her vengeance, for fear of her retribution.

Everything was silent.

Dead.

The world went numb and gray as the cold finally settled on her, seeping into her tattered clothes, moist with death. A snowflake fell on her bare arm and she started, suddenly aware that the bonfire was dying.

To the side, she heard a groan, but it didn't refuel her rage.

She was empty in the aftermath.

A shell.

An empty husk, she shambled over to where the sound came from.

There, next to the cart, a man crawled. One arm hung awkwardly at his side, elbow facing the wrong direction. Both legs appeared useless, though they did not look injured. As she approached, he moved more frantically, muttering in that filthy language of theirs.

With no emotion, she stepped on his remaining good hand, bare foot meeting rough flesh.

He rolled, gritting his bloodstained teeth. She remembered that face, old and wrinkled. It was this man who had killed her husband and put her into the cell, yet she found that there was little emotion left inside of her.

She felt nothing.

He spat at her, his crimson spittle hitting the smooth whiteness of her upper thigh and dripping like a bloody teardrop, stretching out amongst the small hairs of her skin.

She knelt next to him, turning her head to the side in curiosity. He pulled back, eyes shaking in the firelight.

This was fear.

This panic-stricken expression that painted his face, making him almost appear a caricature of his former self. This was what they had desired the most out of her while she lay for them night after night.

This is what he had wanted and she had given it to him.

Now he gave it back.

For a long while she stared at him, emotionless. He cried out at her in his language, hurling demands and accusations that she couldn't understand.

Finally, after several long minutes, he struck at her with his good hand in a panic. She caught the fist in a hand and crushed it to a bloody pulp, watching his face the entire time.

Nothing.

She stepped away, looked around for a moment, found a large rock and returned. He looked up at her pleadingly, desperation thick in his voice.

No doubt, she had looked much this way during the first few days. She'd lost count of the days, let alone the weeks.

She did what she had hoped, begged, them to do to her.

With a single, fluid motion, she crushed his skull.

*   *   *

Alex patted the sweat off Dervy's forehead and cast an angry glare toward where Simon sat, still driving the ambulance.

After her attack, Nathan had ordered Alex to the side and strapped Dervy down to the table by herself. Additionally, he had given Alex a small blanket and his own jacket after some insistence on Alex's part. The blanket covered Dervy's convulsing form while Alex covered himself with the latter.

Once Simon had injected her with whatever had been in the syringe, Dervy had begun speaking and cursing in various tongues as well as shaking, face contorting in anger and despair. Whatever nightmare the substance had induced, it must be horrible. Alex found himself seated next to her, watching her small body wrench against what he now saw were freight straps. Soon after, he was holding her hand and wiping away her tears, sweat, and bloody spittle, speaking soothingly to her and trying to calm her tormented mind.

Nathan still sat in the back with the two of them, but the longer he observed her condition, the more uncomfortable he looked. He sat, large arms crossed across his chest, his eyes locked on her face. A few times he jumped to his feet, panic crossing his face, as a particularly powerful spasm rocked her body.

A bloody hole remained in the center of his button down shirt--tie removed following the attack--revealing dark skin covered in a thick layer of curly black hair. Despite the obstruction, Alex could not help but notice the extensive definition of his musculature. He'd assumed that Nathan was just big in the way large men tended to be. Alex was wrong. Nathan had corded muscle across his entire body.

Dervy sputtered something in a guttural language, gnashing her teeth and spitting bloody chunks of what Alex could only assume were parts of her cheeks, tongue or lungs. Brow furrowed, Alex reached out with the cuff of his jacket and wiped away the mess, taking care around her eyes.

He found himself tracing a finger around her cheek, delicately wiping away a few droplets of spittle, and yanked his arm back, shaking his head.

Nathan snorted, head moving back and forth. "Don't even try it, boy."

"What?" Alex asked, cursing at himself.

"If Kevin's right--and he usually is--that beautiful young woman in your lap is just a little bit younger than the Pyramids," Nathan said, picking at his nail, absentmindedly.

"I don't know what you're talking about," Alex said, shaking his head. "She spit all over herself--I was just wiping it off."

Nathan shook his head ruefully, "Uh-huh."

"Don't you feel bad about this?" Alex burst out suddenly. "If Weynie was telling the truth, this," he pointed at Dervy, "shouldn't be happening."

Nathan glanced over at Simon. It was just a quick flick of the eyes, but Alex caught it.

"Things are changing, boy," he said quietly. "Some strigoi are gonna get what she's getting."

Alex frowned. He needed more than that. Maybe he could convince Nathan to tell him more. Silently pleading, he asked a question. "Some?"

"Yeah, some," Nathan said, shifting on the short bench that ran along the side of the ambulance. "Others are gonna be a lot better off."

"Like you?" Alex asked, carefully. He was beginning to feel a little faint and lights were beginning to swirl in front of his eyes.

Nathan eyed him, eyes narrowing suspiciously. "Are you Scrying me, boy?"

Scrying?

Alex shrugged, but shook his head in a panic, trying to clear his thoughts. "I don't know what you're talking about."

"Ten, nine, eight..." Nathan started counting backwards rapidly, voice growing quiet as he did so.

Alex felt a buzzing just above his right eye and he put a hand to it, rubbing away the pressure. The lights started flashing rapidly, images flitting in front of his face.

A moment later he was on his back, head against the rear entrance, the left side of his face sore and bruising. It felt like his cheekbone was broken and blood trickled down his cheek.

Nathan was standing over him.

"Don't *ever* Scry me, boy," Nathan said menacingly, pointing down at him.

Alex nodded quickly, hands up defensively, and Nathan sat back down, plucking at his pants as he did so.

Squinting as his eye swelled, Alex got to his feet unsteadily as the truck bounced along the road. He took a seat along the bench opposite Nathan. He sat there quietly, trying to ignore the throbbing on the side of his face and think through what Nathan had said.

Alex had questions, but the first he needed answered was what had just happened. Nathan claimed that he had been Scrying him? Was it some type of mind control or mind reading? Maybe it was like 'scanning' someone--

Alex gasped as his cheekbone suddenly set, flaring to life with new pain as it pushed bruised flesh out of the way to regain its place. Gingerly, he touched his face and felt the swelling go down until there was no trace of the wound.

Across from him Nathan grunted. "That was quick," he muttered.

"My face?" Alex asked, still touching at it, amazed at how normal it felt.

"No, you're goddamned foot," Nathan spat. "Yeah, you're face. Usually takes a few decades for regeneration to get that advanced, if at all. It's just a little weird if you haven't..."

He trailed off, narrowing his eyes at Alex again.

"Haven't what?" Alex asked, shrugging. He certainly wasn't doing anything to raise the other man's ire besides asking a few questions, unlike the last time. He hadn't known that something strange was happening at the time, but in reflection, there had certainly been a feeling of invasion--like he was entering a place he wasn't welcome. There was nothing of that sort going on now.

"Nothing," Nathan said firmly. "I don't want to hear so much as a cough out of you for the rest of drive, understood?"

Alex nodded, taken aback by the shift in tone. Quietly, he moved back to Dervy's side, wiping her face as a particularly violent spasm passed, but he was no longer thinking of her. Instead, his mind was strolling down a walkway lined with unanswered questions, desperately searching for the keys to those glimmering doorways.

*   *   *

"Weynie, please exit the room. We have much to discuss," William Searle said, voice overtly calm as he addressed her, yet somehow still projecting throughout the Primatri--the Ankousti Council chamber.

Weynie nodded and inclined her head first to William, then to the group of Elders before her. "Thank you, Primator. Elders."

She turned and left, leaving the dark room lined with benches polished smooth by time and bodies and the embedded scents of ancient incense and modern oils. The heavy oak door--bound with thick metal bands--fell shut behind her with a sound of finality.

Weynie sighed then, letting her anxiousness wane and dissolve into the familiar, controlled air of Heathshome. Everything here had the slightest twinge of cinnamon, a smell that used to aggravate her, but which she came to associate with home as the years crawled by. Breathing it all in, she started walking away from the Ankousti chambers and toward the residential area of Heathshome. The hallway was lit every few paces by natural light, projecting downward as if there were true skylights in the ceiling. It was impossible to have "natural" light down here. On the surface, Heathshome appeared to be a sprawling ranch with a few dozen farmhands operating it.

The bulk of the facility was actually two hundred and forty feet below ground. Heathshome was a sprawling series of hallways, amphitheaters, and residences--a small city existing entirely inside a structure that could withstand the most advanced weaponry known to mankind. Sunlight was captured aboveground and redirected by an elaborate series of mirrors into the hundreds of miles of hallways that connected the facilities of Heathshome to each other.

Weynie nodded to others as she moved toward her rooms, but showed no interest in actual discussion. Still dressed in the firefighter's clothing, Weynie just wanted to get home and get in the shower. She just couldn't think with the filth of the plane glistening on her like a sheen of calcified ash. She had taken a few minutes on the way back from the disastrous Taken retrieval to splash water on her face and scrub her arms, but she still itched everywhere.

"Weynie? Are you all right?"

She glanced up and noticed Jalal approaching, his ever-present tablet in hand and concern etched on his ebony face.

Weynie smiled at him as he approached. "Yeah, I just need a shower."

"Good God," he said as he reached out and took off her hat, exposing her baldness.

Weynie always kept her curly hair long.

Weynie was surprised she let him touch her, but Jalal had a way about him that calmed the nerves even when they should be on edge.

Especially hers.

"Yeah," she murmured, taking the hat back and securing it.

Jalal frowned. "Fire?"

Weynie nodded and he shook his head.

"I was just summoned by Elder Searle," Jalal said quietly. "Am I to assume it's because of all of this?" He waved at her, indicating her new attire.

Weynie snorted, surprising herself at the outburst of lightheartedness. "Probably, but you know I can't say."

Jalal nodded. "Well, get a shower. You look like hell." He patted her on the shoulder reassuringly as he passed by.

Weynie found herself smiling and watching him walk away, shaking her head slowly. He was always such a sweet talker.

She turned and continued on toward her rooms, stopping only to grab an orange and sandwich from the mess hall since she was passing nearby anyway. One of the first things she had learned upon being Taken was that a strigoi never argued with their stomach and not for the typical reasons--missing too many meals was dangerous. The last thing anyone needed was to go into a frenzy. Practicing self-restraint was not worth becoming a Feeder.

Taking a bite of the sandwich, she entered the residential area, the Pasa Tiempo. If Weynie recalled correctly, it had been designed and built under the guidance of a Spanish Youngling in the sixties. Though his name escaped her at the moment--it was very average, like Pedro or something similar--he had beseeched the Ankousti to remodel what had been, up to that point, a rather drab and depressing area in comparison. He'd tried to recreate a more natural environment that reflected his youth in the countryside, though there had not been a major push to recreate the Spanish countryside so much as to merge a natural, calming atmosphere with the utilitarian attitudes that currently dominated the Arktois.

The result wasn't breathtaking, but it was relaxing.

The ceilings were higher here than the rest of Heathshome and painted to look like the morning sky, inspired in the mid-nineties by the casinos in Las Vegas, or so Weynie had heard. She certainly couldn't argue with the result--the introduction of a fake day and sunset had brought about a sense of normalcy while living inside what was for all intents and purposes a bomb shelter.

The main plaza was an open amphitheater with a few stores scattered about that provided the basic necessities for free as well as some fringe items like flat screen televisions and food processors for those who had some disposable income. With somewhere around two thousand Sirgili maintaining residences in Heathshome and a little under one thousand who could actually say they "lived" there, the park and facilities were rarely crowded. Right then there were maybe one hundred people spread out amongst the trees and rocks, leaning against benches while speaking to others. Some sat alone with a book or portable device of some sort.

If it weren't for the slight hum of the climate control system, Weynie would have believed she just stepped into Central Park or the like. As it was, she simply walked through the area quickly, avoiding eye contact and taking the quickest path she could think of to her rooms.

Even though she moved quickly, Weynie's sensitive ears could still pick up the faint buzz of hurried whispers left in her wake. One would imagine that with a mean age of two hundred years, the amount of gossip would begin to fade, but it was actually quite the opposite.

It was a wonderful day in the Pasa Tiempo when some scandal rocked the home front. Lately, the talk had been mostly about Kevin O'Ceallaigh's disappearance, but her sudden reappearance in clothing that was obviously not hers--and completely bald to boot--would either merge with the old gossip or become an entity all its own, stimulating the mind and tongues of aged strigoi for many months to come.

If she wasn't in such need of a shower, Weynie may have taken the time to actually listen in on a few conversations--that was part of her job in the AIC, after all--but she just didn't have the patience right now. Sighing, she exited the plaza through one of the many side passages that dotted the periphery of the circle. She only needed to go a dozen feet more down a hallway before coming to her door. It was painted a nice "Road Work" orange that made her sigh in relief, but there was something new where the door handle used to be that made her frown.

It appeared to be a thumb print reader of the same type they used in the AIC offices with a note hanging off of it. She had spent the past four years rattling the bars of the AIC bureaucracy with study after study showing that finger print biometric scanning methods were unreliable and exceedingly vulnerable to the simplest workarounds.

Weynie had even gone so far as to force the AIC directors-- the small group of three Sirgili that reported intelligence progress to the Ankousti--an episode of a popular television show that managed to bypass fingerprint scanners using Silly Putty. Of course, the twenty-four hour guard shift made everyone else a little more relaxed than they should be, but at least funds had been reallocated to alternate biometric devices for the past few years.

The note itself was from Jalal. She scanned it quickly, a grin spreading across her face as she did so.

The thumb reader is inconsequential, just one part of a three part authentication system. Place your thumb on the plate, a needle will puncture your thumb, draw a blood sample and compare it to the existing record. Additionally, state your first name only.

First and last initiates the Panic Mode; anything else simply fails.

These things need to be tested before implementation, right? We need to get a good sample set so we know where we need to set the lockout.

I'll be breaking into your apartment sometime in the next week, by the way.

Jalal

She folded the piece of paper, but hesitated before putting it inside one of the pockets of the overalls or the coat. These clothes were going in the trash as soon as she could get out of them and Weynie kept every bit of work-related correspondence if she could help it. You never knew when someone would go through your trash and find some piece of sensitive information.

Not that this was sensitive, really...not in a professional sense.

Smiling, Weynie put her thumb on the reader. Immediately, the surface grew warm as a short scanner passed over her print, followed by a quick pricking sensation. By the time she pulled her thumb from the plate, the wound had already healed.

"Weynie," she stated clearly.

The distinct sound of a sliding bolt echoed in the hallway and she stepped inside, pulling the door shut behind her. As soon as it closed, she calmly set the folded piece of paper on the side stand and proceeded to tear off her clothes.

Literally.

She moved purposefully toward the bathroom, not taking the time to turn on so much as a lamp--the dull glow from her sleeping computer lit the room enough for her night vision. The clothes fell into the wastebasket inside the bathroom as she passed it.

A few short minutes later, Weynie slowly lowered herself into a steaming hot bath, lavender soaps filling the room with their flowery aromas. The near-scalding heat was liberating--melting off the greasy residue and cleansing her every pore.

Quietly, the room silent around her, the air hot with steam and scent, Weynie closed her eyes and let the currents wash away her worries for a time.

7
Somewhere, PA
9:31 PM August 21, 2010

    Alex leaned against the cell wall and wondered how the hell he got there. He was finally wearing clothes, so that was a step in the right direction even if they looked and felt like someone had cut a burlap sack into a vague clothing shape.

    He half-heartedly scratched himself and spat in the corner. At least he was finally starting to feel normal again, despite the wretchedness of the situation.

    When Alex got depressed it always took so much out of him, leaving him drained and empty. This time he was feeling much more in control of himself that usual. He wouldn't go so far as to say he was "hopeful," but whatever he was, it was better than the usual alternative.

    Alex sighed. It was hard to be hopeful when you were in a concrete prison with a locked steel door acting as your only portal to the outside world. There wasn't even a proper bed--just a filthy pillow and some layered pallets of cloth in a somewhat bed-like arrangement.

He stood up, stretching and yawning as he did so. His mind wandered back to Dervy as he began pacing the circumference of the room for the hundredth time.

Where they had taken her was a mystery. A few men and women--older than any strigoi he had met thus far--had met them at the front gate to a small, walled compound and taken her away on a stretcher. They had all been speaking so quickly, ignoring him completely, as they rolled the gurney away toward an even tinier building further inside the complex.

Nathan had taken him to this cell, returning only once a few minutes later to give him the clothes he now wore. The big man made sure to retrieve his coat, shaking his head in distaste as he did so.

Since then there had been nothing. Not a sound other than the disturbing echo of concrete chips falling from the aged ceiling. The moldy air and persistent dampness gave the place a very convincing aura of doom and despair, but it must have went just a little too far, since Alex just wasn't feeling it like he guessed he was supposed to.

Turning to the left, he stepped over some refuse that just didn't need to be identified.

Doom? Check.

Despair? Check.

Full out depression and self-loathing triggered by the aforementioned qualities? Nope.

Another turn, this time stepping on his "bed" as he did so. With a grimace he noticed that some of the filth from the corner had followed him onto the bed. The next trip would not include stepping on his mattress that was for sure.

At the end of the day, Alex just wasn't sure what he should be feeling. Over the previous twenty-four hours he'd gone from a Systems Administrator at Nawat Industries in San Francisco to a kidnapped prisoner of a ragtag collection of science-fiction characters out in the middle of nowhere. He was pretty sure they were now in Pennsylvania, near the New York border, but even that was a guess. The road they'd taken to get here had been full of bends and twists. He could be West Virginia for all he knew.

Normally, this would be life shattering--Alex hated the East Coast--but in-between those two extremes, he'd learned he was apparently immortal, able to read people's minds and was developing these powers much more quickly than he was supposed to if Nathan was correct.

At the next corner he turned a little earlier than he had previously. This was the corner he was using as a bathroom, after all.

So what should he do? That was the question he kept coming back to and the one he couldn't answer. Well, not completely, anyway. He felt pretty certain after his incredibly short discussion with Nathan that whatever they had in store for them, it wouldn't be pleasant. With that in mind, escape seemed like a pretty attractive option, but since no one had swung by to say "Hello" yet, it seemed pretty weak.

Alex turned again. There was nothing special about this corner.

Maybe he should test the door again? It certainly couldn't hurt.

As he passed, Alex turned toward the door. It looked to be a solid piece of steel, though he wasn't entirely certain. For one, he wasn't really sure what a steel door looked like. The thing had been painted at one point, but the side facing him was worn clean a dull gray, some small dings and dents alongside long scratch marks marring its surface. He barely resisted the urge to examine those gouges for signs of fingernails.

There was a small grate near the bottom, about two inches tall and nine or ten inches wide. It looked kind of like a mail slot, but he assumed they used it for a food tray or something similar. A mail slot just didn't make any sense given the décor.

Besides that, there was also a very small opening at about eye level. It was large enough that he might have been able to fit his arm through the tiny portal, but with six vertical bars guarding against that, there was little chance of escape presenting itself there.

And that was it.

As far as he could see, the door didn't even have any hinges, though he assumed they were just on the opposite side, away from any would-be escape artists. Grunting, he gave the door a frustrated kick.

Pain flared up through his leg as his bare toes slammed into the surface.

"Sonuva!" He yelled, hopping around on one foot. Taking care, he fell against the wall, the foot with the broken toe cradled in his hands.

Alex's big toe was bright red and swelling quickly.

"That was stupid," he chided himself, shaking his head in annoyance.

Abruptly, pain flared once again and, shocked, Alex watched his toe straighten with a click as the bone fused back together. The swelling subsided shortly after. He wiggled the toe experimentally, feeling nothing but normal movement and a little bit of euphoria.

All of Alex's other injuries he had been unable to see, but this one, as simple as it was, made the whole ordeal believable. Even before, after feeling his face reconstruct itself he still had some nagging doubt.

"Not anymore," he murmured, getting back to his feet and balancing on his previously injured foot. It was too bad everything still *hurt* when he was injured, though. That probably meant that he could still go into shock and all the niceties associated with that as well.

Alex sighed. He really didn't want to live forever. It was such an overrated idea, full of assumptions that he could only imagine were patently false. Everything he used to love was already gone. Why would he want to live with those feelings of loss for all that time?

He'd grown up as a single child of a half-Vietnamese mother and an American father. His mother had emigrated from Vietnam in the mid-seventies at the age of seventeen, leaving behind any family or history to the tumult of that land.

Alex couldn't even say for certain what her maiden name had been, every piece of documentation on her had just said "Ann Marie Mamsin." She had never so much as mentioned siblings beyond periodic mentions of 'her baby' when she hit the bottle particularly hard, which came much more often after his father died in the late nineties.

His father--Jacob Rupert Mamsin--was still calling himself a hippie despite a dreadfully receding hairline and thinning ponytail when he met his future wife during a field trip away from the commune he helped create. The way they told the story, it was love at first sight; so much, in fact, that nine months after their eyes graced each other Alex leapt screaming onto the scene.

Alex sat down on the pallet smiling. Despite all of the hard times and disagreements, the mismatched pair of his eco-friendly, ultra-positive father with his moody, sarcastic mother had worked exceedingly well. They were opposites of the same coin and Alex liked to think that they had proved the phrase "Opposites Attract."

Much of that stopped when his father died suddenly of a burst appendix while hiking at the end of August 2001. It had taken days to find his body, but when they found it much of it had been taken by the very woodland critters he spent much of his adult life protecting. During the eulogy, Alex had quipped that Jacob Rupert Mamsin had literally died doing what he loved.

No one laughed but his mother. That was all he cared about.

Alex just had not anticipated how deep into depression she would slide. His mother had always been a heavy drinker, but without Jacob there to rein her in, she accelerated quickly into alcoholism and within a year was suffering from liver failure. Ann Mamsin died on March 21, 2003 while under the knife for liver surgery.

He grabbed his head as unbidden thoughts erupted into his mind. There was no need to start thinking about Mary. Alex could look back at his parents' with fondness, but attempting to do the same with Mary failed each and every time. Every memory showed her with that bloody hole...

Alex grunted and wiped his face, trying to push the memories away. Now wasn't the time for these thoughts. He was supposed to be figuring out how to get out of the cell, not reflecting on how alone he was in the world or why he didn't deserve to live in it.

He hopped to his feet, walked back over to the door and pressed his face up against the bars, straining to see what was beyond them. He could see a rather wide hallway, nearly as dilapidated as the room he was in, but little else of note. There were some shallow pools of standing water in the hallway and chunks of ceiling scattered about. Long bars of vermillion light shot across the hallway near the edge of his vision.

Cursing, he turned around scanning his own cell. There had to be a way out of this room. He just needed to figure it out.

Again, Alex started pacing, but this time he let a hand trail along the wall. He had a theory, but whether it panned out was another thing. If one of the walls was warmer than the others, then maybe it faced directly outside and was thin enough to break through. The whole building seemed to be falling apart around him. Besides, if he had been able to break through the packing straps this should be just as easy.

Right?

Unless it was steel reinforced.

Which it probably was...

Moving quickly, Alex passed around the corner with the unidentified pile of mess, fingers trailing over the cool, damp wall. Even if one of these walls was facing outside, what were the chances that it was thin enough to get warm, let alone be broken? And how would he even go about doing it? He didn't have any tools available.

Deftly avoiding his bedding, Alex continued.

It was worth checking at least, that much he was sure about. He could figure it out if...

The wall warmed as he passed the part of the wall directly across from the steel door. Shaking his head, he continued until it suddenly grew cool a couple feet away.

Barely suppressing a smile, Alex took a step back and examined the portion of the wall that was warmer. It looked exactly like the rest of the length--most of the paint remnants lying in little toxic piles on the floor along with fragments of chipped concrete. He rested his hand on the slightly warm surface with a smile.

This was a way out. He just needed to find a way to get through it...

Alex's thoughts were interrupted by the sound of footsteps. They echoed emptily through the hallway, seemingly far away, though Alex was unsure whether that was an illusion or truth. There was no reason to take a chance, though, so Alex quickly moved to his pallet and took a seat.

A minute later, a bespectacled face obscured the tiny portal on his door. It looked like an older woman, maybe in her late fifties, dyed, jet-black hair pulled tightly away from a rather dour looking face.

She stood there looking inside the room and then back at something outside the doorway, acting as if Alex couldn't see her. Maybe he could get some information out of her if he moved quick enough. It used to work in cross-departmental meetings; he didn't see why it wouldn't work here.

"I think I've played this game before," Alex said loudly, grinning.

The woman jumped at his voice. "Excuse me?"

Her voice was thick with an accent of some sort; French, maybe? That could put her anywhere though--Alex had no idea what the difference was between Louisiana French, Canadian French, or any other type of French for that matter.

"Peek-a-boo," Alex said with a smile. "I used to play it with my niece," he lied.

"Hmm," the woman muttered quietly ignoring him once again.

Alex frowned. "What's your name?"

She looked back at him, opened her mouth and then snapped it shut just as quickly. Through the door he heard the sound of something scratching, like a pen on paper.

"Listen," Alex said, standing up with a smile. "If we're going to be intimate, it's only proper that I know your name. I'm not a slut, you know."

The woman snorted, quickly covering her mouth to stifle the laugh that was going to accompany it. She looked at him and he was caught off-guard by what he saw there.

Sympathy.

"Please," she said quietly. "This is difficult enough without exchanging names."

Alex raised an eyebrow at that. What did "difficult enough" mean?

"Well my name is Alex, Alex Mamsin," he said, moving forward until he was near the door. "So, since I've already crossed that line, you might as well introduce yourself as well."

The dim light coming through the window seemed to flicker as she turned toward him, but he blinked it away.

She sighed, looking at him again. "You may call me Doctor Aubin."

Alex inclined his head toward the door. "Nice to meet you, Doctor Aubin."

Doctor Aubin nodded back, holding back a smile, though she quickly followed it with a shake of her head. Pictures flashed inside his head briefly, though they passed by much too quickly for him to understand.

Was he doing it again? Scrying, or whatever Nathan had called it? If he was, he just hoped he didn't get caught this time.

"So what's your sign?" Alex asked, leaning in and raising his eyebrows at her suggestively.

"Since we are already breaking the rules, I might as well just ask you these questions," Dr. Aubin said with a half-smile. "How are you feeling today?"

Alex's stomach growled in response. "Despite ravenous hunger, absolute confusion, and a bit of a crick in my neck from that shameful excuse for a bed, I'm pretty good actually."

Dr. Aubin looked away and he heard the distinct scratching sound again.

She looked him over again. "How about your injuries? Have they healed properly?"

Alex smiled. "Yep. Broke my toe this morning, too," he held up his dirty, yet entirely whole foot awkwardly. "As you can see, everything is right as rain."

Dr. Aubin nodded and scratched out his response.

There was no sense in lying to her; if she was here, there was no doubt she knew what he was. Actually, she probably knew more about him than he did.

"Mind if I ask you a question now?" Alex asked quickly.

"Umm," her eyes flashed down the hallway. "I may not be able to answer, but yes you can."

Alex thought for a moment. He'd fully expected her to turn down his request, so he was a little unprepared. Asking the wrong question might bring her back on her guard, as she was obviously not supposed to be talking to him, let alone answering questions. He wasn't sure how much leeway this Scrying thing could get him and he didn't want to alert everyone to the fact he could do it.

Alex just needed to think of the right question. And hopefully she didn't know he could Scry...but that was doubtful.

Asking about Dervy was certainly not the right way to go and pushing too hard on where he was would certainly be too much.

"Hmm," he murmured, still smiling. "Tell me about yourself."

Dr. Aubin smiled at him. "That was a statement, Mr. Mamsin. Try again."

"Okay, okay. I guess it is," Alex conceded. "Here you go: what do you do for a living?"

The smile on her lips faded a little at the question. Alex cursed himself silently, though he tried desperately to maintain his calm demeanor.

"Why do I feel like I'm being picked up in a bar?" Dr. Aubin said suddenly.

Alex grinned, relief flooding through him. Dr. Aubin shook her head.

"I'm an evolutionary biologist, though I spend most of my time tracking evolutionary development in humans," she said quickly. "While many believe that humans are doomed to suffer the same evolutionary timeline as most primates and other organisms, I believe that we should be able to jump-start that process. Ideally, this means that we would be able to experience this change in our lifetimes."

"Really?" Alex asked, raising an eyebrow. "And why would you want to do that?"

"Why would you not?" Dr. Aubin asked, eyes quizzical. "Enhanced healing ability, extended lifetimes; maybe even telekinesis! Could you imagine life like that?"

Alex's face fell. "Yeah. I can a little, yeah."

"I..." she began, but cut herself off, face surprised.

Alex shook his head and opened his mouth to speak, but she cut him off with a quick shake of her head.

"You are good, Mr. Mamsin," Dr. Aubin conceded, nodding, the sound of pen on paper louder than before. "But I have my questions answered and I must go."

Shit.

Dr. Aubin walked away, her light footsteps echoing like those of a giant in the tight, concrete prison. Alex must have pushed her too hard or something, but he just didn't have any idea what he was even doing, let alone know how to limit his influence.

If he was even doing anything, that is.

Shrugging, he moved back toward the wall, letting fingers trail across its damp, lukewarm surface. What was he even thinking? Was he going to tear through the wall like a giant green monster on a rampage?

Setting aside practicality, Alex had another problem stewing inside him. He knew why at least one person here had kidnapped him: they wanted to make the world a better place. Could he really fault them for that? Wanting to heal sicknesses? Extend human lifetimes?

Of course he couldn't--if Mary had these powers, she would still be alive. Given the opportunity, would he deprive his fellow man of the ability to save their loved ones? When he thought about it, he just couldn't do it and stay true to himself.

And what did he have to endure to make this happen anyway? If Weynie hadn't lied, he was now immortal. It wasn't like he would die from anything they did.

Right?

Gritting his teeth, Alex put his hand to his side and sat down to wait for whatever was going to happen next.

8
Somewhere in the Urals
Evening, Winter, ~2000 BCE
and
Somewhere, PA
11:20 PM August 21, 2010

Wind swept over Dervy's freezing body, snapping viciously at the remnants of clothing that hung around her. Bare feet trudged into drifts up to her waist, leaving red smears in the glistening snow only to be devoured by the ever-shifting surface. Her trail disappeared into the brilliant wall of swirling white behind her, making it appear as if she'd never existed.
    Only moving mattered to her.
    Forward motion.

She forced her body to move beyond where it should have, into the encroaching darkness of yet another frigid night. Shortly, she would collapse into the crisp powder and feel the warmth of death sweep over her. Trembling, she held a hand in front of her raw eyes, recognizing the deep rifts in the skin where it had split and bled, only to freeze into long lines of vermillion strands. Flexing unfeeling fingers, deep crimson fissures appeared through waxy tissue, sending her lifeblood toward the ground, only to join the other decorative strands in their intricate pattern that spread miles behind her, now buried deep under the drifts she'd plowed through.

The arm shook visibly though she could no longer sense the movement. Dark patches of purple flesh turned back to white before her eyes. Shuddering out a sigh, Dervy's legs gave out and she collapsed to the right, feeling the welcoming embrace of quiet eternity once again cover her.

Blinding light shot into her eyes, a screaming cacophony of robotics and voices above her. Dervy squinted, turning her head to the side and feeling it restrained.

"Where am I?"

Is she awake?

She can't be, just keep going, we almost have it.

Pain flared in her chest and she screamed, back arcing in response.

I can't do another one of these with them awake. Put her down!

"Get off of me goddamnit!" Dervy screamed, pulling at invisible bonds, eyes adjusting to the spotlights and knives.

Tearing, gouging.

Just take it!

Her entire body quivered as her chest locked, the feeling of her pumping heart interrupted. Dervy gasped once and fell back to the bed, body limp.

Got it. Bag it.

Her mind went numb, vision swimming into the comfort of darkness. *Please,* she begged.

There was no response.

The familiar feeling of crawling spiders snapped her eyes open. She was facing a doorway, men and women dashing rapidly in front of her vision.

"What?" A voice asked irritably.

Behind her, slightly to the left.

"It's growing back already," a female voice said, stunned.

To the right, by her feet.

Footsteps stopped. Breathing indicated six others, three to the right, three to the left.

The tingling confirmed it.

And Alex was near.

A frustrated sigh. "We've seen regeneration happen this fast before. Snap out of it."

"Doctor..."

Tightness grew in Dervy's chest as her body pushed out the foreign objects they had left inside her. Clamps popped, swabs were swept up and across her chest. Something held her rib cage apart, despite her body fighting it.

She closed her eyes and focused.

While other strigoi could control objects with their minds, manipulate heat to their will or channel electricity by thought alone, Dervy had never gained these skills. It had always confused her that some strigoi never even experienced these gifts, while others used them as if it was second nature, almost like breathing.

One thing Dervy did excel at was regeneration and strength.

Flexing her stomach muscles, Dervy sat up.

Her bonds snapped like rubber bands as she moved, a tray of tools and cutting implements flying to the side in a shower of bloody gauze and shining steel. Pain flared anew in her chest, but she pushed it away, instead leaning to the side.

Right hand still bound, she pulled it toward her chest with a grunt, reaching for what she knew must be holding her ribcage open. Memories of a dank cell--a similar implement in place--flashed through her mind as her hand gripped something cool and smooth. With a scream Dervy yanked on it, feeling tissue and bone scrape as it released.

Immediately, as if waiting for the opportunity, her chest closed, bone, muscle and skin mending seamlessly. Dervy took a deep breath and scowled. She scanned the room, seeing seven people standing slack-jawed around her. The pinpricks at the back of her neck told her none of these were strigoi, including the one behind her.

But Alex was near.

Gritting her teeth, she pulled on the bonds to her right. The table bent toward the ground, but the locking mechanism gave way a moment later, snapping under the force of her pull.

Behind her, she heard and felt someone move in--a slight flicker of light encroaching on her space--but she would be damned if they were going to stick her with a needle again.

Dervy launched herself to the left in an awkward somersault, trailing her arm to the side as she did so. A shock of pain told her that she successfully dislocated her left shoulder as she landed on her feet next to a young woman in green hospital attire. With her free hand, Dervy reached to the side, grabbed her by the throat and threw her into the man that had just been behind her holding a needle. The man looked shocked for just a moment before the woman hit him and they rolled away in a mixed mass of light green and dark green scrubs.

Gritting her teeth against the screams that broke out amongst the remaining humans, Dervy leaned toward the table, willed her shoulder back into place, and tore away the last of her bonds. She looked up and her eyes met those of a man, quivering in the corner of the room. A deep, primal anger filled her as their eyes met and she leapt, landing just in front of him.

She snarled, lifted a bare foot and stomped on his chest. Her toes sunk into his chest as ribs shattered and organs popped like overripe tomatoes. His face spasmed for just a moment before blanching, chin sagging to his chest in death.

Dervy turned and watched men and woman scatter down two separate hallways, further into the dilapidated structure. Off to her right, she heard the distinct sound of someone breathing through punctured lungs--the desperate sound of repeated, soggy breaths.

Moving slowly, Dervy walked toward where a woman lay motionless, just next to the man who had tried to poison her again. He pulled away as he saw her, blood pouring from his mouth as he crawled. She stepped up quickly and stomped on his right leg, feeling it shatter under the force of her strike. He tried to scream, to beg, but only succeeded in choking on his own fluids.

Dervy squatted next to him, eyeing him with more than a little curiosity. His breathing grew heavy, eyes wide and panicked, as lungs filled with fluid and he began to drown.

She waited for a moment and then punched him in the nose to help things along. He fell back sobbing big red tears as he drew his last breaths. She leaned in toward him as his eyes began to roll back into his head and whispered: "Dites-lui...j'ai dit bonjour."

Confusion clouded the man's face just before death overtook him leaving behind an empty shell of what he had been only moments earlier.

Dervy stood with a sigh, glancing down at herself. As seemed to be standard in these scenarios, she was entirely naked. With a grunt, she pulled the dead woman to a standing position, purposefully ignoring the look of shock frozen into her dead face as she did so. They were roughly the same height, so she stripped the scrubs off of her and pulled them on.

Dervy looked around as she dressed. The room was nearly falling apart around her. Old paint flaked off in large chunks to expose crumbling concrete beneath and standing pools of water in one of the hallways. The architecture and layout looked like early twentieth century, but it had obviously been abandoned for some time. Beneath her feet, plastic crackled with each step, but she felt some cool liquid just under the barrier sloshing as she moved. Each movement brought the faint humid scent of mildew and mold.

The images and sounds of a dark room assaulted her.

The moans of the dying mingled appropriately with the scent of the dead. The shackles held tight to her wrists despite her best efforts. She just wasn't strong enough...Dervy fell to her knees.

She covered her eyes, rocking back and forth slowly as the memory passed, like a storm cloud crossing a barren field.

Apparently the poison was still in her system.

Taking a deep breath, Dervy took a moment to unlace the dead woman's shoes--she had triple-knotted them for some reason. She was having a hard time focusing on the present. Poison was something she had grown used to over the millennia, but the effects always passed because of her healing powers.

This was different. Whatever it was, it tore into her mind, pulling memories of helplessness that she had thought long buried. Then again, maybe it was psychotropic and the experience would be different for each person, like LSD exposure, but she couldn't be sure. All Dervy knew was that it kept bringing her to the brink and she was getting more than a little tired of the effects.

With deft hands, Dervy pulled on the shoes and laced them. She shuddered at what memories may have been drudged up had they dosed her another time. With a grimace, she stood and flexed her toes in her new footwear.

What had they been doing before she escaped? Taking her heart?

She turned to look toward where the man had been standing, but was interrupted by the sounds of running footsteps coming from the hallway to her left. Cursing, Dervy turned and fled down the passage to the right.

A hazy memory of a round-faced man, concern written in his eyes, drove her as she ran. Dervy needed to find Alex as soon as possible and get them both back to Heathshome. That was priority number one.

Ahead of her a small group of men with guns appeared and she smiled.

Of course, if she had to kill a few people to reach her goal that might be okay, too.

* * *

Kevin sat next to Simon, wrinkled face dimly lit by the weak glow of the security camera monitor. A figure moved like a blur on the screen, dropping guard after guard with ease. Simon could hear the quick pops of gunfire coming from the facility and, with the delay in the video, it seemed almost live. A guard lifted a pistol and shot, blood poured from a wound in the tiny whirlwind, but like its true counterpart it continued to move forward with little resistance.

The old man nodded, a small smile creeping across his weathered face, gray beard shifting with the motion. A small tuft of hair fell from the back of his head, weaving slightly in the stagnant air until it came to rest on his shoulder with some of its brethren.

Simon covered his mouth as a wave of nausea hit him. The Return was beginning to accelerate. As the hours crawled by Kevin had been growing more and more anxious, though at that moment it was hard to tell.

"Call Nathan," Kevin rasped out without looking at Simon. "Tell him to pick up the heart. We need to get moving."

Simon nodded as he pulled out his cell phone. "No problem, Kevin."

The movement finally stopped on the small screen as Simon scrolled down to Nathan's number and called it. For the first time since the fight had begun, Simon could see Dervy and she looked like hell. She was bald and covered in dark gray splotches--no doubt blood from a number of different sources--across what appeared to be hospital scrubs. Turning carefully, she appeared to take everything in, watching for possible attackers and escape routes.

"Time?" Nathan's deep voice rattled over the phone.

Dervy looked directly at the camera.

"Yep," Simon said.

"All right. Be at the truck soon," the phone went silent.

Dervy looked up at the camera, smiled, and disappeared through a doorway to her left.

Toward the holding cells... and away from them.

Simon sighed in relief.

"We should get moving," Simon said, moving next to Kevin.

The old man stared off into the distance, half smile frozen in place. A deep wheezing sound was the only indication that Kevin was still alive.

Slowly, Simon reached out and touched the other man's shoulder. "Hey--"

And Simon was on the floor, his face pressed into the concrete, his wrist wrenched up behind his shoulder blades.

"Jesus, Kevin! It's me! It's Simon!" Simon yelled in pain, trying unsuccessfully to force his arm down. The man was ungodly strong, even for a strigoi.

"Who?" Kevin asked threateningly, voice thick with an accent Simon had never heard before. "The only Simon I know is dead!"

"Pull yourself together! We need to get out of here. Dervy's loose!" Simon said through gritted teeth.

The pressure lessened, as did the accent. "Dervy is here?"

Simon grimaced into the concrete flakes. "Yeah, she's here. And she's pissed."

"Why?" Kevin asked quizzically. "We're partners...we're..."

Suddenly, Simon was on his feet and Kevin was wiping off his jacket, eyes frantically avoiding Simon's own. "I'm so sorry, Simon. I just...lost myself for a second."

Simon took a step back, putting his arms up defensively, but he flashed his most convincing smile at the pained look on Kevin's face as he did so. "It's no problem, but we need to get going. Okay?"

Kevin nodded, blinking rapidly. "Yes, yes. Absolutely. Let's get to the truck. You called Nathan?"

Simon nodded, still smiling, though he didn't feel it. Despite his sudden, advanced age, Kevin was still a very dangerous man. Usually strigoi lost their powers as the Return advanced.

Apparently not in Kevin's case.

Quietly, Simon watched Kevin look around the room. There were three exits. The man's face grew darker with each pass and Simon felt the hair on his arms beginning to rise in response to Kevin's anger.

Faking a yawn, Simon walked forward and turned down the right hallway that led to the rear of the building and the waiting truck. Behind him he heard a deep sigh followed by the sound of footsteps. They needed to get that heart to the main facility as soon as possible. Simon had a strong feeling that Kevin was nose-diving quickly and it wouldn't be pretty when he finally hit bottom.

Not for any of them.

*   *   *

Doctor Aubin disconnected the rubber strap and withdrew the needle from Alex's arm, placing a small cotton ball on the puncture to catch the bleeding.

"So you just need a couple blood samples?" Alex asked, taking over control of the swab while she carefully marked the vial with a marker.

"If all goes well with the samples, that is correct, Mister Mamsin," Doctor Aubin said as she carefully put the vial in an aluminum case next to three others.

"What do you mean, 'if all goes well,'" Alex asked. He lifted the cotton ball and noticed the wound had already closed up entirely.

A stray piece of fluff had closed up in the wound. He plucked it out absentmindedly.

Doctor Aubin latched the case with a loud clink and turned toward him. "Let me just say that I truly hope we will only need the blood samples. We have made much progress over the past decade, but we are missing something that we hope your blood will provide."

Alex nodded, but eyed her uncertainly. Part of that had to do with the woman sitting out in the hallway, though. Like the others on the plane, he could feel her as a faint pinprick in the back of his neck, just on the edge of sensation. She stood out there silently, picking at her nails with feigned disinterest, but Alex knew she was there in case he was planning anything.

Not that he was. A few hours after their last encounter, another nurse had come by to make observations and Alex had told him he wanted to help willingly, but would like to speak with Doctor Aubin if he was to do so. About an hour after that, the raven-haired doctor was opening the door, leaving her new friend in the hallway while she took blood samples.

"So what now?" Alex asked.

Doctor Aubin smiled. It looked forced. "Now we wait."

She hesitated for a moment and then reached out and touched his arm almost tenderly. "Thank you, Alex. I mean this."

Alex smiled weakly and nodded. "You're welcome, doctor."

She smiled again, then nodded before turning and leaving the room with her small, aluminum case. The woman in the hallway looked at him impassively and shut the door. It closed with a metallic thud, followed by the sound of a bar sliding into the wall.

Sighing, Alex plopped back onto his pallet and leaned against the wall. He really hoped he was doing the right thing. Doctor Aubin promised him that the purpose of these tests was to extend human life, not make everyone live forever. There were just so many possible issues with not being able to die, especially when you needed to...

"Alex?"

His head snapped up at his whispered name and he found himself looking at a pair of purple eyes that were staring right back.

"Dervy?" He asked, getting to his feet and walking toward the door.

She nodded and glanced around quickly. "We're leaving now."

"Well, I--" Alex started, but was cut off by the protestations of the door as it opened.

Dervy locked eyes with him as she pushed the door open. "There is no argument here. We leave now."

She was wearing light green hospital gear, but was covered in what hopefully only appeared to be blood.

Alex grimaced and stepped into the hallway. "That isn't blood, right?"

Dervy shrugged, grabbing his arm and moving down the hall to the left, sloshing through puddles and debris with barely any acknowledgement of their existence. "Most of it isn't mine."

"Well, Jesus, that's reassuring," Alex grumbled. With a quick jerk, he tried to pull his arm free and failed.

"What are you doing?" Dervy demanded, rounding on him violently.

"I'm following, just give me my damn arm back," Alex protested.

Frowning, Dervy dropped his arm, leaving a red smear where her hand had been. "Keep up."

With that, Dervy turned and ran.

Well, technically it was running, but one second she was there and the next she was forty feet away and rounding a corner.

Cursing, Alex followed her, moving as fast as he could, which was nowhere near the same speed as her. She flowed around obstructions without slowing, moving as if they weren't even there. Dervy was always ahead of him, going faster and faster until she rounded a corner and stopped.

Alex caught up to her, lungs on fire. He glared at her, but she barely acknowledged him.

"Why...did...stop?" Alex panted, gripping at the stitch in his side.

Dervy turned and glared at him. "You're pathetic."

Alex looked askance at her, making a feeble attempt at a glare. He failed, coughing instead.

She shook her head. "You need to learn how to run or we won't get away. There are two ways to do it: use your adrenaline or stop your heart. I don't care which one you do, but the sooner you understand that, the sooner you'll get over these human restrictions you force on yourself."

Alex's mouth dropped open. "What do you mean 'stop your heart'?"

Dervy scowled and kneed him in the chest, driving all of the air from his lungs. He hit the ground gasping, hand clutching the spot where she had struck him. She leaned down and grabbed his chin, forcing him to look at her.

"Usually Youngling's get a few years to adapt to these new abilities," Dervy said evenly, pulling his chin straight as he gasped. "You have fifteen seconds to get up and run for the next twelve hours."

Twelve hours? Was she insane?

Alex managed to get a single breath before she stood, pulling him to his feet by his chin. "Time's up. Remember: use your adrenaline or stop your heart. Pick one."

With that, she turned around and ran, disappearing around a corner almost immediately.

Alex gasped a breath and forced his legs to move despite their complaints. He certainly couldn't stop his heart, so how the hell was he supposed to get his adrenaline going? He rounded the corner, breaths coming in sharp, painful gasps, and was greeted with another strike to the chest.

Alex fell backward, feet coming up in front of him as she stiff-armed him. This time she didn't give him any time; Dervy simply picked him up by the hair and pushed him ahead of her.

"I...I can't," Alex gasped out as he stumbled forward, pushing back against Dervy's urgings.

Abruptly her prodding hands were gone and he fell backward, landing with a thud. Alex's head hit the ground hard, sending showers of light into his vision.

"Ow..." Alex mumbled, putting a hand to his head and closing his eyes.

Then there was a pressure on his abdomen, followed by another strike to his chest. He managed to get his eyes open between gasps for air just in time to have Dervy press her lips to his, tongue probing through his lips. A moment later he found himself kissing her back despite the ridiculousness of it all. The strong coppery taste of blood filled his mouth as her tongue darted along his own, sending tingles down his spine and into his legs. His heart started beating faster, his breath coming in more urgent gasps. Her hands caressed his face, moving slowly down his chest and toward...

Dervy stood and held out a hand to him, leaving him with his tongue sticking out a little.

"What the hell?" Alex asked, leaning up on his elbows.

"Can you breath?" Dervy asked pointedly.

"Yeah, why wouldn't I...?" Alex asked, before shaking his head in amazement.

His heart was still pounding and he felt flushed, but he finally understood. Alex's body was filled with energy and power, much like it had been back in the van.

She flashed a dazzling smile at him and he grudgingly accepted her hand. With little effort, Dervy pulled him to his feet.

"Ready?" Dervy asked as she cracked her neck.

"Sure," Alex said. "But we need to do that again without the running sometime."

With a grin, Dervy took off like a shot, leaping like a gazelle through a window--shards of glass following her like a diaphanous cloak. Alex sped after her, finally feeling the strength in his legs as he followed suit, cutting himself just a little on his own way through. The wounds healed within moments, but what surprised him the most was the tinkling sound coming from ahead of them as they broke into the tree line just as night's first shadows stretched across the clearing, covering their exit.

At first Alex thought it was the sound of glass falling from her fleeting form, but then Alex realized what it actually was.

Dervy was laughing.

*   *   *

The thick tree branches obscured the moon ever so slightly as it rose toward its apex in the sky. It sat high, a leftward facing semicircle that bathed the area in silver light. In their camp, Alex stared at the sky as he chewed on the bundle of herbs Dervy had given him when they finally stopped. Despite the apparent rush of adrenaline and the lack of complete exhaustion, the hunger he had been fighting was beginning to wear on his temper. The batch of greens in his hand did little to slate the desire he had for an extra rare piece of beef, but it did lull the demons in his stomach to sleep and for that he was thankful.

Alex had forgotten how beautiful it was outside of the city. Everything seemed brighter than he remembered, no doubt contributed to in large part by the bright moon above. The trees glistened with silver fire in the darkness, waving in the warm summer breeze, leaves rustling and branches tapping in time. The woods were alive with movement as well; the sounds of predators and prey alike shuffled close by, caught in their eternal dance of life and death. Around him he could hear as forest creatures stalked the woods, no doubt searching for whatever the hell had just made that noise next to him.

Nonchalantly, Alex got to his feet and made his way to where Dervy sat nearby, staring up at the moon. He moved close enough that he could speak quietly, but not within touching distance. Dervy continued to say nothing as he got settled. She just stared off at the sky.

"I think there was a mongoose or something over there," Alex said with a smile, trying to strike up a conversation.

"Probably not," Dervy said quietly and without looking at him.

Alex bit his cheek. "Right."

"So," he started again. "Do you come here often?"

"Don't."

"Don't what?"

"Don't do what you're trying to do."

Alex frowned. "I'm just trying to be friendly."

"Well, I don't want to be your friend," Dervy said flatly.

"Fine," Alex said acidly. "Do we need to do a watch or something?"

Dervy glanced at him. "For what?"

Alex raised an eyebrow. "For sleeping?"

She shook her head and looked at the remaining herbs in his hand. "Finish that. Then we run again."

Dervy looked back up at the sky.

Alex sat there for a moment, dumbfounded. He wasn't exhausted, but there was some definite fatigue starting to settle in on him. Yawning, Alex stretched out a leg, feeling the muscles loosen and unknot as he did so.

Apparently being immortal didn't mean you didn't need to stretch. Or sleep, despite what Dervy said.

"We're not stopping?"

"No."

He sighed. "Okay."

It took him a few more minutes to finish the greens, but as soon as he did they were back on their feet and running. In the bright moonlight everything shone as if the noonday sun were above, casting its clear light through the boughs and branches and making it easy for both of them to avoid obstacles.

Well, easier anyway. Alex had rarely spent time in the woods. He'd gone camping once during his childhood despite his father's obsession with the outdoors, or perhaps because of it. Since that trip included such natural wonders as fire ants, poison oak, and defecating into a hole while sitting on a log, Alex had simply avoided all opportunities to spend any real time in the wilderness.

Sure, the occasional trip to Yosemite or Tahoe would come up, but they certainly didn't equate to leaping willy-nilly over fallen trees bigger around than he was or leaping small streams without knowing what lay on the other side. Generally speaking, all of his latest explorations in nature included a beverage from Starbucks and a paved walking path, dark roast aromas mingling with dead leaves.

Ahead of him, Dervy stopped suddenly. Exhaling deeply, Alex walked the last few feet until he was up next to her. They stood at the edge of a field. In the fading moonlight it nearly glowed, silver strands of flax rising toward the night sky. In the distance a white farmhouse sat against a road, it's gray length cutting through the landscape.

Dervy looked at him.

"Do you have any pinpricks in the back of your neck. Here?" She ran a finger across the back of his neck.

Alex shivered as it ran over the spot that vibrated the strongest. He was suddenly very glad that it was dark enough that Dervy couldn't see the flush running up his cheeks.

"Just one."

Dervy nodded. "Me too."

Without any additional warning, Dervy ran across the field, moving as if it was little more than a paved driveway. Alex sighed and followed, taking care not to stumble in the grooves and divots of the field as he did.

He was beginning to feel more than a little uncomfortable with how quickly his body was reacting. When they were racing through the woods, branches would fly toward him and his hand would just be there, pushing it out of the way as if he were taking a leisurely stroll. Fallen logs, entwined branches and vines barely slowed him during the trek. Instead he hurdled them like an Olympic track star, clearing obstructions as if they didn't exist. His body just reacted as if controlled by someone else, some being who could see things happening before they actually did.

Overall, it was creepy.

The wind shifted toward them as they ran, bringing the acrid scent of fertilizer and cows, though there were none of the large beasts in sight. Off to Alex's right, a flock of birds suddenly took wing as they passed, moving away from them as they made a beeline toward the house.

Alex slowed and came to a stop. A few moments later, Dervy did as well, turning toward him and waving him forward impatiently. He shook his head, but walked toward her.

Why were they going toward a house? Shouldn't they be moving away from people?

"What's the issue?" Dervy whispered urgently as she closed in on him. Her violet eyes darted around them as she approached, seemingly looking at everything all at once.

Alex pointed toward where the white house stood. "Why are we going toward the house? Shouldn't we be, like, running away?"

Dervy cocked her head for a moment and then took a deep, steadying breath. "Even at my best I can only run about thirty-five miles per hour. If I had to guess, you're barely pulling twenty right now."

Alex gawked at the statement. He knew they had been running faster than he ever knew he could, but twenty miles per hour? On foot?

Didn't gazelles run at that fast?

Dervy pointed over at the house. "Since they're out in the middle of nowhere, I'm assuming there is a vehicle of some sort that we can take."

Alex did a double take. "You mean we're going to steal a car?"

"Yes. We need it more than them right now," Dervy said bluntly, crossing her arms beneath her breasts. "Will this be a problem?"

"Well, yeah," Alex said with a violent shake of his head. "I mean, can't you call someone or something? Maybe we can just borrow their phone?"

Dervy cocked an eyebrow at him. "You are wearing a burlap sack and I'm covered in blood."

Alex opened his mouth, but stopped. She was bald--short stubble just beginning to make an appearance across her scalp and above her eyes--and wearing a hospital uniform covered in what CSI would identify as "directional blood spatter" as well as obvious holes in the fabric surrounded by additional spilled blood. In short, with the silvery moon glistening off of her skin, she looked like an escaped mental patient.

Dervy nodded at his silence and turned back toward the house. "They're not even home or we would sense them."

She tapped the back of her neck knowingly.

"Like I said, we're going to take their vehicle. At that point we'll head toward Heathshome where we'll report in to the Ankousti and you can finally begin your integration into the Arktois as well as your training."

She started moving toward the house again, though this time at a more measured walk. Alex followed, brow furrowed in thought.

Everything was just so confusing. Only a few days ago he had been whining about management in an otherwise cushy job. Frustrating, yes, but in no way dangerous. Hell, most times no one there could understand what he was saying anyway.

Now he was running for his life with a deranged, bald woman who was about to steal a car from what was no doubt a really nice family. All for what? To escape from... some group who wanted to increase the lot of normal people the world over.

Or did they? In hindsight, he wasn't even running for his life if everything was true--and it certainly seemed that way--so why was he running? And why didn't he want to help?

Alex stopped, fists balled at his sides. A few steps ahead of him, Dervy halted, her head dropping and a clear sigh of annoyance echoing in the night air.

"What?" She asked without turning, the statement clearly meant as a challenge.

"Why are we running?" Alex asked, struggling to keep his voice level.

"We're not," Dervy said as she rounded on him. "We're walking."

"You know what I mean."

"No, I don't," Dervy snarled. "Are you asking why we escaped from a small fortress filled with armed guards and psychotic doctors intent on using you as an immortal guinea pig? Or are you being delusional and asking why the sudden slow speed we are moving at is a 'run'?"

She cut him off as he opened his mouth. "I know that you can't possibly be referring to the former as that would indicate your complete and utter lack of any sort of self-preservation instinct, so it must be the latter which simply says that you're an idiot."

"Hey, fuck you lady," Alex said, stepping forward angrily. "I've had a pretty shitty couple days, most of which can be attributed to you ambushing me and assaulting me in my own apartment. Not-"

"If I hadn't--"

"--Not to mention the fact that I've been beaten, set on fire apparently, and taken to some far off encampment in Pennsylvania of all places for God only knows what. I--"

"You need to shut your mouth before I--"

"Before you what?" Alex yelled, throwing his arms to the side. "Before you crush my head again? Before you feel up my crotch and punch me in the chest?"

Dervy glared at him, but stayed silent, purple eyes reflecting menacingly in the bright night.

Alex didn't care. His anger spilled out at her, a rushing river of frustration and confusion. "The past year has been a roller coaster of expectation and failure. Everything I do fails. I can't even kill myself right--and God knows I keep trying. How do you fail at something so fundamentally easy considering that we're all supposed to--you know--die?

"Shit, I failed at killing myself so badly that I became immortal. For God's sake! Talk about an epic fail!

"The only thing I was ever good at was..." Alex shook his head, holding back tears. "You know what? I don't even give a shit anymore. Why don't you just go back where you came from and leave me the hell alone?"

Dervy didn't move. She stood there, staring at him with that unwavering gaze.

"What the hell are you doing? Just go!" Alex screamed, waving at her as he would a pack of wild dogs.

She didn't respond.

"Fine," Alex spat. "What kind of a name is 'Dervy' anyway? Were your parents retarded or just stupid?"

Dervy sprung at him, shooting forward like a coiled snake. Her arms and legs moved as a blur, leaving streaks of light as they shot forward, each blow slamming into him with the force of a freight train. Dervy was an artist, her body shifted to accommodate her needs rather than the other way around, moves blended together like a tapestry of whipping cloth and flashing skin.

Amazingly, Alex found himself blocking many of the strikes, arms and legs moving to intercept or deflect each blow. He just let his body react--letting unknown instincts flare to life under the incessant onslaught of the tiny woman. Repeatedly, he felt bones crack and heal as she struck and he blocked, hitting him so hard he could feel it throughout his being. Every now and then she would get through his defenses, launching a surprise shot to the body or shoulder, but for the most part he stopped her, halting each move in its tracks.

Dervy looked to slow the longer she attacked, each movement coming toward him as if in slow motion, yet he reacted just as quickly. It suddenly occurred to him as he leaned away from another kick toward his face that he was moving faster than her, though it was everything he could do to keep her from crushing him into a pulp. If Alex had any training, he might actually have a chance against her.

Suddenly, Dervy's face wrinkling in concentration and he was no longer moving faster than her. She was everywhere and he quickly collapsed under the force of her assault, bones snapping as she struck at him. A moment later, the heel of her foot caught him in the side of the face, crushing his jaw and slamming him into the ground.

Weekly, Alex crawled to all fours, only to be placed flat on the ground by another blow to the center of his back. Pain flared throughout his body, a dislocated knee and shattered forearm screamed at him.

"Okay!" Alex yelled as his jaw set and the bones shifted back into place.

He spat blood and dirt from a mouth filled with shattered teeth. Alex turned an eye, half blind from dirt and swelling, toward her. She knelt above him, head cocked to the side, watching him. Considering.

Something about the way she was looking at him, thoughtful, inspective, would have made the small hairs on his neck stand on end. If he still had any.

"What are you doing?" Alex asked hesitantly, spitting a little more dirt from his mouth as he spoke.

The sharp click of teeth snapping against each other offset the regrowth of nerve endings. He tried not to pass out.

Dervy stood and held out a hand to him. He eyed it, leaning on one elbow and rubbing his still sore jaw. Dervy looked at him, still unflinching, but without the underlying rage that had been there a few moments earlier. Grimacing in pain, Alex felt his knee move back into place and his forearm begin to knit.

Dervy took his hand and pulled him to his feet.

Alex clenched his teeth and immediately regretted it--bright forks of pain shot through the left side of his mouth as he bit down on half developed chunks of tooth--causing him to waver slightly as spots danced in front of his eyes.

"Focus on the pain," Dervy said quietly as she reached out toward his face.

He flinched, but didn't step away as her fingers just barely touched his cheek, calloused fingers tickling the fresh stubble from the past day.

"Why are your hands so rough?" Alex asked between flinches as she pressed slightly on his wounded jaw line.

"Shh," Dervy whispered with a rare grin. "Focus on the pinpricks of pain as I push on them and will it away."

Again she pushed, sending bolts of pain through his body amidst waves of nausea. "Won't this...just fix itself?" He asked, barely keeping down the generous helping of roots and other unknown vegetables from earlier.

Dervy nodded, but kept pressing, her earlier haste apparently forgotten. "It will, but I believe you can do it faster. Immediate."

She pushed again, this time hard enough that his cheek pushed into his mouth and her thumb found a broken tooth. Alex grunted and his knees buckled from the pain, putting him back to the dirt. Dervy held his head in her hands as he dropped, keeping him upright with a firm grip, though it still felt gentle.

When she was not pushing down on his nerve-endings anyway.

"Make it go away, Alex," Dervy whispered as she prodded yet another tooth.

Why was she always hurting him?

Breathing heavily, Alex closed his eyes and willed away the pain. For a moment it felt as if something was happening, a lessening of pressure and reduction of pain.

Another prod sent a wave of nausea and he vomited.

He leaned forward, no longer held upright by Dervy, and spit. Awkwardly, he wiped at his nose, feeling the long tendrils of snot and stomach acid smear across his face.

"God..."

Next to him Dervy grunted. "We'll try again some other time."

Alex scowled up at her and spit one more time.

"Come on," she said and started moving toward the house once again. "That's enough of a break."

"You're a bitch," Alex grumbled as he got to his feet.

Ahead of him he heard that tinkling noise from earlier.

Alex spat, but followed anyway, kicking a tuft of turned soil out of his way. The situation was ridiculous.

He watched Dervy move ahead of him, lithely moving across the awkward terrain. The moon lit her up, making her appear as a beacon in the night. She was definitely short now that Alex watched her move without fear of additional pain. She could probably be classified in the 'tiny' category, being just barely five foot tall, if that. The way Dervy usually moved made her seem larger and significantly more dangerous than a woman her size typically was.

Well, she was more dangerous than a normal woman. Alex snorted a little at the thought.

Dervy cast a glare back at him and Alex refocused his thoughts. He hadn't realized how close they had gotten to the house or the fact that Dervy had simply stopped making noise entirely. She made a quick motion, gesturing toward the barn before breaking into a stealthy trot. Dervy rounded the corner of the house and disappeared into the shadows, leaving Alex alone in the back yard of some stranger's home.

Alex glanced around in confusion. Was he supposed to go find the car or something? Maybe he should wait next to the barn?

A second floor window flared to life with artificial light, casting a long, stretched parallelogram of light out onto the yard and Alex. His heart jumped into his throat and Alex ducked to the side, making his way quickly toward the barn. He moved as quietly as he could across the gravel driveway, cursing himself as he scuffed stones.

As Alex reached the barn, he looked back and saw the light turn off, darkness covering the back yard once again. Somewhere in the distance a dog howled. A moment later, frenzied yipping came from the back yard as a pack descended on some unfortunate animal.

So, those were wolves. Alex chided himself, pressing up against the barn, desperately trying to make himself invisible. He really needed to get out more if he thought a wolf sounded like a dog.

A hand touched his shoulder.

Alex screamed, arms flailing around him defensively as he turned toward the hand.

Dervy stood there, a pair of keys dangling from her fingers, an amused look on her face. Alex wilted.

She flipped the keys into her palm. "Do you know how to ride a motorcycle?"

"No."

Dervy grinned as she moved toward the barn door. "Guess you get to ride bitch then."

9
Heathshome, NY
2:29 PM August 22, 2010

The woman across from Alex smiled glowingly as she typed out his answer, pretending to be completely oblivious to his haggard appearance and the fine layer of stubble that covered most of his head. He reached up and scratched at the rough patch above his left eye where a brown eyebrow should be.

It itched like hell.

"All right Mr. Mamsin," the woman--her name was Anne--said happily, "just a couple more questions and we'll get your rooms in order, mm-kay?"

Alex raised an eyebrow despite the complete lack of hair. "Where did they get you?"

Anne's face fell, but she maintained her sweet smile. "Excuse me? I'm not sure what you mean."

With a groan, Alex fished a dead bug out of the back of his throat with his tongue. How did that even get stuck back there?

Anne grimaced and covered her mouth.

Alex shook his head. "I'm sorry. You're just not like any of the others I've met."

"Oh?" She asked, quickly regaining her overwhelmingly pleasant demeanor.

He smiled at her weakly, fighting off the sudden exhaustion that swept over him. "You're actually nice. I was just starting to assume... "

"Oh, they can't have all been that bad," Anne laughed, tossing her dark blonde hair over her shoulder. "Most of the Gatherers are really nice folks. Let's just take a look here...

"Derval?" Anne arched her brows in concern and reached out to cover his hand supportively. "Oh, I'm sorry, dear. She's really a very nice woman once you get to know her, but she tends to be extremely... "

"Violent?" Alex offered.

Anne nodded, maintaining a small smile of reassurance. "Yes, that."

There was a long moment where Anne simply patted his hand, smiling calmly in what Alex was sure was supposed to be a reassuring time. Her fingers were rubbing the back of his hand in a way that assumed just a little too much familiarity.

"If you need anything," Anne said, still smiling. "You just let me know. Anything at all. I'm glad to help folks get settled in."

Alex nodded, smiling wanly. "I'll keep that in mind, but I'm pretty bushed so... "

"Okay," Anne said as she gave his hand one last squeeze. "Let's get this done so you can go take a hot shower in your new quarters."

"About that," Alex asked. "Do I have to stay here? Live here?"

Anne laughed. "No, no, no. You don't have to stay here, but every Sirgili gets an apartment of sorts at Heathshome."

Alex cocked his head. "What's a 'Sirgili'?"

"No one told you... ?" Anne asked, but quickly shook her head. "Of course she didn't.

"We're all strigois--"

"I've heard that one before," Alex interrupted remembering his discussion with Weynie.

Anne nodded and her voice took on a tone Alex was used to hearing from bored professors in college. "Good, good. This whole organization here is called the Arktois. It's the longest running stable government in history--dating back to 634 AD when Laonike called the first Ankousti into being. The Ankousti is a council of elders that manages the Arktois."

"All right... "

"Well," Anne smiled. "A Sirgil, or Sirgili when you're talking about more than one of us, is a strigoi who is a member of the Arktois.

"Simple, right?"

Alex smiled and nodded. "I take it to mean that not all strigoi are, what was it again?"

"Sirgili. And no, not all are, though there is something of a, uh, mandatory enrollment period," Anne said awkwardly, twirling her hair as she did so.

"Okay... " Alex conceded, unwilling to ask the obvious question. "So with all of these folks living forever, you don't run out of room?"

"Nope," Anne smiled, setting her elbows on the table. "Since there are only thirteen lucky folks Taken a year and right about ten to fifteen who enter the Return, it equals out very nicely."

"How many, uh, strigoi are there then?" Alex asked.

"A little over four thousand," Anne stated, smiling. "And every one of them has a set of rooms if they are registered with the Arktois."

"All right," Alex said quietly. "You said you needed some more info or something?"

Anne slapped the table and turned back to the flat screen monitor, placing her fingers on the keyboard expertly.

"Let's see," she scanned the screen, scrolling with the mouse as she did so. "Okay, when is your best guess as to when you were Taken?"

Alex scratched his head. "Umm, that's when I became a strigoi, right?"

Anne nodded.

"Okay, well I jumped off the bridge in March and didn't get hurt, so it would have to be before that," he paused as she tapped quickly on the keyboard. "Can I ask you a question?"

She did not take her eyes off the screen. "Absolutely, Alex."

Alex bit his lip. "Would this... thing cause medications to stop working?"

Anne nodded. "Definitely. Your body no longer needs antibiotics or anything else to maintain your natural state of mind."

Alex's shoulders slumped. "Oh."

Anne stopped typing. "You said, 'jumped off the bridge'?"

Alex nodded. "Yeah. The Golden Gate."

"Oh."

Her fingers tapped away--a flurry of phalanges--across the keyboard. "Do you often get depressed and have suicidal thoughts?"

"Umm..."

Anne smiled and turned toward him. She reached out and grabbed his hand again. "Listen, Alex. No one here is perfect. We all have flaws and we need to work together to make the best of this gift we've been given. For some of us," she rubbed his hand and turned back to the monitor, "that means getting counseling."

"Then yes," Alex said quietly, glancing around the empty room quickly. "I get these thoughts often."

Anne maintained her smile as she typed something out and clicked a few items. "Will you be okay for tonight, Alex?"

He nodded. "Yeah, I should be fine."

"Okay," she said quickly. "We'll get you set up for your entry interview in the morning, then. They'll ask you a couple questions and get you in touch with an appropriate counselor, mm-kay?"

"All right," Alex agreed, scratching at his chest.

Did he even have hair on his chest? He didn't remember having any hair on his chest.

"Your room is 1246. That's just past the Pasa Tiempo--our common area," Anne said with a smile as she slid a keycard and thumb print scanner across the table to him. "Head to the right on your way out of the office and follow the signs. You'll take the hallway on the far right once you get there. The door will be on the left."

"You need my thumb print?" Alex asked as he pressed into the scanner and the green bar crept along the screen.

Anne nodded and pulled back the scanner. "Absolutely. Since we don't have to take into account new scars and such, we can be very exact about our images."

Alex slid the key card into his pocket. "Yeah, but the inherent insecurity of that type of biometric scanning makes it more of a stop gap than anything else."

"I mean, if I had some of my gear from my apartment I could clone this card," Alex held it up, "lift a fingerprint from a glass using Silly Putty and have full access to my room."

Anne shook her head ruefully. "I think you'll probably be working with Jalal."

"Who is Jalal?" Alex asked, pocketing the card.

"Jalal Swailes. He's our Chief of Digital Security and is in desperate need of Sirgil help according to his Gatherer memo," Anne said quickly.

"We'll set you up an interview with him for next week, mm-kay?"

Alex stood, suddenly feeling all of the dirt and grit embedded in his skin. "All righty. Do you need anything else?"

Anne smiled. "Yes. We need your former occupation, family history, place of birth and as much background information as you can provide us."

With a sigh, Alex plopped back into the chair.

So much for a shower anytime soon.

*   *   *

"The Return will have claimed him by now despite--" William Searle held up a hand as Dervy tried to interrupt, "Despite any attempts to the contrary. And if it somehow has not, it will shortly. No one can escape the inevitability of this. Not even the Primator."

Dervy looked around the council chamber. Each member was nodding assent to William's words. He sat in the center of the group, the place of honor where the Primator started and ended each session.

It had taken her four hours to get a session called to order, a fact which had raised her ire to new heights. Even not-so-subtle reminders to William had resulted in nothing, no speed, and no respect for the urgency of the situation. No respect for her.

As Dervy stood there, feeling the heat in her face, watching the children on the raised dais look down at her condescendingly, she felt everything fade away. Someone began speaking to her, a voice muted and unimportant, as she realized that there was such a difference between them--a gulf, a void that could not be mended.

"--and I would propose--"

It was time.

"Quiet," Dervy ordered, placing her arms beneath her breasts and looking up at the five shocked faces of this emergency council. "You underestimate Caoimhín O'Ceallaigh as you have since the beginning when I brought him here before the council."

Aaidan Smith, a three hundred year old Australian man sitting to William's right, scoffed. "You weren't even born when he--"

William Searle's smug smile faltered as she continued.

"And I have repeatedly asked for more supervision levied on his actions during the past century," Dervy stated, loud enough that she could drown them all out.

She let her arms drop and she felt her energy suddenly drain. "Now..."

Dervy paused, letting the weight of her words sink into the room and their minds.

"Now what?" Lerato Arraya asked quietly.

Reverently.

There had always been rumors about her. There were certain paintings in the hallways that Dervy resembled just a little too much...

"Now he is your problem. I hereby extricate myself from the order and forfeit any and all rights and privileges beyond basic cultural immersion benefits."

With that, Dervy turned on her heel and left, ignoring the wasted shouts from the council members and leaving her cares behind. She exited the conference chambers and let the doors shut behind her. Emotion filled her, but she pushed it away and walked down the hall, taking a branching hallway toward the main security checkpoint and the freight elevator--the quickest way to the surface.

She passed dozens of strigoi in the hallways and more than a few humans working on contract for one reason or another. Dervy struggled to keep her anger under control at that. It was no longer her problem--she was no longer a Sirgil. She was just another strigoi.

The time had come for Dervy to take leave once again, leaving the Arktois to tend to its own devices until all had passed. She only needed one member of the council who was there today to be alive when she came back so she could re-establish herself. That was the foundation of her life. No one could know she had what most of them desired. True immortality.

Dervy stepped onto the elevator--a thick, steel contraption installed recently to allow mass transfer of foodstuffs and larger items that Sirgili may require or want. She nodded to the operator, a young-looking man whom she had Gathered a little over two hundred years earlier from a slaver in Africa. Sipho nodded back and enabled the engine.

He was a good man.

The device rose quickly, leaving Heathshome behind once again. Arktois had evolved beyond her and she couldn't keep trying to force it into her own designs.

She was Derval now--as she had been for centuries--though for just a moment another name flitted to the surface, teasing her with its power and purpose.

Dervy shook it off and grimaced.

It was time for a new name. 'Derval' was her true name. She shouldn't have brought it back. It was almost too painful to part with it, but it would soon refer to someone who no longer existed. Again.

At least it was easier than leaving behind Laonike.

She'd really liked that name.

* * *

Alex stepped into the Pasa Tiempo and grunted. He fingered the cloth collar around his neck--which was only furthering the incessant itch present in the back of his neck--and shook his head.

"This is bullshit," he mumbled to himself as he stepped into the common area.

It looked like a Las Vegas casino rip-off with the fake sky and gurgling fountain in the center of the room. He tried to avoid everyone else as he moved along the wall toward the hallway Anne had mentioned, but it was a practice in futility. Despite there being about one hundred people there, the room was packed, various collections of folks seated around either the pools of water or sitting on the benches. He was sure it was just his imagination, but it seemed as if everyone turned to look at him as he passed by.

"Excuse me," Alex said quietly as he passed close by a man in what he could only describe as a suit, even though it didn't look like anything he'd ever seen.

The man turned, face annoyed. He was of average height, though a little taller than Alex, with long, thin hair, deep-set eyes and curling mustaches all of which seemed to match the awkward suit he was wearing, with its lace cuffs and large lapels. His eyes flicked toward Alex's neck and his entire demeanor changed. He nodded, suddenly gracious, and stepped to the side.

Alex nodded, brow furrowed in confusion. "Thanks."

"Not a problem, Taken," the man said with his own nod. "Perhaps another other day we can discuss proper decorum?"

"Sure," Alex agreed cautiously, continuing onward quickly.

The man frowned at the dismissal. "Excellent. Now if you'll excuse me..."

But Alex was already gone, moving as quickly as he could. The pressure on the back of his neck from having so many of these... things nearby was driving him crazy. He just wanted to go to where he was supposed to live and get into the promised shower without any additional distract--

"Alex? Alex!"

A moment later, Alex was off the ground, feet dangling a few inches above the grass.

"Weynie?"

She dropped him heavily and he stumbled. "Sorry, but I was so worried!"

Alex smiled weakly at her. "Well, I made it?"

Weynie leaned in and hugged him again, this time pressing herself against him instead of picking him off the ground. The distinct smell of cloves and cinnamon filled his nostrils and he became overly aware of the softness of her body against his own.

Chuckling awkwardly, Alex pulled away.

Maybe he should get ahold of Anne?

"So how did you get here? Is that other guy with you?" Alex asked quickly, scrambling for something to distract her with.

He immediately wished he hadn't asked.

Weynie's face fell and her voice was filled with concern. "Esok has... passed, I'm afraid, and we can't seem to locate Simon at all."

The image of Simon sticking a needle in Dervy's neck flashed in his mind. "Simon is working with those people who took Dervy and me, I think."

"What?" Weynie demanded, fists going to her hips.

"Yeah," Alex said, scratching at the incessant itching at the back of his neck. "We were kidnapped, taken to this facility where they took some of my blood--"

"Are you all right?" Weynie asked, placing a dark hand on his arm.

Alex nodded. "Yeah, I'm fine--"

"Okay, good," Weynie interrupted again. "I need to go find Dervy and figure out what's going on. You have rooms assigned, right?"

Alex nodded.

"Good, go there, relax, but don't go far. I'll need to ask you some questions."

Oh good... more questions. He nodded anyway.

Weynie turned and ran out of the Pasa Tiempo, hips moving back and forth in a pendular rhythm...

"What is wrong with me?" Alex chastised himself out loud.

"You talk to yourself? That's a new one." A young Asian woman offered from a bench to his right.

Alex smiled at her depreciatingly and moved on, ignoring the laughter that followed him out of the common area.

Why did he feel like he was suddenly back in high school?

Alex entered the hallway, eyes adjusting to the darkened environment quickly. Track lighting wove its way on either side of the hallway, just at the edge of an arched ceiling.

"Twelve forty-six, twelve forty-six," Alex mumbled as he walked on.

The door to his right said 1225, so he continued on, passing by people in such disparate clothing that he was beginning to wonder if he was stuck in a time warp. Did they all dress like time had stood still or was it just something that made them more comfortable while they were at home, like a pair of fleece pajamas on a wintry night?

Alex was still considering the thought when he made it to room 1246. Right above the doorknob was a card slider as well as a thumb print scanner. He shook his head in annoyance and placed his thumb on the scanner. A positive sounding tone chimed, so he swiped the card Anne had given him and he heard the sound of a bolt sliding away.

"Give me a normal key any day," Alex muttered as he entered the room.

"I hear that."

Alex fell back out into the hallway as the door opened. A mid-height black man stood just on the other side of the doorway holding a clipboard and looking incredibly embarrassed.

"What the hell are you doing?" Alex yelled, though it came out as more of a scream than anything.

"I am so sorry," the man said earnestly as he extended a hand to Alex. "I was just finishing up here, I did not mean to scare you."

The man's voice was touched with a slight musical quality--it seemed to roll off his tongue naturally, smoothly. Alex accepted the other man's hand and got to his feet, albeit unsteadily.

"There you are," the man said confidently as Alex got to his feet.

"Thanks," Alex said, extending a hand. "Alex."

The man accepted it, gripping hands firmly. "Jalal."

Alex raised an eyebrow. "Jalal Swailes?"

Jalal nodded. "That would be me. Chief of Digital Security."

"So you were... " Alex indicated the door and Jalal nodded.

"Reprogramming the lock, yes," Jalal said with a frown. "Archaic little monsters. Each one has a hardcoded value that needs changing every time a room is switched."

"I hate biometrics," Alex said with a grunt. "They're never quite good enough for real security."

Jalal eyed Alex for a moment.

"What?" Alex asked, beginning to feel uncomfortable.

"I am just wondering if you would like to try some of the new locks," Jalal asked with the first smile Alex had seen thus far.

Alex hesitated, though. "What type of lock is it?"

"Oh, very similar to this," Jalal said quickly, pulling the door shut and pushing Alex out into the hallway so he could show him the thumbprint scanner and card slider. "But it uses a three part authentication system: voice, DNA, and thumbprint."

Alex snorted. "DNA testing?"

Jalal nodded.

"What, you prick me in the thumb scanner?" Alex asked, pointing at the smooth piece of plastic above the doorknob.

"Exactly," Jalal said. "And we have a specialized voice scanner for comparisons."

Alex frowned, suddenly interested. "What about contamination of the sample? Like if I had a greasy hamburger for lunch and tried to get in the room? Wouldn't it mess up the blood sample?"

Jalal nodded, but kept smiling. "That is what I thought, but the manufacturer claims that it will not. It is for that reason that I need a solid bed of technically proficient users to test this out."

Alex found himself nodding as he considered various issues with the layout and tried to determine workarounds to the system. Abruptly, he shook his head.

"Listen, I would love to help with this, but not today," Alex sighed. "I've had kind of a horrible couple days, so... "

"Oh, sure, sure," Jalal said and stepped out of the way. "I will just install the new scanner at the end of the week after we get the voice sample. You left a DNA sample with front, right?"

Alex nodded. "That all sounds good," Alex added with a wan smile. "Nice meeting you Jalal."

"And you," Jalal said with a nod before turning and moving quickly down the hallway.

Alex watched after him for a moment before stepping into the room and pulling the door shut behind him.

The door opened up into what he figured to be the living room and despite the sparse furnishings it was huge. It stretched nearly twenty feet across and forty feet wide, though for some reason only a single lamp lit the room at the moment. On the far side of the room was a darkened fireplace. Layered brick surrounded it in a traditional pattern that reminded him of Mary's parents' home in Colorado. The floor was hardwood, somewhat gray in the low light, but appeared to be cherry in finish with a central throw rug in front of a long leather couch.

Off to his right was the kitchen of his dreams. It was filled with stainless steel appliances and dark granite countertops. He frowned a little when he noticed the stove was electric, but he wasn't going to look a gift horse in the mouth. Especially not today. To his left, back in the corner of the living room was a door that he hoped went to an amazing bedroom and bathroom.

Moving slowly, he went into the kitchen and opened the cupboards. They were stocked with glasses, plates, and even serving dishes. Alex grabbed a glass and moved over to the sink and turned on the cold water. Clear liquid shot out immediately with that refreshing, 'good plumbing' sound that he hadn't heard since selling his house in Oakland.

A small smile crept across his face as he filled the glass. The place was incredibly homey; comfortable even. Taking a sip of water, he made his way into the living room and glanced around.

There was no television. That would need to be remedied.

"Maybe pick up a game system or three..." Alex mumbled as he moved toward the bedroom.

He let his hand run over a side table with a potted tulip standing atop it. It came off with just a trace of dust and he moved on, opening the door to the back rooms.

Alex smiled at the huge, four posted bed as he stepped in. He flicked on the light switch, triggering the recessed lighting and suffusing the room in a warm, comforting glow. It smelled faintly of vanilla, though the air was a little stale.

To his immediate left was the bathroom. Taking another sip of water, he entered and turned the lights on in there. The bulbs lit slowly, as if designed to allow your eyes to adjust to their brightness.

As with the rest of the layout, this was expertly designed. The floor had slate tiles that ran the length and merged up into a dark, sandstone textured wall and ceiling. There were two brass sinks set into what appeared to be granite countertops. Two large, oval mirrors with faux gold frames were attached to the wall.

Alex stepped up to one and cringed.

"Yikes."

He looked like hell. He felt a little satisfaction that his lifelong aversion to shaving his head was well founded. His bare head looked like a misshapen, brown tennis ball. His clothes were filthy as well, given that he hadn't yet changed out of the burlap rags given to him by Nathan the previous day. He set the glass down and stripped them off, throwing them underneath the sink. The neck strap followed, but he stopped short of tossing it in with the other items. Instead he laid it on the cool counter.

Once out of the clothes and despite the complete lack of hair anywhere on his body, Alex couldn't find much else that indicated the type of hell he'd been through.

"All I need is a shower and some rest," he said to himself and smiled.

Alex pushed back the shower curtains and felt a huge grin break across his face. It was a three sixty shower, with heads along the sides and above him. He'd always wanted one of these. He reached in and turned on the water, noticing with pleasure that it was steaming as it came out of the showerheads.

"Wonderful," Alex mumbled as he stepped into the streams.

10
Somewhere, PA
11:56 AM August 25, 2010

Simon leaned against the wall, eyes locked on the bench across the room. The constant beeping echoed shallowly throughout the room, adding a tinny dissonance to the harsh rasping breaths that filled the air. All around him humans bustled, orderly, but only just so as they worked to keep Kevin breathing those gasping breaths.

As far as he knew, no strigoi had ever deigned to extend their life with these medical tools. There had never been a reason before. Why extend what you had already exceeded? Why cheat God more than you already had?

Nathan stood to his right, eyes locked on Kevin's haggard face, absentmindedly chewing on a thumbnail. They had barely made it back to the main facility when the Return had swung full force on Kevin, dropping him to the ground with barely a noise. As much as he hated to admit it, only the expertise of the human doctors and nurses had stabilized the frail man. How they had kept Kevin going for so long was beyond him.

The longer they stood there, waiting, the more Simon found himself considering, planning. Should they truly be trying to stop the Return? What would happen if they did? How would the world change? More importantly, what would happen if this worked on humans?

That last question was what bothered him the most. The idea of every human suddenly gaining the abilities that made a strigoi superior. How did a world full of Alpha Dogs survive? Someone had to be on the bottom and he'd rather it not be him.

There was another question nagging at him as well, eating away at him like a cancer. Simon narrowed his eyes at the emaciated body and could not help but wonder if they should simply let Kevin die.

An older human stepped into the room, letting a pair of double doors swing shut behind him. Simon recognized him, though he couldn't remember the man's name. He'd replaced Doctor Williamson as head researcher after the other man's death in January; that much Simon remembered. However, things had slowed since then with this new man claiming that Doctor Williamson hadn't been keeping detailed notes of his experiments.

But now he was here and it looked like he was carrying a small vial, hand-scrawled label hastily applied.

The doctor scanned the room, eyes settling on Nathan, and he approached quickly.

"Sir," he began, voice muffled behind the facemask, but obviously strained. "I believe this sample will achieve our results, but without further testing--"

"Do it," Nathan said without looking away from Kevin.

"I... " the man began, but apparently thought better of it.

Instead, he turned away and approached the bed where Kevin was aging visibly. Just in the past hour, his cheeks had sunken into his face, revealing a grisly visage that looked more a skull than the slightly plump face of the man Simon used to know.

"Syringe," the doctor stated and one of the others unwrapped and handed one to him. He quickly filled the syringe with fluid from the vial.

The room was suddenly silent, only the steady digital beat of Kevin's heart and the rasp of his halting breaths breaking the stillness. Simon could see the doctor's hands shaking ever so slightly as he inserted the needle into Kevin's emaciated forearm. In a single smooth motion, he emptied the fluid into a purple vein.

A moment later, a solid tone filled the room and Kevin let

out a rattling breath.

Beeeeeeeeeeeep...

Nathan stood straight, fists balling at his sides as the doctor cursed and the room began to swarm with humans operating their various pieces of equipment.

"What's going on?" Nathan demanded, but was ignored.

The solid tone continued, pealing high and long.

Simon remained against the wall, but he couldn't tear his eyes away from the scene. Doctors crowded around Kevin's body and others moved hurriedly, just a hair away from panic as they tried to resuscitate him. Minutes crawled by as Nathan and Simon stood numbly, humans spouting gibberish, racing around them.

BEEP-beep. BEEP-beep.

A smile crept across Simon's face.

"Jesus Christ," a nurse said suddenly, stumbling backwards and away from the table.

He was too slow. A hand shot out--still thin, but thickening rapidly as muscle and tendon re-grew and restored--and grasped the nurse by the throat. The humans scattered as the man was pulled into the bed screaming, legs flailing for just a moment before Kevin snapped his neck and ripped open his throat.

Simon felt those old cravings fill him at the sight and sounds of Kevin's appetite. Blood flowed everywhere--covering the smooth white linens that rippled with developing muscle and de-calcifying joints--as he devoured the man. Beside him, Nathan licked his lips, blinking rapidly as he did so. A moment later, the body fell to the floor, head lolling weakly, face gone. Only a bloody skull, fleshy remnants still twitching in death, remained.

Kevin sat up, cradling his head with his thick hands. The beard was still a mass of gray, but it would grow back out to the flaming red he was known for.

Cautiously, Simon walked forward, bending to the side slightly so he could get a better look at the renewed man before him. Kevin had always been a thickly built man--up until the last week or so anyway--and from what Simon could tell, that had come back in force. He could see the corded muscle in the man's chest and arms, defined lines showing through skin covered in a thick layer of reddish-gray hair, though that was probably a side effect of giving in to the Hunger.

If it wasn't a side effect...

Well, that would be interesting to say the least.

"Kevin?" Simon asked, stopping short, the memory of their last encounter fresh in his mind. "How're you feeling?"

Kevin looked up, blinking quickly. "I feel... "

He paused, glancing at his arms and flexing. A smile crept across his face as he locked eyes with Simon.

"...Great."

PART II

11
Laramie, WY
4:54 PM January 15, 2011

     Zeke Dunfee sat in the corner of the coffee bar just as he had every morning for the past four months. The familiar scent of roasted beans was comforting--the dark aromas bringing him solace amidst an otherwise unsteady mind. The odors blended so perfectly with the lacquered woodwork of the establishment. Everything was quite rustic, though not close enough to be considered authentic by far. It certainly didn't remind him of the cabin he'd grown to adulthood in, though the weather outside piqued certain memories of Illinois during the winter.
     Zeke sighed and took another sip of his bitter liquid. The warm mixture went smoothly down his throat, leaving behind that trace of sweet and tart from the dark chocolate. A slow, sad smile spread across his face as he set the drink back down, watching the frothy head swirl.
     The tables were interesting, or at least they had been when Zeke first arrived in Laramie and found the Coal Creek Coffee Shop. Across the decorated surface were scrawled quotes, some familiar, some obscure. This table in particular had a series of statutes

outlawing the brewing of coffee and the demonization of coffee houses as places of lechery and sin.

Scattered amidst such phrases as 'dens of iniquity' were quotes attributed to various famous historical figures, though Zeke always gravitated toward the one near the center of the table.

Apparently spoken by Abraham Lincoln, it read:

"If this is coffee, please bring me some tea; if this is tea, please bring me some coffee."

It always made him smile.

The straightforward, yet polite declaration reminded him of the rough looking man with a fondness that surprised him. It had been a long time since the night they fought and then diced the rest of the night away. It happened the day before Zeke had been Taken. Maybe that was why he counted it amongst his fondest memories. It was easy to remember the event since it had left him with a three-inch long scar along the outside of his right eye. Zeke sighed and touched the scar, feeling the raised flesh prominent against his face.

Time moved so slowly now.

Zeke took another sip of his coffee and looked around the room, taking in the small group of college students studying at a table near him, a wizened older man with the look of a professor tapping spasmodically on a laptop in the corner and the barista. She was a young woman with short black hair and a ready smile named Nikki. She caught him glancing at her and he pointed quickly to his glass, hastily indicating a refill. With a nod, she turned and began whipping some more milk for his drink.

He shook his head in annoyance, shoulders slumping wearily. Even after all his years women still made him uncomfortable about his features. Sure, Zeke was tall, but that was about it. His balding pate and the beginnings of a bulge around the middle were persistent. Zeke would look exactly the same as the day he was Taken no matter what he did to try and improve his looks.

Not that he could even try to fix some of it. Zeke's nose was crooked, having been broken in a fight during his youth and he had some deep pockmarks across his entire body, though especially prevalent on his face and hands, from a battle with smallpox as a child.

There was also that wonderful scar running next to his eye,

of course. During his early years he'd kept long mustaches and sideburns--as was the style at the time--but over the past hundred years or so, he'd gone away from facial hair completely, instead going fresh shaven when possible.

The bottom line was that Zeke Dunfee was not a pretty man. Not even handsome by any persons' measure. Not that it mattered--he was just waiting for the Return at this point.

Or for Dervy to catch up with him.

Zeke didn't pretend that a berserker like her would allow him to get away with what he'd done to her in San Francisco. It was just a matter of time before she came and killed him.

The thought made him shudder. Slowly, hands shaking, Zeke lifted the mug to his lips and drank deeply, but the warm coffee did nothing to help.

There weren't that many ways to kill a strigoi beyond incineration. God knows, Zeke didn't have any interest in dying that way. Of course, he didn't want to be locked away in a safe and tossed into the Mariana Trench either. That wouldn't kill him, but it certainly wasn't any better.

Zeke took another slow sip from his quickly draining cup and stared off at a coffee bean sack stapled to the wall. However it happened, it would not be pleasant.

For what seemed like the thousandth time, Zeke chastised himself for listening to Kevin, for agreeing to try and kidnap the Taken. Kevin was now long dead and the only thing Zeke had managed to do was seal his own fate. How Zeke had been taken in by Kevin's claims of real, unlimited immortality dumbfounded him.

Zeke was usually so cautious, so meticulous about the way he lived his life. The very idea that he would give up this life--as meaningless as it was--for something as unrealistic and impossible as living forever astounded him.

What did he have to live for anyway? The Arktois would never let him fulfill his dream. Hell, even if the human nations would take strigoi council now, they could just as easily wipe them out. After they split the atom, everything changed. With a single flick of the wrist, the entire strigoi nation could be wiped out.

Why on Earth would Zeke want to help them now? That just put everyone else in danger.

Sighing, Zeke finished his drink just as Nikki approached his table, carefully carrying a large ceramic coffee mug filled to the brim. Gingerly, she set it down on the table, smiling at him as she did so.

"Here you are: another quad shot, large mocha," she said.

He smiled back, close-lipped so he wouldn't show his crooked, yellowed teeth, and wrapped his hands around the warm mug.

"Many thanks, ma'am," he mumbled.

Still smiling, Nikki nodded, picked up the empty mug and made her way back behind the bar.

There really wasn't much to do except wait for someone to show up, whether it was Dervy or someone else from the Arktois. It was well within their rights to elevate his punishment. God knew he deserved it.

With his rank in shambles there were only a select few punishments left, most involving decades in a small cell. In the latter case, the least Zeke could do in the meantime was enjoy his coffee, savoring the tastes so that he could have something to look forward to when he got out. And if Dervy found him... well, at least he'd gotten his caffeine fix.

The door opened, jingling the quaint reindeer bells wrapped around the handle and bringing in a burst of snow flurries as well as a short man wearing a thick winter jacket, but no hood. Hurriedly, he pushed the door shut, forcing it closed against the strong wind that followed him. With a quick shake, he cleared his jacket of stray snow, creating a small pile of fluff in the doorway.

Zeke went to take a sip of his new coffee and froze as the man locked eyes on him and grinned. Instead of rising panic--as Zeke knew he should be feeling--a wave of calm came over him and for the first time in what seemed like an eternity, he was relieved. The man walked toward him purposefully, unzipping his coat as he came.

It was the same man who had been with Dervy that night. The one who went into the apartment before her. Though his hair was longer, he was clean-shaven, and his cheeks were piping red from the cold, Wyoming winter air, it was him. Zeke Dunfee never forgot a face and that, if nothing else, was part of the problem. In fact, the longer he looked at the other man, the more familiar he seemed, as if he knew him from somewhere other than a failed kidnapping.

Names on the other hand...

"Ezekiel Dunfee?" The man asked, removing his gloves as he approached.

Zeke started at the name. No one called him Ezekiel.

Well, almost no one.

Trying to cover the brief flash of surprise and failing, Zeke motioned for him to take a seat.

"Yeah, I'm Zeke Dunfee," he mumbled, taking a long sip of his drink.

It scalded the roof of him mouth as he drank, but he savored it nonetheless. Who knew when he might get another.

"You go by Zeke? All right," the man glanced around the room, one eyebrow raised as he critiqued that shop. "I'm not sure if you remember me--"

"Oh, I do," Zeke said, locking eyes on the man. "You were with Dervy back in San Francisco."

"Yeah," the other man laughed. "Well, things have changed a bit since that time."

"Oh?" Zeke said with feigned disinterest. "Before you go on, how about a name?"

"Simon," he said with that same grin. "Simon Vanderwell."

Zeke wrinkled his forehead in thought. The name sounded incredibly familiar, but he just couldn't place it. Instead, it floundered in his mind, trying to latch itself to a memory and failed.

"I wish I could say it's nice to meet you," Zeke grumbled, eyeing Simon out of the corner of his eye. Where had he seen this man before?

It was infuriating!

"Well," Simon said as he shrugged off his coat. "Kevin sends his regards."

"Bullshit," Zeke spat before he could stop himself. He immediately chastised himself at the smug look on Simon's face.

Simon rapped his knuckles on the tabletop and looked up at the menu, squinting slightly as he did so. "Anything good to drink here?"

Zeke eyed him warily. There was something off about him, something... unsteady.

"Something wrong with your eyes?" Zeke asked quietly, watching Simon's face intently.

Simon's grin widened and he turned back to Zeke. "That is something Kevin really, really wants to talk to you about."

Zeke snorted. "He wants to talk to me about your bad eyes? Sounds like he's gotten a little senile."

What the hell is going on here?

"Oh a little, but he's better now," Simon said, the grin a permanent fixture on his intense face.

A face that was getting a little too intense.

"All right," Zeke said firmly, but quietly as he pushed his coffee to the side. "What the hell do you want, Simon?"

The smile faded from Simon's face as he leaned in. "I want you to come back to New York with me. Kevin wants you as an advisor."

"For what?" Zeke asked, his curiosity once again beginning to outweigh his common sense.

He would not become a patsy for Kevin again.

"That part," Simon said quietly as he leaned back into the chair. "I can't tell you. Not until we're on the plane."

Zeke leaned back as well and stared at the coffee in front of him. The ridiculous secrecy, the way Simon led him on with impossible lines, it just couldn't be true. It would be insane to follow anyone--let alone a man he had seen with Dervy not five months prior--on the amount of information he had just been given.

That said, the entire thing reeked of Kevin. He was a clever, scheming, conniving sort who enjoyed these types of games. Give the target just enough to need to follow and they will come, dancing on the line like a baby trout.

"Zeke," Simon said, grin springing back easily. "Do you want to live forever, or what?"

The coffee cup swirled in his hands. He didn't have anything to live for. No family, no friends. The only good he had ever tried to accomplish had been quashed and forgotten.

No, he was better off staying here and waiting for Dervy to come and liberate his soul from this prison. At least then the running would be over. No more hiding, avoiding.

No more shame.

Simon's eyes drilled into the top of his head.

One question kept running through Zeke's mind. He wasn't sure if Simon was planting it or not, but deep down, he knew it didn't matter.

What if?

What if it was true?

Zeke sighed. With a tip of his head, Zeke drained most of his coffee in a single gulp before getting to his feet.

"Fine," Zeke said as his conscious screamed at him. "Let's go."

*   *   *

Alex closed his eyes, willing away the sounds of the phone ringing next to him. The alarm shone brightly off to the side, a nice little electronic package that reminded him of one he used to have as a child, intense red numbers turned away so they wouldn't keep him awake at night. The phone stopped ringing, its electronic vibrato silenced by the impatience of the man Alex knew had been on the other end.

With a sigh, Alex rolled on his side so he could face the nightstand where the phone sat. A small band of fabric lay next to it, hastily tossed there the night before along with his black button down. He breathed in deeply, smelling the odd mixture of rose petals and sweat Anne had left behind when she snuck out that morning. At the same time that it was refreshing--giving him a connection to another person again after so long, however tenuous--guilt ate away at him. Even during the pleasurable hours of the late night, the nagging doubt of his actions had torn at his psyche, threatening to overwhelm him in the midst of their lovemaking.

Alex snorted.

Not that there had been any love involved. As Anne stated while they groped each other in the hallway outside his door: "We're just two people fulfilling each other's needs."

Anne's had been fulfilled, but somehow the act left him feeling empty and lost for the first time since his arrival at Heathshome. It wasn't that he was surprised, he'd just hoped it wouldn't.

Alex sat up quickly, rubbing his hands across his face and grunting. He felt filthy, greasy, and defiled, but the strength to pull himself into the shower was conspicuously absent. Instead, he fell back to the mattress, sending the mingled scents of the previous night into the air with the impact.

His mind wandered, only gently touching on Mary--her smooth face causing the first hints of a smile crease his face--before pushing her away. He didn't need that memory coming back right now. Especially not right now. Instead, he reflected on his time at Heathshome and found himself just as confused as he had been the day he arrived.

Soon after being dropped off by Dervy, Alex had been put to work with Jalal in managing the digital security of Heathshome. Much like many of his other technology jobs, it seemed like the keys to the castle had been handed to him before he even had the chance to get comfortable with the systems and infrastructure.

Alex had the feeling that it probably took decades for normal Younglings--strigoi less than ten years in the Arktois--and Sirgili to get an idea of the breadth of the Arktois. Those things had been laid bare to him because of his previous experience. Apparently, Alex was the first pre-trained System Administrator ever to be Taken. Even Jalal had had to be trained after the need arose. Apparently, Jalal used to be in charge of physical security. He'd been part of some elite guards someplace in Africa, but he didn't talk about it much.

The work had let Alex fall into a world of repetitive action, just as he had done in San Francisco. It was mind numbing, mentally exhausting work and it left him drained and apathetic by the time he made his way back to his rooms. Regular system maintenance had given him glimpses into an archaic file system structure filled with recently digitized documents spanning millennia and spread across hundreds, maybe even thousands of nations and languages, many of which he didn't even know existed.

He still had no idea what Goust was or, if it was a place, where it was located.

The backend work had certainly been eye opening, though not nearly as much as the Youngling training sessions.

That was where Alex really got to know Anne over the past weeks.

It was also where he regularly felt inadequate.

Being a newly risen Sirgil, Anne helped train the Younglings and Taken a few days a week in a capacity that reminded Alex vaguely of a teaching assistant, but without the usual restrictions.

Obviously.

The classes ranged from history to power control and while Anne taught some of the introductory classes, she didn't teach them all.

History was one of those that she didn't teach. The instructors rotated every few weeks as did the teaching styles, but overall Alex found it all incredibly interesting. The classes reminded him a lot of high school history courses. Each day tended to be information dump sessions, dates and events were dropped off in the order they happened and with little consideration of the 'why' behind each event.

Still, despite that, Alex soaked it all up. He just wished he could spend more time doing that than the power classes.

Thus far, all he seemed to be able to do was heal passively. The other Taken and Younglings all appeared to have full control over their abilities to some extent, but he couldn't even show them the insane strength he'd used to break the straps in the van. That was to say nothing of the other things these... people could do. Some of them could control objects with their minds, play with fire by rolling it around in their hands or, Alex's favorite, control electricity. Some seemed to show some capacity for extreme strength as well, but very few.

Anne called their powers the Six Gifts. Animi Sustuli, telekinesis; Animi Ignis, the power of fire; Animi Fulminis, the power of electricity; Animi Pellegi, the power to read thoughts; Cutus Curatis, the power to heal oneself; and Cutus Viris, the power of strength. Every strigoi was able to use Cutus Curatis to some extent, but there had been strigoi in the past that claimed to control up to four of the powers. Typically, the more powers you had, the weaker you were in each one.

When Alex asked Anne or one of the other teachers why, the best answer they could give was something about a person's chi, which was apparently the aura a strigoi is filled with when Taken. The stronger the aura, the more powerful the strigoi, and that manifested in their strength in the Six Gifts.

Thus far, Alex assumed his chi was pretty tiny since he'd been unable to manifest it at will.

Alex would walk into the powers classroom each day and sit down next to Li Li. She was an elderly woman who wore the same

Taken strap he did and was just as quiet in the classroom. Li Li reminded Alex a little of his mother, though he hadn't told her that. Well, he hadn't told her anything since she didn't speak much English and had her own translator. That was just strange to speak through to someone via proxy.

On the other hand, the instructors were in awe of her control of the Animi Sustuli as well as Animi Ignis. Li Li would make the most beautiful swirling patterns in the air by combining the two abilities. During one class she sprinkled the ceiling with fire and spun them around like dancing fairies.

Everyone had been very impressed. It was certainly one of the most beautiful things Alex had ever seen and he hadn't been able to stop himself from clapping in delight.

On the same day Alex had succeeded in doing absolutely nothing to a candlewick.

There was a sudden knock on his door, jarring Alex out of his reverie though it hadn't been unexpected. In all likelihood it was Jalal, which just made Alex roll back over into his pillow. The problem with being immortal and immune to disease was that there was no easy way to call in a sick day. The hammering grew louder, a muted voice beginning to accompany it.

It was definitely Jalal. And he was very upset.

Grunting, Alex finally pulled himself out of bed, taking a moment to pull on a pair of pants and a shirt from the floor before heading out into the living room. As he approached, Jalal's voice became clearer.

"Alex! Alex Mamsin!"

"What?" Alex yelled at the door, annoyance like a throbbing ache behind his left eye. Each strike against the door aggravated it, making the room turn red.

It was not an unusual transition for him, going from depression to immediate anger. Sometimes it was the only way Alex could get out of bed in the morning.

He would thank Jalal later, though. For now, there was some yelling to do. With a yank, Alex ripped open the door, revealing Jalal, ever-present tablet in hand, fuming.

"What the hell is your problem, Jalal?" Alex asked, putting himself in the doorway.

Jalal grimaced. "My problem, Mr. Mamsin, is that you were

supposed to be at work an hour ago."

"Sick day," Alex said bluntly, shrugging as he spoke.

He moved to shut the door, but Jalal put out a hand and stopped it. Alex attempted to force the door shut, but Jalal stood his ground. The door didn't shift an inch. Jalal's primary power was Cutus Viris, the power of strength.

Which meant that Alex might as well try to move a mountain than close that door.

Alex's shoulders slumped and he stopped fighting. "What do you want from me Jalal?"

"I want you to work on time," Jalal said quietly, voice stern. "I want the only other person in this facility with the skill level to perform this job to show me that they can handle the responsibility."

"I know," Alex sighed as he wiped his face again. "I just had a long night."

"I heard," Jalal said quickly, face disapproving, though he tried not to say anything.

Jalal grew up during a time when sex hadn't become just another exercise. While he wouldn't stand against the will of other Sirgili to do as they wished, this South African man felt no need to humor them with feigned approval. After all, doing so would infringe on his own will to do as he wished.

That didn't mean it was any less annoying to Alex, however.

"Don't show up to my place and judge me," Alex said tiredly.

Jalal put his hand up in apology. "I am sorry, but you know Anne is something of a loose woman--"

Alex cut him off. "Jalal."

So much for keeping it to himself.

"Okay, okay," Jalal said quickly. "The bottom line is that I need you today, Alex. We are migrating the database backend and you wrote the scripts."

Alex slapped himself on the forehead. "Damn, I forgot about that."

"Just get ready," Jalal said, motioning back into Alex's rooms as he did. "We may have a few Elders showing up for a tour and I do not want you looking like a common thug today."

Alex snorted, feeling the haze of depression fading with the recent anger. "I don't ever look like a thug."

"Just brush your hair before you come today, at least," Jalal said dismissively as he turned around. "I expect you in thirty minutes."

"Fine," Alex said as he shut the door and turned back toward the living room.

It was almost exactly the same as it had been the day he arrived, though the addition of a widescreen, 3D capable television, a few newer gaming systems, and a couple old standbys resided on the shelves of a large stand.

Even the side table, tulip barely clinging to life in the darkened room despite his best efforts, sat in the same place as it had when he had arrived. Two long streaks through the dust that covered the tabletop were faint reminders of his touch on that first visit.

"Let's get this over with," Alex muttered and walked to the bathroom.

*   *   *

Mary Smith walked along the crowded Mission Street in San Francisco, mouth turned into a scowl that seemed to fit her face, despite her youth. The crowd, regardless of race or creed, seemed to part for her as she moved forward, as if frightened of what might happen should her course be diverted for whatever reason.

She spat to the side and grimaced inwardly.

Mary Smith.

What a ridiculous name. Why hadn't she decided on something more articulate, more mysterious? Had she truly been in such dire need of supposed normalcy that she'd adopt a name with absolutely no character?

Derval had been a good name, a strong name. It had history--though from a time and place few were alive to remember. Despite that, it was still remarkable, unique.

Mary Smith was a weak name.

Ahead of her, three Latino men in matching colors walked toward her, ignoring her save for the size of her breasts and the smooth motion with which she walked. Apparently they mistook her grace for attractiveness rather than what it was.

"Damn," one of them whistled as he approached, bringing the other two to attention.

"I'd like to hit that," another said gesturing rudely with one hand. His only significant feature was a thin line of hair going from chin to sideburns.

Mary Smith simply ignored them, adopting the weakness and frailty that the name provided. She'd walk by, ignoring their advances. Why had she decided that the place that made her sick would be the best place to hide?

She shook her head. Dervy hated cities, that was why.

Mary Smith loved the camaraderie and human interaction.

As the last man passed, he grabbed her arm and pulled her light form around so that she was pressed up against him. Alcohol was ripe on his breath, though the others hadn't smelled the same. "Hey chica, you want to come back with us. We'll show you a good time."

She tasted bile as she glanced around.

Mary Smith didn't fight. Mary Smith was a normal woman.

One of the other men, the one with the tiny effeminate beard, laughed and tapped his friend on the shoulder.

"Hell yeah," he grunted out, thrusting his pelvis suggestively.

The third man looked uncomfortable, but could not stop himself from licking his lips, regardless.

"Let go of me," she whined weakly.

Mary Smith did not fight.

Around her, people continued moving as if it wasn't happening. There were stray glances from some passersby, but not a single one stepped up to help.

Mary Smith does not fight.

"Yeah," the drunken man said, leaning in so that his filthy lips were close to her ear, breath hot on her neck. "We're gonna show you a real good time, chica."

Mary Smith does--

"Fuck it."

Dervy broke the man's arm. Before he could scream she reached an arm up around the side of his neck, kicked his legs out, squeezed, and jumped. A sickening crack resounded through the street as his neck snapped.

Suddenly, everyone cared.

She dropped the body and rolled her small shoulders. With a low growl, she turned toward the other men.

"Did you kill him?" The man with the facial hair yelled in disbelief as he took a quick step away.

Maybe it was quick enough to get away from Mary Smith.

But not Derval.

Derval leapt forward, a primal scream erupting from her lips. One fist struck him in the throat with a well-placed jab, crushing his trachea and dropping him to the sidewalk, gasping for air.

The third man froze, arms up in surrender, but eyes full of panic.

"What about you *chico*?" Dervy asked menacingly, enunciating the last word with disgust as she approached him slowly. "You want a good time like your friends?"

He ran.

Dervy turned around, noticing with disgust the shocked humans surrounding her. A mix of most modern races, they showed the same expressions she had learned to expect from panicked animals that found out they were being hunted.

None of them came forward to help the gasping man.

Cowards.

A few of them, however, had cell phones out and had probably recorded the entire confrontation. She growled, low and deep. It hadn't been a good idea to move to a city when she was this far gone--this separated from humanity. Dervy turned around and found more dumbfounded humans sprinkled with tiny video recorders capturing the moment.

She snapped.

"What!" Dervy screamed suddenly, feigning a lunge toward the nearest man with a phone.

He pulled back, fear flashing across his face, and the phone fell to the ground. Instead of fleeing right out, he leaned forward, as if avoiding a dog on a leash, and grabbed the small device.

"You want a show?" Dervy screamed at the crowd. "Do you want to be entertained?"

Someone near the back of the gathered group shouted yes.

For just a moment, she let herself simmer in the possibility of it. She could picture them all screaming, scattering to the winds as she tore them apart, one after another, their weak bodies collapsing easily under the power of her blows. There was nothing they could do about it if she attacked. Everyone within ten feet of her would die.

There would be no escape.

Dervy's fingers twitched in anticipation and a droplet sweat born of eagerness traced the small of her back. The rage filled her... she could feel them all, hear their blood pumping, taste their fear. She shook her head, dismissing the thoughts before they overwhelmed her.

She scowled and spat. "You're all goddamned pathetic."

With that Derval turned and walked into the mob. As always, it split before her, though this time it was done with deference.

As it should be.

*   *   *

The roar of the equipment nearly drowned out Jalal's voice as he led the four Elders into the server room.

"As you can see here Primator Searle, we have a fully redundant system put up that manages not just our data, but also the climate control, security, and overall system operations of Heathshome," Jalal said loudly as he turned back toward the exit, speaking more slowly than he did when it was just he and Alex.

William Searle frowned as he looked over the full racks of blade servers, mass storage and fiber networking equipment. "Is this wise?"

Jalal stopped short, turning back to the head of the council, the question causing him to forget the appropriate formalities. "Excuse me?"

Primator Searle raised an eyebrow at him.

"Primator," Jalal added hastily, just barely keeping the annoyance out of his voice. "Excuse me, Primator."

Primator Searle nodded and looked back to the hundred million dollars of equipment. "Are we putting all of our eggs in one basket, so to speak?"

Jalal hesitated for a moment before answering. "In a way, yes we are..."

The other elders began looking at the equipment

disapprovingly. Alex found himself staring at the group from his small workbench a few feet away. They were all a bunch of sycophants, always kowtowing to the council leader whether that person knew what they were talking about or not. They had all conveniently forgotten that he and Jalal had penned a proposal for an offsite emergency data center a month ago and this very man had disapproved it. He snorted in annoyed amusement.

"Do you have something to say, Taken?"

Alex froze. *Had it been that loud?*

Oh boy. Alex turned toward a group of some of the most powerful bipedal beings on Earth. *Just keep calm and everything will be all right.*

"Ah," Alex began, smiling. His mind blanked.

What was he going to say?

Primator Searle narrowed his eyes thoughtfully. "You are the Taken from San Francisco. The one recovered by Dervy before the Return took her, are you not?"

Alex nodded in assent, but his heart sank.

The Return? Dervy was dead?

Why hadn't anyone told him?

Primator Searle's face filled with compassion. "No one told you, my boy?"

Alex shook his head, barely suppressing the urge to point out that Alex was older, which, of course, he wasn't. Primator Searle looked like he might be in his early twenties. He had a full head of well-maintained dirty blonde hair and piercing blue eyes, but he certainly was not younger than Alex. He reached out and placed a gentle hand on Alex's shoulder and for the first time, Alex realized that Primator Searle was much taller than him.

The prickling vibration at the back of his neck--a constant companion nowadays with the thousands of strigoi nearby--grew intense for just a moment as Li Li walked by the server room. That always happened whenever she passed by. Apparently other strigoi felt the same thing when he was nearby, but Jalal assured him it would pass.

Alex wasn't as sure, however, since he not only felt Li Li, but other strigoi in much the same way, though he couldn't tell them apart.

He frowned. Or could he... there was something... unique

about Primator Searle.

"Perhaps this young strigoi should take time to grieve, Jalal?" Primator Searle said abruptly, interrupting Alex's thoughts. He was still looking down at him, tapping Alex's shoulder reassuringly.

Alex looked up, taking a moment to steady himself before locking eyes with the man. "That's okay, Primator Searle. I'll be fine. We have a lot of work to get done today."

Primator Searle smiled and squeezed his shoulder. "You are sure?"

Alex nodded. "Absolutely."

"Good," Primator Searle said, looking back at the server racks. "Then I believe you had some input to add to our discussion a moment ago?"

Alex cursed himself mentally. Behind the group of elders, Jalal was staring at him, flat faced, but eyes wide in alarm. They both knew that Alex had a certain impatience with those who pretended knowledge. They agreed after the first incident that Jalal would handle all things administrative for just that reason. They both knew what needed to be said, but Jalal preferred a certain patience and tact be applied.

Alex had never invested much in either.

So when Alex smiled, Jalal's shoulders slumped.

"Well," Alex started, suddenly growing relaxed. "Back in November we petitioned for an increased budget to cover offsite storage in the event of catastrophic failure."

Primator Searle's face darkened, though just enough to be noticeable. Alex assumed that most Sirgili would stop there, but he was feeling good for the first time that day.

Smiling, Alex picked up the thin tablet he used for various basic functions like reading or note taking. It was a great little device and even better for proving a point.

And it was a wonderful place to keep documentation.

With a few taps he pulled up a digital copy of the proposal. "Since we wholeheartedly agree with your astute statement a few moments ago, I assume that the second review of the proposal will go far better than the first, Primator."

Alex turned the tablet toward Elder Searle. He glanced down and nodded, but didn't take the device. The two men stared at each other, neither flinching, Alex smiling his most charming smile while Primator Searle considered him.

Just as Alex began to wonder if he'd pushed Primator Searle too far, the other man broke into a smile. "Well said, Mister... "

"Mamsin," Alex said, exhaling slowly to cover the sigh of relief that came with it. "Alex Mamsin, Primator Searle."

A brief look of recognition flashed and then disappeared. "That is right, Alex Mamsin. No middle name."

Alex smiled and nodded.

Primator Searle glanced back down at the notebook. "Resubmit it today and you will get your authorization, Mister Mamsin."

Jalal looked dumbfounded.

Alex smiled. "Thank you, Primator."

"Thank you, Mister Mamsin," Primator Searle said as he turned away.

The other elders glanced at Alex on their way out, one going so far as to nod his head in approval.

"Just this way, Primator," Jalal said as he opened the door and Elder Searle left. He cast a quick glare at Alex before following and closing the door behind him.

Alex stood there smiling like an idiot as the group of five men made their way down the hall toward the security offices. Within a few minutes, they faded entirely from the back of his neck.

"Still got it," Alex said to himself and sat back down at his workbench.

With a quick glance around, he leaned back and put his feet up on the desk. Jalal hated it when Alex did that, but he earned it.

*   *   *

Dervy sat in the small one bedroom apartment, an empty can of soup in front of her and nothing but the sounds of cars on the streets, passing pedestrians, and the periodic rant of an angry neighbor to entertain her. The door was unlocked, though leaving it that way in this neighborhood was a horrible idea. She was liable to wake up with her throat slit and the few possessions she had brought with her missing.

Maybe she wanted someone to try. If they tried to kill her, then the rules of combat stated that their life was forfeit.

Right?

Dervy remained sitting as she had for the past six hours, unmoving, stoic, statuesque.

Mary Smith was dead.

It was not the first time a new persona had failed, but this one was different. It hadn't been the persona that failed, but her. Through her own dehumanization, Dervy had become something less than she'd ever been.

She licked her lips. Save for during that first night. It seemed as though the swirling snows surrounded her once again, jagged flakes tearing flesh anew.

There was no purpose to these humans' existence save to make hers easier. They were like cattle to be herded or mules to leverage as pack animals. Sterilization of the weakest of the breed was not unheard of in history...

They are too dangerous to rule this planet without guidance.

She breathed in through her nose and out through the mouth. Those words kept creeping back into her mind, words of a man she had punished, a man who'd humiliated her not a mile away from her current location.

Zeke Dunfee.

Dervy blinked slowly, eyes tearing at the pain that accompanied the movement.

One blink every thousand-count.

Strength. Determination. Concentration. Dedication.

If she wasn't strong enough to control her own mind, she couldn't be trusted to walk amongst them. Without total control of her thoughts Dervy was an unstable weapon, just waiting for someone or something to trigger the rage that had been building over the last two centuries.

She considered leaving San Francisco again. Reconnecting with humans in cities always presented certain... challenges, but they had always been manageable in the past. Of course, that had been before there were cities that housed millions of humans; a web of presences that made her neck sore from their vibrations.

If only they could all be silenced at once.

She knew how.

She knew where the silos were.

They can't stop me.

Another deep breath; another thousand-count.

The pain in her leg was getting unbearable. Dervy released the pressure and blood flowed from her self-inflicted wound for just a moment before it sealed up.

Without flinching, Dervy dug her fingers back into her leg.

Deep breaths.

Eyes closed.

Calm thoughts.

Eyes open.

One.

Two.

Three...

12
Heathshome, NY
10:12 AM January 20, 2011

"Derval is dead, Weynie."

Weynie grimaced at the words. She set her tablet down on Elder Searle's desk, pulled up YouTube and spun it around as the video loaded.

"If Dervy is dead, then who the hell is that William?"

The pixels on the screen streaked as a small woman kicked a man's legs out from under him and snapped his neck. A split second later, another man fell to the ground, grasping his throat though the video hadn't picked up any other movement.

Despite the tinny quality from the low quality of the recording, the voice that followed was unmistakable.

What about you chico? You want a good time like your friends?

William picked up the tablet and handed it back to Weynie, face flat.

"It is not her," he said firmly.

Weynie's jaw went slack. "Well, if it isn't, then you can't say it isn't an undocumented strigoi."

William didn't move.

"Someone needs to go gather this person before they draw attention to us!" Weynie yelled in sudden annoyance.

William frowned at her. "Control yourself. You are an Elder. Behave like one."

Weynie took a deep breath and pulled away from him. When had she gotten so close to him? She had been right in his face.

"I'm sorry, I'm not sure what came over me," Weynie said, head bowed slightly.

William smiled at her deference. "Do not worry, my dear. Regret and sorrow sometimes foster disbelief and, at times, insubordination.

"I would not be a leader if I could not forgive such indiscretions."

William reached out and touched her arm, still smiling.

Weynie held back the sudden urge to swat it away.

"Know that I--and the rest of the Arktois--are here to counsel you through these trying days," William said smoothly. "The months immediately following this type of loss--especially of one Derval's age--can be hard. Sometimes you need contact and reassurance to readjust to these times.

"I know that I certainly did with the departure of our former Primator, and my close friend, Kevin O'Ceallaigh."

Weynie nodded slowly, avoiding William's eyes. She considered his carefully chosen words; his warning. It should not have come as a surprise that he knew--and cared--that she was spreading the story of Kevin's assault on the Arktois jet, but for some reason Weynie found herself without words. William wasn't one who mentioned things without meaning, especially not personal relationships.

The urge to reach out and touch his mind almost overwhelmed her. To delve into his thoughts and see what he was hiding from her and, maybe, from the Arktois would almost be worth it. She glanced at his hand, sitting unmoving on her forearm in what should have been a comforting gesture. The warning felt more like shackles, a reminder of her ultimate subservience to the Ankousti and to William as the current Primator.

With him touching her, though, she could more easily pull on his thoughts, find out what he knew, what he was hiding...

William smiled and moved his hand almost as if he knew what she was thinking.

He wasn't Scrying her. Was he?

Panic filled her for a split second. If he knew that she doubted him...

"I trust this meeting is over, Elder?" William said formally, pulling a sheaf of papers in front of him and eyeing them.

He lifted a pen as a wry smile crossed his face and proceeded to sign the top-most document.

Weynie smiled wanly and nodded. "Of course, Primator."

She bowed her head and backed away before turning and exiting William's office, quietly shutting the door behind her.

Walking casually, Weynie made her way toward the security offices. William Searle was a powerful strigoi, especially where it came to Scrying, but Weynie was not a novice. One didn't become a member of the AIC without a certain expertise in Scrying and most of that expertise came from the knowledge of what it felt like to be Scryed.

Weynie moved a little quicker, shaking her head in refusal. No, there was no way he'd Scryed her without her knowing. *It wasn't possible.*

But still, she doubted herself. What if William had been Scrying her? What would he have gotten from it?

Weynie wracked her brain as she maneuvered the long hallways, absentmindedly waving to other Sirgili while she contemplated. There was only that moment of doubt in his office that could be construed as incriminating. Just the brief consideration of Scrying the Primator...

Weynie cursed herself. What had she been thinking?

She'd acted like a child. She'd shown her hand. Of course he wouldn't trust her if she persisted in doubting the word of the Primator. How could he? William said that Dervy was gone, Returned, and when the Primator spoke, it was law. Or at least as close to that sort of thing as one got in the Arktois.

There was no reason to doubt him.

Except Weynie recognized Dervy.

She heard her friend's voice shouting across the bits of the internet. The post date was from less than a week ago and a news posting in a local San Francisco paper substantiated it.

Yet William hadn't wanted to hear any of it.

Why?

Weynie frowned as she put her thumb on the fingerprint scanner for the security offices. She nodded at a woman who looked little more than a teenager, though she was actually closer to fifty.

There was a short, sharp beep and the red light above her thumb didn't change. The door remained shut.

Weynie frowned, looked at the woman at the desk and pointed at the locking mechanism. The lady looked surprised for a moment, but then hit a button and the light turned green.

The door slid open with a gasp and Weynie approached the desk.

"Good afternoon, Janine," Weynie said with a smile. "What's wrong with the door?"

Janine smiled, trying her best to avoid flashing her large buckteeth, and shrugged. "Issues with the servers, I guess."

Weynie hissed dramatically. "Jalal's probably not very happy then, huh?"

Janine shook her head and changed the subject. "Haven't seen you around in awhile, how are things going?"

Weynie nodded. "Things are going well," she lied. "Is Jalal in the server room?"

"Yep," Janine said, pointing to her left, though Weynie had been there hundreds of times. "Just down the hall on the right."

Weynie smiled in thanks and moved on, still thinking about her encounter with William.

"Um, Elder? Ma'am?"

Weynie turned back to Janine. "Yes?"

Janine shifted uncomfortably. "Jalal asked that you stay outside of the server room in the future after what happened last time."

Weynie rubbed her forehead in annoyance at herself. The last time she'd gone in, she'd accidentally shorted out an entire rack. Sometimes it didn't feel like Animi Fulminis was actually a gift. Not in this age, anyway.

"That's right. I forgot. Thank you Janine."

Janine smiled, letting her teeth show beneath a lip. "Not a problem Elder."

"I'll stay outside the door this time Janine. I promise." Weynie called out as she continued on.

The bottom line was that Weynie was more worried about Dervy than any scandal the Primator might be trying to hide. While Dervy had been trying to hide it for decades, Weynie had noticed a gradual increase of her hostility toward others, particularly humans. It had recently become worrisome, like with the man from Nawat Industries.

The video just gave substance to that concern.

Weynie paused and slapped herself on the forehead. She had never reported the incident with Nawat Industries. With all that had happened it'd slipped her mind...

The sound of fans and a rushing HVAC told her she had reached her destination. Weynie steeled herself as she knocked on the server room door, its rough wood surface scraping her knuckles. There was little she could do to help Dervy by herself. She needed help. She could feel a Taken inside, probably Alex.

A long tone came from the card swipe next to the door and a moment later it swung open, revealing a surprised Alex Mamsin.

"Weynie?"

She smiled, looking around the Taken. "Is Jalal here?"

"Yeah," Alex said, turning around. "Jalal!" He turned back to her. "You want to come in?"

Weynie smiled. "Not allowed."

"Fulminis?" Alex offered hesitantly.

"Yes. How did you know?"

Alex shrugged. "I had a theory about it. Jalal didn't want to go over it with me."

Jalal made his way toward the door, tablet suspended on one hand while typing furiously with the other.

"Well that is *not* happening right now," Jalal said without taking his eyes off the computer. "We're in the middle of a major hardware failure--"

"No we're not," Alex interjected testily.

"--and," Jalal said quickly, glaring at Alex. "Mr. Mamsin here needs to somehow come above this failure and get the database server back online before everyone finds out they can no longer get into their homes."

Alex threw his hands up and walked over to a terminal in the corner where he began typing just as energetically as Jalal had been a moment before.

"What do you need, Weynie?" Jalal asked, eyes still locked on his tiny screen.

Weynie hesitated. Should she really be interrupting something that sounded so critical? If the roles were reversed, would she want to be interrupted?

"Dervy is alive," Weynie spurted out, much louder than she planned.

"What?"

Jalal stopped typing, but it had been Alex who spoke.

"Dervy Returned," Jalal said with a frown, staring at his screen blankly, hand suspended just above the digital keyboard.

Weynie shook her head. "Can I come in? I have a video to show you two."

"Yeah," Alex said, jumping to his feet and nearly running to the door. "Come in."

Jalal's eyes opened wide. "Um. That might not be a good idea--"

As the door shut behind her, Weynie wondered if she was doing the right thing bringing them into this.

Alex took her to the furthest corner away from the server racks. There was a small table and fridge set up. Crumbs from a sandwich littered the tabletop. Weynie wiped them on the floor.

It was too late now.

Weynie laid her tablet on the table, bringing up the YouTube video.

"Now listen to the voice... "

*   *   *

It was nearly midnight by the time Alex made his way down the now empty halls toward the Pasa Tiempo and home. At least the clock on his tablet said it was midnight.

Heathshome was several hundred feet below the surface and despite many areas being lit by a rather impressive light redirection system, after sundown or when it was simply overcast, the entire community took on a sterile, hospital inspired ambiance. The fluorescent lights buzzed overhead, the periodic failing bulb popping at him as he passed.

Alex ran his fingers through his hair and sighed. The database server was back up, people were home, and it was his turn to sleep.

He wasn't sure if sleep would come, though.

It was less the fact that Dervy was alive that troubled him and more the reality that Primator Searle had lied to his face. Politicians lied all the time, but for some reason Alex had let himself believe that in a community of a few thousand people--a community where people had to live together for centuries--that there would be integrity.

Well, maybe not integrity, but honesty at the very least.

Now Alex knew that didn't even exist.

Alex stifled a yawn and looked at the small screen of his tablet again, flipping through various windows until he came across the monitoring application. He let out a relieved sigh at the subsequent graph and lowered the device to his side. Everything was working perfectly, though he wished he had some wood to knock on for good luck.

Alex stepped out into the Pasa Tiempo, fake moonlight scattering around him, tingeing the foliage and wandering Sirgili with an azure glow. At least they managed to make the light seem natural here. The now familiar scents of wildflowers intermingled with the various culinary delights wafting from the dozen or so restaurants that dotted the periphery of the public area. As he passed by one-- an establishment owned by an Italian strigoi and staffed by humans-- Alex found himself salivating at the scent of Alfredo sauce and biscotti.

He shook his head at the thought, pretending to ignore the sounds of discussion and laughter of the patrons as he passed. As Alex understood it, he currently had no disposable income. He'd assumed on arrival that his time at Heathshome would be akin to a free ride, at least in regard to finances. However, after purchasing the new entertainment system in his home it became clear that there was a restriction on spending concurrent with income generated by daily duties.

If it could even be called income, anyway.

Immortal

When it came to the Arktois there was no actual currency, but more of a credit system put in place. As you worked in the organization, you gained credit that could be applied to any of the delights available to you in the Pasa Tiempo or through the vendors of Heathshome. All actual money was owned and operated by the Ankousti who invested, spent, and hoarded the finances in ways that no one outside the small group could identify.

For the most part though, no one really cared. The Ankousti contained possibly the most trusting body of constituents Alex had ever heard of, though "constituents" was the wrong term given the lack of a constitution of any sort. This trust was infectious and over the course of four months even a pessimist like Alex had become assured of the goodwill of the Ankousti.

Or maybe they all knew and just didn't care.

Alex spit into the neat flower arrangements as he left the Pasa Tiempo.

Anyway, now it was over for him. He couldn't help but care.

He walked through the false light, leaving the artificial landscape behind, the gentle buzzing of fluorescent bulbs in the low hallways almost as frustrating as the itching at the back of his neck.

Li Li must be nearby. It felt a little different though. Maybe the Gatherers had finally found another Taken?

Alex made it to his door and pushed his thumb onto the scanner, feeling the familiar pain as the needle took a small blood sample. A faint chime sounded, indicating that he should speak his first name.

"Alex," he said clearly. Immediately, he stifled a yawn.

A second later the door unlocked and he stepped in. This was one of the systems that had broken during the downtime, though most of the residents had no idea yet.

Shutting and locking the deadbolt on the door behind him, Alex moved toward the kitchen, shedding his shirt and pants as he moved and leaving them in uneven heaps along the way. Flicking a light on, he opened a cupboard and found himself staring up at a half bottle of rum. It was hard to remember, but he thought there had been more in there the night before...

"You're still drinking, Alex?"

Alex spun around, heart pounding.

Simon reclined on Alex's couch, swirling a glass in his hand.

The clink of ice quietly filled the room as he tipped it back.

"I'd have thought the counselors would have gotten you to stop by now," Simon added, smacking his lips in satisfaction.

Alex focused on the sensations at the back of his neck. The loudest one, for lack of a better term, was coming from right in front of him it wasn't Li Li... it was Simon.

What was going on? How did he get in here?
And why was his vibration so intense?

Alex knit his brows together in concentration.

And what was wrong with it?

"You're front door was kind of open," Simon said nonchalantly. "Without that fancy little lock, it pretty much just opened up when I knocked."

Restraining himself, Alex focused again, concentrating on his thoughts and feeling for anything different, foreign. It was part of the standard training, being able to identify when you were being Scryed--the more mundane term for Animi Pellegi--and stopping it. While he wasn't very good at much else, Alex had what Anne called a "protective personality."

There.

With something Alex could only describe as a mental flexing, he severed the connection Simon had established with every ounce of power he could, causing the other man to choke slightly.

"Yikes," Simon said quietly, blinking rapidly for a moment. "Usually it's just proper etiquette to give some warning when you break a Scry, Alex. God--"

"And usually people ask before Scrying," Alex said acidly. "What are you doing here Simon?" He asked, moving forward slowly.

"What?" Simon said with a smile, getting to his feet suddenly. "A guy can't swing by and say 'hi' to an old friend?"

Alex shook his head in disgust. "At what point were we old friends?"

"There were a few hours there... " Simon said with a wave as he stood and started walking around the apartment.

He motioned to the entertainment system. "Love what you've done with the place, what with the games and such.

"So adult of you."

"What do you want Simon?" Alex asked again in frustration,

taking advantage of Simon's movement so he could grab and pull on his pants.

Simon ignored the question, instead pausing next to the painting near the side table. "Did you know Kevin painted this in 1904? Yep, placed it right here in 2002 when they upgraded his quarters."

Alex frowned. "Kevin lived here?"

Simon looked back at him innocently. "Oh yeah, they didn't tell you?"

Alex shook his head and pulled on his shirt quickly. "I guess they didn't think it was important."

Simon sighed, setting his glass down on the side table. "How quickly the youth forget their elders."

With a disapproving shake of the head, Simon ran his fingers through the thick dust on the table.

Alex's anger flared. "What do you--"

"Want?" Simon interrupted, turning around and facing Alex quickly. "You're so single-minded sometimes, Alex. It's really annoying, actually. Oh!"

Simon stopped for a moment as if remembering something and grabbed his glass. "Doctor Aubin sends her greetings."

"She made me promise to say that," he added with a smile.

"Can you get to the point?" Alex asked in annoyance while he desperately tried to think.

What was Simon doing there? How did he get into Heathshome, let alone into his apartment?

Alex didn't buy the idea that the door was open--he always locked it first. Even if the DNA tester had been offline, there was still the voice and thumbprint reader and those used a local database...

Alex cursed. Except they didn't. The old ones used a local reference, the new ones used the database server for all points of authentication.

It should have just locked people out, not let everyone in.

"Excuse me?" Simon asked as Alex swore, walking toward him casually glass once again in hand. "Did you say something?"

"What do you want?" Alex yelled suddenly.

Simon smiled and scratched at his chin. "I want Dervy, Alex."

Why?

"Then go find her," Alex grunted, keeping his question to himself and doing his best to lie. "As far as I know she's buried up on the surface."

"The surface, eh?" Simon asked, finishing his drink and setting it on the side table gingerly. "So she Returned?"

Alex shifted uncomfortably and cursed himself for it. "As far as I know, yes."

"As far as you know?"

"Right."

"She's dead?"

"Yes."

"Derval is dead? As far as you know?"

He wasn't buying it.

"Right."

Simon nodded and picked up the glass again, twirling it in his hand. "So she is dead up on--"

Alex who barely avoided the glass as it whistled by his ear.

The next moment, Simon had Alex by the throat with one hand and was punching him in the face with blows that rang against his skull like swings of a sledgehammer. Blood poured from his nose and mouth.

Simon let him go and Alex collapsed on the floor, gasping for air. Alex knew how to focus on regeneration now, but he wasn't very good at it and practice sessions never included a vicious beating by a madman. Every time he grasped at the idea, flaring pain distracted him and he lost focus.

"All right," Simon said as he smoothed his shirt, grimacing at some of the blood he'd gotten on himself. "Maybe you can answer the question now."

Simon leaned down and grabbed Alex by the chin, sending a flash of pain through his neck and into his skull. "Where is Dervy?"

Alex sobbed in pain as Simon squeezed his broken jaw, keeping it from mending as his regenerative powers began working.

"Where."

More pressure.

"Is."

Alex cried out in pain.

"Dervy?"

Weakly, Alex swatted at Simon's hand. The other man released and Alex hit the floor with a thud.

After a moment, Alex mumbled into the floor while he cursed himself silently.

"What was that?" Simon asked, coming closer.

"San Francisco."

*   *   *

"Auckland, New Zealand."

"Let me see here," the woman on the other side of the counter--Jill, according to her nametag--said as she tapped on a keyboard. "It looks like we have something for you tomorrow at six in the morning."

Dervy nodded.

"You can order tickets online in the future," Jill said in a sweetly condescending voice. "We tend to have longer lines--"

"I wanted to wait in line," Dervy interrupted, perhaps a bit too hastily. "Do you need anything to get me on that plane? ID? Maybe even money?"

Jill frowned. "I'll need a valid U.S. Passport for verification purposes first."

Dervy fished out a passport and slid it across the counter. Jill opened it up, revealing a stoic Dervy. The name Mary Smith was plastered beneath it.

Jill glanced at her screen, then waved the passport underneath a scanner of some sort before frowning. "This isn't an enhanced passport?"

Dervy shook her head. "No."

"I didn't know they were still giving these out," Jill said, looking at Dervy suspiciously. "When did you get this?"

"Why don't you call the number in the front and find out for yourself?" Dervy asked, gesturing rudely at the document. "Or, I don't know, look at the issue date? Are you always this inept or have you been practicing for my edification?"

"Ma'am, I need you--"

"You know what?" Dervy asked impatiently, taking the passport back forcefully. "I'll just go fly a different airline that has a lower bitch-to-assistance quotient."

Dervy turned away, ignoring the murmured curses that followed her and made her way to the exit. If she were lucky, she would make it out of SFO before the woman had the sense to call security.

She just needed to get out of the country. Why was that so impossibly hard?

Dervy cursed at William Searle for the thousandth time that day.

Dervy's first attempt to purchase a plane ticket out of the country had resulted in a similar experience, though she'd tried leaving from Oakland first due to her encounter with the men in San Francisco earlier that week. That time she'd left nicely, excusing herself with a fake phone call and a sudden taxi trip.

Dervy's passport apparently didn't have an RFID, though she had no idea what it meant. Whatever it was, not having it made her look suspicious as apparently all new passports came with one. That, her strange accent, and a recent bulletin released by the police looking for someone remarkably like Dervy had made it nearly impossible to get out of the city.

Dervy cursed angrily and pictured a smiling William Searle. *One thousand and one.*

This was her first attempt at fading back into the woodwork since the Industrial Age began and it was quickly beginning to look like these departures might no longer be possible. If that was so, it certainly begged the question of how Dervy was supposed to maintain her anonymity in this new world.

Of course, that was why she chose New Zealand. In a country littered with pristine wilderness she could disappear for centuries, only reemerging when most of those she knew were already Returned. Dissolving into wild forests had worked twice before, it should work this time.

Dervy growled, causing a young child on the arm of his mother to look at her in fear. It would work if she could *get* there, anyway. Instead of leaving, Dervy walked toward the car rental area and approached the kiosk, pulling out her useless passport.

Hopefully she could at least rent a car with this thing...

13
Somewhere over the Midwest, USA
3:45 AM January 21, 2011

    Simon grimaced at the sleeping woman next to him. Her somewhat pretty face was turned toward him, mouth agape, a slight snore filling the small space they shared. He did his best to readjust himself in the tight seat of the passenger plane. Not for the first time, Simon wished he had been a little more in shape when he was Taken. It was annoying that he was quicker than a cat and stronger than a bull, but couldn't squeeze into a pair of thirty-six waist men's jeans, let alone a coach airplane seat comfortably.
    Sighing, Simon stared out the window, the rolling plains of middle America passing beneath him in the black of night. The moon was more than enough light for his strigoi eyes and despite his general abhorrence of nature, he found himself smiling. It was like watching an interactive painting and he could find the beauty in that, especially with the increased sensitivity of his vision since taking the Cure.
    Now if only it hadn't made me a little near-sighted...
    Below him a meandering river cut across a long swath of the wild, untamed landscape. Rising mountains, rough and uneven in

their glory, faded into the distance as the plane moved ever onward. The land was speckled here and there with scattered pins of light that interrupted the utter blackness of the wilderness. Those lights expanded year over year, filling the land with artificial light. They created beautiful backdrops of civilization amongst the harshness of the earth.

Unlike Kevin and most of the others that followed the man, Simon had no hatred for humans. Quite the contrary, he actually respected them more than most of his strigoi counterparts. In the space of three hundred years they had pulled a species from relative barbarism to a realm of technology and culture that had never existed. No empire of the ancients could measure against even the smallest nation of this new world.

That was impressive and it was a drive Simon wished the strigoi--whether through the Arktois or another entity, such as the one Kevin imagined--would embrace and work to further. Unfortunately, the longer Simon remained a member of this group and as Kevin became coherent for longer periods of time, the more Simon doubted that was the goal of either body.

That brought up the problem with Kevin's lucidity, which made Simon shudder. The side effects of stopping the Return had not been readily apparent during that first week. The excitement had been so infectious that both Nathan and Simon had taken the injections without so much as a worried glance. The burst of power was amazing--both of them became faster, stronger and their powers were amplified.

For two strigoi who had never given in to the Hunger it was new, thrilling and ultimately addicting.

Kevin should have told them there was something wrong.

Simon shook his head, doing his best to banish the thoughts from his mind, though he couldn't remove them completely. Things got... fuzzy every couple weeks now, but it was worse for Kevin.

Kevin needed to feed every day.

"Goddammit," Simon mumbled to himself as the plane roared across the world, a bullet in the night.

Kevin had found Simon in February of 1929, just a few short months before the United States fell apart for a good part of the next decade. At that point, Simon Vanderwell--still unconcerned about the fact that he hadn't aged a day in five years--was working as an agent between country farmers and the financial boom that was Wall Street. All for a very reasonable fee of course.

If he knew then what he knew now, Simon never would have pulled over his Model A to pick up a disheveled man with an army satchel tossed over one shoulder.

How Kevin had determined that Simon was a strigoi was still a mystery to him, but the relationship continued in much the same way until another Sirgil found him out in 2010. During those interim years, he and Kevin met often and discussed topics ranging from world politics to the details of whiskey distillation. When the second World War broke out and America began the draft, Kevin got him relieved from service even though he was going by Simon Vanderwell Junior at that point and was pretending to be thirty-three years old.

It was hard for Simon to admit that Kevin knowingly cursed him with this... this sickness, but when he looked at the facts it became increasingly clear that Kevin had known the cost as soon as he tore into that nurse in August. Knowing how he felt when the Hunger came upon him--a ravenous thirst and appetite that tore at his mind and nearly drove him mad--Simon just couldn't let that nagging thought go, despite Kevin's assertions to the contrary.

He just kept seeing their faces...

Simon took a deep breath and pulled down the plastic shutter, blocking his view of the world below and leaving him in the cramped space. Absentmindedly, he found himself looking for a stewardess as his stomach began to growl.

Suddenly, the proximity of the woman to him was incredibly unnerving. She was sitting there, facemask in place, head tilted to the side exposing her long, tanned neck. He could almost see the artery move with each heartbeat, a slight rising of the skin as it continued its offbeat, perpetual rhythm. It drew him in, pulsing, subliminal, insistent.

Simon shook his head violently and stood up. He pushed past the woman, triggering a series of slurred curses as he did so, and made his way to the toilet. The light showed vacant so he pulled the tiny door open and squeezed inside, locking it behind him.

"Relax Simon," he told himself as he stepped away from the door and sat down on the plastic toilet. "Take a deep breath, count to ten and everything will be okay."

Simon followed his own advice, taking a deep breath and beginning his count, but his heart jumped as someone pulled on the door.

"Occupied!" Simon screamed, voice raising an octave near the end of the word.

"Sorry," a muffled voice responded.

Footsteps led away from the door and Simon breathed again.

He rocked back and forth on the toilet, counting over and over again as his stomach rumbled. There was a chance he was simply hungry for normal, everyday food.

"It doesn't always have to be bad," he whispered to himself.

But he wasn't sure and that made the caution necessary. It was a fine line between the usual appetite that came with being a strigoi and the Hunger that beset him since taking the shot.

They felt similar up until the first bite, but then it was over. If he tried to eat and it turned out that peanuts and turkey sandwiches would not sate him, then...

Simon shook his head. He looked up into the mirror to his left and saw the same face he had seen every morning for the past one hundred and thirty-two years. Every gray hair was still gray, every frown line was as worn as the day he purchased his 1928 Ford Model A. Something was different this time, though. Just on the edge of sight, like a faint star in the night sky.

He couldn't see the change, but he felt it every moment of every day. The Hunger had changed him, made him at the same time stronger and yet more infantile--driven more by desire than need.

Simon laughed. It went long and hard, growing more hysterical with each passing moment, his voice rising--becoming louder and more varied in pitch and tone. It was a laugh filled with self-loathing, panic, hatred, disgust, and realization. As his throat began to ache from the effort--his trachea raw and eyes red and puffy--Simon reached out to the mirror and carefully traced his own cheek.

"So what are we then?" Simon said aloud, remembering a conversation with Kevin all those years ago.

He could remember the sardonic smile the short Irishman had flashed him as they drove through the noonday sun on a California highway, flasks of whiskey in their hands. The answer had made them both laugh at the time. It seemed utterly ridiculous as they drove through the day, feeling the dizzying effects of alcohol.

"Technically," Kevin had said with a grin as he took a quick pull on his bottle. "We're vampires."

* * *

Alex sawed viciously at the rare piece of beef in front of him while doing his best to ignore the bustle of the cafeteria. It was noon and dozens of Sirgili swept in to take advantage of the free food.

"Alex!"

He cringed.

"I'm talking to you!"

It was a lot harder trying to ignore Weynie.

"Listen, I already told you that I don't want to talk about it anymore," Alex snapped back at her. He took a big bite of the steak and took care to look right at her as he did so.

She gave him a look--one filled with utter revulsion--and turned on her heel. "Come talk to me when you are finished, Taken."

Alex snorted and put his head back down, focusing on the bleeding meat.

Taken. It was never used fondly, only as a reminder of social status, or rather, the lack thereof. Most people referred to him as a Youngling even if he still had another eight months before he could officially be called that.

Weynie had never called him Taken or Youngling before.

He must have really pissed her off with the steak thing.

Alex shook his head and continued eating, mixing some potatoes into the bloody fluids swirling into the dripping butter. Weynie was one of the few Sirgili he had met that had maintained some semblance of religious dedication. While she was no longer devout, somehow she avoided beef and pork despite the cravings that came with the territory.

Taking another bite and feeling the bliss that accompanied it, Alex couldn't for a moment fathom why someone would consider being a vegetarian as a human regardless of religious practice. It was just... delicious.

That combined with the discipline one would need to avoid any kind of meat as a strigoi were two reasons why Alex didn't even consider it an option. In fact, he was sure avoiding meat would drive him insane, though that was unsubstantiated.

Alex set down his fork and stared into the discolored mashed potatoes. "Why did I do that?"

He didn't receive an answer, though he wasn't really expecting one. There were only five or so people in Heathshome that he even spoke to, let alone had friendly conversations with. The saddest part was that number included Weynie and she only started talking to him again the day before.

The potatoes definitely were not part of his core group.

Alex stared at his plate, watching the sanguineous fluids pool and eddy around grease and white mounds. To his right a small tone from the tablet told him that he had an email from Jalal. Alex had taken the extra time to specify a sound for him so that he could identify incoming messages that were potentially critical.

He sighed and pushed the potatoes around with his fork. He could almost hear the sound of Frieda watching her stories...

Nothing had changed. Financial freedom, change of scenery, magical abilities and immortality of a sort... and Alex was still pushing around boxed potatoes and wishing he had a beer. He couldn't even protect someone by keeping his mouth shut. It wasn't like he could die so why did he say anything? Why had he told Simon where Dervy was?

His fork rattled against the plate, hands shaking.

Alex knew why.

It was the same reason he'd thrown himself off the bridge and it was the same reason he'd abandoned all of his friends after Mary's death. People had still cared for him; they had tried desperately to help him and he tossed them to the side. He preferred to wallow in the bottom of a bottle instead of cry on the shoulder of a friend.

The truth was that Alex was a coward.

It was a simple realization, one that made his hands stop shaking. Everything in his life revolved around that one fact, leading him by the nose, training him to respond in practiced, predictable ways.

His father died in a freak accident and his mother had

needed him, but how had he helped? By leaving her alone in a home filled with the remnants of the only man she had ever loved? A man she had given up her previous life for?

Alex felt the tears welling and he let them come.

He killed his mother. Alex saw what the loneliness was doing to her and he did nothing because he was afraid of what the conversation would bring. It didn't matter that he had no idea what to say... saying anything would have been better than the months of silence and avoidance that followed his father's death.

Alex didn't have to be the one who administered the dose of anesthetic that ultimately caused her fatal allergic reaction during her surgery. He put her in that bed. He let her destroy her liver and then he tried to follow suit when the same situation became his.

"Oh Jesus," Alex cried, putting his face in his hands.

"Are you all right?" A familiar voice said.

Alex looked up, wiping away tears and sniffing back some loose snot. Anne stood across from him, food tray in hand. Her face was contorted with concern though she didn't make any move to sit down.

"Yeah," Alex said quickly, adding a fake smile for effect. "Just some heavy spices today. I'm no good with hot sauce."

Anne nodded slowly, eyes glancing away uncomfortably. "All right."

Alex smiled and picked up his fork. He jabbed at some potatoes with faked interest.

"If you need anything," Anne said, "just call me, all right?"

"Sure," Alex said. "I'll do that."

Anne smiled reassuringly. "Good."

The subsequent silence dragged on for a few moments before Anne turned away. "I've got to be going--"

"All right, talk to you later," Alex said quickly, eyes dropping to the mess on his plate.

"Bye."

Alex watched her leave, following her movements as she dropped her tray off at the counter, flashing a suggestive smile at another strigoi he didn't know. Alex shook his head and sighed as he picked up his own tray. There was definitely nothing there for him either. Jalal was right.

Grabbing his tablet with one hand, Alex took his tray over to the counter and left it with the human contractor. The man nodded at him, letting free a fake smile and a thank you before Alex left with a nod.

Alex exited the cafeteria, taking a left as he went. He looked at his tablet. Technically he was supposed to be going to meet with Weynie, she was an Elder and had given him a direct order, but he just couldn't bring himself to face her accusing eyes right now. Besides, Weynie already knew that Simon knew where Dervy was, everything else was just superfluous questioning.

Tapping on the touch screen, Alex brought up Jalal's email. He read over it quickly and found himself frowning. It was a statistical analysis of system reliability and uptime, but that wasn't the only reason Alex was glowering at the screen. The truth was that he just no longer cared. Why should he? All it did was remind him how much he hadn't changed.

He'd rather be washing dishes.

Alex stopped and blinked.

There was nothing stopping him from just leaving. The only indicator of what he was consisted of a small strap he wore like a collar and his own mind. During his two months in Heathshome he'd learned a few things, first and foremost of which was that punishment generally consisted of loss of rank and tenure instead of incarceration or physical punishment.

But he was a Taken, the lowest of the low in the eyes of the masses. Why should he care whether his punishment consisted of losing a few months of clout? Alex smiled suddenly at the feeling of empowerment. He turned on his heel and headed back the way he came, taking the first left at the next hallway.

He moved quickly, though not fast enough to arouse suspicion. As Alex passed other Sirgili, he nodded amiably and continued, doing his best to avoid conversation, which wasn't hard considering his lack of associates.

Within a few minutes he found himself at the main foyer of Heathshome. Shocked, he realized it was the first time he'd been back since his initial arrival. The room was bustling with activity as the weekly supply shipments arrived. Hundreds of humans and dozens of strigoi were unloading pallets and wheeling them deeper into the compound. The narrow hallways of Heathshome did not lend well to forklifts or pallet trucks, so most supplies were hand trucked to their destination after being pulled from the freight elevator off to the right of the foyer.

All he needed to do was walk out the front door and away from here, though he wasn't entirely sure what he'd do once he got out there. Where was he going to go? It was winter in New York, it wasn't like he could just go for a jaunty walk in the snowdrifts.

Alex frowned. The need to leave Heathshome was eating at him, a nagging voice in his mind that he couldn't ignore.

He cursed. Outside of Heathshome he had no money, no transportation and, for all he knew, no identity. When a Sirgili left Heathshome, most had to check in at the front desk to get their papers and access to Arktois finances in the form of cash and credit.

He looked over at the desk. A young man was facing off with an older, red-faced human. The human was wearing a uniform of some sort--khakis and a polo shirt with a logo of a face surrounded by fire on his left breast. He kept holding out a clipboard at his side, but from where Alex stood and due to the commotion around from the unloading process, whatever he was saying kept arriving as nonsensical gibberish.

Of course, that could be a very good thing. If he could speak with the strigoi at the desk while he was distracted, maybe he could get funds, ID and maybe even an Arktois vehicle of some sort.

It was worth a shot.

He took a steadying breath and then made his way over to the counter, an easy, self-assured smile cemented in place.

"For the last time, just because you think a product isn't good enough doesn't mean you get to cut the price on the fly!" The human yelled, gesturing violently with the clipboard. "Listen. Erol. You purchased at the price we agreed on. I'm sorry it was subpar, we can work on that for the next shipment, but you need to pay up or we'll stop delivering."

Erol raised an eyebrow. Now that Alex was up close, he found himself feeling a little sorry for him. The faint buzz at the back of Alex's neck told him this man was a strigoi, but he appeared to be sixteen or seventeen years old with rosy, peach fuzz covered cheeks. It was always a little sad when someone was taken before full adulthood. As they aged they generally became much more bitter. At least, that seemed to be the trend in the strigoi Alex had met.

Erol didn't disappoint.

"How do you anticipate we resolve this in future shipments, precisely?" Erol asked evenly, in a carefully controlled voice that seemed on the edge of cracking. "Shall we over-package all subsequent products so that the glassware is not a menagerie of shards that would look appropriate on the mantel of a madman? Or perhaps we can work through the spoilage of the produce by creating a biomass engine to enable creation of a food replicator so that we no longer need Hope Foods' services?"

The other man said nothing, but a red flush began to creep up his neck.

Erol shook his head, face still innocent and honest. "No? Then maybe--just maybe--you can accept the reduced payment now and we can work out future reparations moving forward. Thank you and once again, Heathshome appreciates your dedication. Yes?"

Alex blinked and his grin faded away as Erol turned toward him. The human growled very quietly though Alex could still hear it above the chaos of the room. With a huff, the man turned and left, yelling to a couple of his employees as he passed.

Alex smiled, regaining his mental balance and opened his mouth.

Nothing came out.

Erol raised an eyebrow again. "Are you the newest deaf-mute Taken, by chance?"

Alex looked at him questioningly for a moment before laughing. "No, no. I'm here to pick up, uh, ID, money and the keys to a vehicle."

Erol looked askance at him as he tapped at a keyboard. It was obvious he didn't believe him.

Alex's mind raced. "I'm heading to, uh, Buffalo for an IT conference."

Erol kept typing and didn't acknowledge that comment.

Alex was reasonably sure he was being ignored.

"It's the National Network, um, Administrators of America conference," Alex leaned in, fake smile held in place despite his rising panic. "Jalal wants me to go since he's really busy and, let's face it, I'm doing all the networking since I got here anyway."

"Do you have authorization?" Erol asked as he tapped the Enter key before crossing his arms.

"Um," Alex mumbled. "I don't have... "

A light bulb flashed on and a true smile split Alex's face.

"... a paper copy. Will digital approval work?"

Erol looked at him suspiciously. "I... would prefer paper, but digital is fine."

Alex tapped on his tablet and pulled up the notice of budget approval for the offsite storage project. It lacked line items, instead just providing a quick overview of the things it did cover. Alex grinned as he scrolled down to the one marked "Training and Offsite Services."

He turned the tablet around and slid it across the desk to Erol.

The baby-faced strigoi looked at the document and awkwardly scrolled down until he got to the approval area. Shrugging, he handed the tablet back to Alex and turned toward a flat screen monitor to his right.

"This will just take a few moments, Mr. Mamsin," Erol said quickly.

He picked up a thumb reader without turning his head away from the screen and slid it toward Alex. "We just need a quick ID for our records."

Alex pressed him thumb onto the plate and sighed.

It appeared that there would be no quiet, anonymous departure from Heathshome after all. He was really beginning to dislike the idea of constant monitoring and control that the Arktois exerted over strigoi. It was frustrating when he couldn't leave the compound without a fingerprint scan.

"Very good," Erol said mostly to himself.

A minute later the printer behind him--a monstrous beast of a machine that looked like something out of a mid-seventies mainframe commercial--began vibrating. After a moment, a small card resembling a driver's license popped out of the machine. Erol grabbed it, inserted it into a card reader and slid it across the table to Alex.

Alex picked it up and took a look. It was a New York State driver's license with a picture of him when he first arrived in Heathshome. He was bald and looked exhausted, but otherwise appeared exactly the same. At the top the words "Enhanced Drivers License" were printed. The name Alex O. Mansim was printed along with a fake address in the "town" of Heathshome, New York.

"Will this hold up if someone needs to check it?" Alex asked as he flexed the card, watching iridescent waves of color ripple with the twisting motion.

"It should," Erol said. "It's an actual license."

Alex looked up and considered asking how they could do that, but Erol was sliding more documents toward him.

"Since this is your first time out, we created a new identity for you," Erol pushed across a small paper card. "It isn't very original, but should be memorable enough that you won't have trouble. Alex O. Mansim. The 'O' is for Oliver. This is your Social Security Card and before you ask, yes, it is legitimate. Additionally, if anyone needs it your birth certificate is on file at the Heathshome Hall of Records. You were born at home in Heathshome--you grew up here, moved away, and moved back only recently."

Alex nodded as he scooped up the Social Security card. "Okay."

Erol tapped out a few keystrokes and a drawer opened beneath him. "Do you need the entire line item in cash, credit or just a portion of the total?"

Alex blinked. The line item was for forty thousand dollars. "Umm, how about four thousand in cash," Alex said while he shouted down his conscience. "And sixteen in credit. We'll leave the rest for the offsite services."

He suddenly felt horrible.

Erol quickly began counting out one hundred dollar bills. "You want big bills or small?"

"Umm, how about two thousand in hundred and the rest in twenties?" Alex asked.

Erol nodded, hands moving quickly as he organized four piles, each of one thousand dollars. He counted out the amount like it was no big deal--just another transaction. It made Alex wonder how much money a typical strigoi took with them when they left Heathshome and where the Arktois got their funds. When twenty thousand dollars left a building without paperwork confirmation-- four thousand of it in cash--you had to wonder how much money the organization had, let alone how much was kept in the drawers.

"Excuse me?" Alex interrupted Erol as he finished stacking the first pile of twenties. "Can I get the last one in hundreds? I didn't realize it was going to be so damn big."

Erol nodded, putting away the stack of twenties and pulling out ten one hundred dollar bills. Expertly, he stacked all of the cash and then counted it back to Alex.

"--and twenty, forty, sixty, eighty, four thousand."

Alex reached out and took the pile. He pulled out his wallet, put the license and Social Security card in place and wedged the stack of money in as well, though he had trouble closing it afterwards.

Erol pressed a couple more buttons and the printer spat out another small card. This time it looked like a gift card of some sort. Erol took the card, swiped it twice and handed it over to Alex.

"Sixteen thousand, even," he said as Alex took the card gingerly. "It works much like a normal credit card, but the funds are preloaded. Any questions?"

Alex shook his head. "No, wait," he said. "Can I borrow a car or something?"

"That's right, I'm sorry," Erol said quickly, turning back to his terminal. "Do you have a preference?"

Alex blinked. He had four thousand dollars cash and sixteen thousand on a preloaded credit card.

He'd lived in San Francisco and grew up with hippies for parents. There was one thing he'd always wanted to do.

Did he have a preference?

Alex smiled. "Yes, yes I do."

*   *   *

"Where is he?" Weynie threatened.

Jalal glared at her before turning back to a laptop he rarely used. "I don't know, he's not answering emails, he's not at home, and no one has seen him since lunch."

Weynie turned on her heel as she approached the wall and paced in the other direction purposefully. She'd been doing that for nearly an hour before Jalal finally showed up with the news that Alex was gone.

"Check the exit records, please," Weynie nearly whispered.

Why would he be avoiding her? She was just trying to help him and the boy was acting like she was the one who invaded his space and beaten him. If he weren't immortal, Alex would be dead.

Alex didn't even seem angry with Simon!

"I found something," Jalal said.

Weynie stopped pacing and walked over so she could look over his shoulder. What she saw didn't make her happy.

Apparently it upset Jalal a little as well.

"That son of a bitch," Jalal cursed, slamming shut the lid on the laptop with a sharp crack. "He used the offsite backup budget to get that money."

She was shocked. He never cursed.

"It said he was going to Buffalo?" Weynie asked, moving the subject away from the misuse of the budget. "Why Buffalo?"

Jalal glared at Weynie. "Because they have IT conferences there," Jalal said angrily. "If you read the rest of the entry you would have seen that."

"Jalal, calm down," Weynie said, putting a hand on his arm. "The money isn't important, but Alex and Dervy are."

"Pot. Kettle. Black," Jalal spat back at her.

He shook his head. "Yes, I'm aware of the irony of that statement."

Weynie sighed and stalked away. "Listen, we need to find him. He's like a beacon out there. They took both of them before. Why wouldn't they do it again?"

"Because they would have taken him last night if that were the case?" Jalal suggested with an annoyed flick of the wrist.

"You know they couldn't have," Weynie shot back. "Even with the authentication system down, they wouldn't have been able to get an unwilling strigoi out of Heathshome quietly."

Jalal nodded and plopped down into a nearby chair.

"If it was Simon," Weynie continued, "then he knows more about Alex than most of us. According to Alex, Simon Scryed him pretty deeply back in San Francisco. He probably expected something like this."

"Or he just wanted Dervy," Jalal said. "I mean, there is so much more going on here than just a runaway Taken. Even removing the idea that Kevin is alive and running some sort of clandestine kidnapping ring as you keep suggesting," Weynie frowned at that, but Jalal continued, "something is very, very off. In any other time, in any other place there would already be a team of

Enforcers tracking Simon down for imprisonment, but I have not heard of a single action brought against him or that other strigoi--"

"Nathan."

"--right, Nathan," Jalal acknowledged. "And you reported Alex's attack this morning, right?"

Weynie nodded. She was beginning to feel more and more uncomfortable as Jalal went on. The South African man was staring off into the distance, hands moving as if he were putting together an invisible puzzle.

Which he was, Weynie admitted.

"I mean, why is that?" Jalal asked. "There is only one entity who has the authority to stop due process and that is the Ankousti. That said, what are the chances that the entire Council is involved with this? It is not out of the realm of possibility that they could pass some motion to censure the response to these attacks."

"But we'd hear about them from someone," Weynie interrupted. "Some of the Elders wouldn't even go along with something like this. Erol certainly wouldn't stand for it. He's a really good man."

Jalal nodded. "Agreed."

He stood and walked over to the bench where Alex typically sat. He ran a hand over the Formica top.

"Then that only leaves one option," Jalal said quietly.

Weynie nodded, but said nothing. Neither of them had to.

There was only one person who had that type of authority. And that one person could mandate a complete and utter silence on any issue or topic within the Arktois without a majority vote in the Ankousti.

The Primator.

William Searle.

Jalal went back to the laptop and opened the lid long enough to see the shattered display. With a grimace, he left it on the table and turned toward Weynie. For the first time since she met him nearly a century earlier, Weynie saw fear and doubt written on his face.

"We should probably leave for Buffalo as well," Jalal said quietly. "The training session would be great for me and I know you have an interest, right?"

Weynie nodded slowly. It felt wrong, but she knew there

was little else to do.

Jalal nodded. "We should get going then if we are going to catch up with Alex."

"Right," Weynie said.

As they exited, Jalal turned and looked back, eyes scanning the room to finally settle on his tablet. His eyes lingered there for just a moment before turning and leaving.

Weynie followed and wondered if they would ever be back.

14
Northern Pennsylvania
4:54 PM January 21, 2011

    Zeke Dunfee sat quietly in the tiny room, eyes closed, lost in thought. The space seemed akin to a janitors' closet, though without the usual maintenance tools you'd find in such a place. The drifting snow outside the building obscured a small window, but gray sunlight managed to struggle through the piled flakes, bringing diffused light into his place of temporary solace. The strong scent of mold and mildew permeated the air causing him to sneeze periodically.

    A sudden chill raced through his body and Zeke pulled his jacket tighter. He wasn't entirely sure if the feeling came from the weak insulation surrounding the window or from the knowledge he'd gained since arriving at Kevin O'Ceallaigh's base of operations the week before. Another chill ran through him at the memory of the incinerator and the bodies piled before it, showing various stages of decomposition.

    There were dozens of strigoi within the compound. Inside Dóchas.

    It was an Irish word for 'hope'.

Zeke didn't dare to.

He hadn't seen such a collection of his fellow outcasts since the days of the revolution, but this group was different. Most of them had taken Kevin's offer of 'true immortality' and with rare exception, they were thrilled with the results, regardless of the price. As the days crept along, other strigoi, some Zeke recognized from his earlier life and others he had never met, trickled into the compound. They sought support, companionship and that sense of trust each and every one of them had lost when they were either ejected from or willingly left Heathshome and the Arktois. There were a select few who hadn't chosen to accept the shot for whatever reason, whether that was morality, concern at the cost, or disinterest in true immortality, but they were a minority.

Zeke was a member of this group. Upon arriving at Dóchas, he had been sorely tempted to accept Kevin's offer, but something had held him back. Maybe it was the frantic light in his old nemesis' eyes or the nagging question he had about Simon's eyesight, but regardless of the reason he'd abstained despite Kevin's obvious displeasure. Gaining a bunk in the staff quarters, Kevin had then dismissed Zeke and moved on with only a vague promise of future meetings about "plans," voice tinged with anger.

The following day, while at breakfast with the rest of the strigoi Zeke found out the cost of Kevin's offer.

He'd been taking a sip of the vile brew the kitchen staff claimed was coffee when the whisper of a voice had caught his ear. It was an urgent, insistent thing--begging, pleading for release. Zeke narrowed it down to the kitchen, using his enhanced hearing--better even than most other strigoi--and got to his feet, flimsy coffee cup held loosely in one hand.

As he approached, the desperate pleas grew more intense, panicked. Whoever was in the kitchen, it was a man, given the deep tone to the voice.

"Please," the voice had begged. "Don't do this, I won't do it ever again."

No voice answered.

Casting a glance around, Zeke saw that no one was watching him. In and of itself, that was odd, but what they were doing was even stranger. All of the strigoi in the room--men and women who had taken Kevin's offer, all--were sitting stock-still, eyes focused intently on the table in front of them, hands flat on the table.

The voice screamed, bringing him around quickly. "Just fucking say something!"

Quietly, Zeke pushed open the door to the kitchen and froze as the sharp scent of spilled blood tickled at his nostrils and awakened those deep urges that followed him through the Life.

In front of him were two strigoi and a short, naked Hispanic man. The short man was strapped to a table, head moving quickly back and forth between the strigoi on either side of him, tears streaming down his now terrified face. The table showed visible signs of sawing and chopping and a drain sat directly beneath it, the grout tinged burnt sienna. Two large rivulets ran alongside the man's head and out to the side. Two more ran along the inside of his legs. Each of his limbs were held fast by thick straps to restrict his movement.

The strigoi on his right picked up a long chef's knife and ran it quickly through a 'V' shaped groove built into the countertop just next to him. Each swipe rasped out, finishing with a sharp exclamation as the tip slashed outward and away.

"Please... " the man on the table pleaded as the defiance faded at the sight of the blade. "I'll do any--"

With a sudden motion, the strigoi with the knife drew it across the man's throat, cutting off his plea and leaving a deep red ravine behind. A moment later, blood began seeping out and spilling to either side. Moving with practiced accuracy, the strigoi made four other quick incisions--one on either side of the neck and one on the inside of each thigh. The man quickly began to spasm, body writhing against the restraints as his lifeblood drained to the floor--crimson streams striking and spattering onto the mud boots of the two other men.

"My God," Zeke managed as a wave of nausea hit him, overwhelming the hunger that had been building as he watched with disgusted fascination.

The man with the knife turned toward Zeke and frowned.

Zeke caught his breath as he recognized a man who'd served him during the revolution. "Will? How could you do this?"

Will Stone had followed him faithfully for more than a decade, both as a guerrilla fighter during the early years and finally through the very halls of Old Heathshome during their final push.

He'd been Zeke's third in command--a lieutenant, deferring only to Nathan Potts and Zeke himself. As with many of the strigoi who had joined him, Will Stone had been a good man.

Will shook his head slowly, eyes glancing down at the blood stained knife as if he had no idea how it had gotten there. He opened his mouth as if to say something, but quickly snapped it shut. Their eyes met for just a moment and Zeke took a step back. The Hunger was visible, tangible in that glance in a way Zeke had never seen.

"You took the shot, didn't you?" Zeke asked as he backed out of the kitchen.

"General, I... " William began, blinking furiously and rubbing at his forehead with a hand covered in arterial spray, leaving a grotesque red streak behind.

Zeke dropped his coffee as he put up a warding hand, body growing hot as his defenses began to kick into full gear. "No, you stay the hell away from me. All of you."

With that, he turned and ran, eventually finding this small room set away from the staff quarters in a corner seldom visited by others.

Kevin came to see him later, somehow tracking Zeke down to the closet. The dialog quickly degenerated as it became clear that this new self-proclaimed Primator of Dóchas was well aware of the sacrifice necessary with the application of the immortality drug. The conversation ended with Zeke calling the other man a murderer and casting him out of the room. Kevin left peacefully, but promised to return in a few days once Zeke had time to process everything. The next day Zeke had followed the smell of burnt flesh, oily and foul, to the incinerator where they tossed the carcasses of their victims.

Zeke turned and looked at the window. He focused, feeling his body warm and pushed that heat outward, toward the window and slightly beyond. Snow began to tear up on the other side of the pane as it melted, pile shrinking more rapidly as he gradually focused his Animi Ignis.

A sliver of silver light shot through the room as the snow collapsed in on itself, temporarily blinding him with its intensity. Zeke blinked away the sunspots and narrowed his eyes. A blue sky greeted him beyond the small snow bank, skeletal trees standing stark against the dark cerulean backdrop. Long shadows from the building he was in stretched across a parking lot that he could barely see as he stood up, though it was filled with vehicles of varying makes and models.

Zeke had forgotten the floor he was on happened to be just below ground level. As you entered the main entrance, there was a small descent before walking into the facility proper. He shook his head; Zeke had assumed the drab color of light to be indicative of a tearfully despondent sky, not due to him being underground.

A knock at the door brought his focus back to the room. He suddenly felt claustrophobic as Kevin entered. Zeke reached up and scratched at the long scar next to his eye while Kevin pulled a small footstool closer to him before sitting down. The so-called Primator smiled affably, but there was that same hint of madness and Hunger that tinged the other strigoi who had taken his 'gift'.

Zeke couldn't put his finger on it, but that instability seemed much more pronounced within Kevin. Zeke could still remember what the Irishman had looked like during most of his life--red-faced, thick beard the shade of rust and smooth skin around his eyes--but this Kevin O'Ceallaigh looked older. There were streaks of gray touching his beard--which appeared to have been shortened significantly--and fine lines touched his face wherever you looked-- around the eyes, mouth and nose.

"Ezekiel," Kevin said quietly before lowering his head and sighing. "Ezekiel. You know that I highly value your judgment in all things, right?"

Zeke frowned slightly before nodding hesitantly despite feeling quite the opposite.

Kevin smiled, nodding. "Good, good."

He paused again, drumming his fingers across his leg. "I want you on my side in what will happen next, Ezekiel."

Zeke nodded. "Okay."

"'They are too dangerous to rule this planet,'" Kevin said quietly, bringing a frown to Zeke's face. "You said that in 1886 during your exile trial."

"Alone. I said 'They are too dangerous to rule this planet alone'. I know what I said, Kevin," Zeke said in a measured tone. "I was suggesting taking on an advisory role. That tends to be forgotten. That's why I was exiled."

Kevin nodded thoughtfully. "And I'm sorry for that. You

were right and we were too weak to accept your vision."

Zeke almost choked in shock. Had Kevin O'Ceallaigh just apologized to him?

"That's why we need you," Kevin said with a reassuring smile. "Dóchas needs you."

"Dóchas needs to get itself under control, first," Zeke spat. "You're right. I don't think humans should be running this planet without us, but I certainly don't think we should be eating them, Kevin.

"What's happened to you?" Zeke asked in disgust. "How could you let something like this go on under your own roof?"

Kevin waved dismissively. "It's become apparent that humans are little more than cattle and tools to be used, Ezekiel. Like comparing a prize-winning race horse and a lame mule, some are more useful than others in the larger scheme of strigoi domination, but both have their uses."

"Your cooks chopped up a man in the kitchen a couple days ago!" Zeke yelled, pointing off into the distance as if he could pinpoint the exact location of the room.

On subsequent trips out of his room he had smelled that crisp scent of blood as well, but he managed to convince himself that it was the stagnant stink of aged fluids. The alternative would have driven him mad with guilt for lack of action.

Kevin shrugged.

Shrugged!

"He had no chi. He was a lame mule--a drain on the society that supported him," Kevin said casually. "He was a death row prisoner, if you care. Killed and raped two children in front of their mother before doing the same to her."

Kevin paused. "Do you still feel indignant?"

Zeke struggled to maintain his anger at the revelation, but felt it falter. Instead he clung to the morality of the choice. "It's still not right," he said weakly and Kevin smiled.

"The truth is rarely easy, Ezekiel," Kevin said quietly, placing a hand on his shoulder reassuringly.

"You know that."

Zeke nodded, but still pushed away the hand. "Tell me truthfully, then," Zeke said quietly. "These strigoi, these immortals, do they need to give in to the Hunger to continue on?"

Kevin leaned back and exhaled deeply. He waited, eyeing Zeke and it was obvious he was carefully weighing his words before answering.

"It's an easy question, Kevin," Zeke said quietly, yet forcefully. "It requires a 'yes' or 'no', nothing fancy. No flowery language or deceit."

Kevin leaned forward shaking his head. "It's not as easy as that--"

"Yes or no," Zeke repeated.

"We don't know, Ezekiel," Kevin said pleadingly. "It's... hard to describe the feeling."

A shadow passed over the Primator's face. "It's even harder to deny it."

Zeke exhaled. "How can you give this shot to them if it makes them into--into monsters?"

Anger flashed across Kevin's face, contorting his features into a mask of hate and violence, but it was gone as fast as it came. "I force no one, Ezekiel."

"Then leave," Zeke said as nausea rolled across his very being. "Leave and I will get out of here."

Kevin stared at him, confusion and something else clouding his face. Was it sadness?

"Okay," Kevin said, getting to his feet. "I'll leave."

Zeke nodded and released the breath he had been holding. "Thank you."

Kevin smiled weakly, then turned to leave the small room.

"What happened, Kevin?" Zeke blurted out so suddenly that he surprised himself.

The short Irishman stopped and he seemed to... shrink. His shoulders collapsed and his head, covered in light brown hair interspersed with orange lowered. Kevin turned slowly, eyes full of sadness and loss, mouth slightly open and downturned as if carefully considering his words.

Abruptly, Kevin smiled, though the sadness remained. "I don't know. Huh. Nothing important anyway."

With that, Zeke's old nemesis turned and left, leaving Zeke alone with his thoughts and concerns.

"I wanted to help them Kevin," Zeke mumbled to himself. "Not kill them."

Deep down, Zeke knew that Kevin must have done what he did out of a concern for the betterment of the strigoi, but he had gone too far. Cheating the Return was one thing--it was a dream of nearly every strigoi since the dawn of time--but the price was too steep, too... wrong.

Another knock interrupted his thoughts and for a moment he panicked, but then he saw the small sheet of folder paper on the stool where Kevin had been sitting. It looked like Kevin had forgotten it in his haste. Reaching across, Zeke picked up the sheet of paper and stood, walking the few steps to the door. Idly, he flipped the sheet open, eyes glancing down onto the handwritten text.

I'm sorry.

Panic flooded him, defenses kicking into full strength--the paper in his hands lighting into flame as he focused--but he was too slow. The metal door exploded inward, bowing in at the center as it was released from its hinges by an incredible force. It slammed into Zeke, tossing him to the left and against the bare wall.

The sound of falling cement chips, the creak of cracked wood and shouting greeted him a moment later as multiple strigoi charged into the room.

Zeke screamed in anger and unleashed a wave of flame, pushing the fire away from him with bonds of air and force. It struck like a concussive ball of flame. Zeke felt his eardrums pop and crack as it exploded. Blue flame writhed around four figures as they were shoved against the opposite wall, colliding with it under such a force that Zeke found himself crushed against his own wall, his entire body vibrating, shattering ribs, and puncturing more than one organ.

Grunting, Zeke pulled himself to his feet, forcing his body to heal faster. It was hard to ignore the sensation of bugs inside of you--dancing across destroyed tissue and bone--let alone the experience of having one of those ribs suddenly pop back into place, but it did allow him to push out his chest and breathe again. He struggled forward toward the open doorway.

He was almost out of the room when something gripped his foot. A moment later he was weightless and then he struck the wall with the window. Zeke's head rebounded off of the glass, shattering it with the force of the collision.

Grunting in pain, Zeke looked around, trying desperately to find his target, to clear the way for an escape.

He shouldn't have trusted Kevin. He was evil... untrustworthy.

Despair washed over him as a form rose in front of him out of the thick dust and growing smoke from the smoldering fires he'd lit. The hulking black man reached forward, grabbing hold of Zeke's throat with a single hand and lifting him into the air.

Zeke pounded at the other man's arm, feeling bones and muscle give and then immediately reform without so much as a twitch. Lights flashed in front of his eyes as he choked, but he continued to strike at the man using arms and legs. A dark face leaned in--clean-shaven, hair tightly controlled with a buzz cut--and Zeke stopped fighting back. His second-in-command. His Right Arm. The man he had trusted beyond a doubt before and after the revolution failed.

Zeke couldn't beat him.

"Na--Na--than?" Zeke managed to choke out.

Nathan Potts nodded, face impassive. The grip increased, squeezing, muscle tearing and veins beginning to break under the force of the choke.

"I'm... sorry, Zeke," Nathan said quietly, eyes darting quickly to the left.

The world was growing black. Already he couldn't feel his legs and his left arm had gone limp. Zeke wanted to scream at him, to tell Nathan what Kevin was doing was wrong. That it was never what the revolution had been about.

They had dreamed of something greater--something benefitting both races, something that brought the wisdom that age fostered to the innovation a short lifetime demanded.

Zeke tried to say something, but then he met Nathan's eyes.

The Hunger. It was there, just on the edge of vision, dancing in the skin around the whites of his eyes, almost like a tiny twitch.

But it wasn't anything so mundane. He had seen it in Kevin's face as well. This is what true immortality really brought-- madness and death.

As the darkness swept upon him, tears rolled down Zeke's face for the first time in a century as realization struck him. It tore at him, screaming into his soul. They would use him as an excuse--a banner to wave. They would martyr him. Alone, Kevin could rally a few hundred strigoi, but with Zeke murdered by the Arktois or the humans--whoever--Kevin would have an army. All of his old soldiers. All of his friends. Almost a third of the strigoi nation could rally...

That was the reason Zeke had disappeared in the first place. To avoid something like this.

It would be his fault.

"I'm sorry," Zeke managed to choke out.

Nathan Potts blinked and squeezed harder.

The world went black.

15
Nevada/Utah Border
8:41 PM January 21, 2011

The wind tore through the windows of the car and the engine roared as the Dodge Charger flew through the night. Dervy didn't look at the speedometer, preferring to keep her foot to the floor instead. All around her the world was a blur of flat landscape, moonlit terrain flying by at a breakneck pace. She smiled at the sharp scent of salt and earth that filled the cab.

Dervy reached down calmly and picked up her now chilled coffee. She drank deeply as she crossed the Nevada-Utah border. A pinprick vibration sparked at the back of her neck as she entered the new state. A human was ahead of her, a good ways down the highway.

Slowly, she eased on the brakes, bringing the speed back down to seventy-five miles per hour. A minute later she passed a highway patrol car in the center divide. She wasn't followed. As the minutes crawled by, Dervy accelerated again, quickly topping out the speed limiter on the car and relaxing.

There was a certain peace to be found in driving, especially when traversing such a barren landscape as that of the Nevada and

Utah desert areas. Adding breakneck speeds to the equation made it a bit more entertaining as well. Dervy set the cup of coffee in her lap, keeping one hand on the steering wheel. She let her mind rest as the car sped along the luminous road.

The lines were hypnotic. Long reflective spreads of light vibrated under some unknown force, drawing her ever onward along the shifting path. Memories of banners flapping in the breeze, screaming men and women--the scent of burning pitch and flesh heavy in the air--shifted effortlessly into the moaning agony of a city under siege by an unseen foe, rose blossoms decorating their skin as she wandered alone, helpless against their plight.

Bright light flashed in her eyes--the mushroom cloud spewing upward and outward as radiation burned her skin despite her distance from the city.

"Fuck!" Dervy yelled, pulling the car back into her lane as a horn honked, loud and long.

The Charger fishtailed as the tractor-trailer sped by, a gust of wind kicking the backend of the car violently. Dervy tapped the brakes and counter-steered, putting the Charger into a sideways slide, wheels skipping across the pavement. Out of the corner of her eye she saw a blow over point, sand spreading across the road in a narrow band a few feet wide.

Dervy closed her eyes as the car struck the sand. The wheels on the right side folded and the car flipped, careening into the air like a toy until it landed twenty feet away. Despite herself, Dervy screamed as the ceiling crumpled in onto her, pushing her down into the steering wheel. The movement continued, each flip slamming her harder, sending sparks through her vision.

She pushed on the steering wheel as the vehicle leapt again, stretching out the roof of the car in panic, but it landed upside down, slamming her back downward and delivering her to oblivion.

16
Somewhere near Elmira, NY
7:33 AM January 22, 2011

    Alex shook the gas nozzle before hanging it back up and securing the cap. He gave the 'No' button a light flick as the machine asked him if he wanted a receipt. Humming, Alex jumped in the cab of his F150 and turned the engine over. With a grin, he pulled away from the gas station.
    Dawn was breaking through the trees on the horizon as he made his way west. Huge swaths of deciduous and evergreen forests covered either side of the four-lane highway, interrupted only by the infrequent town or gas station. Any open land was a glittering sheet of snow, iridescent as the sun rose, violet and magenta sparks of light showering the countryside.
    Alex reached down and turned the heat up a notch even though the truck wasn't warm yet. It was a futile attempt at warding off the deep chill of an Upstate New York winter. He shivered inside the thin coat he'd brought and muttered quietly. San Francisco might not be warm, but it certainly stayed above freezing. He shook his head at the temperature gauge in the dash that read five degrees Fahrenheit.

Merging onto the highway from the exit, Alex leaned back into the seat and relaxed. He set the cruise control at the speed limit and smiled as vehicles began passing him. As they sped by, Alex found himself looking at them and wondering. What were they in such a hurry for? The woman doing her makeup at 70 miles per hour... the man eating breakfast at 80... the old couple arguing vehemently at 72.

Was their hurry worthwhile? What was wrong with the world when multitasking interrupted your safety and brought you within an inch of dying at any moment?

It was the expectation of more, Alex conceded to himself. There was always one more thing to do--one more task that begged for completion. No one took the time to experience life in modern America. Everyone was too busy preparing for the always ephemeral 'tomorrow' and the unattainable 'future'. Would it be worth makeup applied, meal eaten, or argument won if any of those people lost control of their vehicle?

The obvious answer was no, but Alex found himself remembering doing similar tasks while in bumper to bumper traffic in the heart of San Francisco. How many meals had he eaten in his car over the past five years? How many emails had he read and text messages had he sent?

Alex sighed. It just wasn't worth it. Just as it hadn't been worth the years of misery he put himself through after Mary's accident. He tapped the steering wheel thoughtfully at that, feeling strangely optimistic despite the memory of his dead wife, lying still and silent on the cold, silver slab of the morgue. It had been such a long time since he'd allowed himself to really feel anything besides grief. What did happiness even feel like anymore?

Alex flicked on the radio and started seeking through the channels, searching for distraction. His first attempt located a station playing some sort of cheerful rock tune, so he left it. In a few moments Alex was tapping away on the steering wheel in time, swinging back and forth to the beat without really listening to the words. A gray SUV sped by and pulled in front of him, swerving slightly as it did so.

"Idiot," Alex mumbled, reaching down to change the channel as it became clear he was listening to a Christian music channel. "Why are there so many of these around here?"

Red lights flashed in front of him and the SUV fishtailed. Alex slammed on the brakes, cursing, and swerved toward the left lane. The truck lurched as he collided with another vehicle in that lane and then the world exploded as he rammed into the back of the SUV, airbags deploying all around him with a resounding pop. Something slammed into him and there was a sudden moment of vertigo and complete silence. It was as if he were suspended in a vacuum.

Then the world shattered.

Alex was tossed toward the passenger seat, though, luckily, his seat belt kept him firmly in place. The sound of tearing steel and plastic boomed within the encompassing blanket of airbags as the world spun, crinkling the cab up around him.

With a final thump, the truck came to a stop on its side, Alex suspended in the air by a seat belt, the ground slowly becoming visible through the passenger side window as he batted away airbags. Grunting, Alex released the harness and fell the few feet to the ground where he landed with a crunch, digging into the shattered glass of the window. He looked around quickly, cuts and scraps already beginning to close on his face and hands.

Alex sat down on the ground and gave the windshield a kick, popping it free of its mountings easily. He reached out and pushed it away, ignoring the shower of crystalline fragments that fell on him. Adrenaline pushed him through the glass and into the snowy drift where he had landed.

Slowly, Alex rolled over into the snow and took a deep, steadying breath. Closing his eyes, he focused on the soreness in his chest, the cuts across his body, and the pain right behind his left ear and willed it away. Bruised ribs healed and chips of shattered glass were forced from his face and hands almost immediately. He tried not to think of why it finally seemed to be working. Instead, he let the healing complete.

A moment later, a sharp pain indicated that the object in the side of his head had been pushed out as well.

Cursing, he sat up on his elbow and looked for the last object. He found it melting into the snow, a small flattened ball of metal covered in blood and skin. Squinting, Alex rotated it in his fingers, uneasiness sweeping over him as he realized what it was.

A bullet.

Alex cursed again and scrambled to his feet and crouched behind the hood of the overturned vehicle. "It's okay, it's okay," he reassured himself as he slowly raised his head above the edge of the wreck. "It's not a bullet. No one shot me..."

Two SUVs were pulled over on the side of the highway nearly a hundred yards away. There was a clear trail leading from where his truck had slid off the road to where it landed as a smoldering wreck. Four figures were scaling the side of the steep hill, all wearing thick winter jackets and hoods. One of them was incredibly tall and looked to be in a gray suit and a long black fabric trench coat. Alex's heart sank as he saw a pistol in the hands of one of the others coming down the hill.

"Oh shit," Alex muttered, dropping back to snow and leaning against the snow.

Alex had no desire to find out what they wanted, least of all from the tall man. If he was right, that was the guy who had grabbed he and Dervy a few months earlier. Even if the ultimate goals of that group were philanthropic, adding "getting shot in the head" to the list of offenses did little for Alex's trust. The only thing he was considering at that moment was getting the hell out of there, but there was a major hurdle of which he was only too aware.

He was Taken, which meant he might as well have been jumping around with a spotlight on him and a loudspeaker yelling "Over here! Over here!" Getting away would take a lot more than simply turning tail and running. The only way Alex Mamsin was going anywhere was either with the four strigoi.

Then again, maybe he could outrun them and get ahold of the Arktois. Neither option seemed very attractive, but they were all he had.

"Oh god," Alex whined as the four tingling dots danced closer to him.

What would they do this time if they took him? Dervy had barely mentioned what she had been through, but the little she had made his skin crawl. They had cut her open. Taken samples. At the time, Alex had simply thought he was helping humanity, but in hindsight he had to wonder what type of organization would do such a thing to a living being. Would he be the one cut apart like a lab rat? Diced and chopped like a never-ending sample?

And then there was Simon. He worked with them. For

them. The man had broken into his home and beaten him mercilessly for information. Sure, Alex hadn't been kidnapped then, but he'd been in Heathshome where it was safe. Where he was protected.

Now he was alone. Alex's only escape was sitting useless next to him and the only chance he had beyond that was to outmaneuver four strigoi with decades, if not centuries, more experience than he had. He could barely use any of his powers. If his encounter with Simon had taught him anything, it was that he certainly couldn't even hold up regeneration under any real pressure.

"I'm screwed," Alex grunted, sliding his back down the hood of the truck as the four dots began moving more quickly, their vibrations growing more intense as they closed the distance.

He looked out across the snow-covered field where his truck had come to rest. It spread away from him, an undisturbed sheet of ice and snow until it faded away into a tree line in the distance. Behind him, he heard the crunch of boots as they approached and he bit his lip.

Did he run for cover and have a chance or make a stand and fail?

"When you say it like that..." Alex muttered, getting to his feet, but keeping low.

His heart was pumping, but the panic that typically overwhelmed him was conspicuously absent. Instead, he felt a rising excitement as the footsteps drew closer.

Alex licked his lips, a small grin creeping across his face.

Behind him, the footsteps stopped.

"Alex," a deep voice called out. "Can you come out on your own or do we need to get you?"

Alex took off, bolting off toward the tree line, a string of curses erupting behind him as he sped forward. Each step pounded through the drifted snow, making his progress infinitely slower than his sprint through the Pennsylvania forest, but it was also inhibiting his pursuers.

"Alex!" The deep voice screamed behind him as he ran. "Stop or we'll stop you!"

It was definitely the man from before.

Nathan.

Alex grimaced. *Balls.*

The sounds of multiple feet pounding through crunchy snow followed Alex as he pressed forward, adrenaline rushing through his veins. He pushed forward as quickly as he could, feet hammering into the thick, icy crust that covered most of the field. A sharp pop echoed around him--sounding much like someone had detonated a firecracker--and he heard something whiz past him.

Alex screamed despite himself and forced his legs to move more quickly, but they were already starting to give away. He cursed himself for not continuing to run after being delivered to Heathshome. Since that night, Alex hadn't been able to channel that same infinite vigor Dervy had forced out of him.

"Come on," Alex urged his aching body and burning lungs, but the tree line remained far away, taunting him with the safety of its boughs.

Another pop and this time a flaring pain shot through his shoulder, dropping him to the ground in a roll. Alex pulled himself back up and focused on the pain for a moment, forcing the wound closed. Gasping, he pulled himself forward, fighting for every step against the flaring pain in his chest and legs.

"I can make it," Alex grunted through gritted teeth.

A moment later a bullet tore through his other shoulder, followed by another in his upper back and a third in his upper thigh. Alex hit the ground unceremoniously, gasping as the pain wracked his body. He focused on the pain, closing the wound in his thigh and shoulder, but his chest was more difficult. Each attempt brought agony as the bullet shifted through his body.

"No, no, no," Alex spat at the deep azure sky as the sounds of gasping and boots crunching through snow surrounded him.

One of the strigoi stepped over him. He was an Asian man who appeared to be in his mid-twenties. He was gasping heavily, too. Shaking his head, the man kneeled down and brought the pistol forward, dangling it just above Alex's head, steam drifting off the hot barrel in the frigid air.

"You're a pain in the ass, Taken," the man said in a voice tinged with annoyance and disgust.

Alex grimaced, still trying to force the bullet out of his chest. He failed again.

"You want to say something?" The man said, leaning in with an ear forward, tauntingly.

"Get away from him," the man with the deep voice yelled, though it was apparent he was pretty far away still.

He still had a chance.

The Asian man turned toward the voice. "What's he gonna do?"

Alex grit his teeth in anger and pain as the bullet finally pushed out through the hole in his back. He reached up and grabbed the shocked man by the jacket and pulled him toward him. Alex then slammed his forehead into the other man's face. Bright lights flashed in Alex's eyes for a moment, but soon the sound of cursing and angry yelling resounded around him. Something slammed into his head, pummeling him back to the snow and cutting a long gash across his cheek.

Alex cursed and tried to sit up, but a foot slammed into his chest, forcing him back down to the snow violently.

The man he had head butted--nose twisted and flattened across his face, blood splattered everywhere--stood above him, pistol pointed down at him.

Shocked, Alex raised his hand defensively, the familiar panic finally springing to the fore. "Wai--"

A bright muzzle flash and everything went black.

17
Nevada/Utah Border, UT
7:42 AM January 22, 2011

The world was empty.

It was a place void of color or emotion, of sound and light; weightless, quiet.

Peaceful.

Everything felt as she had always hoped. The world was gone, left behind in a rental car used to let her escape. She smiled into nothingness, only wondering briefly at her ability to do so.

How long had she hoped for this time, this solitude? How many times had she sobbed silently, wishing for it all to end?

And now it was.

It was... beautiful.

But something was wrong. It was a nagging thought--a worry without substantiation. It was there nonetheless and if Dervy had learned one thing through her long life, it was to trust her worries. Tentatively, she reached out to it, though she was unsure how. It was more of a stretch of the mind--a near instinctive reaction to her desire than a practiced act.

Ahead of her, a pinprick of light flickered into existence. Dervy squinted as it grew brighter, forms merging and flowing inside its depths, every changing and morphing. She reached forward in that same way, letting her mind react to her need, caressing the light, bringing it into existence, and forming a picture.

It began as a whisper. There was a murmur of nonsense in an otherwise empty world, drawing her forward, urging her toward the light. She stepped toward it, curiosity guiding her steps as much as the instinctual responses her mind facilitated.

What was it? Dervy wondered as she approached, stretching out toward the floating globe of light and sound.

She pulled back in shock as feeling flowed into her, harsh and poignant. Dervy hesitated as the sounds and light urged her forward, begging her to reach out again. What if this was Valhalla or Heaven? Would she stay back because of fear or step forward bravely?

Hesitantly, Dervy reached forward, cringing as the sense of touch flooded back into her. She gasped in pain as the light sped toward her, filled with sound, angry and violent. She tried to run, to flee, but the light wrapped around her.

As it slammed into her, tearing her apart, she did something she hadn't done in a century.

Dervy screamed in fear.

*   *   *

Holy hell. She's alive. Get the stretcher.
Yes, sir.
The world was a spinning globe of lights and sound.
Blue and red.
Red and blue.
Flashing, spinning.
Nausea hit her and she vomited, blood mixing with the contents of her lunch. Everything was so distant, so far away.

Where was she? How did she get here?

"Can you hear me?" A voice erupted in her ear like an explosion and she screamed in response, slamming hands against her ears, but missed on one side, a sickly stump slapping weakly against her cheek.

Her face was hot with her own blood as it gushed.

"We need restraints!" The voice pummeled her and she writhed in agony, light swirling and spinning in the night.

Voices were more distant behind her, off to the side. "She just crossed the line, I don't know... "

Weak human hands gripped at her wrists, forcing her still as her body reacted, pushing blood, flesh and sinew out through the open hole at her wrist.

"Get off me!" Dervy screamed, sitting up against the gripping hands.

She looked around in panic, men she didn't recognize, some concerned, some scared, some...

"Jesus Christ... " One man said, pulling away as if he'd touched something unholy.

Dervy screamed in pain as her body reformed bone first, followed quickly by sinew and muscle. The flesh burned as it touched her pants and the stretcher, but she reached out with it anyway, ignoring the pain and grabbing one man by the throat and tossing him away like a rag doll.

The others backed away quickly, backpedaling as she screamed and cried, rocking back and forth while her body regenerated. Everything was ruined, a torn, bloody mess where it had been smooth and flawless. Her face burned as it was healed, bones popped as they reset into old, torn joints.

The ants seethed on her body.

The world was silent agony. She shut her eyes, wishing and begging for it to end as they crawled across and through her. The world gained balance as her right ear grew back and the eardrum stretched taut. Her left nostril slowly formed, pulling on the skin around it, tugging on the slash through her cheek.

"Please, stop," Dervy cried.

She wasn't sure what exactly she meant. Did she want the pain to stop or something else?

Did she want it to be permanent?

"Please," Dervy begged as she rocked back and forth.

Her skin began closing, sensations dulling as fingers were wrapped in dermis and bare tendons were covered. Dervy let out a shuddering sigh as the hole in her cheek stitched back together, closing up with a sickening sound like that of a slurping straw.

"What are you?"

Dervy looked up, eyes tearing up against the grating sand from the wind-swept desert. She looked around, counting quickly.

Seven men.

Men who had seen her come back from the dead.

Men who needed to die.

She leaned to the side of the stretcher, tossing the loose black bag they had bagged her in. She was sick of killing; sick of lying and hiding and pretending she didn't exist. It used to be important in the days when she established the rules, but was it still? Did she need to hide in this world, this place filled with so many that had lost touch with themselves?

In many ways, Dervy was just another human in the world; lost, estranged, and lonely.

Dervy looked ahead of her where a police officer was standing slack-jawed next to a larger man, red flares coloring them dangerously in the deepness of the night. She hopped to the ground and stumbled slightly.

One of her shoes was missing.

She walked over to the police officer, but turned toward the other man first. "You the guy in the truck?"

He nodded, but didn't say anything.

Dervy smiled. "Thanks for stopping."

"No problem, miss," he said quietly.

She turned back to the police officer that had moved a hand to his gun, a slightly panicked look on his face. "Don't do that," she said casually. "It'll just piss me off."

The officer nodded and took his hand off the pistol slowly.

Dervy sighed. "Thank you."

She looked around into the empty wastes around her, the rotating lights reverberating across the tiny dunes, dissipating and spreading their glow as they went. In the distance, the horizon had brightened, dulling the lights of the police car.

"Can I get a ride to Salt Lake City, by any chance?" Dervy asked, flashing her most charming smile at the group of dumbfounded men.

*   *   *

"Over there," Weynie said, tapping Jalal on the shoulder and pointing to the shoulder where a police car was pulled over, its lights flashing silently in the afternoon sun.

They had been driving all morning, stopping at various areas to check and see if anyone had seen Alex. They had finally gotten a stroke of luck from a nearby gas station.

Now it looked like those hopes might be dashed.

Jalal nodded and eased the sedan to the side of the road behind the police car. The field below was pristine, an undisturbed palette of glistening ocher in the fading light of day except for a long shadowed scar that ended at the crumpled mass of a pickup truck. Tracks were visible from the side of the highway down toward the truck as dark pockmarks in the snow. As Jalal rolled the car to a stop, Weynie's heart leapt into her throat.

Putting the vehicle in park, Jalal took a moment to make sure that traffic had passed and opened his door to exit. Weynie followed suit, taking care on the slippery shoulder. Shutting the door behind her, she made her way quickly to where the other car sat idling.

As they approached a tall policeman exited, motioning to the back of his vehicle and glancing behind them as if to verify that there was no one else with them. He was well above six foot with a heavy build though there was some prominent buildup around his midsection. Despite being clean-shaven, he wasn't handsome in any way. A prominent jawline and a crooked nose that looked like it had been broken and set incorrectly dominated his face. Weynie and Jalal stepped up closer to him, both looking toward the wreck.

"I'm Officer Phelps," the man said, nodding at each of them in turn.

"Weynie Dixit," Weynie lied, flashing a smile at the officer. "This is Jalal Ebbs." She added pointing at Jalal, who nodded.

"Do you know this vehicle?" Office Phelps asked, pointing off at the mess in the field.

Weynie nodded, but Jalal spoke. "It looks like a truck issued to an associate of ours from work."

"His name is Alex," Weynie added, looking off into the distance as if in a trance.

There was no smoke, no steam. Frigid air swept across the plain, causing her eyes to tear from its harsh bite. Footsteps went down to the wreckage, then some more beyond the truck... toward the tree line in the distance.

"I went down, but there's no one in the vehicle," the officer said. "It looked like a couple folks stopped and... picked him up."

Weynie cocked an eye at him. "You paused."

Officer Phelps shifted uncomfortably under her stare and Jalal shot her a sudden glare. "I'm afraid I can't say much else until we process the sce--"

Weynie focused on Officer Phelps, pushing her mind into his, forcing away folds of defenses as if they were papier-mâché--stiff, but inflexible and thus fragile. The man stumbled slightly as she delved into his mind, vicious and relentless. Distorted images flashed before her, half-formed thoughts merging haphazardly with the walk down to the truck. Chaos ensued for a moment--pictures of people she didn't know, places she'd never been.

Usually, Weynie would take more care, use patience and a soft touch to help the process, but she was in a hurry. She pushed harder and something gave way allowing the memory she needed to snap into focus. She grabbed it.

There is blood everywhere as he approaches, though it grows more prominent when he reaches the vehicle. The front window looks like a torn sheet of paper, folded upward at an odd angle as if someone had kicked it free from the inside. Phelps leans forward, carefully holding himself upright while he peers through the window. He notices small traces of blood, nick and scratch stuff, but nothing to explain the pools he saw on his way down. Phelps bites his cheek and carefully walks around the front of the truck, doing his best to avoid the blood pools and existing tracks. The last thing he needs is to get in trouble for disturbing a crime scene. He's still on probation for the hooker incident.

He peers around the front of the truck, balancing himself with a gloved hand and his breath catches. About a dozen yards out toward the tree line is a red patch in the snow. From there it moves back toward the highway, each subsequent pool or splatter smaller and more faint...

Weynie blinked and put a hand to her head at the sudden headache that assaulted her. In front of her, Officer Phelps had collapsed against his squad car, arms and legs splayed haphazardly. Jalal sat over him, urgently trying to wake him with a few quick slaps to the face, but to no avail.

Jalal turned and glared at her. "You could have just asked!"

Weynie said nothing. Instead she stared for a moment at the motionless man on the ground, her heart empty of sympathy. What good were beings so frail that they could simply collapse like this? She'd hardly pushed him--only the one thrust had been anywhere near forceful--so why was he catatonic?

Weynie looked back out at the broken truck, Officer Phelps' memories as clear in her mind as they had been in his, though the mixing magentas and vermilions colored it in a way that made it seem softer, less dangerous. Less foreboding. That would end once the sun finally set behind those trees, casting shadow upon the world and flooding the wreckage in darkness.

"Let's go," Weynie said, walking back to their car.

Jalal hesitated for a moment, trying to wake the man one more time, though the effort was futile. Weynie sighed and got into the car, taking care to belt herself. Something about the sight of the car crash made it seem important. Jalal was there a moment later, plopping himself down into the driver seat with a grunt.

They sat in silence for what seemed like an eternity, Officer Phelps sitting motionless to the side of the police car where Jalal had moved him. Weynie chewed her lip, glancing askance at Jalal who sat next to her, taking deep, even breaths.

Weynie broke the silence. "Maybe we sh--"

"If you ever do something like that again," Jalal interrupted, still facing forward, unmoving. "I will never speak to you again."

Weynie felt tears welling. "Jalal, I'm--"

"Do you understand?" He asked, finally looking at her.

The disgust and shame present on his face made her sick, nauseous.

Slowly, Weynie nodded.

"I am glad to hear it," Jalal said quietly, emotionlessly.

They sat in an awkward silence again, Weynie wanting to apologize, but not wanting to see that face again. She wanted to crawl in a hole and die.

"There are a lot of strigoi that hate humans," Jalal said suddenly, voice even and calm. "I am not entirely sure why, but I guess I can understand the need to demonize something you can no longer be."

Weynie didn't move. She bit her lip in silence.

Jalal sighed. "Just because we can't die does not make us better than them. We ignore that, relegating them to the importance of serfs and peasants, while at the same time forgetting that the entire system fails without those very people. The lords and ladies, the emirs and kings, they live on the backs of the peasants, squeezing the life out of them, eking away a life of luxury and respite.

"But that has nothing to do with why I stayed with the Arktois after my Youngling years. I stayed because I felt like I belonged. I had a family. I found real friends for the first time in my life."

Jalal looked at Weynie, face sad. "And I left the hate behind. All were equal in the Arktois and I managed to avoid most of the unpleasantries associated with human-strigoi relations. But at the end of the day, whether you believe that what we are given is a gift or a curse, the simple fact is that we were all human once and, as the Return falls upon us, we will be once again. It's just a matter of time."

Weynie nodded, trying desperately to resolve the conflicting hate and shame that warred inside of her. It wasn't that she hated humans--because she didn't... this was the first time anything like this had every happened. It had always been Dervy sitting on the edge, staring at their massing numbers with barely concealed abhorrence as the decades crawled by. She was nothing like that; like Dervy.

But when compared to the worst, you always came out looking pretty good, didn't you? Her heart sank at the realization.

"I'm sorry, Jalal," Weynie muttered, feeling much like a chastised child. "I... "

She looked over at him and chewed her lip. "We should get going... "

She slid the fabric of her scarf between her fingers rapidly.

Jalal looked at her for a moment before nodding and starting the car. Flicking on his turn signal, he pulled the vehicle out onto the road, leaving behind the flashing lights of the police car, still spinning as night settled on the scene.

18
Unknown
Unknown

"Heart rate is up."

Alex screamed in his mind as another tube was pushed into his abdomen. A moment later they turned a nozzle and fluid rushed into his body. It felt like when you get hit with a stream of water while playing in the back yard during a hot summer day. The slight dimpling of your skin, that hairpin of pain as the fountain runs across nerve endings. But instead of flowing off onto the ground and allowing you to dance away giggling, it breaks through you. Into you. Flooding your body with a foul liquid that reeked of tar.

"Sedate him."

Faceless forms, masks pulled tight to anonymize them while they shuffled around the table monitoring beeping machines and taking samples.

A pinprick in his arm... the world became fuzzy, dulled. Alex retreated into his mind, falling backwards into his head as if looking through an infinitely deep tunnel.

"Where is the list?"

"Right here."

The high-pitched whine of a bone saw flared to life as the world faded.

"How is his medulla oblongata supposed to help?"

How indeed...?

*   *   *

Simon turned away from the window just as the high-pitched whine turned into an abrasive grind when blade met bone. A shudder ran through his body at the sound. Distant memories of Vermont, a chainsaw in hand and ten men pulling a tree with straps away from him--the smell of the pine and sickly sweet fragrance of decomposing foliage underfoot--flashed in his mind. A moment later, it was gone, replaced by the dull sound of something hard and wet cracking.

The four others in the room looked askance at him, while still trying to monitor the events just beyond the glass. They were all human--three women, one man--and their ages were scattered along the prism of life. One was a pre-med student kicked out for performing unlicensed surgery, two of the women had been partners at a successful cancer institute, and the last man had lost his license due to a malpractice suit during an emergency room mix up that left two people dead.

They were all geniuses. Paragons of skill and intelligence all. And they had all lost something.

Simon looked at the young woman staring out the window, eyes wide and excited, curly brown hair barely contained in a tight ponytail and pock-marked cheeks flushed at the sight.

They called her Doctor Sterows, despite not having finished medical school. Her father and mother had been soldiers--stationed in Afghanistan and Iraq, respectively. Both had died within an hour of each other from insurgent roadside bombs. She received the news while finishing up her second year at Stanford Medical. Within the next two years, Sterows had been ejected for performing research on the hardening of cellular tissue without consent, in a way deemed amoral, and for impersonating a doctor. She avoided criminal charges when Kevin recruited her in 2006. He made the federal inquiry disappear.

The two older women had a much less maligned history.

Doctor Williams--the shorter woman with salt-and-pepper hair and transparent framed glasses--had joined forces with Doctor Penheimer--the taller woman with dark brown hair and a long hawkish nose--in 1986 after losing her longtime partner to throat cancer. Throughout the years the two woman spearheaded cancer research and developed various treatments, but always fell short of their goal. They wanted a cure, though not a vaccine. They were pragmatists and didn't believe they could actually prevent something like cancer from happening reliably, but they both believed wholeheartedly that it could be stopped just like an infection. When their funding was cut, Kevin stepped in and offered them limitless resources in their search for a cure.

The man was Frank Heathrow, not a doctor anymore, but rather a biochemist and bioengineer of some renown. Simon's brief research on the man had turned up that he had won the Nobel Prize for Chemistry earlier in his life before turning to more extreme applications of his mind. If the news was to be believed, Heathrow had been cloning children and integrating cybernetics into their bodies as early as the fetal stage. These projects--despite showing actual promise--caused him to be expelled from the scientific community and he lost everything in the subsequent local, state and federal lawsuits that ensued. Kevin claimed he had literally pulled the man off of the ledge.

All four had been lured in by Kevin's promises--biological discovery or freedom from oversight committees--and each quickly fell into step with the mantra of the organization. They ingrained the message that the ends justified the means and each had learned, in turn, how to filter the screams out of their scientific inquiries. Simon wondered if they still heard the cries in their sleep like he did.

Abruptly all four of them rushed to the window as a nearby monitor began spewing data onto its flat screen. They muttered amongst themselves all while scribbling furiously at their boards for a few minutes before Heathrow handed his to Sterows for review.

"That might work… " 'Doctor' Sterows mumbled, handing the clipboard over to one of the elder doctor duo.

Simon shook his head and left as the saw spun back to life, it's high-pitched whining as painful as if the blade was tearing into his own skull. He shut the door behind him as their chattering reached a dissonant crescendo with the bone saw. The steel barrier muted the cacophony, but couldn't eliminate it.

Eager to get away, Simon sped down the hallway toward a nearby exit. Large windows flashed by as he jogged, the brightness of the noonday sun glistening off the snowy accumulation outside. It shone pleasantly, invitingly. Simon longed to be outside, away from the vibrating din of the saw and the wavering itch at the back of his neck.

Ahead of him, standing aloofly near the exit was an average looking strigoi with medium length brown hair, nondescript features and no defining facial hair. He wore the strigoi uniform as mandated by "Primator" O'Ceallaigh, the same one Simon refused to wear. The outfit managed to make him look like one of the other hundred and fifty strigoi who had trickled in over the past few months. It consisted of a collared red jacket with an emblem sewn over the man's left breast. It was an emotionless, half-shadowed blue face surrounded by what appeared to be flames. Under the jacket, the man wore a white shirt and sported pressed black pants.

To Simon this strigoi was just another eternally youthful face in the crowd. Right now, he was in the way.

"Move," Simon spat as he approached, waving the other man to the side.

If Nathan was Kevin's right hand man, Simon was the left. Everyone in Dóchas knew who Simon was; hell, he'd invited most of them into the facility over the past few months.

Now, instead of stepping to the side, this strigoi stepped between Simon and the door.

Simon stopped at the obstruction and ground his teeth in barely concealed anger. Both men flinched suddenly as Alex's vibration strummed violently and Simon found himself sighing in relief. There had been a moment where he thought that maybe it was all in his head--that he alone had been cursed with the fluctuating vibration. It certainly wasn't normal.

Simon still needed out of there, though.

"Please," Simon said, taking a deep breath and motioning the man to the side.

"No one is to leave the building today," the strigoi said firmly, standing his ground. "By order of Primator O'Ceallaigh."

Simon was aghast. "I'm third in command at this facility. I'm Simon Vanderwell."

The other man stared at him blankly.

"Are you kidding me?" Simon asked.

"No, sir," the strigoi said calmly. "I'm sorry, but I have no idea who you are or your standing within Dóchas."

Behind this nameless strigoi, a brisk wind swept up the loose snow atop the drifts and scattered it past the doorway teasingly.

Simon glared at the man standing between him and freedom. "What's your name?"

His back straightened slightly as he spoke. "Corporal Frank Abernathy, sir," the man said with a restrained smile.

"Corporal?" Simon asked. "Since when?"

"Since last Wednesday, sir," Corporal Abernathy said in response.

Why was the door blocked? When had they started giving out ranks?

Apparently last Wednesday.

Simon looked around in confusion, suddenly feeling as if the building was entirely foreign, alien.

Where was he?

"Fine," Simon spat, eyes teasing along the snowy mounds just beyond the annoying man. "Where is Primator O'Ceallaigh now?"

Corporal Abernathy pointed back down the way Simon had come from. "I believe he's still in the war room back the way you came, sir."

Simon raised an eyebrow. "War room? What war room?"

Abernathy cocked his head quizzically. "It's, um, near his private rooms, sir?"

"The big room with the fluted columns?" Simon asked, feeling stupider with every question.

"Fluted columns are the ones with the grooves, right?" Corporal Abernathy asked and Simon nodded. "Then, yes, sir. I believe it is the only room with those types of columns."

"Thanks," Simon spat and headed back the way he came, passing an eerily silent medical bay on his way.

A shudder ran through him at the lack of sound, though he could still feel Alex's pulse in his neck. He wasn't sure what bothered him more, the tearing of the saw or the silence of those scientists thinking. Shaking his head, Simon continued past urgently.

As he progressed further into the compound--the medical bay was situated on the periphery of the facility for some reason--the halls became crowded with a mixture of humans and strigoi. There was a tension in the air and he noticed that the humans tended to group together in pods of four or five as they went about their business.

They presented a false aura of confidence, or at least it seemed so to him, laughing and joking as they passed by him in the hallway. Their eyes looked away too quickly, their backs tensed, the person closest to him would move away slightly, whether they would have touched him or not.

Their heart rates increased.

Simon could hear it.

He grunted and moved on, trying to ignore them as best as he could, but he was haunted by the sounds of their beating hearts. A few minutes later he came to what was now called the "War Room" and was surprised to find it blocked off by four strigoi in their black and red Dóchas uniforms. There were three men and one woman.

All sported the new uniforms--each with patches worked onto their left shoulders instead of on the chest--with a strange pride that bothered him immensely. Three of them--two of the men and the woman--had two gold stars inside of a white-bordered box, while the third man had three stars similarly bordered. All four had close cropped haircuts and the men were clean-shaven. Their apparent age ranged from early twenties to early thirties, though the strigoi man with the three stars had a wicked scar cutting across his left cheek and across his mouth that caused his face to pucker off to the side slightly.

Shrugging, Simon quickly fitted himself with a bright smile and walked up to the man with the three stars, hand extended, before they thought about him overly much.

"Simon Vanderwell," Simon said, grasping the man's hand and giving it a good shake. "I'm here to speak with Kev--Primator O'Ceallaigh."

Simon cursed inwardly at his misstep, but maintained a smile. It didn't help, though. The man with the scar scowled at him--or at least Simon thought he did.

"Primator O'Ceallaigh is meeting with the generals right

now, sir," he said politely. "He left explicit instructions that no one be allowed into the War Room."

Simon's smile faltered. "If you'll just tell him that Simon Vanderwell is here, fresh off the plane from a San Francisco round trip that *he* ordered, I'd be very appreciative."

"I'm afraid I can't do that, sir," the man said and all four strigoi stood a little straighter.

Simon scoffed. "Are you serious?"

"I'm sorry, sir."

"I built the goddamn Dóchas with Kevin and Nathan!" Simon yelled, getting a little too close to the man with the scar. "Without me, you wouldn't be wearing these ugly uniforms or those stupid patches."

Simon slapped the man on the patched shoulder and felt the four of them grow tense.

"What?" Simon asked, getting in his face. "Are you going to subdue me?"

"If we have to, sir," the man said brusquely, eyes flashing.

This one was dangerous, for sure.

"Then try, asshole," Simon whispered and jumped at him.

Simon struck out while Scrying the man violently and managed to get a few good hits in before the other three were able to pull him away, legs flailing wildly.

"Kevin!" Simon screamed as they wrestled him to the ground. "Get your ass out here!"

The woman in the group raised her fist and punched him in the face, causing his head to rebound off the floor, scattering his vision. Simon cursed quietly as warmth crept along his forehead and into his eye, stinging and coloring the spinning world red.

"Ambrose, get him on his feet," a deep voice ordered quietly.

Abruptly, Simon was lifted upward until his legs were beneath him. They set him down as his vision began to clear and his forehead and scalp began to itch. Still cursing, Simon wiped the blood out of his eyes, though he knew who had ordered him picked up.

"Nice timing, Nathan," Simon said while blinking away stars. "Couldn't have come a couple minutes earlier, could you?"

"Shut up, Simon," Nathan snapped, shaking his head. "I

came out as soon as I heard you making a commotion."

Vision steadying, Simon looked up at Nathan for the first time and found himself laughing. Nathan stood in front of him wearing the same uniform as the strigoi holding him place. The only difference was that his rank patch was a bright red circle with crossed swords surrounded by arching feathers of some sort.

"What's funny?" Nathan asked, frowning.

Simon wiped his eyes as much for the tears as the remaining blood. "You look almost as bad as these monkeys. I got used to seeing you in a suit all the time, but this," he motioned in Nathan's general direction, "this is priceless."

Nathan shook his head and then motioned at the four strigoi surrounding Simon. "Return to your posts. I'll deal with him."

The four of them saluted by bringing their right hands to their foreheads stiffly and then returned to the door. Simon returned the gesture loosely, but transitioned it into a rude gesture as the man with the scar--Ambrose apparently--glanced back at him. Nathan slapped Simon on the shoulder and gestured down the hallway.

"Things are changing, Simon," Nathan said as they moved on.

"No shit," Simon muttered.

Nathan glared at him and then turned straight ahead as he continued. "That isn't what I meant. Primator O'Ceallaigh has plans that will change the world and we're going to be a part of it. This plan requires finesse and patience," Nathan held up a hand, "as well as a structured military element."

"Then why aren't I part of either of those things? Why did Kevin call me back?" Simon asked.

Nathan paused for a moment, his angular face thoughtful. "I honestly don't know," he said finally, but he hesitated before continuing. "I just know you should go hang out in your room and wait until he needs you."

Simon stopped in the hallway. "You want me to go to my room?"

Nathan sighed. "I didn't mean it like--"

"What the hell is going on here, Nathan?" Simon asked, throwing up his arms. "We've gone from scientific foundation to kidnapping ring to cult to, what, military dictatorship? Or is this just a natural progression of the cult thing?"

"Simon, I--"

"I'm just not sure what is supposed to be happening here, but I know," Simon turned to Nathan, poking a finger at his chest, "that you are not telling me something."

"Zeke Dunfee is dead, Simon."

"What?" Simon asked, confused. "Who the hell is Zeke Dunfee..."

A pockmarked face in a coffee house, waiting for death.

Simon rubbed his neck. "Oh."

"Yeah," Nathan said.

"But I thought..." Simon started.

"So did I, but it wasn't why he was here apparently," Nathan finished quickly, eyes downcast.

Simon frowned. Zeke Dunfee was dead. A *strigoi* was dead. That hadn't happened since the bomb fell on Nagasaki. No one had killed a strigoi in the past hundred and fifty years except for Kevin O'Ceallaigh, but that was during the Dunfee Rebellion.

Well, except for Esok and the pilot.

Time to reset the count, he guess.

"Did he induce the Return at least?" Simon asked, though he already knew the answer.

"No," Nathan said quietly. "I don't think... it occurred to him at the time. Zeke was incinerated."

"Was it public or quiet?"

"Quiet."

Nathan was lying about Kevin considering using the Return drug, but the fact it was kept quiet meant only one thing. Kevin used Zeke's death to further this crazed goal of his, whatever it was anymore. Kevin had manufactured a martyr for his cause by murdering one of the last heroes of the rebellion.

Simon wondered whom Kevin had blamed for that death. *The Arktois? Humans?*

He shook his head and took a deep, steadying breath.

"Well, thanks for this," Simon said quietly. "I'll head back to my room and wait for, well, wait for orders, I guess."

Nathan nodded and turned back toward the War Room, but motioned for Simon to follow. "I'm going to have to send someone back with you to make sure you go there, Simon. I'm sorry."

Simon shrugged. "No problem, Nathan."

Nathan nodded and motioned to the woman who had beaten Simon a few minutes earlier. "Sergeant. Escort Mr. Vanderwell back to his room over in the orange sector."

She saluted and stepped up next to Simon's side.

Nathan extended a hand to Simon, who accepted it. "Good luck, Simon."

"Thanks," Simon said, but then pulled Nathan a little closer. "I'm curious. What rank are you?"

Nathan smiled. "Brigadier General. Stay out of trouble."

Simon nodded and released Nathan's hand. "I will, thanks again."

"Let's go, Mr. Vanderwell," the woman said, indicating that he should lead the way down the hallway to his left.

"How gallant," Simon mumbled and stepped out in front of her. "Just try not to punch me in the back of the head while you're back there."

She cleared her throat, but said nothing else.

A few twists and turns later and Simon was standing in front of a thick oak door fishing out a key ring. Whistling, he picked out the correct key and unlocked the door. Simon turned around and backed in, waving to his escort as he shut the door behind him.

She did not smile back.

Simon let out a breath as the door closed. He pulled a chair from a small folding table and sat down next to the door intent on waiting for her departure, but he frowned when he heard the wall creak as she leaned up against it. Apparently he was going to be guarded at all times.

Great.

He stood and stretched, causing bones to pop and his neck to crack, before collapsing on the small bed on the other side of the room. The air was stale and the sheets were covered with a fine sheen of dust that tickled his nose and brought out a violent sneeze. Cringing, Simon sat up and leaned against the wall directly across from the door. He stared at the thin line of light visible beneath the frame and watched as his personal guard paced back and forth infrequently.

Everything was different now. He'd only been gone a couple weeks and now Dóchas was filled with dozens of strigoi he had never met and everyone was active military except for him.

And strigoi were dying. Simon grunted and ran his hand through his thinning hair. Everything was different when you had to wonder about losing your life. Suddenly every moment was precious and each breath seemed surreal in its infinite complexity. Even if you didn't necessarily need to breathe.

Sitting there leaning against the cold concrete wall and breathing in the musty scent of stale air, Simon wondered if he was going to die for the first time in nearly a century. The thought left him chilled to the bone.

19
Northern Pennsylvania
9:31 AM January 22, 2011

    The sky was bright as they approached Salt Lake City. It transitioned gently from a blue halo around the city to a cloud dispersing white before fading into the salt flats, the brightness of the land nearly blinding her with the morning sun. Dervy stared off to the side, watching the terrain speed by, scattering red and blue light from the police car as it neared the city. The car held a deeply ingrained crisp scent reminiscent of Old Spice that tickled her nose slightly, though it wasn't unpleasant.

    Sergeant Jensen sat quietly in the driver's seat next to her. His fingers tapped lightly on the steering wheel in a futile attempt to pretend he was unfazed by the events from earlier. Jensen was an older man, moving steadily into his fifties, with a thick mustache that was more gray than brown. He had deep lines around his mouth that made it seem like he was about to break into a smile. Dervy glanced over at him again and felt a wave of shame wash over her again. She looked away quickly.

    Since waking up Dervy had found her hate was muted. She wanted to attribute it to dying--no matter how brief it had been--but knew it wasn't that. It was the fact that so many people--*so many humans*, she corrected herself--had stopped to help her. It didn't matter that she was obviously dead when they arrived, it was the fact that they had tried. The torn shirt that she covered with Sgt. Jensen's jacket was proof enough of that. Even though she'd been mutilated, they still tried to resuscitate her. It was something she just couldn't get over.

"Why would you help me?" Dervy wondered aloud for the first time.

"Excuse me?" Sgt. Jensen asked, fingers finally going still on the steering wheel.

Dervy looked over at the man and bit her cheek. "I was dead when you all arrived."

"Quite dead, ma'am," Sgt. Jensen laughed, his mouth breaking into a sudden smile, though he stopped himself with a grimace. "Sorry."

Dervy waved off the concern. "That's fine. But why did you do it?"

"You act like you've never had anyone help you before," Sgt. Jensen said, glancing at her with a smile.

Dervy looked at him curiously. "It isn't that I've never been helped, but I'm rarely in need of help."

"Everyone needs a hand every now and then," Sgt. Jensen said.

"Some more than others," he added quietly, snickering to himself.

To her complete surprise, Dervy found herself laughing as well. She shook her head ruefully. It was a great feeling. Warmth flooded her body as she continued, slapping her knee to accentuate each guffaw. After a few moments, she composed herself and wiped her eyes, short titters still wracking her body.

"I don't think I caught your name, Miss... "

"Mary," Dervy said quickly, but then corrected herself. "Derval, actually. Dervy, depending on the company."

"May I call you Dervy?" Sgt. Jensen asked.

"No--err, sure, yes," Dervy said, confused at her indecisiveness.

Sgt. Jensen looked askance at her, but did not mention the hesitation. "Dervy. That's an interesting name. And if I may say so, that's an interesting accent. Is it European?"

Dervy nodded, but didn't offer the information he was looking for. She wasn't even sure why she had given him her name. Dervy was supposed to be dead. Just like Laonike and every other identity she had ever worn. These lives were temporary, like a pair of shoes or a jacket. If you held on too hard, you got absorbed and made mistakes. Everyone would find out and strigoi and human alike would try to worship her, just as they had back then.

"Well," Sgt. Jensen said quickly, trying his best to keep the conversation cordial. "Where are you from?"

Dervy looked at him and bit her lip, considering her answer. "It doesn't exist anymore."

Sgt. Jensen glanced at her. "What do you mean?"

Dervy looked straight ahead as she spoke. "I think it was someplace in the Urals, but the last time I went back I couldn't find it."

Memories of rising mountains and a long flat valley flashed in her mind briefly. That's where she was reborn.

"When was the last time you went back," Sgt. Jensen asked.

"1682," Dervy said quietly and immediately cursed herself.

What was wrong with her? Why was she answering these questions?

"Excuse me?" Jensen asked as the car swerved from side to side for a moment. "You can't be over twenty."

Dervy saw him glance at her, but she kept staring straight ahead out into the early morning light. If she told him, it was over. Everything would stop being simple and become chaotic. They would worship her and she would need to disappear again...

Dervy stared at Sgt. Jensen for a long moment. He'd helped her. She was dead and he called the paramedics. Why couldn't she just tell him? What was stopping her? Some ancient fear of worship?

She looked down at her hands, folded neatly in her lap, and pulled the thick police jacket tight around her shoulders. Things had changed since Laonike had come to an agreement with the first Ankousti that her lifespan should never be revealed. People had changed.

Laonike had changed.

And things couldn't get any more complicated.

Could they?

"I'm four thousand years old."

Dervy was surprised at how easily the words just rolled off her tongue. It was like discussing something entirely innocuous, like the weather or a muffin recipe, but the words were life changing. She sat still, rubbing her calloused hands together in her lap and waiting for the expected exclamation.

But it never came.

"Okay."

Dervy raised an eyebrow and looked at Sgt. Jensen. "'Okay'? That's it?"

Sgt. Jensen shrugged. "I already saw you go from dead to fully functional and threatening in just under three minutes," he snickered, "adding something as trivial as you being four thousand years old is just... kind of expected."

Dervy snorted and smiled off into the distance.

"Hell, I'd be kind of disappointed if you weren't immortal," Sgt. Jensen added.

"Oh, we're not all like this," Dervy said. "Most only live three to five hundred years before dying."

Sgt. Jensen did a double take and then shook his head. "So there are more of, um, I mean, more people like you?"

Dervy nodded stoically. "A little over four thousand, actually."

Jensen whistled quietly and they sat in silence for a few minutes. Salt Lake City grew on the horizon as they approached, like a second sunrise in the middle of this barren land.

"Tell me about you, Dervy," Sgt. Jensen said suddenly.

"What do you want to know?" Dervy asked as she readjusted herself in the seat, eyes locked on the city in the distance.

"You said you don't remember where you were born, that is was somewhere in the... where again?"

"The Urals."

"Right, the Urals," Sgt. Jensen said. "But you remember your parents, right?"

"My mother died at birth and my father was killed while I was still a child," Dervy said quickly. "I was... married off, if you want to call it that, to a young hunter whose name I can't remember."

Etu. There was no reason to give out everything.

"How old were you?" Sgt. Jensen asked.

"I don't know exactly, but it was late enough that my breasts were beginning to show," Dervy paused for a moment and snickered. "Everyone thought my hair and my eyes made me special."

"I guess they were right, huh?"

"No," Dervy said firmly, still staring off into the distance, though she was no longer seeing the road. "When I was the age I look now, I had just become pregnant after years of trying. Then the Life chose me and I could no longer bear children."

Dervy rubbed her fingers together roughly. "Soon afterward, a roving band attacked our village, killed all of the men and took the women as prizes."

"Jesus," Sgt. Jensen said quietly.

"He hadn't been born yet," Dervy said with a smile. "And no one had parted any seas at that point either."

"Right," Jensen said with a quick exhale of breath. "I'm sorry you had to go through that."

Dervy gritted her teeth and then continued. "I'm not. I killed every last one of them and left them to rot in a long, flat field between two mountains."

Dervy paused and then smiled. "I found that spot pretty easily when I went back."

They sat in silence for a long time. Buildings began to spring up on either side of the highway as they came closer to the city.

"Where do you call home now?" Sgt. Jensen asked haltingly, as if carefully considering each word.

Dervy opened her mouth and quickly shut it. She had been about to say that she didn't have one, but that wasn't what he had asked.

Where did she call home? No one had ever asked her that question. That was something different altogether, something much more visceral and spiritual. Each time she asked herself the question--the airport growing closer by each crawling second--the same name popped into her mind.

"Heathshome," Dervy said quietly.

Jensen smiled. "What's it like?"

Dervy looked askance at him again, his smile persistent

beneath the thick mustache and his affable nature outweighing the uniform and gun at his side. It was obvious he had other questions, things much more important to him, but he was avoiding them.

What was the point? Why didn't he just ask?

Dervy shook the suspicions away and turned her thoughts to Heathshome. "It's a modern marvel, though I preferred it when we were situated in the Vendée region of France, on the west coast."

"Yeah? Why is that?" He asked politely.

Dervy smiled and shook her head. "Technically it's still there, but it isn't defensible in the event that someone crazy decides to drop a nuclear bomb on our heads."

Sgt. Jensen laughed. "Are you always this negative or is it just my company?"

Dervy snickered. "I'm always this way. It's part of my charm; my je ne sais quoi."

Jensen laughed.

"But it's a real danger," Dervy continued. "Up until Fat Boy dropped, we could only be incinerated and it is really hard to do that. If you think my regeneration was bad, I've seen strigoi regenerate from a sliver of bone four inches long."

Dervy laughed. "Boy was he angry at that Inquisitor."

"Heh," Jensen snickered half-heartedly.

"Anyway," Dervy said, smiling. "The new Heathshome is out in the middle of nowhere and a few hundred feet below ground, but it is amazing. There are nearly two hundred miles of interconnected tunnels. Effective emergency systems, housing, administration.

"It's beautiful."

"I can't quite imagine something like that being beautiful," Sgt. Jensen said cautiously. "I think I'd get claustrophobic."

"No, no, no," Dervy said dismissively. "Natural light is funneled down into every corner of the structure and there is a large amphitheater built into it, the Pasa Tiempo. It was modeled after a Spanish garden by a strigoi back in the sixties. It's gorgeous."

"Maybe it does sound beautiful," Sgt. Jensen said with a smile.

Dervy nodded. "It is."

"Well," Sgt. Jensen said, changing his tone abruptly. "I think we should probably get you some new clothes before putting you on an airplane. What do you think?"

Dervy smiled and nodded. "That is probably a good idea."

She pulled on the top of a pant leg and it came free, brown from dried blood. "Your boss is going to think you had a dead hooker in here."

Sgt. Jensen laughed out loud and shook his head. "That was horrible Dervy."

"Funny though, yeah?" Dervy said, sitting back in the seat. "To the nearest department store, please."

"How about the nearest Wal-Mart?" Jensen asked with a smirk.

Dervy waved into the air. "If we must."

"Yes, m'lady," Sgt. Jensen snickered as he pulled off the highway.

"Jensen?" Dervy asked quietly.

"Yeah?"

Dervy smiled. "Call me Enyo. That's what everyone called me first."

Sgt. Jensen smiled and nodded, though she noticed his lips were pursed thoughtfully. "Enyo, it is. What does it mean?"

"Look it up sometime. It should be easy to find," she said with a grin.

"Will do, ma'am," Sgt. Jensen said with his ever-present smile.

Dervy--Enyo--nodded to herself and watched the buildings flit by as they crawled further into the city. Her smile grew as she plotted her next course.

She was going home.

20
Unknown
Unknown

    Alex lay awake in the gray room staring at the cracked ceiling above him. There was an itch at the corner of his nose that was driving him insane. His first attempt to scratch it had resulted in a cacophony as the steel chains holding him in place shifted. A man wearing a black uniform with some ridiculous patch had come in and told him to keep it down.
    "Scratch my nose and I'll be quiet," Alex had begged, but the man--a strigoi if the buzzing in his neck was right--just turned and left, locking the door behind him on the way out.
    Alex wished he were dead.
    It occurred to him that there wasn't any need for flaming forceps or water boarding. All a torturer needed to do was tie you to a bed for a few days without food or water, then come in while the prisoner was sleeping and sprinkle some dust in their face.
    Pure agony.
    Alex wiggled his nose ineffectively. He desperately tried to distract himself by looking around the room... again. It was an interesting bonus that they hadn't strapped down his head like in the

van, though looking around an empty room had soon lost its thrill. The hum of a fluorescent lamp above the single door in and out of the room was persistent, interrupted only by a periodic popping noise and a flicker of light. There was only one bulb working in the enclosure as the second had already burnt out. Its time was quickly running out as well.

Unlike his.

Alex could be there in that room, waiting in fear, for decades before the chains and fabric rusted and rotted to the point that he could break them. If he even had the strength at that point. Were there others like him? Were they trapped in some inescapable dungeon, filled with perpetual hunger and thirst, clawing at the walls of their cells as their minds rotted and twisted?

What would happen if no one ever came for him? Alex had left without telling anyone where he was going. No one knew where he was or why he was gone, only that he had stolen money and a car from Heathshome...

"Oh God," Alex moaned.

He pulled at his bonds again in futility, straining against them with all of his strength, but they held fast. And the itch on his nose returned with a fury, sending Alex's face into spasms as he desperately tried to dispel it with simple muscle movement.

A polite knock resounded on the door to his lonely cell. Alex grew still, turning his head slowly so he could see who might be coming in. He waited like that for long moments before the knock came again, just as polite--three light strikes in quick succession, emphasis on the final tap.

Alex wrinkled his nose in confusion--and in another attempt to destroy the damnable itch--before calling out: "Come in?"

A man walked through the door, but took care to shut it tight behind him. Alex thought he was short--it was hard to tell from his current angle--but he moved in a way that piqued a memory. When the man turned around, the feeling of familiarity intensified. Bright red hair with short streaks of gray, neatly trimmed and parted on the left, merged with a thick beard of the same color. A mustache covered his lips almost entirely, but he still managed to smile warmly in the slight shifting of his beard and walked over to the bed to which Alex was secured.

"Do I know you?" Alex asked, raising his head against his

restraints uncomfortably to get a better look at him.

The man frowned. "I don't think you were conscious during any of our encounters, so no."

Alex let his head fall back to the bed. "You certainly look familiar."

The pressure on his chest released suddenly. Alex inhaled deeply and looked at the man as the sound of jingling chains filled the air. The straps and restraints loosened and fell free with a clatter. Alex was amazed at the number of bands holding him in place. There were six straps and three or four thick steel chains there to keep him in that bed.

"No wonder I couldn't move," Alex mumbled as he sat up, grunting. "You could hold an elephant with those."

Triumphantly, Alex raised his arm and scratched his nose, letting out a quiet moan of pleasure. The man sat at the end of the bed, unfastening the final strap as he did so.

"There is nothing better in the world than scratching an itch after being locked down for three days," the man said with another bearded smile.

Alex snorted approval and sighed, eyeing the man across from him quizzically. "Who are you?"

The other man smiled. "I'm Kevin O'Ceallaigh, Primator of Dóchas."

Alex took a deep breath and let it out, shoulders slumping in the process. Hazy memories of surgeries--doctors and nurses cutting and removing parts of him--danced in front of him hauntingly, just on the edge of memory. He could remember vague words and feelings, a strange tightness in his chest, the sensation of air caressing places it shouldn't be able to reach, but there was nothing substantial to grab hold of and focus on. It was like watching a bizarre television show, something Pink Floyd would direct, and trying to remember it years down the line.

Despite all that, Alex knew one thing for certain.

He knew that name.

"You're supposed to be dead," Alex said without emotion, though panic rose within him. "You Returned. I... remember seeing you old."

Kevin laughed at that. "You were passed out, so I don't think so, but if you did see me somehow and you thought I was old, it was because I was."

Alex raised an eyebrow. "And now you're not?"

"Now I'm not," Kevin agreed. "Do you want to know how?"

"I'm not sure," Alex said hesitantly. "I'm pretty sure it has a lot to do with you guys cutting me up while I'm tripping balls on an operating table."

Kevin nodded and leaned in slightly. "And I'm sorry about that, but it was a necessary evil."

"I get you're trying to live forever," Alex said, glancing around furtively. "But without going into why that's a bad idea, why do you need me? Aren't you already immortal?"

"We're not sure," Kevin said frankly, leaning back again. "But we know that we were able to stop the Return in mid-step and reactivate the genes that make us strigoi."

"Being a strigoi is a gene thing?" Alex asked.

"Absolutely," Kevin said, eyes bright. "What else could it possibly be? God? Gods?"

Alex shrugged, but felt empty all of a sudden. There had been a certain mystique to it all, he'd never denied that. Despite being atheistic most of his life, he had finally begun to believe that maybe there was something out there; something with the power to make strigoi the way they were. Something *like* a god if not *actually* a god.

"Well, what about the thirteen strigoi a year thing?" Alex asked. "If it were all about genes wouldn't it be hard to only have thirteen?"

Kevin waved it off. "The only reason we say thirteen a year is because that is the most Taken anyone has ever seen in one year. There are so many variables and other sources to consider that it's almost impossible to determine the cause. It could be cosmic radiation from a far off star causing it when we pass through a specific point in our solar orbit for all we know."

Alex looked at Kevin oddly. "Isn't that a comic book premise... "

"Regardless," Kevin continued dismissively. "You're focusing on the wrong question, Alex. At Dóchas we're interested in the 'how' and 'what', not the 'why'. 'Why' is for philosophers and toddlers."

"What makes a strigoi live for so long? What gives us these strange powers? What causes the Return? And how do we turn these things on," Kevin made a motion as if turning on a light switch.

Kevin flicked downward and Alex felt a shiver run through him, "Or off."

"That sounds... great," Alex conceded weakly.

Kevin considered him for a moment, blue eyes intense. "Did you know that Dervy is four thousand years old?"

Alex's jaw dropped and Kevin nodded solemnly.

"Yes, she is four thousand years old, give or take a century," Kevin said. "She built the Arktois back in the early days of this era. Every few centuries she disappears until every strigoi she knew Returns. She only comes back when there is a single person who knew her--someone who is invariably an Elder by then--and they transition her back into the new Arktois.

"Back when the Egyptians were just getting on their feet, she called herself Enyo. She and a few others burned and pillaged their way across the Steppes and down into Macedonia, leaving behind rubble and death," Kevin snorted and shook his head. "The Greeks called her a goddess. A goddess of war and destruction."

Kevin was thoughtful for a moment. "I guess it's only appropriate. When Dervy fights, it's like watching a master painter spread oils across a fresh canvas. But instead of paint, Dervy uses blood, lots of it, and she paints the ground."

Alex stared at Kevin, not sure whether he should believe him or diagnose him as a madman corrupted by whatever drugs Alex had unwittingly helped create. He was about to do the latter when he saw the fondness written plainly on Kevin's face. For just a moment, Kevin stared off at nothing, a small smile playing at the edges of a mouth that Alex could finally see, being so close to him. Just as he was about to mention it, Kevin stood up and began pacing.

"Dervy shows us that true immortality is possible," he said hurriedly. "But that wasn't my original goal with this research. At first, when I was still Primator... " Kevin paused and then corrected himself. "Primator of Arktois that is, we decided to start measuring the abilities of some of the newly Taken after I witnessed a feat of strength I'd never seen from one so young. This was back in the early eighties."

Kevin stopped and turned toward Alex, tongue flicking along his lips. "He just picked up this Buick and threw it. It was amazing, but he wasn't alone.

"Every Taken located that year was way ahead of the normal, established curve; a curve based on nearly two thousand years of observations and possibly the largest observed data set in the history of the world. As the years crept by, we knew we had something important happening so I ordered covert studies performed on a few of these Younglings and Taken to confirm it. The tests did.

"It was amazing, but a few of us in the Ankousti were interested in the 'how' of it, so we decided that it would be best to begin comparisons of what were beginning to be termed the 'Old Generation' with the 'New Generation' of strigoi. These comparisons were nearly fruitless, but when I brought in a human doctor, Scott... " Kevin hesitated for a moment, stopping in mid step, but quickly resumed his pacing. "Doctor Scott Kelly saw differences, important differences. They weren't between the strigoi, but rather between strigoi and humans. Strigoi have higher iron content in their blood, overactive neural signs, various glandular secretion differences amongst a host of other things--"

Alex snorted and Kevin's eyes went wide in surprise.

Kevin scowled at him. "What?"

"You... " Alex started and hesitated.

"I what?"

Alex bit his cheek for a moment before deciding there wasn't much more Kevin could do to him than what had already been done. "Well, you reminded me of Dr. Moreau there for a minute."

Kevin stared at him and then laughed before turning his intense eyes away from him. "Vivisection. What a strange old practice, wouldn't you say?"

Alex smiled, but quickly found his humor waning as dreamlike memories floated in his mind's eye. "Yeah... "

"As I was saying," Kevin said, beginning his pacing again. "All of this was fine, but it wasn't until the human genome project was completed in 2003 that we made true progress. We hired a few people from a private firm who had been competing with the public program and had them compile diagrams of both Dr. Kelly and I for comparison."

Alex bit his lip. Every time Kevin mentioned this Dr. Kelly, there was a hesitation. It was just a hair too long, but it was enough.

Who was this doctor?

Kevin was still going on, completely unaware of the fact that Alex had become distracted. "--was a hard choice, but it was--and is--the right choice. I'm saddened by their loss, of course, but the knowledge we have gained is immense."

Alex shook his head. "Whose loss?"

"The loss of strigoi," Kevin said unemotionally. "Without their sacrifice, we wouldn't have developed the Return drug or the cure. But we have. Though there have been some complications with the cure."

"You tested on strigoi?" Alex asked. "Like you've tested on me?"

Kevin shook his head. "No, no. We haven't tested anything on you. In fact, the only test run on you was to determine whether you had the same gene sequence as Dervy. You see, we needed to isolate it. Dervy is a sample size of one. I hadn't expected to see it again, but we did. In you."

"Wait a damn minute," Alex yelled, getting to his feet suddenly. "What does that mean?"

"It means that you, like Dervy, will live forever without my help," Kevin held up a finger as Alex prepared to protest. "That is, unless you are killed by incineration, live to some age beyond four thousand years when the Return comes on you--we can't predict that--or I give you the Return drug."

Alex tried to speak, but succeeded in only letting out a tiny squeak before collapsing back down onto the bed.

Kevin sat down next to him and put a consoling hand on his shoulder. "Listen Alex. If you help me now, then I'll help you when my new order is in place."

Alex looked up, hopelessness filling him. He didn't want to live forever. Hell, not six months ago he had tried to end it, why on earth would he want to live forever?

Alex blinked, something Kevin had said sticking in his mind. "What new order?"

"That's not important right now," Kevin said, rubbing his shoulder. "But if you continue helping me, I'll make sure everything turns out all right for you."

Kevin leaned in toward Alex and looked him in the eye. "All right?"

"Why me?" Alex asked.

"Because your genes hold the key," Kevin said urgently. "Without you, all of these... side effects will drive each and every strigoi insane."

Kevin pulled away and walked toward the door, turning back to him when he reached it. "Make no mistake, my plans will proceed with or without your cooperation, but I would rather move forward as a savior instead of as a tyrant."

Alex looked away, eyes tracing the familiar lines of cracked plaster and contours of the doorframe. He could feel the two strigoi standing outside as well as maybe a hundred or more nearby. There was no escape from this; no brave, glorious getaway. If he declined, Kevin would just tie him back down on the bed he was sitting on and leave him to scream into the still, pale room until his mind cracked under the pressure.

That didn't mean Alex trusted Kevin; not even the slightest. Everything the man said was laced with obfuscation and lies. There was no doubt as to what Kevin meant when he said everything would turn out all right for him. It meant Alex would be killed, though he really wasn't sure it was that bad of an option. Live forever or die at a time and place of his choosing? He already knew his answer, but it didn't make it any easier to say it out loud.

Every time the words came to his lips, he pictured Jalal or Weynie or Anne walking the hallways of Heathshome. He pictured Dervy. That crazy, crazy bitch that had lived for so long with the curse he now inherited.

Was it really up to him?

Savior or tyrant, Kevin had said. In Alex's mind, he didn't see that Kevin could be perceived as anything but the latter, though he kept that to himself. Kevin was going to do this whether Alex wanted him to or not, so it really broke down to a much simpler choice.

Be tied to the bed or be allowed to get up and walk?

"I'll do it, don't worry."

*   *   *

The door opened revealing a sharp-faced woman with black hair and a prominent mole over her left eye. Simon choked a little at the sight of the brown protrusion and the speech he had prepared over the past twelve hours disappeared in a fog of mixed curiosity and disgust.

"I... " Simon started and then closed his eyes to focus. "I need to speak with Primator O'Ceallaigh about a mission he sent me on recently."

"Really?"

"The mission was to bring back a certain strigoi," Simon said, opening his eyes and focusing on hers. "Now that strigoi is dead."

She raised an eyebrow at that... it looked like the mole was breathing when she did that.

Simon shuddered.

Apparently the news had gotten around about Zeke Dunfee's death. Simon was just hoping that he could use it to speak with Kevin.

The woman sighed, pulled a small walkie-talkie off of her belt and pressed the transmitter. "Vanderwell has requested transfer to the Primator. Requests debrief."

She shook her head and took her finger off the button. "If you're screwing with me--"

"Primator confirms debrief," a somewhat surprised voice called back. "Bring him down."

Simon smiled, just barely concealing his own surprise at the approval. "Shall I follow you or do you want me to lead?" He asked politely.

The woman frowned and motioned him ahead of her. "Let's go, sir."

Simon stepped out and proceeded down the hall at a fair clip, causing the guard to do a stutter step to keep up. Simon had no intention of giving Kevin any time to reconsider the offer. He had too many questions to ask.

Like what the hell was going on.

Simon grumbled as he walked along, ignoring the small packs of humans and uniformed strigoi entirely. Soon he approached the War Room and was only slightly surprised to see the man with the long, wicked scar--*Ambrose was it?*--standing in the way.

A deep rasping sound filled Simon's throat at the sight of him and he narrowed his eyes threateningly. He could picture tearing the man's throat open, blood spilling freely from the fresh wound, pain and shock twisting his face, yet mocked by the persistent scar...

Simon blinked and the sound stopped. He shook his head and rubbed his eyes, anger fading rapidly and, just as quickly as it had come, it was gone.

"Primator O'Ceallaigh is waiting for you, sir."

Simon looked up quickly. Ambrose was looking at him curiously, head tilted to the side slightly.

"What?" Simon asked, disoriented for a moment. "Oh, right."

Blinking rapidly, Simon stepped forward past the man and pushed open one of the double doors. As he passed through, Simon heard the man and his escort discussing his sanity, but he didn't have time to dwell on their words.

"Jesus," Simon said in awe as he looked around.

When he, Kevin and Nathan had first located what would become Dóchas, it was an abandoned and entirely unfurnished 1950's hospital. There had been a few squatters on the premises, but those had been easily removed. It had cost nearly two million dollars to get it to the point that humans could even work in the environment. Even then the room Simon stood in now had always been relegated to a storage area, despite once being an auditorium of some sort.

Now it really was a War Room, though there were odd combinations of old and new technology. Large maps were spread across tables next to transparent, flat displays with digital maps flickering and outlined with washable markers. Monitors were infrequently placed; large, thin screens that seemed to serve as repositories for paperwork and coffee cups. Simon couldn't tell what the maps were of--they were unlabeled--but wherever it was, it appeared to be out in the middle of nowhere. It only looked like there was one road heading into the town. In the far back corner, Kevin leaned back in a chair looking at one of those huge screens and rocked back and forth as if in deep thought.

Simon's own thoughts darkened at the sight of his former friend. He felt that rage building inside of him, but he took a steadying breath, pushed it firmly down into his stomach, and walked over. Kevin spoke as Simon approached, though he didn't look up.

"We both know there is no reason to debrief and I'm busy," Kevin said tersely before looking up at Simon, his eyes full of that new mad intensity. "So why don't we cut the bullshit and get everything out in the open?"

Simon glared at him for a moment before nodding. Kevin got to his feet and typed a key on a keyboard. Instantly, all of the electronic maps disappeared, leaving behind the illegible scribbling of Kevin and his generals.

"I didn't give you a rank because you aren't good with structure," Kevin said, passing by Simon brusquely. "Right now I need soldiers who will follow orders without question and I need officers who have experience plotting military movements, regardless of size."

"I can--" Simon started, but was cut off.

"No. No, you can't, Simon," Kevin said simply. "I've known you for eighty years and at no point would I have ever consulted with you for military help."

"But you'll use me as a spy all day long," Simon shot back.

Kevin shrugged. "Absolutely. That said, the time for stealth is gone and you aren't useful to me at the moment."

Simon opened his mouth to respond, but shut it. The words stung more than he ever imagined.

You aren't useful to me.

"Come on now," Kevin said, voice softening as he moved toward Simon with a small smile. "This is no different than any of the other projects we've worked together over the years. I've never involved you in the fighting."

"This is different," Simon said firmly, backing away from Kevin and walking toward one of the transparent displays. "I helped build this, Kevin."

"And you'll be involved again," Kevin said quietly. "Just not right now."

Simon turned around suddenly. "Why? Why not right now?"

Kevin's face darkened. "Because I said so, Simon. That's enough of a reason."

"Not this time it isn't," Simon said. "I'm sick of your

secretive bullshit. You're always like this and I always just back off and accept your explanation."

Simon smiled smugly as he continued. "But not this time. I need to be involved or maybe I'll bring the info I know to the *other* Primator and let him know what you've been up to.

"And," Simon waved a hand in the air dramatically, "if I'm feeling particularly nasty, tell him how to get to Dóchas so he can swing by and say 'hi'."

He wouldn't do it, of course--it was a bluff. Kevin would have him killed before he could even exit the facility.

Simon's confidence was shattered as Kevin laughed. "You think he doesn't know?"

"What?" Simon asked in confusion.

"It takes more than pure force of will to finance something like this, Simon," Kevin said, motioning to the transparent displays and the various monitors in the War Room. "You know that."

Simon put his hands up in a warding motion. "Are you saying he's known about this the entire time?"

Kevin stepped toward Simon quickly, closing the distance between them in just a few steps.

"Known?" Kevin snarled. "It might as well have been William's goddamn idea!"

Simon took a step back. Kevin turned with a dismissive snort and walked back to the monitor where he'd been working. For some reason, the idea that William Searle would finance the type of activities that the three of them--Simon, Kevin and Nathan--had taken part in left him with a sour taste in his mouth. That surprised him immensely, though it all broke down to simple idealism. Deep down Simon had always hoped that the Arktois wouldn't approve of what they were doing, that they would chafe at the idea of kidnapping and forced experimentation.

Or was the Arktois another example of an organization that believed in the ends justifying the means? He couldn't accept that. Yes, strigoi the world over would benefit from their work because Kevin had strength to do what was necessary, but the organization as a whole shouldn't have to be tarnished because of the acts of the few.

That's why they had split off. *Right?*

"Let me see," Simon said firmly.

"What?" Kevin asked as he finished typing something. "See what?"

Simon walked over to Kevin, face flat. "I want to see that William is involved. I need to know."

Kevin stared at him thoughtfully for a long moment before getting to his feet. "Fine," he said before continuing threateningly. "But if you push too far I will hurt you in ways that will leave you wishing that I had killed you."

Simon nodded and extended his hand. Physical contact made a Scry much more coherent and less painful for the recipient. Kevin reached out and grasped Simon's hand firmly, locking his deep blue eyes on Simon as he did so.

"Do it."

Simon closed his eyes and pushed his mind outward. The physical connection made everything easier; their minds met quickly, a blinding flash of light behind eyelids and then they were merged together. Simon focused, forcing himself beyond barriers Kevin had unconsciously erected--blowing through them like paper doors. There wasn't much to see when outside of a memory, just a myriad of threads, like an immense game of Cat's Cradle with globes of light dancing between the strands. Regardless of the target, important memories almost always consist of heightened senses caused by intense emotions or continued revisiting. The more someone relived a memory, the more vivid it was to the Scryer.

Simon thought about William Searle; pictured the man's smooth, handsome face, his chiseled physique, the measured, lyrical tones of his voice... a thread began pulsing just in front of him and he reached out...

The air is thick with decay and wood sap; the sharp scent of pine offsets the decrepit leaves and merges smoothly with the late autumn breeze that flits through the trees.

"Are you sure?" William asks, leaning against the pine tree.

A thick yellow jacket lies on the ground next to him, a leather-bound book sitting on top of it. William's hair is long in the back and short in the front, which he claims is the up and coming style, though Kevin thinks it looks ridiculous. Absentmindedly, William flicks small pinecones off into the distance, disturbing some small rodents who had been hiding in the underbrush.

"He picked it up and threw it at me," Kevin says, rubbing his arm. "I've never seen a Taken do that before, Will."

Immortal

William nods and stares off into the distance. "Did you tell the rest of the Ankousti?"

"Yes," Kevin responds, letting his eyes wander the tree line. "Primator Yu thinks that I'm exaggerating, but most of the other Elders agree that this is abnormal."

"That is because it is," William says quietly. "Maybe he is... what are they called when something is abnormal in science?"

"An outlier?" Kevin offers.

"Right," William agrees. "An outlier."

"I don't think so," Kevin says, worried.

William nods...

The memory spun away, but Simon held fast to the connection and began digging through Kevin's memories, searching for telltale emotional attachments and rage.

Ahead of him, a thick red band oozed importance. Purposefully, Simon grabbed hold of the memory and nearly screamed as it slammed into him.

Vanilla mixes with stale urine and citrus, a putrid bouquet made lovely, reminiscent of something he can't remember. The room to the side is finally quiet, but soon it will begin again.

A man stands off to the side of a gurney. He wears green scrubs, but they are streaked with arterial spray. Rubber gloves come off violently, each snap a stab in Kevin's heart.

The man shakes his head and Kevin moves to touch him, to reassure him, but a hand comes up in warning.

"Don't," he says firmly.

The hand doesn't wear a glove anymore. Liver spots are present on the skin. He will die soon. As all humans do.

"We all die, Scotty," Kevin says in what he hopes is a reassuring manner.

"No," Scotty says. "Not everyone does."

Scotty turns around, face full of fury and hatred. His eyes dance around Kevin's face, not stopping anywhere in particular, just rabid and pained.

He no longer looks like the freckle-faced child in the black and white picture Kevin carries in his wallet, but it makes no difference.

He is still Scotty.

"Do you want me dead Scotty?" Kevin asks, barely keeping the choke from his voice.

Scotty stares at him for a moment before sighing and hanging his head.

"No, I don't want you dead. But don't call me Scotty. No one has called me that since before mom died."

"I'm sorry, Scotty--Scott," Kevin says, laying a hand on a blood streaked shoulder.

"Are we doing the right thing here?" Scotty asks, eyes looking up at Kevin pleadingly.

Suddenly, he is the freckle-faced child again, eyes wide and vulnerable. They are begging for approval, for acceptance. That all this pain will be worth something. Kevin has to make it okay. He has to make it worthwhile.

"Yes, we are."

Scotty nods.

They both shiver as the screaming begins again...

Simon pulled away from the memory, shedding the panic and sadness like a second skin, but still feeling shock and awe. Despite the intensity, the memory did not help justify anything Kevin had done, let alone implicate William Searle.

He needed more.

Simon looked around. The environment was beginning to feel hostile as Kevin's patience wore thin. There was no way for Kevin to know what thoughts Simon was delving into beyond getting the general feelings that accompanied each memory, but Kevin was no longer the patient man he had once been.

Simon needed to hurry.

It was always so much more difficult Scrying an Elder because there were so many memories to dig through. Simon had been lucky thus far to at least get two related memories--at least he was pretty sure the last one had been pertinent--but there were dozens of throbbing strands in this mental web. It would take hours for him to go through them all without Kevin's help.

Without opening his eyes, Simon spoke. "Think about the memory you want me to find."

In response to his question, a strand began pulsing with red light--an artery in the distance. Simon sped toward it, moving formlessly through the void until he collided with it and the memory enveloped him.

Polished wood, lightly tinged with lemon, aged lacquer, and boot black.

"Primator," William Searle says, taking a moment to look at each member of the Ankousti. "You have been performing these tests for nearly two decades. Do you have any information to share with us?"

Immortal

Kevin looks out across the gathered group. He knows what they want to hear, but he doesn't have that information yet. What he does have, they won't want to hear about. William pushed him to tell them earlier, but Kevin isn't sure they can handle it. He is still unsure as he sits at the head of the table.

"We've had some progress," Kevin says hesitantly.

Esok Johnson snorts in disbelief and William makes a noise to silence him.

"What progress, Primator?" Elder Cortes asks in his thick accent. "Your team has brought great knowledge to the Ankousti--and through us, the Arktois--but I believe I speak for everyone when I say that your methods cause us to become sick."

Others nod around the table and they begin mumbling things like, "Enough is enough," and, "These are strigoi, not guinea pigs."

"We have a Return drug," Kevin spits out and William smiles as he looks around the table.

"Excuse me?" Esok asks hesitantly. "A 'Return drug'?"

"Yes," Kevin says. "We can induce the Return in an otherwise healthy strigoi with little more than a shot, not unlike getting vaccinated."

"My God," Esok mumbles and stares off into the distance.

William gets to his feet. "I, for one, applaud Primator O'Ceallaigh's continued progress on this matter and look forward to the culmination of his research."

A muted response follows, but is by no means a consensus, though it is clear that William believes it to be so. William flashes a wink at Kevin as he sits back down...

Simon pulled away from the memory easily. It no longer shone brightly, indicating that Kevin was no longer reliving the moment with him. There was no denying that memory... William Searle knew along with everyone else in the Ankousti. Hell, even Esok had known. Maybe that was why he'd resigned?

Simon just couldn't believe that the Ankousti, the moral compass of the Arktois for millennia, would accept what they had done. There it was, plain as day. Not even Kevin could plant a memory that vivid. There was no timing involved in it, but regardless, it had happened. Simon began pulling out, slowly disentangling himself from the strands of Kevin's mind and taking care to avoid any others.

Something caught his eye as he went to disconnect; a bright, pulsing memory. It almost vibrated with power, a rotating red and black strand that stood out against the backdrop of his mind. Cautiously, Simon reached out and made contact...

Sharp, acrid, copper. Biting darkness and bile filled teeth.

"I'm so sorry," the voice sobs.

The van rumbles through the flat landscape. His eyes catch the birds circling ahead.

He wants pain.

"Please," the voice again. "I have children."

I had one, too.

The engine revs, closing the distance quickly.

Salt. Brine.

He pulls off the road, sending the pallet shifting and the voice screaming. He drives straight toward them, pulling off the road nearly a mile into desert. He goes at the birds and they scatter away from the carcass of some large animal.

The van goes in park. He gets out and walks around the back. The stench of rotting flesh fills his nostrils. The bones are not yet white. The kill is still fresh.

He grips the handle of the rear door and stops. A line of blood stretches across his forearm. For a moment he panics, but then he wipes away the mess, revealing unblemished skin. There is too much left to do for the Return to get him.

The door opens and the screams begin again. He grips the side of the pallet and pulls it out onto the desert, tossing up clouds of dust that soon stifles the voice of the man.

"Please," the man pleads again, the nicks across his naked body oozing small droplets of blood as he strains against the bonds holding him in place. "Don't do this... I didn't mean to kill him..."

Kevin stares at him for a moment, considering what he is doing, but the memory of a hand covered in liver spots interrupts it.

Whispered assurances to a dead body.

He shuts the door to the van and walks back around to the driver's side, ignoring the mixture of pleading and cursing. He pulls his door shut and pulls away, but soon turns slightly so that he can see where he left the man.

After a few minutes the vultures return to the carcass. They are intrigued by the man, but avoid him at first. No doubt he is screaming and flailing as best he can.

A few minutes later the first vulture moves over to the pallet. Kevin turns around as three others join in.

He can still hear the screaming in his head as he pulls back onto the highway...

Simon screamed as Kevin threw him to the floor violently. "Get out of here," Kevin said, running a hand across his eyes. "And stay away from me. You understand?"

Simon climbed to his feet, but Kevin struck him suddenly, sending him crashing through one of the Plexiglas boards, sending shards of plastic throughout the room.

"Get out!" Kevin screamed, voice cracking, waving wildly toward the door.

Simon scrambled away and broke into a run, pushing open the doors and dashing down the hallway, leaving confused guards behind. He ran in a panic, heart pounding until he reached his room, slid inside and slammed the door behind him.

Simon stood with his back against the door for many minutes, reassuring himself that he wasn't going to die.

Kevin wasn't coming to kill him. They had been friends for too long.

Simon couldn't get the image of Kevin's face out of his head.

Taking deep breaths, Simon walked over to his small chair and sat down. He tried to calm himself, but his heart would not stop pounding. He needed to be calm now. He needed to be logical.

With a deep breath, Simon forced his heart to slow. He felt it dragging, felt the lethargy take it as the pumping slowed.

Slower.

Kevin's face flashed in his mind.

Slower.

The man's screams as the vultures tore into him...

Stop.

The world went dull. The colors in the room became muted as Simon opened his eyes. Everything looked drained of color, just as it always did when you stopped your heart.

With a start, Simon realized the ever present hunger was just as muted now. He smiled.

A few moments later, footsteps made their way toward his room, stopping briefly on the other side. The sound of the old wall creaking indicated that his guard had returned to her post.

Letting out a breath Simon didn't realize he was holding, he got to his feet and paced around his room. He didn't take another breath. He no longer needed to.

21
East of Hornell, NY
10:39 PM January 22, 2011

The short, thin waitress swept toward them, glass decanter full of dark brown liquid in hand. The acrid smell of strong coffee swept ahead of her, mixing easily with the aroma of diesel fuel and pungent sweat that filled the truck stop. A smile split her aged face when she stepped up to the table.

Her nametag said 'Sheryl'.

"More coffee, hun?" Sheryl asked.

Jalal shook his head and smiled back. "No thanks, I am fine for now."

She turned to Weynie. "How 'bout you sweetie?"

"No thank you," Weynie said with a forced smile. "I don't think I can have much more."

"Just let me know if you need anything else, all right?" Sheryl said cheerfully and then added: "And I love that shawl."

"Thanks," Weynie said warmly, rubbing the dark orange fabric between her fingers reassuringly.

Sheryl turned and left. On her way to the kitchen she scooped up a pile of plates and somehow managed to slip a tip into her pocket with both hands full. Weynie stared after her and wondered what it would be like to have a job like that. Come to work, give your all and then go home, leaving it all behind. What would it even be like to have the ability to forget about work and just focus on yourself or your friends. Your family?

Centuries ago, Weynie had known what that was like, though it had all been couched in fear and violence. The Life had seemed a blessing then, but now she wasn't so sure...

"Jalal?" Weynie asked, staring at her coffee.

Jalal glanced up from his own cup. He looked exhausted; his dark eyes were bloodshot and puffy as if he had been crying.

"Yes?" The response quickly turned into a long yawn, which he stifled with a fist.

Weynie stared at him for a moment, considering her question. Did he feel the same way at the end of a day? She wasn't sure it was comparable--Jalal's day-to-day work probably didn't keep him up at night, guilt-ridden--but he was constantly fretting over this server or that configuration. At the end of the day, they both had the same level of investment. But did he realize it? Would she be doing him an injustice by even bringing it up?

"Weynie?" Jalal asked, raising an eyebrow in concern.

Weynie sighed and decided against asking. Some things were better left alone.

"Did, uh, did Alex get tagged when he was checked in?" She asked instead, taking a sip of her coffee to cover her indecision.

Jalal considered the question for a moment before shaking his head. "I'm not sure, but I do not think so. That is something Alex would have complained about."

"Why?" Weynie asked.

Jalal smiled. "He is heavily invested in personal privacy."

"Huh," Weynie grunted, looking back down at her cup.

It was horrible... and very, very strong.

"Regardless," he added quickly, getting her attention. "It is only an RFID tag and the range is significantly less than that of his Taken aura."

"Oh," Weynie grumbled. "I'd hoped it had GPS or something."

Jalal shook his head again. "No, it was decided that was a bit too invasive. Even if it had GPS, though, we would not be able to access the information since it would require permission from the Primator."

"Can't you just hack it or something?" Weynie asked, taking another sip of her coffee.

Jalal glared at her for a moment.

"What?" She asked.

"That's insulting," Jalal said with a grimace. "I do not 'hack'. The only person with authority to access that data is Primator Searle."

"You didn't leave in a back door or whatever you people call it?" Weynie asked in slight disbelief.

"No. I left no 'back door'," Jalal said, seemingly taken aback by her suggestion to the contrary. "I build systems to be secure and follow stringent protocols; I don't do this to feed my ego or--"

"All right, all right," Weynie interrupted. "I'm sorry I even suggested it."

"You should be," Jalal muttered, looking back down at his own coffee.

Weynie smiled and shook her head slightly, but didn't say anything else. They sat silently for a few minutes; letting the bustle of the truck stop surround them. Humans sat at the counter, mostly big men with well-worn clothes. There were a few women as well. Some joked raucously, while others sat quietly watching the small television hanging just off the corner of the kitchen. Like Weynie and Jalal, they sipped at their coffee slowly, only in the truck stop physically. Their minds were elsewhere, drifting along the road or maybe at home in a favorite chair, a child asleep on the couch across from them or a pet curled up in their lap.

Weynie sighed. They probably weren't still traversing the highway outside, looking for any sign of a man no one out here knew. After the incident with the police officer earlier, they spent the rest of the day driving up and down the highway searching for Alex. For nearly ten hours they looked; questioning gas station attendants, scouring side roads and scanning police frequencies for any information on a kidnapping or car accident. They were hopeful at one point, when they heard the scanner broadcast that a black SUV had been abandoned on the side of the road, but there had been police present when they arrived and Jalal forced them to continue onward. He hadn't wanted to find out whether the officer had left a description of them.

The smooth, orange fabric of her shawl flit between Weynie's fingers as she wracked her mind, trying to find any indication of where these kidnappers may have taken Alex. When he and Dervy had been kidnapped a couple months earlier, the AIC had been told not to investigate the location of the facility they had been held at despite Weynie and a few of her associates protesting. Instead, all resources had been focused on assisting the Gatherers in locating the remaining batch of Taken, though none had been found. Alex had been the last.

Jalal lifted his head as if to ask Weynie a question, but was interrupted as her cell phone began ringing. She pulled it out and looked at the number, but it wasn't one she recognized.

"Albany area code," Weynie said.

"Is that Usher?" Jalal asked, raising an eyebrow.

"Really?" Weynie frowned at him, then hastily answered the phone.

Jalal shrugged.

"Hello?" Weynie asked.

"Weynie?"

Weynie's eyes went wide in surprise. "Dervy?"

"Dervy?" Jalal mouthed, but Weynie held up a finger.

"Yeah," Dervy said, the sound of traffic making her hard to understand. "It's me. I was wondering if you wanted to get some dinner?"

"Dervy, they said you Returned," Weynie said, heaving a relieved sigh at the sound of her friend's voice.

"No," Dervy said quietly. "I can explain more in person. If you want to meet up, that is. If not, that's okay, too... "

"Absolutely," Weynie said, though something in Dervy's tone made her uncomfortable for some reason. "But Dervy... "

Jalal waved his hands warningly. "Don't tell her until we're face to face," Jalal said urgently.

"Yeah?" Dervy asked.

Weynie hesitated, biting her lip for just a moment before blurting out: "They took Alex again."

Jalal shook his head.

"What?" Dervy said, voice anxious. "They took Alex?"

"Yeah," Weynie said, flinching at the admission. "But let's

talk more in person, all right?"

"Where are you?" Dervy asked.

Once again, Weynie hesitated for a moment, but this time decided against telling her everything. "You know that Olive Garden near Elmira?"

There was a pause. "On 17?"

"Right."

"I remember, yes," Dervy said. "You want me to meet you there?"

"Yeah," Weynie said. "Let's meet there and we can talk some more."

"I'll be there in a few hours," Dervy said, then, after a short pause. "Be careful Weynie."

"I will. You too," Weynie said confidently, though she didn't feel it.

The phone clicked silent, leaving Weynie and Jalal staring at each other.

"Well," Jalal said impatiently. "What did she say? Why did she let all of us think that she Returned?"

Weynie shrugged and put the phone away, tucking it inside her pants pocket. "I don't know; she didn't say, but she's hiding something, Jalal. I know it."

"So what now?" Jalal asked.

Weynie shrugged and got to her feet. "Feeling up to Italian food?"

* * *

Dervy pulled into the restaurant parking lot and eased her rental car into a vacant spot. She cut the ignition and the vehicle went silent, leaving her alone in the darkness of the small cab. The fresh scent of vanilla just barely covered the harsh odor of industrial cleaner emanating from the back seat. It had been growing stronger the entire trip as the fabric warmed.

Taking a deep, steadying breath, Dervy opened the door and stepped out into the crisp night air. A biting wind swept up from across the highway, dragging with it the deep-fried scents of fast food restaurants and gas stations along the way. The wind shifted direction briefly and the smell of garlic and pasta sauce danced by.

Dervy sighed, shut her door and made her way toward the Olive Garden entrance. She'd wanted to have a chance to actually talk to Weynie. Dervy wanted to talk about her age, about living for four thousand years.

She wanted to talk about, well, everything. She'd kept so much hidden for so long that it was threatening to burst out now that she had a taste for it thanks to Sergeant Jensen.

But Alex had been kidnapped again.

Why couldn't he just keep himself safe?

His kidnapping probably meant that Simon and Nathan were still trying to do whatever it was they had been trying the first time. Dervy steeled herself. She couldn't let them torture Alex like they had her. She would find him and make sure that they couldn't run these experiments on anyone ever again.

Dervy pushed open one of the double doors easily and stepped inside the main foyer of the restaurant. There were cherry stained benches along the sides--all empty at the moment--and a similarly colored pedestal standing directly in front of her. Beyond that, she could see most of the tables had chairs set on top of tables. The sound of a vacuum came from the left.

Behind the pedestal was a tall young man who smiled as she entered. He was wearing a white button down that tucked into a pair of black pants, partly obscured by a short, black apron. He set a bottle of cleaner on the pedestal as she approached, tucking a cleaning rag into his apron.

"Can I help you, ma'am?" He asked as she stepped forward, looking around for a glimpse of Weynie and Jalal.

"I'm looking for two people," Dervy said distractedly, narrowing down their position based on the vibration at the back of her neck. "A tall, black guy and an Indian woman?"

The young man nodded. "You must be Dervy then?"

She nodded.

"They asked us to stay open for awhile for you," he smiled and Dervy realized for the first time that he appeared exhausted. "We have a limited menu available for the next couple hours. They're right through the right there."

"Thanks," Dervy said and went the way he pointed.

"You're very welcome, ma'am," the young man said as picked back up the cleaner.

Dervy followed his directions and soon found Weynie and Jalal. They were both hunched over a small four person table, apparently so deep in conversation that they didn't hear her approach. When she was nearly on top of them, Jalal looked up, shocked.

"Dervy!" Jalal said in that lyrical voice of his, amazed. "I half expected this to be a joke."

He looked down quickly, muttering to himself so quietly that most strigoi would not have been able to hear. "I half hoped it would be... "

Dervy looked askance at him, but Weynie stood, face filled with mixed emotions, and gripped her in what would be a rib cracking hug to a human. As it was, Dervy's back popped as the other woman squeezed.

"Sit down, sit down," Weynie said, letting go and motioning Dervy to the chair next to Jalal. "I was really beginning to doubt my sanity for a little while."

Dervy smiled at both of them as she sat, though she was disturbed by Jalal's comment. "Well, no need to worry. I'm not dead."

Weynie smiled and took a sip of water just as a waiter approached the table. He smiled politely despite also looking exhausted. Not everyone could force stamina like she could.

He pulled free a black notebook as he spoke.

"Are you folks ready to order?" He asked.

"Yes," Weynie said. "This is it."

"Great," the waiter said cheerfully. "Well, our specials for today are--"

"Let's just have two bottles of wine. One of your house red," Dervy interrupted. "And one of the house white for right now."

His smile faltered for just the briefest moment, but it was back again immediately. "Yes, ma'am. Shall I take the menus?"

"Nah," Dervy said, flipping through the pages. "I'm hungry still, but we need some time alone before eating. Sound good," she glanced at his nametag. "Chris?"

Chris smiled. "Yes, ma'am. Two bottles of wine--one red and one white--coming up," he paused, glancing around the table for just a moment before turning and leaving.

Dervy watched him go and focused on the vibrations of the other humans--there were only four others in the building--until she was sure they were alone. She turned to them again.

"Now what happened to Alex?" Dervy asked quietly.

Weynie went through it all in a rush. She began with the Ankousti decree that the AIC should not investigate their kidnapping. Dervy frowned, but said nothing and Weynie quickly moved on, touching on a few things that had piqued her interest during those few months before finding the video of Dervy on the internet and taking it to Primator Searle. She paused long enough to let Dervy interject, but when she didn't, Weynie continued on, transitioning to Alex's encounter with Simon. That got Dervy's attention.

As Weynie moved on, Dervy stopped her.

"Wait," Dervy said. "Simon knew I was alive?"

"Yes," Jalal said simply. "Since we did not even know, we also found it hard to believe, but Alex said that he was quite insistent."

Who told him? Kevin or William? Dervy wondered, but didn't comment. Instead, she motioned Weynie to continue.

"Well," Weynie said, shrugging. "Soon after that, Alex took almost twenty thousand dollars from the Arktois and a truck and took off using the excuse that he was going to Buffalo for a technology conference."

"And then we found his truck flipped over off the side of the road about two hours east of here," Jalal said quietly as Chris returned with the two bottles of wine.

Chris made the rounds around the table, filling Dervy and Jalal's glasses with the red and Weynie's with the white before asking if they need anything else and leaving. Dervy swished the red liquid around, gave it a sniff--it had a slightly fruity scent, with just a hint of oak--and took a sip before setting the glass down.

"It's not bad," Dervy said absentmindedly. "Wine just isn't the same as it used to be... "

Weynie nodded as she sipped at her own glass. Dervy closed her eyes for a moment and let herself bathe in an ancient memory of a summer day in Tuscany, the bright scent of jasmine in the air as she savored a glass of wine next to a wrinkled, old man she had known for decades. It had not been called Chianti then--she forgot what he'd called it--remembering only the wine. It had a crisp fruity pallet, with a slight biting flavor at the end. Mostly she remembered the laughter and the company.

Dervy opened her eyes and realized that Weynie was talking and Chris was gone.

She frowned. She had been looking to order some pasta.

"... I Scryed the police officer and it doesn't look like an accident. There was a lot of blood and signs of multiple people," Weynie said with a frown as she swirled her glass, bringing the white wine a hair's breadth away from spilling out onto the table.

Dervy stared at the table for a moment. *What did they want with him? He was only a Taken...*

She could remember the first time she saw him; nose crinkled at the smell of her smoldering flesh, purple eyes wide at the sight of her...

"A Taken with purple eyes," Dervy muttered, setting her glass down. "Weynie, I never got a chance to talk to Alex about what happened to him. Did he ever tell you?"

Weynie nodded. "He said they took some blood samples."

"That's it?" Dervy asked, the memories of her escape flashing through her mind. "Just blood samples?"

"Yeah," Weynie said slowly. "What'd they do to you?"

Dervy shook her head and looked at her glass of wine. She considered lying or waving off the question for just a moment before shaking her head.

"They cut me open and took stuff out," Dervy said sullenly. "The last thing they took was my heart before... "

She shook her head and finished the drink in front of her in a single gulp.

"Anyway," Dervy said quickly, setting the glass to the side. "We need to find him since they're probably doing the same thing to him."

Jalal shuddered next to her, but did not say anything.

"Could you help us find where the facility is that they took you to?" Weynie asked hopefully.

"Do you have a map?" Dervy asked and Jalal nodded, pulling out a small, smooth screened cell phone.

He tapped the screen and then set it in front of her, one finger still in place. "What was that highway you were picked up on again?"

Dervy shook her head and pulled the phone closer to her. "It was just south of the Pennsylvania border... "

*   *   *

The room was freezing, but he didn't notice. Physical things tended to fade after you stopped your heart. After Scrying Kevin, Simon had begun to realize how far his powers had evolved since taking what Kevin referred to as "the Cure." Over the first few hours following his encounter, he had begun Scrying his guard lightly, dexterously, and was amazed to find that he could do so nearly as well as if he was touching her.

It had taken Simon decades to learn how to distinguish memories without physical contact. That wasn't to say that it was truly different--the fundamentals were the same--but rather, it was like searching for those glowing strands with your eyes closed and a pair of thick logging gloves covering your hands. Each thread was there, but the telltale colors were missing and the pulsing was faint, even for the most intense memory. The further away the target, the thicker the gloves.

That was no longer the case. When Simon closed his eyes, he could see the memories as if he had reached out and touched someone. There were pounding hoses of emotionally charged thought intermingled with the faintest glimmer of a recollection, hovering just on the edge of sight, waiting to be viewed.

And view he had. Simon was certain that if he stayed another night at Dóchas, he would face the same fate as Zeke and he had no interest in leaving the world in that manner. The woman with the mole had become his target. Her name was Gretchen Matthews and Simon had unraveled her. He was burrowed into her thoughts, implanting himself in her deepest memories.

Simon would wager that he knew more about Gretchen than she did. He could recite, word for word, the vow she had sworn to Kevin the previous week. He could also discuss nuances between the various plays of the Medieval dramatists, though he wasn't sure why anyone would really want to know about that.

Regardless, after nearly ten hours of constant Scrying and modification, Simon was finally beginning to feel that it was time to test his plan. Eyes fluttering open, Simon got to his feet, taking only a moment to run a steadying hand across his face before knocking on the door.

A moment later, Gretchen Matthews opened the door. She took a moment to glance past him before nodding him out into the hallway. Simon's heart leapt as he stepped into relative freedom, but he took care to keep it from showing on his face.

"How is he doctor?" Gretchen asked, concern only barely detectable in her voice.

Simon shook his head and looked to the floor. "Well," he brought his eyes back up to catch hers, though he didn't raise his head entirely. "It looks like the Return."

Gretchen shook her head sadly. "That's too bad, but it's better than what was planned, I guess."

Simon nodded, remaining outwardly calm. Inside he was panicking and rejoicing in equal parts. He was ecstatic that his ruse was working. Luckily, with his heart stopped, he wasn't jumping at every sound.

"Well," Simon said, just a little too quickly. "Would you mind escorting me out, Gretchen?"

Gretchen Matthews eyed him for just a moment before shaking her head as if clearing her mind. "Absolutely."

"And do you mind if we avoid any populated areas right now?" Simon asked casually, with just a hint of sadness in his voice. "I'm feeling... vulnerable."

Gretchen reached out and rubbed Simon's back comfortingly. "No problem, George."

Simon let a small smile flit across his lips as he passed through a shadow on his way to freedom. *Thank you Mr. Clooney.*

22
Near the New York/Pennsylvania Border
5:44 AM January 23, 2011

The snow crunched beneath the tires of the car as they pulled behind a decrepit Volkswagen off to the side of the road. Dervy killed the engine and sprung out in a blur. She rushed to the driver's window of the car in front of them, but it was empty.

She motioned for Weynie and Jalal to follow her before focusing on the small automobile. Despite her night vision, Dervy could barely make anything out. There was a small fast food bag and what appeared to be the bloody remnants of some butcher-packaged meat. She moved forward, running her hand along the cold trim of the vehicle until getting to the hood. There had been no snowfall here tonight, but there was still condensation building up around the hood supports so she reached out and placed her hand on the center, feeling the waning heat of the engine beneath.

Without speaking, Dervy caught Weynie's attention, pointed at the hood and pointed down the snow-covered trail. Pulling her shawl tightly around her, Weynie nodded and motioned Dervy to lead the way.

Dervy made her way down the trail, leaving the Volkswagen

behind. She broke through new snow parallel to a fresh set of tracks that appeared to be made by the sole passenger of the car. Carefully, she retracted a foot and compared the tracks. Whoever it was had slightly larger feet and weighed significantly more than she did, which probably meant it was a man of average height who was a little overweight.

Weynie stepped up next to her and glanced down at the tracks expertly. "Any idea?" She mouthed.

Dervy looked up at her and shrugged. "Simon?"

Jalal soon joined Dervy and Weynie and the three of them set out down the path, crunching through the snow as they plodded along. There was nearly two feet of snow sitting in smooth drifts across the path and throughout the woods off to their sides. The snow glittered in filtered moonlight, casting detailed patterns that wove in and out of each other as branches swayed in the light wind. In any other situation, it would have been beautiful, hypnotic, but at that moment it infuriated Dervy. Each glistening step threw her back into her own mind and into those memories she was desperately trying to avoid.

The cutting snow, tearing across her skin as she plodded ever forward, a red smudge spreading behind her as she went, a scar in the pristine tundra. The sound of the saw as it tore through her chest; the pressure of her heart being removed and the utter calm that accompanied it as she faded...

Dervy gritted her teeth and dug her nails into her palms.

"One, two... " she whispered, trying to center herself.

Weynie glanced over at her and then back at Jalal, expressing everything with that look. Dervy ignored it, instead focusing on her count as they moved forward.

The three of them continued like that for nearly an hour before the trees widened into a familiar clearing. By that time the eastern sky was progressing with surprising quickness from a deep purple to the shaded crimson of morning. Long shadows spread out toward them from dilapidated buildings--many of which had collapsed--as light began filtering through the trees. Dervy could feel another strigoi nearby, a few hundred yards away and to the right, most likely in one of the buildings. There was something odd about this vibration, though; something different that she couldn't put her finger on. It did remind her of someone, but she just couldn't tell who.

Weynie and Jalal stepped close to her as she stared off toward where the other strigoi was situated.

"If there's only one guy here, whether it's Simon or not, I don't think this is where they are keeping Alex," Weynie whispered, glancing around furtively.

Jalal nodded. "Agreed. But Dervy," he asked quietly. "Is this the place where you were taken in August?"

Dervy frowned and looked around the clearing. "There were a lot of people here then. Lights. Electricity. No cars, though," she recalled quietly.

She paused for a moment, letting her eyes wander and feeling familiarity in a collapsed building and the bent bough of a tree.

Dervy nodded assuredly. "But this is the place. I'm sure of it."

"Okay," Weynie whispered.

The three of them looked around for another moment before Jalal pointed at the tracks in the snow. "Shall we continue to foll--"

At that moment a horrendous grinding noise sprang to life. It sounded as if plates of metal were being twisted together by a giant. The three strigoi dropped to their knees in the snow, each trying to find the source of the piercing sound.

"What the hell is that?" Dervy whispered as she put her hands over her ears.

"I don't know," Weynie called back, cringing and forsaking silence in the cacophony. "Maybe it's a--"

The sound faded abruptly, dropping away until it became a low, pulsing roar off in the distance. Dervy got to her feet, though she was a little unsteady as she did so. For a moment, she couldn't remember where she was or what they were doing, but the feeling passed quickly as a cold winter breeze swept by her, chilling her cheeks and ruffling her short blond hair.

"What is it?" Jalal asked, looking around.

Weynie shrugged, "I don't know. Maybe a snow blower or something... "

As the hum stabilized, it picked at the memory of her escape--the sound of her heart, the pounding of her feet as she ran.

Gunfire.

Behind it all there had been a constant thrum, like the building had a pulse of its own, persistent and immutable.

"It's a generator," Dervy said as she stomped forward toward the nearest building.

Behind her, Weynie and Jalal looked at each other abashedly. "Oh. A generator makes sense," Weynie said quietly.

A few minutes later Dervy squeezed into one of the buildings that was part of the larger complex, taking care not to touch the door or disturb any of the refuse in the hallway. The vibration at the back of her neck hadn't shifted from where she'd originally located it, so Dervy was relatively sure they hadn't yet been detected despite the noise they had caused by tromping through the snow and yelling back and forth. Most likely the unknown strigoi deeper in the complex wasn't expecting anyone to follow.

Dervy smiled and stepped forward, taking care to move quietly. Weynie followed suit behind her--as silent as a mouse--but Jalal clomped along, apparently unaware of their attempts at stealth. Dervy and Weynie turned around and glared at him, but he just looked back at them blankly.

What? He mouthed, shrugging.

Quiet, Dervy mouthed back.

Jalal opened his mouth to respond, but snapped it shut. Instead he pointed at the doorway and made a motion indicating that he would wait. Dervy nodded and continued on, Weynie in tow.

The halls were much like she remembered. The plaster was flaking visibly and millions of tiny particles hung in the air as the barest glimmer of morning seeped through the cracks and windows of the building. It looked as if it had become a squatters' palace. Trash was scattered everywhere--bottles and cans littered the floor--and the scent of stale urine grew stronger as they proceeded, moving ever closer to the sound of the generator and the buzzing at the back of Dervy's neck.

After a few minutes and a couple dead-ends, Dervy turned a corner and stopped as the sound of the generator suddenly amplified in the compact corridor. She threw up a hand to halt Weynie, stepping around the corner. Carefully, she peeked out just enough to get a good view of the room a few feet away, near the end of the hallway. The door had been left ajar and yellow artificial light streamed out into the walkway.

The strigoi with the familiar vibration was in that room. Dervy could hear him walking back and forth just to the right of the door, muttering. She desperately tried to make out what he was saying, but only managed to pick up the word 'vial', which he used multiple times.

Dervy turned back to Weynie and motioned her to stay. Weynie swept her hand horizontal to the ground and shook her head, instead indicating that the two of them would go. Dervy shook her head and repeated her first gesture. Weynie locked eyes with her for a moment before nodding.

Breathing smoothly through her nose, Dervy stepped out into the hallway, moving silently until she reached the doorway. She took a moment to evaluate the entrance, searching for any traps, makeshift weapons or pretty much anything else that might slow her. Determining that they would be alone, Dervy poked her head inside and looked to the right.

Directly to the right of the door was Simon. He stood with his back to her, a drawer to a filing cabinet open wide. His clothes were disheveled and covered with stains, but most disturbing was the smell that emanated from him. The coppery scent of fresh blood rolled off of him in waves.

Various papers and folders lay discarded at his feet as if he had looked at them briefly before tossing them to the side like so much trash. Dervy cocked her head slightly to read one, but was only able to make out what looked like various metric measurements--five milligrams of one item, forty milligrams of another and others like that.

Simon cursed suddenly, throwing another folder the ground. He leaned against the filing cabinet, arms atop it, and his entire body sagged in apparent defeat.

"Where the hell is it?" Simon muttered. "I've got the list, but I thought he left a copy... "

Dervy stepped into the room. "A copy of what, Simon?"

Simon spun around, eyes wide in shock and panic, and Dervy hissed despite herself. The whole front of his once gray shirt and the fringe of his thick jacket was covered in dried blood. His unshaven face was speckled with red droplets, but the space around his mouth had a decidedly pink sheen as if he had tried to wash away some of the mess.

Dervy took a step back in disgust. "Have you been *feeding*?"

"I-I..." Simon stuttered, looking around wildly. "You don't understand what its like, Dervy. And it's easier without the heartbeat, believe it or not. I just still had to..."

Dervy spat. "What is there to understand? Feeding is prosecuted for a reason, Simon. It's never justified. What the hell were you thinking?"

"No," Simon said, blinking fast. "It's different after you take Kevin's Cure. You can't deny it anymore... this isn't even human," he motioned to the blood on his shirt. "This is deer blood... and a chuck roast. But it's not enough."

Simon stared down at his hands, red lines under his fingernails. "It's never enough."

Dervy narrowed her eyes and began circling Simon to the right, cutting of his escape route through the other side of the building. If he tried to go the other way, Weynie could slow him down until she could get there and help. The vibration at the back of her neck pulsed slightly.

Why was his vibration different?

"What 'Cure' are you talking about?" Dervy asked.

Simon's eyes snapped away from his hands and he stared around the room for a moment, disoriented. "Yeah, Kevin has a shot that stops the Return. Makes you more powerful."

Simon snorted. "Makes you hungry, too."

"Bullshit," Dervy spat. "You can't stop the Return."

Simon looked at her smiling and moved toward her slowly, his usual swagger coming back into his steps. "Come on Dervy. We both know the Return doesn't take everyone, now don't we?"

Dervy glared at him, firmly keeping herself between him and the exit.

Simon frowned as he realized what she was doing and turned around abruptly. "He has a shot that can cause the Return, too."

He turned back and looked her straight in the eye, a slight grin on his blood-spattered face. "You wouldn't know anyone interested in something like that, would you?"

Dervy stared at him, mouth agape, and let herself dare to hope for just a moment. And at that moment, Simon lunged at her,

Scrying her violently as he did so.

Images flashed through her mind; nonsense pictures of intertwining lines and maddening forms. These were coupled with powerful thoughts and emotions that slammed into her from all angles. Sadness, anger, lust, love, depression; they all warred inside her mind as Simon attacked, just barely visible beyond the swirling lights and fake dreams he was pushing at her.

Dervy's body responded more out of instinct than any conscious instruction on her part. As Simon tried to rush by her, she tackled him, dragging him to the floor where he pounded on her mentally and physically. Her head snapped back as he kneed her in the jaw, trying desperately to break away from her and reach the door. But her grip remained tight.

"Let go of me," Simon yelled, kicking wildly, but she held on despite the cacophony in her mind.

"Simon," Dervy said threateningly as she dug her fingers deep into his thigh, causing him to scream. "If you don't stop Scrying me, I'll tear your leg off and beat you to death with it. And then, when you regenerate, I'll tear the other one off and do it again."

Almost immediately, the images ceased, leaving her alone on the floor with Simon, who was no longer struggling. He was just lying there on his back not breathing.

"Thank you," Dervy said through gritted teeth as she sat up, pulling her bloody fingers out of his upper thigh.

Simon grunted as he sat up, looking at the near bloodless wound on his leg as it healed up. "No problem. Oh, hi Weynie."

Dervy glanced toward the door, taking care to keep Simon in her sight, and saw Weynie standing there in confusion, orange shawl wrapped tightly around her. Idly, Dervy motioned her forward and Weynie did so, albeit hesitantly.

"So," Dervy said, turning back to Simon who was sitting forlornly next to her. "Was all that bullshit just to distract me?"

Simon shook his head. "No. Every word was true, actually."

Dervy sighed and wiped her hand off on Simon's leg. "Even Bloodless still bleed a little, eh?"

"Yeah, apparently so," he said curtly.

Dervy smiled. "Mm. So I guess this means Caoimhín is still

alive?"

Simon nodded. "Yeah, Kevin is still alive."

Dervy cursed. She couldn't believe that he would go to such mad lengths for something as ridiculous as immortality. Why couldn't anyone understand that immortality was not a blessing; it was a curse. Being a strigoi was bad enough. Having to live for hundreds of years and watching your family and friends die off as you continue unchanged was torture. It was something else entirely to watch strigoi do the same.

The thing that truly infuriated her was that Dervy had told Caoimhín that decades ago. He had approached her with a suggestion that they try to figure out what made her live so long and it had resulted in the same dialog. At the end, she'd thought he understood, but now Dervy realized he had just ignored her. Instead, he decided to kidnap her and force her to do what he wanted instead.

For some reason that made her more sad than angry.

"So," Simon said slowly, interrupting her thoughts. "Can I go now?"

"What?" Weynie said. "No. You broke into the Arktois and assaulted a Sirgil. You don't just get to walk away from that Simon."

"You can't put me in one of the holes," Simon said, panic in his eyes as he mentioned the old Arktois prison--a series of holes drilled forty feet into the earth. "You don't understand what this new Hunger is like. I *will* go mad. I'm barely keeping it together out here where I can eat squirrels and shit."

"You deserve it," Weynie spat.

Simon cursed. "No, I won't do that. I'll fight you right now--"

"And lose," Dervy said irritably. "Just relax. You're not going into the hole."

Dervy turned and locked eyes with Weynie. "He's not going into the hole."

Weynie huffed, but nodded, though she began rubbing her shawl in annoyance. Simon sighed in relief.

"How about this," Dervy offered, turning back to Simon. "You tell me everything you know about Caoimhín and his plan."

Simon eyed her warily. "Or what?"

Dervy narrowed her eyes at him. "Simon. Don't mess with me. I am not playing with you."

Simon held up his hands in surrender. "Okay, sorry."

"How about we start with where you are keeping Alex?" Weynie asked urgently.

"Whoa," Simon said defensively. "Kevin is keeping him, not me."

"Whatever," Weynie said in frustration. "I just want the location."

"Hold on a damn minute," Dervy interrupted. "I want to know what the hell is going on first. We need to know what we're dealing with."

She got to her feet and extended a hand to Simon. "Why don't you start at the beginning?"

Simon looked at her hand for a moment and then shook his head and accepted it, getting to his feet unsteadily. "The beginning is a long time ago."

"How long ago?" Weynie asked.

Simon shrugged. "About eighty years, I guess. Kevin found me, though technically he didn't Gather me since it wasn't reported to the Ankousti."

"There's no way he has been kidnapping Taken for eighty years. I gathered thirteen in '49 and '67 personally," Dervy said incredulously.

He shook his head. "No, the kidnapping started in the early eighties."

"But why?" Weynie asked.

"Because they're getting stronger, quicker," Simon said. "We've all seen it; it's not really a big surprise to find out that the Ankousti wanted to know why, right?"

Dervy narrowed her eyes at Simon and stepped forward, causing him to back away cautiously. "The Ankousti ordered this?"

"Well, not *all* of it," Simon said, gesturing around the room. "But most of it. Kevin let me Scry him and from what I saw, most of the Ankousti was more interested in the results than the process."

Dervy shook her head in disbelief. How could they sanction something like... like this? She had worked too hard to make an organization that would be a safe haven for the strigoi, not a place that used them for testing. Her hands were balled into fists at her side as she recalled the names of the Ankousti elders over the past twenty years.

Each one would pay for their support.

That was when Dervy realized Weynie was staring at her suspiciously.

"What?" Dervy asked harshly, anger bubbling to the surface despite her best efforts.

Weynie bit her cheek. "Weren't you a member of the Ankousti then?"

Dervy shook her head. "No, I resigned in '76. Esok Johnson was nominated to replace me."

"I wonder if that was why he resigned?" Weynie asked.

Simon shrugged. "It doesn't matter. From what I hear, he's dead."

"Thanks to you," Weynie snarled, taking a step forward threateningly.

Dervy put up a hand. "Okay. Stop it. I get you're angry--I am too--but we need to work with Simon if we're going to get anywhere."

Weynie stepped back and shook her head. "Fine. You talk to him. I'm going to go get Jalal."

Dervy nodded as Weynie left and turned back to Simon. "Tell me more."

"You know that most of this is your fault, right?" Simon asked as he pulled a rickety chair away from an old desk. "If you'd just done what Kevin asked, all of this probably could have been avoided."

Dervy paced in front of him. "Don't start pointing at me. This is Caoimhín's mess. I told him that immortality was a mistake."

"Kevin," Simon said. "His name is Kevin. He hates it when you call him Caoimhín."

"*Caoimhín,*" Dervy spat. "Or Kevin. It doesn't matter. He's still a fool."

"Fool or not, he's done it," Simon said purposefully. "And ideally he'll be able to fix the problems with Alex's help."

Dervy stopped and stared at him. "Why are you here then? Why dig around in old, abandoned paperwork instead of sitting by his side like the lapdog you've apparently been your whole life?"

Simon stood, face indignant. "I am not a lapdog. I don't

bow and scrape when he's around and he's going to find that out the hard way, regardless of whether he fixes this, this," he stopped, searching for a word in the midst of his anger. "This mistake."

"And how do you plan on doing that, Simon?" Dervy asked, getting close to him again. "Really. I want to know."

Simon looked at her, a grin spreading across his face, madness dancing in his eyes for just a moment. "I'm going to kill him and everyone who helped. The Cure is a gift, but the process... the process needs punishment. You can't just do this and get away with it. He needs to be stopped before he can get--hurt more people."

Dervy held her tongue as he finished; there had been a hesitation near the end. "'Before he can get' what, Simon?"

Simon smiled, but it quickly faded as she maintained eye contact. "Before he can get the Cure. The real one, I mean."

Dervy looked at him long and hard, but Simon held the gaze, albeit a bit unsteadily. She was sure he was lying, but doubted the lie was malicious. Staring at him, his mouth twitching in anxiety, Dervy was sure that the lie was much over something much more mundane. Survival, most likely.

"Fine," Dervy acceded reluctantly. "Tell me where they are and we'll help you."

Simon looked aghast. "You want to go to Dóchas?"

"Dóchas?" Dervy asked. "Isn't that 'hope' in Irish?"

Simon shrugged. "Yeah, but it's also the name of Kevin's base. And it's filled with strigoi like me."

"Well, no offense," Dervy said with a small smile. "But you weren't that hard to take down."

"Right," Simon said with a sneer. "I stopped because I value my limbs and I respect you, Dervy. Most of these others won't know you and don't give a damn about your age. Hell, if any of them find out who you are, they might try and kill you on sight."

"Why?" Dervy asked, flabbergasted.

Simon threw his hands in the air. "You still don't get it do you? This is all because of you. Kevin rushed the Cure because he didn't have any more time left and you were gone. We've been dealing with this for months because you decided not to help."

"That's crap and you know it," Dervy said dismissively. "None of this would have--"

"But it did, didn't it?" Simon said angrily.

Dervy just stared at him for a moment, smoldering rage held carefully in check. It was obvious that Simon blamed her for the state he was in and she didn't have time to deal with his paranoia or finger pointing. She needed to get to Alex.

"Listen, Simon," Dervy started, but the presence of two strigoi in the doorway distracted her.

Weynie entered the room with Jalal in tow. She stepped forward, apparently ignorant to the tension between Dervy and Simon; or perhaps she just did not care.

"Do we have a destination yet?" Weynie asked.

"Nice seeing you again, Jalal," Simon said with a small wave.

Jalal grimaced. "Go to hell."

Dervy looked at him in shock. It was the first time Dervy had ever heard Jalal swear.

"You see?" Simon said with a small grin. "How am I supposed to work in these conditions?"

Dervy covered her face. "Simon. Shut up."

"Where is Alex?" Weynie asked again, anger tingeing her voice.

"He's at Dóchas," Simon said simply, looking away.

"What is 'Dóchas'?" Jalal asked.

Dervy glanced back at him. "It's the name of his stronghold or whatever it is."

An idea occurred to Dervy and she turned back to Simon, grinning as well. Simon's smile faded quickly.

"And Simon is going to take us there," she said sweetly.

He paled as she spoke. "What? I didn't say that."

Dervy shrugged and motioned to Jalal, who stepped forward eagerly. "Then I guess you're going in one of the holes, huh?"

Simon cursed, backing away in a panic. "But, you said--"

"I know what I said," Dervy interrupted viciously. "But the fact is that we need to get Alex and you know where he is."

"I can tell--"

"No," Dervy interrupted. "You are going to *show* us because you don't want to get caught either."

"I... " Simon dropped his chin to his chest and sighed in defeat. "All right. I'll do it, but then I'm gone. Understand?"

Weynie looked askance at Dervy. She could feel the Scry

happening, the message Weynie was trying to pass along. A series of pictures flashed in her mind--Simon in shackles in a pit, hot brands pressing into his skin. It was an easy message to decode.

Simon couldn't be freed. He had to pay.

Dervy bit her cheek for a moment. Her entire life she had given no quarter. When given the choice between mercy and violence, Dervy always chose the latter, though she wasn't sure why. She'd earned her reputation amongst the Greeks and Romans, but it never fulfilled her; never satiated the desire for more pain.

Maybe it was time to try something different.

"All right, Simon," Dervy said. "You take us there, you get us in, help us find Alex and get us back out again--with him--and you can go free."

Weynie sighed, shaking her head, but Simon was smiling widely.

He held out a pink hand toward Dervy. Hesitantly, she reached out and accepted it, feeling the cold skin beneath.

"Deal," Simon said.

23
Dóchas
8:14 AM January 23, 2011

What was he doing here?
It was crazy. If Kevin found him, Simon was dead. Like, dead-dead. Full, no regeneration dead.
Simon wasn't even sure if Kevin would take the time to torture him before inducing the Return and putting a bullet in his head.
Oh god.
Thankfully, Simon's heart was still as he led the three strigoi through the wilderness surrounding Dóchas. The closer he got to the facility--gray walls slowly becoming visible through the overgrown brush--the more anxious he became and, strangely, the hungrier he became. It had been four hours since he had killed and eaten that deer, but despite the short time the animal's flesh did little to sate this new Hunger. Every time he looked at any of the others his stomach turned and rumbled at the same time, begging for sustenance. Thus far he'd held the cravings at bay, but it had been nearly three days since the last time he'd eaten at Dóchas and his mind was starting to tear under the pressure.

Behind him, Jalal crushed a small bush, causing Simon to cringe in annoyance. He turned around for what felt like the twelfth time that morning and addressed Dervy.

"Do we have to bring that oaf?" Simon hissed. "He's going to get us caught."

Dervy cut him off with a quick chopping motion and pointed forward.

Quiet and move.

Sure, why not?

Simon made an irritated noise and moved forward with renewed urgency. With Jalal lumbering through the snow like a crippled mammoth, they might as well get some speed out of it.

Dervy stopped him as they approached and whispered, "There are people right over there."

Simon looked askance at her. "I told you there would be--"

The sounds of truck engines roared to life, cutting him off. Confused, Simon and Dervy moved slowly forward until they came to the edge of the clearing where they could peer out through the heavy brush. Just beyond the thicket were nearly a dozen delivery trucks, each with the logo of a half-shadowed, blue face surrounded by flame. The words "Hope Foods" were emblazoned just underneath the logo.

"What the hell is this?" Weynie whispered angrily as she crawled up next to them.

Simon shook his head and glanced around. There were dozens of humans in Hope Foods uniforms walking around the parking lot. Some loitered about, but most appeared to be wheeling fifty-gallon drums around onto large pallets. There were maybe twenty strigoi that appeared to be coordinating the activity. They walked around in black uniforms, though Simon couldn't see the blue patches on their breasts.

"I've seen that symbol before," Weynie whispered as she appeared silently to his left. "I just don't remember where."

The cracking of a branch indicated that Jalal had stepped forward as well. "It's the same as the new supply company," Jalal said in hushed tones.

Simon craned his head around and got a look of the somber African man, face set in concern. "What supply company?" Simon asked.

Dervy suddenly grabbed Simon by the front of his bloody shirt. "What's in those barrels Simon?"

"I have no idea," Simon mumbled in annoyance, pushing her away roughly. "He wouldn't tell me anything. Only that something big is going to happen."

Dervy looked away in disgust, eyes lingering on the trucks for just a little too long before shaking her head. "We need to get to Alex and then we'll figure this out."

Weynie looked askance at Dervy. "What about the trucks?"

"We leave them," Dervy said, motioning Simon to lead them onward. "And hope that we can figure this all out in time to stop it."

Simon raised an eyebrow at that, but moved ahead regardless. Somewhere along the line, Dervy's motivations had changed, though he wasn't sure how. He was certain that the Dervy of four months ago would have abandoned Alex and moved to destroy the obvious threat--especially given that it was a much more present danger.

As he led them toward the side door near the medical wing, Simon wondered if she was making the correct choice. While not entirely sure what Kevin had loaded inside those barrels, Simon felt confident that it had something to do with the Cure. At that point, he wouldn't have been surprised to find out that Kevin intended to forcibly infect every strigoi with his serum.

"God help us," Simon mumbled when he reached the edge of the clearing.

Dervy glanced at him sharply, but he simply shook his head and pointed toward the door a few feet away. She nodded back and, after glancing around for roving eyes, cleared the distance between the tree line and the door in a flash. Simon motioned Weynie across, then Jalal--who lumbered past like a crippled mule--before joining them.

By the time he reached the door, Dervy was withdrawing a small knife from the keyhole and gesturing the rest of them behind her. Simon shook his head and snuck up next to her.

What? Dervy mouthed.

"The medical rooms are down the hall about forty feet on the right-hand side," Simon whispered. "That was the last place I saw him. We should start there."

Dervy nodded and motioned Simon behind her. He stepped gratefully into place. Dervy pushed the door open and slid inside, disappearing from view. Cursing quietly, Simon followed.

He entered the hallway in time to see Dervy setting a tall strigoi soldier down to the ground gently, right forearm wrapped tightly around his throat; face purple. Simon shook his head in disbelief at the sight of the petite woman as she straightened easily.

To think, he had once considered trying to fight her.

He would have lost.

Dervy looked back at him irritably. *What?* She mouthed.

Simon smiled and motioned for her to continue onward, pointing down the hall toward the double doors that led to the medical area. She glanced past him at where Weynie and Jalal were crouching and motioned Weynie forward. Dervy looked at Jalal and pointed him to the guard. Jalal nodded and approached the man, taking care to keep close enough that he could debilitate him if necessary. Last, Dervy motioned for Simon to follow her before continuing down the hallway.

As Simon passed the guard, he noticed the wicked scar that ran down the side of the man's face. Smiling, he leaned down and whispered into Jalal's ear: "Give him hell for me."

Jalal glared at him, but said nothing. Simon moved forward, allowing himself the pleasure of picturing that smug strigoi's face being pounded into the ground, even though he was sure Jalal wouldn't do it for him. Simon would be lucky if Jalal gave the man a bloody nose. Jalal was a big kitten.

A big, bumbling kitten.

Simon snickered, moving with a silence perfected over nearly a century of practice and soon found himself at the open doors to the medical room. Dervy was already inside rummaging around and Weynie was standing next to the door, watching for others. He entered, feeling a little queasy as his eyes passed over the operating table just past the thick, plate glass window on the far side of the room.

"Simon," Dervy whispered urgently, waving him over to her. "Come here."

Simon nodded, tearing his eyes away from the glass and walked up to where Dervy was standing, shuffling through some papers.

"What?" Simon asked.

"I don't know," Dervy said as she held a piece of paper up and then turned it sideways. "What is this?"

Simon shrugged, but looked closer anyway. It appeared to be a list of chemicals and mix ratios for something.

"Maybe it's the formula for the Cure?" Simon offered, glancing around the room uncomfortably.

"What's today's date?" Dervy asked, looking up at him.

Simon shrugged noncommittally. He was happy enough knowing that it was almost morning. What day it was mattered more to humans.

Weynie stepped toward them, pulling a cell phone out of her pocket. "January twenty-third. Why?"

"It's dated yesterday," Dervy said, turning it over and pointing toward a timestamp saved in the header region of the paper. "This is new."

Simon turned away from the sheet as Dervy and Weynie began fussing over the contents. It really didn't matter to him what was on that sheet--there was nothing that could help him now. A grim smile spread across his face as his eyes wandered across the room to the storage fridge. Maybe there was something he could do about it, though.

Silently, Simon moved toward the fridge and located a small portable cooler that had been left nearby--like the kind you would use to put lunch in for work--and set that next to the fridge. He glanced back to see Dervy and Weynie entirely preoccupied with their find. Licking his lips, he cracked open the fridge, which sighed slightly as the rubber released from the edges of the metal.

There, sitting on the middle shelf and labeled clearly in permanent marker was a small collection of vials--thirteen in total-- each marked with the word 'Return' in quotes.

"Simon, what are you doing?" Dervy asked as he reached toward the small rack.

He glanced behind him in a panic. "Um, looking for some of this stuff. Figured it would help if we run into Kevin."

Simon reached out and grabbed a handful of the vials as he spoke and shoved them into the small cooler, next to what appeared to be a ham sandwich. He had no idea if they needed to be climate controlled or not, but if he was lucky he could get outside and refrigerate them. If Simon's heart weren't stopped it would have jumped into his throat when Dervy stepped toward him.

Dervy eyed him warily as she approached. "Step to the side, Simon. What did you put in there--"

A yell in the hallway turned her attention away from him and toward the door. Figures in black uniforms ran past and the sounds of fighting broke out from down the hall.

Where they had left Jalal.

One of the figures glanced toward them as she passed and Simon saw the telltale mole on the face of Gretchen Matthews.

Desperately, Simon shook his head and tried to Scry her, to bring back the memory of a handsome, yet deeply troubled doctor who fed upon a certain celebrity crush. This time Gretchen was prepared and cut off his attempt viciously, forcing him out of her mind. Simon's shoulders slumped and he cursed as she pointed into the room and motioned to some unseen people behind her.

Gretchen stepped inside, livid, the sound of pounding feet close behind, her eyes locked on him. He could already feel the needle tearing into his skin and old age thrusting itself upon him, decalcifying his bones, loosening his skin, making every movement a living agony. Simon would wish for death without torture--would welcome it when it came.

If Kevin would even allow that. The Cure could stop the Return in its tracks--reverse it. What if Kevin decided to use the chemicals as a form of torture? What if you aged and grew young, felt agonizing pain and then brief bliss for eternity?

Simon stood frozen in place as she moved toward him, three other strigoi in their black uniforms at her back.

And then she was gone, leaving behind fluttering loose-leaf papers that hung casually in the air.

Simon's jaw went slack as the solid metal desk settled to the ground on the far side of the hallway, a small cloud of dust scattering in the streams of morning sunlight. Small rivulets of blood began flowing from around the mangled collection of limbs beneath it.

A deathly silence fell upon them all at that moment. Simon turned, as if in slow motion, to look at where Dervy stood amongst raining paperwork, face furious--a mask of war that promised certain death--feet planted wide as she recovered from the throw. Weynie stood near her in a defensive position, arms in front of her face, eyes locked on Dervy and a look of pure terror glued to her face. At that moment it didn't seem strange to Simon that Weynie was posed as if protecting herself from Dervy.

Not strange at all.

For a moment, Dervy stood there like a goddess of war--daring anyone to stand in her way.

And then everything went to hell.

Dóchas soldiers flooded into the room--Simon quickly lost count of how many--and Dervy screamed in fury, launching herself full into the fray like a whirlwind. Weynie followed suit, though her style was substantially different from Dervy's. Weynie could use Animi Fulminis and it became apparent that she knew how to use it in a fight. Arcs of blue lightning scattered amongst the uniformed strigoi, causing heads to snap backward as current coursed through their bodies, legs locking in pain, and muscles twitching uncontrollably.

Dervy plowed into the center of the group, heedless of the fact that these strigoi--these Cured members of Dóchas--were supposed to be stronger, faster and overall more powerful than her. In the hallway, Simon saw a figure fly past the door, careening slightly as it collided with the stray desk. Apparently Jalal was much more useful in a fight than Simon had thought.

Weynie unleashed an arc of lightning that exploded past him, raising the hair on his arms and searing a purple scar in his vision; Dervy's screams were punctuated by the cries of pain coming from the Cured strigoi as she quite literally tore them limb from limb; Jalal hit another strigoi in the chest hard enough that the entire cavity collapsed.

And Simon just sat there, crouched into the corner of the room, small freezer bag clutched tightly to his chest. Simon Scryed furiously, watching everyone's eyes and tugging on their memories when they did see him... it was risky, but if he could just last until the fight was over...

For a few breathless moments, Simon wondered if the Sirgili could overcome the massing Dóchas force. Dervy was nearly to the exit, leaving behind a line of crippled, broken and otherwise incapacitated strigoi. Weynie was beset by three Dóchas soldiers, but seemed fully capable of keeping them away. Dervy glanced behind her, toward him, and her eyes narrowed.

Simon felt his still heart sink again.

And then she was in the air, hanging there by the neck as Nathan Potts stepped into view. He was wearing the same uniform Simon had seen him in last. Nathan would have blended in with the rest of the soldiers if he didn't stand nearly a foot taller than the next tallest person in the room. Dervy became a blur once again, fists and legs flailing around--many of which connected solidly with Nathan's thickly built body--but they were ineffective. After a minute, Dervy's strikes grew weak as her face went from bright red to a sickly blue and then to purple.

Nathan squeezed then, corded muscles showing beneath the fabric of his jacket, and a resounding crack echoed through the hallway. Dervy's head went sideways unnaturally and Nathan lowered his arm, though he kept her firmly in grasp, neck forced apart by one large hand. Nathan knew how good her healing power was and wouldn't be so cocky as to think he had debilitated her for any extended length of time.

A moment later, disbelief plainly written on her face as her feet were taken from beneath her, Weynie disappeared beneath a pile of Dóchas soldiers. Within seconds, those who had tackled her were taking her unconscious body out of the room.

With the other two down, Jalal quickly succumbed to the overwhelming numbers he faced, collapsing as a blast of force crushed him into the wall, the impact sending a spider web of cracks through the concrete.

Simon prayed to whatever god would listen that they not find him. Nervous sweat spilled down his back and soaked his clothes. He carefully Scryed a soldier who glanced his way, pushing an image of a shadowed desk to replace that of the filthy man in the corner. A glazed look passed over his face for a moment and then he shook his head, turned and left. He took only a moment to salute Nathan before continuing past. Soon, a small group of Dóchas soldiers passed by carrying the beaten body of Jalal. The man with the scar, Ambrose, followed behind rubbing his neck tenderly.

That left Nathan Potts in the hallway, Dervy dangling from his massive fist.

Simon didn't breath. His heart was still.

But his eyes were locked on Nathan in the hallway. The

large man was staring after his soldiers, but didn't move an inch. Nathan looked almost comical. With their differences in size, it almost looked as if Nathan was carrying a large rag doll. Dervy's feet lay limp on the ground, her face a violet and crimson abstraction.

The urge to laugh rose inside of him, but Simon forced it down. He needed to stay silent.

Invisible.

They stood like that for nearly a minute, Nathan staring into the distance and Simon paralyzed. Then Nathan finally shook his head.

Almost casually, Nathan turned and looked directly at him, locking eyes with him. Simon Scryed expertly, but he knew that there was no chance. It was over. Nathan saw him and his life was forfeit. He would feel pains that he had never imagined.

He was dead.

Just as Simon was about to stand and give up, Nathan turned and walked away, leaving Simon alone in the sparsely lit room with nothing but his disbelief and a small cooler filled with a dozen vials of the Return drug.

Simon choked down a sob as Nathan's footsteps drew away. After a few minutes of utter silence, Simon left the medical room, turned left, squeezed out the exterior door, and disappeared into the trees.

24
Dóchas
10:57 AM January 23, 2011

The lights came and went quickly, accompanied by the sound of rolling wheels and rapid vibration. A high-pitched squeaking railed against Alex's temples from somewhere to his right. He struggled to focus, to even open his eyes, but the burning fluid in his veins kept him on his back. Another round of testing; another bout of fitful dreams and lost memories. Alex groaned against the helplessness, but if there were anyone around him, they showed to recognition.

He could hear their heartbeats, though.

Ba-dump, ba-dump, ba-dump...

The cart stopped at the sound of running footsteps. The lights were bright, burning into his mind. He tried to shy away, but was paralyzed.

"Primator O'Ceallaigh wants to see him," said a deep, officious sounding voice that warbled in the haze.

"We just finished the testing, sir," a feminine voice from behind him said. "We aren't sure if it is working yet. We need to monitor him; he could be unstable."

"That wasn't a request, doctor," the other voice said angrily. "Take him to the war room and get that shit out of him. He needs to be coherent."

There was a tentative pause. "Yes, sir."

"Good," the deep voice said.

Footsteps went away from him and once again Alex was moving, the squeaking to his right suddenly back and incessant.

"If we're taking him off the narcotics, I'm out of here," the feminine voice said.

There was a waver in her voice that hadn't been evident a moment before.

"We don't do this and they'll eat us," another voice said from behind him. "If this works, we don't have to worry. What would you rather do?"

"I don't know," the woman said, confused. "I just wish I'd known..."

"Yeah," a third voice, this one younger, if Alex could guess. "If we'd all known. But we didn't and now we're here."

A moment later, Alex felt something removed from his right forearm. It was as if a giant splinter had been pulled and almost immediately the burning sensation faded. The flashing lights began to dim, the screeching normalized. Slowly, Alex opened his eyes, a groan escaping from his lips as he did so.

"Hello Alex," the female voice said.

Squinting his sensitive eyes against the bright fluorescent bulbs above him, Alex looked at the woman above him.

"Dr. Aubin?" Alex asked, tentatively pulling on his straps. They held firm.

She nodded, smiling hesitantly, eyes flicking to someone near his right arm. "Yes, it's me. How do you feel?"

At that moment, Alex's stomach rumbled and he cringed in sudden pain. "Hungry."

*   *   *

Dervy knelt in front of Nathan with her back to him and her arms crossed behind her head. Weynie and Jalal were similarly situated next to her, each with their own small 'honor guard'. The room they were in looked as if it had been hastily rearranged. Tables were shoved to the sides, large standing maps and transparent acrylic drawing boards stood haphazardly off to the sides. This left a large open space in the center of the room with a clear path to the double doors that led out.

Dervy couldn't believe it, but in the center of the room stood Caoimhín O'Ceallaigh. He paced back and forth impatiently, fidgeting with the hem of his black jacket as if waiting for something splendid to happen.

Just as he had been doing for the past twenty minutes.

Caoimhín showed certain signs of aging that Dervy had recognized immediately. There were gray streaks in his hair and beard, some more prominent hair on the backs of his hands, and deep wrinkling of the skin around his eyes. He certainly didn't appear old, just *older* than he had over the past five hundred years. Instead of a flush early-twenties youth, Caoimhín appeared to be a man in his late thirties who was still in the prime of his life.

There was one very definitive difference between the man in front of her and the strigoi Dervy had once called friend. A certain unstable glint lay just behind each glance. Like the shifting of a dark shadow at the corner of your eye, it was there one moment, but gone the next, replaced with a man who was both confident and dangerous. He was also very nervous.

And his vibration was different... just like Simon's had been.

Caoimhín was wearing a uniform similar to the others, but bore no insignia, not even the blue face that adorned everyone else's chest. Caoimhín simply wore black from head to toe. Dervy wondered at that. It seemed that a general who didn't wear his own colors would be demoralizing. Though that certainly didn't seem to be the case given what she'd seen so far.

Dervy was just about to ask about it when, not surprisingly, Weynie broke the silence.

"What are we doing here Kevin?" Weynie asked in annoyance.

Her guard immediately struck her in the back of the head with a thick baton. Weynie fell forward and remained there for a moment before pushing herself back up.

They all carried batons now. Apparently they weren't so sure of their ability to overwhelm the three Sirgili tied up on the floor.

Dervy grinned.

"You will address the Primator with his proper title," the guard behind Weynie growled, gripping the baton tightly.

Caoimhín stopped pacing and turned toward her, waiting for Weynie to clear her head from the blow before approaching her.

"Who are you again?" Kevin asked quizzically, head to the side slightly.

Weynie frowned and glanced askance at Dervy. "Weynie Chakravarty. I presented several security reports to you during your time as the Primator--"

The soldier behind her kicked her solidly in the back, sending her sprawling forward. Caoimhín looked menacingly at the soldier, who took a cautious step backward.

"I *am* the Primator," Caoimhín said firmly, making sure to catch Weynie's eyes as he said so. "Currently of Dóchas, soon of the Arktois as well. That's already assured."

Dervy narrowed her eyes but didn't say anything.

Jalal, however, did.

"What does that mean?" Jalal asked cautiously before quickly adding, "Primator."

Caoimhín smiled and turned away. "It means what it sounds like. I've beaten it. The Return. The Cure."

Caoimhín looked at the doorway as if hearing something none of them could, though Dervy could feel the pulsing of a Taken nearby, coming closer by the second. The vibration was incredibly strong, but she didn't have time to concentrate on that.

"I've even outmaneuvered Searle," Caoimhín said quietly, a small grin shifting his thick mustaches.

"William knew what you were doing," Dervy stated suddenly, not really directing it at anyone in particular.

Everything suddenly fell into place for her: the Ankousti assigning her to find the missing Taken, Simon's apprenticeship under her, every last thing. It made her wonder for a moment if William's little whore was actually with child or if he had just said that to try and break her.

"Yes," Caoimhín said simply, but without further elaboration.

His eyes locked on the doors as the sounds of squeaky wheels approached.

To Dervy's right, Weynie's shoulders slumped and she seemed to wilt at the confirmation. Weynie had suggested that William might be involved in some way, but Dervy didn't think Weynie truly believed it. The verification seemed to drain her.

Apparently Weynie had dared to hope.

Jalal on the other hand sat up straighter, jaw set, and stared directly at Caoimhín as if challenging the assumption, or maybe just challenging *him*. Dervy felt a small smile creep across her face at Jalal's defiance.

There was more to him than she'd given him credit for.

"Here we go," Caoimhín whispered to himself as the double doors opened inward.

Dervy watched as two people in green scrubs--a man and a woman--brought Alex in on a gurney. A third remained out in the hallway, a tiny buzz indicating that it was a human. The white sheets on the faux bed appeared speckled in a fine red sheen, no doubt remnants of their last extraction. Dervy felt her ire rise as the two people, humans by their minute vibrations, glanced around warily. With a sharp motion, Caoimhín waved them away and they left quickly. Apparently they were only too happy to do just that.

Caoimhín walked over to the gurney and with a few quick flicks of the wrist, disconnected the straps holding Alex in place.

Once that was done, Caoimhín stepped backward, stopping a few feet away.

"Greetings again, Alex," Caoimhín said in a friendly tone, arms at his sides. "Can you sit up?"

Alex groaned and Dervy felt her heart jump, but then he sat up.

"Good, good," Caoimhín said reassuringly.

Cautiously, Caoimhín licked his lips before his next question. "How do you feel?"

Alex looked toward him, obviously unsteady and under the influence of some sort of powerful drug. "I'm hungry, man."

Alex paused and rubbed his face. "Jesus, I'm hungry."

Caoimhín's smile faltered for just a moment before he called out to someone beyond the doors and told them to bring some food.

Dervy went numb.

If Alex were one of them, she would have to kill him along

with the rest, but for some reason that possibility bothered her. It had nothing to do with the unlikelihood of her success, but rather with the idea of killing *him*. Why did that bother her? What was it?

Dervy chewed on her cheek as footsteps approached from the hallway. Something wasn't right. It was right there, just on the edge of her thoughts. She just needed to focus...

His vibration was steady, Dervy realized.

The rest of these corrupted strigoi pulsed chaotically, just as Simon had. Just as Caoimhín did.

Not Alex. He was a single, pure constant in the back of her neck, a beacon of light that drew her in and called out to her.

Her eyes went wide as another realization struck her.

It was not the call of a Taken; there was something else there, something she had never felt before.

"What... ?" Dervy mumbled, staring at Alex as a man approached him with a plate filled with a bloody section of meat.

The smell of freshly spilled blood caused Dervy's stomach to rumble and the Dóchas soldiers around her to shift uncomfortably. One of them took a step forward before Caoimhín stopped him in his tracks with a look.

Alex, however, responded quite differently. He looked at the man and a look of abject horror filled his face. "What the hell is that? Can't I get it cooked a little?"

A near frenzied Caoimhín threw his hands in the air in triumph and a roar of approval rang throughout the room, causing Dervy, Weynie, Jalal and Alex to look around in confusion.

It was a near riot. Soldiers lifted batons and screamed, tears pouring freely down their faces. Strigoi hugged each other. Cries of glee filled the room.

Victory clear on his face, Caoimhín turned toward Dervy, his eyes maddened in glee. "Kill all three of them. We have it."

Dervy barely felt the needle, but the fluid Nathan Potts injected into her neck burned as it coursed into her bloodstream. Almost immediately she felt a fatigue wash across her body that she'd never experienced. Suddenly weaker than she'd ever been, Dervy leaned forward, face toward the floor as Weynie screamed and Jalal fought.

In the distance, Dervy thought she heard Alex shouting as well, but everything was secondary to the rushing of time and the subtle differentiations in her body as everything caught up with her. Dervy let out a deep breath she hadn't realized she had been holding.

How long had she kept that inside?

Slowly, calmly, Dervy let it happen as the room broke out in violence around her. As a small pain shot through her stomach, she closed her eyes.

Slowly, a smile broke across her face.

*   *   *

Hands like vices gripped Weynie around the arms, but she flailed anyway, screaming wildly, gutturally, as they tried to inject her with something. She cried at them to let her go, but more hands pulled at her in response.

A face that was puckered by a long scar appeared just above her, mouth turned into a permanent scowl. She could see the needle wavering in front of her as he tried to get it into her neck.

"Stay still goddammit," he grunted in frustration as he grabbed her around the neck and squeezed.

Weynie choked, her mind erupting into a buzzing haze and watched as the needle descended in slow motion toward her. She tried to move, but hands held her firmly in place; locking her to the floor.

No, please...

"No."

The air *rippled* in front of her and the man was gone, torn away by a burst of energy the likes of which she had never seen. Everything stopped for a moment and the room became silent, only the sound of Jalal struggling to her right audible. Weynie picked up her head to see where the strike had come from.

Alex stood just next to his gurney, one hand extended ahead of him. He was shaking visibly and sweat was beginning to dampen the light hospital gown her wore.

To his right stood Kevin, mouth agape. His eyes were wide, though what emotions they portrayed were lost to her. Kevin seemed conflicted at that moment--at once amazed, proud and angry. And afraid. That was the only thing she was sure of. He was deathly afraid.

Unfortunately, Weynie didn't have the benefit of figuring out exactly what happened so she pushed outward with Animi Fulminis suddenly. Her short hair rose and the hands released as electricity poured into their bodies.

Weynie launched herself to her feet, kicking out at her captors viciously and connecting with something solid. She lashed out with Animi Fulminis, hearing the distinct sizzling sound as it connected with another soldier and hurtled toward where Jalal still lay pinned beneath the Dóchas strigoi. There was no needle visible as she approached. Weynie just hoped she wasn't too late to help him as she jumped at the man kneeling on Jalal's chest.

*   *   *

Alex blinked rapidly, still stunned by what had just happened. He watched as Weynie broke free of her captors, tossing lightning as they sat stunned, and ran toward where Jalal lay. Directly across from him, a strigoi was crumpled against the wall, smoke rising from his body. The man was trying to move, or heal maybe, but without great effect. The only thing he was successful at doing was groaning in pain.

The haze was fading finally as he turned to his left.

Instincts Alex didn't know he had kept him from having his brains dashed out. He pulled back at the last moment as a black baton swept through the space where his head had just been. Stumbling, Alex backed away, trying desperately to get his bearings as the narcotics were filtered out of his system by his regenerative ability.

Kevin stepped forward twirling what looked like a police baton and smiled though there was no kindness or mirth in it.

"What are you doing?" Kevin asked simply as he began to circle around, putting himself between Alex and the others. "Huh? What do you think you're doing?"

Alex shook his head and backed away, but though it shifted under his weight, he was blocked by the gurney.

"I don't know," Alex said, shaking his head. "What did you do to me?"

"I saved you," Kevin said. "And through those efforts, you've saved us."

Alex pushed lightly, but the gurney flew away as if he had put his whole body into it.

"What's going on?" Alex asked as he stepped backwards hastily, panic rising and threatening to overwhelm him. "What did you do to me, Kevin? I thought you were just taking samples. What's happening?"

"I Cured you. And now I need you to calm down so we can finish this," Kevin said calmly.

The spinning baton didn't help calm Alex at all.

"How do we finish this?" Alex asked, mind still reeling.

Kevin smiled, his eyes seeming to quiver. "I just need you to relax so that we can deliver the Cure to everyone. They need it or they'll continue to Hunger. They'll continue to feed."

Alex stepped to the side of the gurney. He gestured to where Jalal and Weynie were struggling with a guard. "Okay, then call everyone off. Have them stop doing whatever you told them to do!"

Kevin's smile faded.

The red haired man charged, baton whipping toward Alex's head.

Balls.

*   *   *

Dervy hacked and spat something thick and dark onto the floor. The world was spinning around her, threatening to overwhelm her with a maelstrom of emotions and sensitivities that roiled inside of her. The smile faltered as her body began to burn; sweat started rolling down her body and she reached up and tore at the hem of her shirt, desperately trying to get it away from her neck.

Dervy froze as she saw Caoimhín attack Alex, moving like a frantic blur. Alex danced out of the way, narrowly avoiding getting pummeled with the piece of wood, but he looked as unsteady as she felt. To the left of the two men more strigoi entered the room, a few with automatic weapons though most had clubs similar to Caoimhín's. Strangely, instead of jumping into the fray, they paused.

Gritting her teeth--and almost falling over in shock as a tooth shifted slightly--Dervy got to her feet. Dervy needed to move quickly if she was to stop them before they shot the rest, she needed to--

Instinctually, she ducked into a roll and spun away as Nathan attempted to grab her from behind. Dervy landed in a crouched pose, ready for battle, but cringing slightly at as her hip popped. She narrowed her eyes at Nathan, but the man didn't move. There was something strange written on his face as he stared her down, eyes locked, but unmoving.

Dervy cocked her head and straightened up, wiggling her leg a bit and feeling a satisfactory crack as whatever had shifted went back into place. She wasn't sure if it was a still active healing process or just something normal, but regardless Dervy was happy to move again.

Something about Nathan seemed off as she began circling him, taking care to keep an eye on the small group that had just entered the room. He seemed somehow smaller than even a few minutes earlier, as if he was shrinking.

Nathan smiled wanly at her and nodded, small smile lines creasing a once smooth face as if his skin was made of putty. "There you go. You got it."

"Why?" Dervy asked in sudden confusion. "Caoimhín is on the verge of some supposed great victory, we're all here in relative defeat. Why Return? Why now?"

Nathan glanced over to where Caoimhín was chasing Alex and toward the strigoi who had entered the room. "This is wrong, Dervy."

He sighed heavily. "I hated you for so long that I just, I, I don't even know anymore. But I'm tired and it's not right."

Dervy nodded slowly. "Okay."

"The final straw was Simon though," Nathan said, gazing off into the distance. "He just looked like an animal. The only difference between him and me was a towel and a change of clothes. And who cares if Alex's blood fixes it? We weren't meant to live forever, so why do it?"

"I've been saying that for a long time," Dervy said quietly.

"I know that," Nathan smiled. "So I'm going to leave, take as many of these fools with me who will follow and die someplace quiet."

Dervy smiled back at him. "Good luck."

Nathan turned away, grimacing a little bit as he twisted his right knee the wrong way. "You too. You'll need it."

"Thanks," Dervy mumbled as he moved toward the armed group near the door.

Nathan turned around as the soldiers saluted. "One more thing. It goes faster if you get it in the neck."

With that, he threw a small pouch toward Dervy. She snatched it out of the air, hearing the sound of glass on glass as she caught it.

Nathan nodded at her and turned toward his soldiers. A moment later the group left and although a few cast looks of concern behind them, none stopped the march.

"Should have worn the uniform," Dervy said with a smile as she pulled out a small glass vial with a single word scrawled on it in permanent marker.

'Return'.

*   *   *

Stars flashed in front of Weynie's eyes as her head rebounded off of the cement floor with a sharp crack. She lay there dazed for a moment before crawling forward, eyes blinking out of sync, trying to get away from the soldier behind her. Her head snapped back as the Dóchas strigoi grabbed her skull and lifted her off the ground.

Weynie screamed unabashedly as she was picked up, fingers digging into her scalp. A strigoi with a huge mole just above her shattered right eye covered Weynie's mouth with one hand and leaned in close, eyes twinkling.

"Die, bitch."

Flame roared from the palm of the woman's hand and down Weynie's throat, searing her from the inside out. Weynie felt like she was exploding as the fire raged through her body. It sputtered from her nose, singing the skin of her face, but the woman somehow kept it contained. Weynie spasmed as the flames tore into her, flailing against the man holding her.

The woman's head disappeared as Jalal punched her in the side of the head. She went spinning, a trail of flame following after her hand as she tumbled away. A moment later, Weynie was tossed to the side, landing heavily against something large and hard, but she had no interest in finding out what it was.

Smoke from Weynie's smoldering insides escaped from her lips. Everything tingled--a deep numbing that extended everywhere, leaving her body useless, though she could turn her head. Weakly, she looked toward where Jalal was beating on the man who had held her. He wasn't nearly as quick as most strigoi--especially not these ones--but what he lacked in speed Jalal made up for in intelligence and strength. The strigoi kicked out, but Jalal caught it, struck him in the solar plexus and then dropped an elbow down into the man's knee, shattering it completely.

Weynie smiled as Jalal knelt over the man, intent on keeping him from getting back up, but, sadly, the darkness took her before she could watch him follow through...

*   *   *

The blow shattered Alex's cheekbone and sent him sprawling across the hard floor. Dazed, he pulled himself to his feet, but Kevin was already there, hammering at his back and legs mercilessly. Each blow dislocated or broke something, but Alex's regeneration healed it within moments regardless of the damage.

Frantically, Alex rolled away as Kevin's baton slammed into the floor where his head had just been. Somehow, Alex found himself on his feet, taking only a moment to wipe the blood away from his eyes before setting his mind to dodging Kevin's now-frenzied blows.

Alex was amazed to find that when he focused, Kevin's otherwise blurred swings and powerful strikes became like slow motion film. He watched as Kevin brought the baton up from the ground, going for Alex's groin. Alex made to grab the stick, but at the last moment, Kevin leaned in to grab him around the neck. Instead of waiting for the attack, Alex abandoned the baton and stepped to the side, avoiding both the baton and the grapple attempt at the same time. While he had no idea why it was happening, there was one thing Alex was positive of:

Whatever he was doing was making Kevin really angry.

Kevin stepped back, rolling on the balls of his feet like a professional boxer, and swung the baton up into his armpit. He shook his head in an anger he didn't even try to conceal anymore and wiped away a layer of blinding sweat.

"God you're fast," Kevin said, voice thick with a strange Irish accent Alex hadn't heard him use before. "You're really starting to pess me right the feck off, ya know?"

"Sorry?" Alex offered helpfully, shrugging his shoulders for emphasis.

Kevin laughed derisively. "Oh, by Jesus, boy."

Angrily, Kevin waggled the baton at Alex as he ran his tongue over dry lips. "I dunna give a shite how fast you be. I'll kell ya."

Kevin hefted his baton again, waving it back and forth like a baseball player, but his eyes went wide suddenly as something flashed at the right side of his neck and he spun around, swinging the weapon wildly. A figure rolled under the blow and to the side, coming to rest in a crouch off to Alex's right.

She was an older woman in her fifties, short blonde hair streaked with gray at the roots, but otherwise in amazing shape for her age. She turned and glanced at Alex and winked at him, purple eyes almost black in the lighting.

"Dervy?" Alex asked in shock, barely able to reconcile the older woman in front of him with the teenager who had beaten and then rescued him a few months earlier. "You're dying... "

Dervy shrugged and smiled at the statement. "We all die, Alex. Some of us just aren't as good as it as others."

"But--" Alex tried to say, but was cut off by a terrible scream from in front of him.

Kevin tore something from his neck and threw it to the ground, where a hypodermic needle bounced against the floor. "You stupid bitch."

Dervy smiled at Kevin and began circling him carefully. "Language, Caoimhín. I'd hate to have to take the strap to you again."

"Then again," she added, face thoughtful. "Maybe the lack of a beating made all of this possible," Dervy turned to Alex. "What do you think?"

It took Alex a moment to realize that she was trying to put Kevin between them. He began circling the other way as well.

Alex nodded, smiling uncomfortably as Kevin's face began to age visibly and his chest started to heave. "A good beating goes a long way. At least that's what my mom used to say."

"Shut up boy," Kevin spat and began moving counter to the two of them, keeping himself from getting pinned easily. "And the name is Kevin, you twat."

"You say that," Dervy said stoically. "But I heard Caoimhín a minute ago when you were screaming at the lad here."

Kevin roared and launched himself at Dervy, bringing the club to bear expertly. Dervy danced around the blows, flowing past frenzied swings and weak grab attempts as if she were simply shadow boxing. She slapped him at each attack and spat what sounded like training tips as if they were practicing instead of fighting to the death.

As Dervy batted each attack away, she called out like a trainer.

"Too slow."

"Shift to your right foot when you lunge."

"Eyes up Caoimhín."

"My name isn't Caoimhín!" Kevin screamed wildly as he launched into a furious barrage of attacks.

Both had been given the Return drug and, as they continued their fight, it began to slow down visibly. Kevin's swings came slower, with less power. His chest rose and fell heavily as he pressed the attack and sweat soaked through his black uniform, making large rings of color that were darker than the rest of the fabric.

But Dervy was beginning to show signs of the Return as well. Her hair was beginning to thin--each sudden twirl leaving a little more blonde hair behind--and her skin was getting looser around her face and neck.

However, as liver spots became prominent, Dervy leaned into Kevin, raised a forearm to block another wild swing, and struck him for the first time.

It was also the last.

Kevin seemed surprised when it happened. His right arm was held out of the way, completely useless, and he had put his left hand on his hip for balance in the strike, leaving his entire core open for attack. It looked like he expected another slap, another training guide instead of a full strength, stiff palm to the chin.

Kevin's body lifted into the air, baton falling from suddenly loose fingers, and it seemed to Alex as if he hung there, suspended on transparent wires for an eternity; body limp, weak, frail.

And then Kevin came back down and landed on part of the gurney, sending it flipping over and off the side with a crash.

Alex stared at the man's body for a long time before a whimper brought his attention back to Dervy. She knelt on the floor, jaw set firmly. Tears streamed down her face. Dervy cradled her right arm tenderly. Alex rushed to her side, sliding next to her.

"Are you all right?" Alex asked, eyes flicking back to where Kevin's body lay.

Violet eyes were nearly unseen beneath the thick bags that had formed over the last few minutes, but the glare she gave him was no less potent. "Get over there and finish him. Then we'll worry about me."

Alex nodded and ran over to where Kevin's body lay. He hesitated long enough to grab Kevin's blood smeared baton before moving forward.

"Kevin," Alex called out hesitantly. "Just lay there and let me crush your head, all right?"

When Kevin didn't respond Alex stepped forward, baton raised above his head, and prepared to brain him.

And he prepared... and prepared.

But Alex couldn't swing. He licked his teeth in uncertainty and stood there, baton held high above his head for a long moment.

Cursing, Alex lowered the baton to his side and knelt next to Kevin's body, the shallow rise and fall of the old man's chest just barely visible. Alex reached out cautiously and gave Kevin a shove, rolling him onto his back.

Alex screeched in terror and fell backward, baton rattling on the stone.

Kevin's face was a mangled red and purple thing interspersed with bright red hair. His jaw had been slammed up into his skull, pulverizing his once strong face into a mass of flesh and gray hair. Kevin's eyes were open, flicking back and forth wildly in panic as he struggled to continue breathing through a nose that was partially blocked by skin from what used to be his upper lip.

"God," Alex whimpered and made to back away, but Kevin grabbed his forearm, squeezing painfully.

Their eyes locked and Alex's head swam as Kevin's memories and thoughts swam into his mind. They were violent at first--an old van spattered with blood as a man screamed--but they moved away quickly. The room shook as Kevin forced Alex into his memory.

Scotty sits next to him, legs crossed and arms stretched out across the back of the bench. Since his graduation from medical school earlier that day he's had that same shit-eating grin on his face as he used to get when he stole cookies as a toddler. The long robes that Scotty wore earlier--elaborate things that reminded Kevin of some of the old university professors from his youth--are gone now, replaced by tight fitting bell bottoms and a rainbow-striped t-shirt.

Kevin snickers at how ridiculous Scotty looks, which draws a somewhat annoyed stare. Scotty hates it when Kevin points out that he'll regret these fashion choices later in life, but his usual indignant attitude is tempered by the unwavering happiness he must be feeling. Instead of issuing a sarcastic retort, Scotty simply shakes his head ruefully and looks back over the sprawling park just outside of Heathshome.

"Feeling pretty good now, huh?" Kevin asks without looking at his son.

"Yeah," Scotty says, his grin evident in the tone of his voice. "I'm feeling really good."

"Shrooms?" Kevin asks with his own grin.

Scotty laughs. "No, not shrooms, dad. Where the hell did you even hear about them?"

Kevin shrugs. "Read it in the paper. Sounds like fun if you ask me."

"Eh," Scotty says before flashing Kevin a smile. "There's some indication there are side effects after the fact so, obviously, I've never tried them."

"Right," Kevin says, stretching out the word knowingly.

Scotty nods, smiling widely. "Right."

Scotty's smile is infectious; Kevin finds himself joining in and enjoying the scenery with his son.

"I'm proud of you," Kevin blurts out suddenly, his chest aching strangely at the words. "I don't know if I've ever said that to anyone."

Scotty's smile fades a little and he turns to Kevin, voice thick with emotion. "Thanks dad."

Kevin nods vigorously, sniffling awkwardly. Scotty knows who he is. What he is. Scotty has known since he was a teenager.

He's always been too goddamned smart, Kevin thinks with an approving smile.

"Now if only we can figure out a way to fix your attitude," Kevin says in faux sincerity, tapping his foot. "Then you might be worth my time."

Scotty laughs, turning eyes back to the park. "You're an asshole, dad."

"Yeah, Scotty," Kevin says, joining his son in the aimless observation. "I know."

Alex reeled back, trying to pull away, but Kevin held fast. It was too much information, too intense; too much emotion. He'd only been told how to touch another person's memories. Alex hadn't even done that successfully. This was wrong.

You have to know why, a deep voice, filled with pain, erupted in his mind as new images flashed in front of his eyes. Alex tried to fight it, but failed.

The room is stifling despite the cool, climate controlled atmosphere. The screaming, though muted by thick walls and solid doors, is still coming long and loud from the other room despite them having left nearly thirty minutes earlier. Kevin covers his ears and looks across the room to where a figure is pacing back and forth.

Scotty is old now--nearly seventy--and it shows in the lines on his face, the liver spots on his arms and hands. Even his chin has grown slack, skin hanging heavily toward the floor like an inverted sail. The cancer that ravages his body has left him thin and weak, though the straightness of his back shows a defiance that still makes Kevin smile.

Kevin is so proud of him, but pride will not save his son. Scotty will die soon if they cannot figure out the next formula; if they cannot find a way to activate the Life in a human.

"I can't do this anymore," Scotty says, turning toward Kevin. "I--I just can't keep doing this."

Kevin stands and walks toward his son. "Scotty, you just need--"

"Stop calling me that!" Scotty screams at him angrily. "I'm not a goddamn child anymore, dad. I'm almost seventy years old, for Christ's sake."

Still a child, Kevin thinks, but says nothing.

Scotty closes his eyes and takes a deep breath, only the slightest quiver of his cheek indicating the pain involved in the process. "I'm going to die."

"No," Kevin says defiantly, getting up and taking a step forward, shaking his head vigorously.

Scotty keeps his eyes closed. "There isn't anything we can do about it. Even you."

"That's bullshit," Kevin says. "I refuse to believe it."

Scotty opens his eyes, a familiar grin dancing across his face. "It doesn't really matter if you believe it, dad. It's happening."

Scotty turns to leave, but Kevin grabs his shoulder, fingers digging in just a little too hard. Scotty curses and whips around as Kevin pulls away, ashamed.

"Just... just stop," Scotty says, trying desperately to keep a smile on his face, however difficult. "I'm going to go home now and give my son a call. I'll... I'll talk to you later."

Kevin feels tears building in his eyes, but forces them back, though it means that he can barely see his son. For just a moment, he imagines that the figure before him is an eight-year-old boy, hair a fiery red in the summer sun. The boy smiles and Kevin smiles back... and then the image is gone as the tears fall from his eyes.

"We'll talk later, then," Kevin says haltingly, just barely keeping the sobs back. "Yeah."

Scotty turns and makes it to the door as the screams finally subside in the other room. He pauses for a moment and turns around.

"Stop trying to find this," Scotty says thickly, sniffling slightly. "Not everyone needs to be like you."

Kevin nods. "Okay."

"Okay," Scotty says with a smile before opening the door and leaving the room.

"Okay," Kevin says to an empty room.

Alex blinked away tears as Kevin's emotions flooded away from him, leaving him feeling hollow and empty. Whatever Kevin was trying to tell him, Alex just wasn't getting it. What did this person--Scotty--have to do with the Life? Scotty was Kevin's son and it sounded like they had been trying to find a way to activate the Life in regular humans, but what did that have to do with the Cure? What did that have to do with his attack on the Arktois?

Kevin's hand loosened and the whistling noise coming from his face slowed. Alex looked down at Kevin's mangled face and saw that the man's eyes were starting to roll around in his head.

"No," Alex said, suddenly angry. "I need to know why. Tell me why!"

Alex grabbed the sides of Kevin's head, causing the other man's body to spasm in pain, and Scryed him. Alex had only been taught the basics of Scrying during his training, but it was enough to try the process. They said Scrying usually involved a moment of awkwardness and resistance as you pressed against someone else's psyche before you received even the slightest connection. After that, you could kind of see the memories, but it was incredibly confusing and it involved a lot of trial and error.

This was nothing like that. Alex pushed with his mind and instead of the gentle give of Kevin's barriers, he felt something snap and he was enveloped in a bright white light.

Shit.

            *   *   *

"Hey, wake up."

Weynie cringed as she woke to a sharp slap across her cheek. "Stop it."

"Okay," Jalal said.

Groaning, Weynie sat up and, for a moment, she forgot where she was, though that feeling fled fast.

"Dervy," Weynie said, getting to her feet unsteadily.

Jalal was there to support her, grabbing her arm as she rose. "Careful. They hurt you pretty badly."

Weynie nodded, but made to pull her arm away from Jalal regardless. "Thanks, but I don't have time for that."

Sudden flares of pain in her chest made her rethink that choice. Jalal nodded and she put more weight on him.

She looked around the room quickly, but only saw three figures. Alex was kneeling over a body and an old woman was rocking slowly back and forth a few feet away.

"Where did the soldiers go?" Weynie asked as she stepped toward the woman.

"They scattered," Jalal said. He steadied her as her next step faltered.

"Why?" Weynie asked, grunting as much from the pain as the tiny ants crawling through her body, repairing charred tissue.

Weynie squinted as she neared the woman on the ground. It looked like... no.

"Dervy?" Weynie asked, releasing Jalal's arm and kneeling down next to her.

The old woman looked up at Weynie, violet eyes flashing in the fluorescent light. "In the flesh."

"Oh my... " Weynie sighed.

Dervy shrugged, though the action made her flinch.

Looking down, Weynie could see a deep purple swelling in her right arm that went up to the elbow.

"Let me see that," Weynie said, reaching out to take her arm carefully.

Dervy shook her head and pulled away. "It's destroyed. Just a sack of flesh. I don't want anyone to see it."

Weynie sat back on her haunches and nodded. "All right."

"Thank you," Dervy said, eyes turning back to stare straight ahead of her.

Weynie followed her line of sight and found herself staring at where Alex sat, face locked as in some kind of a trance. Immediately, she tried to get to her feet and move over, but Dervy stopped her.

"Sit down Weynie," Dervy said chidingly. "Let the man have his final words."

"But what if--"

"What if what?" Dervy asked. "I plugged him with his own drug and crushed his head."

A small smile creased her wrinkled face. "Frankly, I'm surprised he's still breathing."

As the last word left her mouth, Alex shook his head and looked down at the body in front of him. He lifted his hands away from the body, shaking his arms in frustration before reaching out and grabbing Kevin's mutilated face. Alex leaned in close to the man.

"Tell me why!" Alex screamed.

Everything suddenly went blurry as a force slammed into her, dropping Weynie to the ground heavily. She blinked and tried to focus, but her eyes wouldn't cooperate.

"What the hell was that?" Weynie grunted as she sat up next to where Dervy lay, sprawled out.

"I don't know," Dervy moaned as she sat up slowly.

Again, a small smile split Dervy's face. "I really have no idea."

*   *   *

Alex blinked and the world suddenly came back into focus. Well, kind of.

Everything was a brilliant white that ran away from him in all directions and into infinity. There were no edges, just pure existence. Instead of a feeling of immensity, Alex felt claustrophobic as if the light was tight against him. If he squinted, it was almost as if the whiteness was swirling, but when he tried to focus the world became flat and uniform once again.

Around him, Alex began to see flickering images of people. To Alex's right he saw a crouched form that he thought might be Weynie flash to life and then disappear. Next to where she appeared an old woman came and went just as quickly followed by the form of Jalal, confusion written plainly on his face.

A moment later, a man appeared in front of him, but he was standing with his back to Alex. A head of bright red hair stood out against the uniformity of the rest of the area like a torch.

"Kevin?" Alex asked, stepping forward.

Kevin turned around, whistling in appreciation at the surroundings. He was entirely in one piece and appeared to have become young once again; face flush with health and life.

"This," Kevin said, motioning around him. "This is impressive Alex."

"What is this?" Alex asked in confusion. "Did you do this?"

"Me?" Kevin asked in disbelief. "I could never do something like this. Never."

Alex rubbed his head. Everything was starting to get fuzzy. What was he trying to do? Why was he here?

"I was asking you something," Alex mumbled, shaking his head vigorously. "Why. I was asking you why."

Kevin nodded, though he continued looking around, eyes darting continuously as if he, too, could see the swirling just on the edge of his vision. "I'm afraid you'll be disappointed. I told you that we don't focus on the why."

"Tell me anyway," Alex said through gritted teeth.

Alex felt like the world--this world--was pulling on him in all directions. As the seconds crawled by, he felt like it was trying to tear him apart.

Kevin closed his eyes. "A human killed my son."

"Scotty?" Alex asked. "Someone killed Scotty so you waged war on the Arktois?"

"Yes," Kevin said simply.

Alex shook his head. "That doesn't make any sense."

"It does if you have a large enough vision, Alex," Kevin said.

Kevin held up his pointer finger. "Step one: Make strigoi truly immortal."

He flicked up a second. "Step two: Unify the strigoi."

Another finger.

"And step three," Kevin said evenly. "Subjugate the humans."

"All of this because someone killed your son?" Alex asked in disbelief.

"Yes," Kevin said firmly.

"You're insane," Alex said, shaking his head.

Kevin held up a hand. "To the victor go the spoils, so enjoy making your own history and demonizing me, but remember one thing."

Kevin stepped forward quickly, closing the gap between them effortlessly. "You'd do the same thing if our positions were reversed. Think about what that means."

"No I wouldn't," Alex said reflexively, but even as the words came out of his mouth, he recognized how false they sounded.

Kevin smiled and turned away. "Right. Of course you wouldn't."

Alex shuffled his feet as a memory flickered through his mind. Small hole under the eye...

He felt like he was missing something important as his eyes searched the mists. "That can't be all of it."

Kevin laughed harshly. "You wanted motivation and you got it. What else do you want to know?"

Alex looked at the back of Kevin's head. "How."

"How," Kevin turned around, a real smile on his face for the first time. "Now that's the right question."

"Then tell me."

The pulling sensation was growing exponentially as the seconds ticked by. Alex groaned despite himself, causing Kevin to turn and look at him in concern.

"You should go, Alex," Kevin said, voice suddenly comforting. "I think I'll just stay here. It's... peaceful."

"I need to know," Alex grunted as his head split.

Kevin sighed and turned away. "Know then that there are a

lot of people out there who don't want us as much as we don't want them. Know that they're trying to get rid of us. All of us."

"Who?"

Kevin smiled. "Maybe you should reconsider what I was doing. It was the best plan I could come up with."

Kevin's smile turned to a grin. "The best plan always wins. Come up with a better one if you can."

The pressure was building and Alex fell to his knees, grabbing his head as pain began to build in the back of his head.

"Who!"

"It all rests on you now Alex. Make good choices, or we'll all suffer."

Alex groaned. It felt like lightning was writhing around his brain. "What does that mean?"

"Alex?"

Alex forced himself to look up at where Kevin was standing and caught his breath. The air around Kevin shimmered as his body seemed to lose form. Light filtered through him, highlighting the content smile on his face.

Kevin smiled at him. "Tell Dervy she's right."

Kevin laughed suddenly as he turned away from Alex and started walking, shaking his head ruefully. "She's always right. Adh mór ort, Alex."

The world tore apart and Alex shattered.

25
Dóchas
1:29 PM January 23, 2011

"Wake up."

Alex groaned, but didn't move. His head was killing him.

A quick slap across the face did nothing to help that.

"Alex, wake up!"

"God," Alex grunted and opened his eyes to see Weynie crouched over him. "Really? A slap?"

A smile of utter relief filled Weynie's face at the response despite the red puffiness around her eyes. "Get up, Taken."

"Is that an order?" Alex asked, but he sat up anyway.

"Yes," Weynie said with a smile, rubbing at her eyes with one hand.

Alex shook his head, trying to get his bearings, but then his eyes fell upon a still body a couple feet away. Kevin lay sprawled out where he left him, but there was no longer any motion or vibration indicating that there was life of any sort left in the body.

Caoimhín O'Ceallaigh was dead.

Alex grimaced and got to his feet, a haunting memory of the man standing in pure white light dancing in his memory.

"Dervy wants to talk to you," Weynie said, voice cracking, pointing over to where the now ancient woman was laying on the ground, head propped in Jalal's lap. "She's dying and she won't let me go find Kevin's Cure."

Alex approached Dervy as Weynie turned away and walked the other direction. Alex's breath caught in his throat as he knelt down next to her. Her once fair skin was a mass of wrinkles and liver spots that hung loosely on her thin frame. Dervy's right arm was mutilated, a stunted, purple mass; long sinuous bruises running up her forearm and under the short sleeve of her shirt. If it weren't for her eyes, Alex would have had a hard time identifying this frail person in front of him as Dervy.

Dervy locked eyes on him and she smiled. "Hi Alex."

"Hi," Alex said awkwardly.

"He's dead?" Dervy asked.

Alex paused, considering his answer. "His body is," he finally said.

Dervy narrowed her eyes for a moment before nodding. "That's good enough, I guess."

"Yeah," Alex agreed. "He told me to tell you that you were right. That you're always right."

Dervy laughed and immediately broke into a gasping coughing fit. When it was over she looked at him with a smile.

"'I'm always right', eh?"

Alex smiled back. "Yep."

She shook her head ruefully. "Five hundred years and he finally realizes it. What a stubborn asshole."

Alex snickered, but a sudden gasp from Dervy caught his attention.

"Alex," Dervy said urgently, grabbing at him.

He reached out and grabbed her hand without even considering what might happen.

As her hand touched his, she smiled, purple eyes clouding as death's hand crept over her. "Live well."

"Okay," Alex said with a small, sad smile.

Dervy nodded and then grit her teeth as another coughing fit wracked her body. This one didn't subside like the previous one. Instead, it kept getting more intense, as if her body was trying to expel some poison.

Dervy gripped his hand fiercely and Alex squeaked in pain as his pinky broke under the pressure. A sudden image flared into his mind--a pyre; bodies lain atop it delicately--and then it was gone, replaced instead with Dervy's ancient, pleading eyes.

Alex nodded. "Okay."

Dervy smiled wanly as the coughing reached its crescendo and suddenly stopped. Her body went limp, a small telltale smile permanently stuck to her aged lips. Empty, violet eyes staring off into the distance.

Jalal reached down and gingerly closed her eyelids. Behind Alex, Weynie broke into a sob.

They sat like that for a moment before Alex got to his feet.

Weynie looked over at him, confused, vulnerable, and aimless.

As Jalal stood, he turned to Alex.

"What now?" Jalal asked.

"We burn this place to the ground," Alex said. "We make this place a pyre for her.

"Okay," Weynie said, pulling her shawl tight around her. "Okay."

Epilogue

Alex, Weynie and Jalal burned Dóchas to the ground, taking care to create a proper pyre for Dervy's body prior to watching the place disappear. They experienced no resistance as they coated the halls with gasoline and any other accelerant they could find. They were further surprised to find that the trucks had been left behind, fully loaded with their cargo. It was as if the troops had simply packed up and left, abandoning the stronghold and their mission without a fight.

The cargo, crates of weapons and refrigerated boxes filled with bottles of the Return drug as well as the Cure, joined the rest of the pyre.

After returning to Heathshome the three of them brought their accusations of Primator Searle's wrongdoing to the Ankousti, but were dismissed after a council vote cleared him of all charges. Following the vote, Weynie and Jalal monitored Alex closely. Besides an unprecedented increase in his abilities and an unsurpassed expertise with all of the Six Gifts, there seemed to be no side effects. There was certainly no hint of the hunger that had plagued Caoimhín O'Ceallaigh's followers.

Weynie and Jalal decide not to tell anyone that Caoimhín had developed a new Cure and used it on Alex. After long deliberation, Alex agreed with them.

Soon after Primator Searle was cleared of all charges, Weynie was reassigned to a newly established West Coast division of the AIC. She transferred under protest.

Jalal retained his position as Lead Information Security Officer, but became bogged down by an appointed Ankousti member under the title of Chair of Technology, Kevin Lindsay. Within weeks, both Jalal and his new boss realized that the position had been created to stifle any further complaints about the Ankousti or the Primator.

Alex continued his training, but was forbidden from working with technology or having access to Arktois funds due to his actions. Given his circumstances, the only punishment placed on Alex beyond this was his mandatory attendance of extensive psychiatric counseling. Haunted by Kevin's final words to him, Alex begged the Ankousti to give him a task and was finally assigned to a newly assembled special division of the AIC specifically designed to hunt down and capture ex-Dóchas members who had taken Kevin's Cure.

Alex Mamsin happily accepted the task.

* * *

Simon opened his eyes as he retracted the needle, making only the most delicate of sounds as it cleared William Searle's neck. He turned and left the large bedroom, his night vision allowing him to step over the small pile of clothes next to the bed without issue. A quiet snore came from the pregnant woman lying in bed next to William, her dark skin shining in the dim light.

Silent as a shadow, Simon slipped out of the room, passed an in-progress nursery--a crib only half assembled in the corner of a room in what appeared to have been a study--and left through the front door. He stepped out into one of the many hallways of Heathshome and pulled the door shut behind him with just the barest of clicks. Only then did Simon let go of the Scry he held in place on both William and the woman.

Simon smiled, his heart still quiet in his chest, and pulled out a small list and pen. He chewed on the end of the pen as he turned toward the Pasa Tiempo. He followed the list past nine names that were crossed out until he came to one of the last.

William Searle.

Simon scratched the name out with a flourish and a smile.

The next name gave him pause.

Alex Mamsin.

Simon stopped in the hallway and tapped his lips with the pen. He stood like that for a few minutes, completely alone in the depths of Heathshome. The small pouch at his side jingled as he shifted his weight in consideration.

Finally, after what seemed like an eternity, Simon scratched Alex's name off the list.

"Live well," Simon whispered into the empty halls of Heathshome.

As he approached an intersection, he turned to the right. Simon whistled happily as he proceeded to the rooms of his final target.

About the Author

Michael J. Wyant Jr. is a fairly eccentric guy who vacillates rapidly between overused verbosity and an almost complete dependence on profanity in order to express himself.

When not writing, Mike is an avid video gamer and tech geek who also has a soft spot for cats and Chihuahuas. No, he will not accept any more pets into the household.

Four is enough.

Immortal is the first book of **The Sundering Trilogy** and is Wyant's first published work. He is currently working on the second novel in the series as well as a standalone quasi-post-apocalyptic novel, **Soundless**.

Made in the USA
Charleston, SC
25 April 2013